VISIONS

*Luncheon scene, with Andreyev (self-portrait)
sixth from left.*

VISIONS

Stories and Photographs by
LEONID ANDREYEV

Edited and with an Introduction by
OLGA ANDREYEV CARLISLE

HARCOURT BRACE JOVANOVICH
San Diego • New York • London

HBJ

English translation
copyright © 1987 by Olga Carlisle and Henry Carlisle
Introduction copyright © 1987 by Olga Carlisle
Photographs copyright © 1987 by the Estate of Leonid Andreyev
"The Seven Who Were Hanged" is reprinted from
An Anthology of Russian Neo-realism,
translated and edited by Nicholas Luker,
© 1982 Ardis Publishers

LIBRARY OF CONGRESS CATALOGING-IN-PUBLICATION DATA
Andreyev, Leonid, 1871–1919.
Visions : stories and photographs
Translated from the Russian.
Contents: The thought—The red laugh—
At the station—[etc.]
1. Andreyev, Leonid, 1871–1919—Translations, English.
I. Carlisle, Olga Andreyev. II. Title.
PG3452.A23   1987   891.73′3   87-8605
ISBN 0-15-193900-4

Designed by Beth Tondreau Design

Printed in the United States of America

First edition

A B C D E

CONTENTS

INTRODUCTION

Olga Andreyev Carlisle

*Self-portrait with children.
Olga Andreyev Carlisle's father,
Vadim, is seated to the right.*

As a child I lived with my parents in a small modern apartment in a remote suburb of Paris. My father's study, with its single window overlooking well-tended vegetable gardens, was a sunny, quiet room, walled with books and journals. The thin, light-colored ones were collections of contemporary poetry in French and Russian. There were heavier books in dark bindings, among them four identical volumes bound in violet cloth. My father told me that these were the works of his father, my grandfather, which I would read when I was older. In the meantime I could look at pictures of him and of my father as a young boy. He showed me three tasseled, tooled-leather albums containing black-and-white and sepia photographs, and glass color plates kept in small, carefully crafted boxes labeled in a rounded hand. I spent hours leafing through the albums and holding up the glass plates to the light. They opened for me the world my father had known when he was a child.

My grandfather, Leonid Andreyev, was the man with the black eyes who never smiled at the camera.

There was the house in which they had lived, an enormous wooden castle with a tower. St. Bernard dogs at play. A boating party gliding down a river. The family and guests assembled at the sun-flecked tea table, presided over by my grandfather in a white linen summer suit—a young male standing behind him to his left, mysteriously double exposed with the small-paned window overlooking the garden. And again and again there was my grandfather, dressed as a sea captain, a medieval prince, an artist, a Russian peasant. And with him sometimes was a slender, proud boy who looked very much like the adult my father had become.

Though Leonid Andreyev died in Finland eleven years before I

3

*Vadim Andreyev, Olga Carlisle's father
and Leonid Andreyev's son.*

was born, his presence haunted my early childhood. Besides the photographs, there were massive possessions that my father put to daily use: a tall Remington typewriter, a gigantic wooden German camera, and (my favorite) a monumental bronze Empire inkstand that stood on the desk in the study and that I often drew in still lifes.

And there were Andreyev's own paintings and drawings.

His self-portrait dwarfed our dining room. My grandfather had been exceptionally handsome, talented, famous, and yet in this picture he appeared doomed, like the Russia he had loved—Russia, his country and ours as well, which had been lost to us in the days of October 1917. The eyes were downcast, as if mourning that loss and other losses enigmatic to a child, the unbearable losses caused by death. With his dark, closed face, he seemed to know more about loss than anyone else. The portrait, done in brown pastels, was romantic and yet remote: Andreyev looked like a stranger not only to the world around him but to himself as well.

These pictures and objects spoke of Andreyev; they suggested that the arts to which he had devoted his life—writing, painting, and photography—had the power to bring the past to bear on the present. They suggested, too, that Andreyev's life had been overshadowed by death. My father's mother, Andreyev's beloved first wife, Alexandra Mihailovna Veligorskaya, his hope and inspiration, had died when my father was only three. My father would sometimes read "Annabel Lee," one of Andreyev's favorite poems. It was my first encounter with American literature—the lilting lines that I believed were written about my grandmother.

I have a vivid memory of a painting by my grandfather that had made its way into the hall of our apartment. It was part of the shipment of heirlooms—my father's inheritance—that had arrived from my grandfather's house in Finland sometime in the mid-thirties. It was a charcoal study of devils trimming their toenails, an enlargement of Goya's engraving—though of that I had no idea. I found it frightening. My mother and I persuaded my father to relegate "the devils" to a storeroom. They disappeared, but still I

Andreyev with The Devils.

5

knew that they were there in the darkness of the storeroom. Andreyev's paintings had lives of their own. They filled me with a special dread, which I recognized again years later, when I first read some of his stories and plays.

When my father, Vadim—an émigré poet then in his early thirties—assumed the literary legacy of his once-celebrated father, Leonid Andreyev was all but suppressed in the Soviet Union and—outside of a small theatrical milieu (the Pitoëffs had staged him in Paris in the twenties)—unknown in France. Before the October Revolution he had been one of the most successful and controversial of Russian writers. He and Alexander Blok—the prose writer and the poet— were the two charismatic literary figures of that era, foretelling as they did an ominous future for Russia and for all of Europe. Andreyev had died at the age of forty-eight in 1919, at the time of the civil war, the Red Terror, and the famine—at the time of the collapse of a whole culture, which seemed, then, to have engulfed him as it swept Russia into an unknown future.

When I was a child the new society that was developing in place of the old in the USSR was the central concern of our family. My father was possessed by a longing to return to Russia that had little to do with reason or politics. But when would the time be right? We read Blok's *The Twelve* aloud. The poet's vision of Christ crowned with roses leading the twelve Revolutionary Army men through frozen Petrograd seemed intelligible. I understood that my parents embraced Blok's view. But even as a child I discovered that Andreyev had not shared the vision of the Bolshevik's ultimate vindication. Political editorials he had written at the time of the October coup d'état had culminated in *SOS*, his appeal to the Allies to intervene in Russia and drive the Bolsheviks out militarily. I knew that this publication dismayed my parents. They detested the Bolsheviks, but they found the notion of calling for foreign intervention against one's own country unacceptable It seemed to me that the *SOS* pamphlets, like the painting of the devils, had a life of their own in the depths of our storeroom.

I was born in peacetime in Paris and had enjoyed a carefree childhood, yet I felt a personal involvement in the catastrophic events that had marked my family's past— World War I, the revolution, the civil war. My parents as adolescents had had extraordinary adventures. After his father's death, my father had fought in the civil war in the Caucasus. My mother had been born into a family of revolutionaries with populist roots. They were the non-Marxist socialists to whom Leonid Andreyev had been close. They had staged the moderate February Revolution, only to be destroyed by Lenin as soon as he seized power. The Socialist Revolutionaries (SRs) were in the majority in Russia then. They had been especially threatening to Lenin because their political party had had a wide popular appeal, which the Bolsheviks lacked and envied.

My Chernov grandmother, my mother, and her two sisters were arrested and imprisoned. In the usual course of events, they would have perished, as did virtually all other SRs, but they were saved by a miracle. That miracle—their release with permission to leave Soviet Russia—was wrought by a man who played important roles in the lives of both the Andreyevs and the Chernovs. He was Maxim Gorki, foremost among the Russian writers who aligned themselves in the early years with the aspirations of the new society.

There were several photographs of Gorki in our apartment—some in the company of Andreyev, one with my father as a young boy in Capri. In these he appeared good humored. He had wide cheekbones, bushy eyebrows, a smile that contrasted with Andreyev's solemnity. Gorki had been my grandfather's closest friend for many years. He had helped launch Andreyev's literary career, and he was my father's godfather. But as I was growing up, I came to understand that the two writers had become estranged over philosophical and political issues—issues that were still very much alive in my childhood, ardently debated and quarreled over in my family.

Andreyev had spoken for freedom and individual responsibility, for a moderate revolution, for a constitutional government. He had explored the dark side of man. He put the search for truth ahead of

Maxim Gorki.

all values. Gorki in contrast, was an optimist who believed in man's perfectibility. To achieve it, in his view, it was necessary to submit to party discipline. A radical revolution would bring social justice and happiness to Russia and eventually free all mankind from oppression.

Andreyev had died, defeated yet lucid and outspoken to the end. Gorki's ideas had apparently won out, though; as Andreyev had foreseen, the reform of the social order had soon been subverted into a new authoritarianism beyond Dostoyevski's darkest fantasies. In the thirties, however, before the revelations of the killings, of the Gulag, the Soviet Union appeared to many liberals in the West (and most poignantly to certain Russians, like my parents, who had been forced into emigration) as a land of promise that would one day emerge after the storms of the revolution—the Soviet Union as it

8

appeared not in Andreyev's vision but in the dreams of Maxim Gorki.

Ever since the turn of the century, Gorki had been a beloved public figure in liberal circles. His charm, his decency, his legendary kindness validated his convictions, even if they appeared at the same time naive. As was Gorki himself, they were so very appealing. It was heartening to know that in the thirties he was alive and well in Russia. From time to time we had news of him through his first wife, Yekaterina Peshkova, who on occasion came from the USSR to Paris, or through the writer Isaac Babel. Babel, a friend of my father, visited us twice in those years, before he disappeared in the terror of the late thirties. He had encouraged the publication of my father's first work in prose. *Childhood*, which came out in Paris in 1938, was a candid study of his difficult yet loving relationship with Leonid Andreyev and of the predicament of being the motherless son of a celebrated author.

In 1928 Gorki, the writer who was to coin the term "socialist realism" had returned in triumph from a self-imposed exile on Capri, to be glorified as the father of Soviet literature. Once or twice, in oral messages to my father, he urged my parents to return to Russia. Then came the news of his death. Two years later, during the last of Stalin's great show trials, it was alleged that Maxim Gorki had been poisoned by his doctors. Photographs of his kindly face again appeared in the newspapers. There were more agitated conversations among the adults. It was all very hard to understand, very upsetting. Afterward there was no longer any question of our going to live in Russia in the immediate future. The Russo-German pact and the German invasion of France followed soon thereafter.

We left our apartment for a seaside summer vacation in 1939, expecting to return in the fall. The war kept us away for five years. During that time Andreyev's books, his pictures, and the great Empire inkstand stood undisturbed in the apartment, the painting of the devils and *SOS* in the storeroom. I was nine when we left Paris, and during those years on an island under German occupation, I no longer felt Andreyev's spell.

Only in the sixties was I to become fully aware of him again. For the first time in my life I went to Russia, on a literary assignment. In Moscow I met people who had known Andreyev and had loved him—Peshkova and especially Kornei Chukovsky, then Russia's most famous writer of children's books and a distinguished man of letters. They remembered my grandfather's generosity, his willingness to give of his time to worthy political and social causes, the support he lavished on younger colleagues, including Chukovsky himself and Alexei Remizov. As for the younger Soviet intellectuals I met, they regarded Andreyev as a Russian classic, far more important for his existential insights and formal inventiveness than the realist Gorki, enshrined though he was in the official Soviet pantheon.

During my several visits in Russia during the sixties, no one was able to bring me closer in spirit to my grandfather than Chukovsky; no one knew better how to evoke a sense of life's continuity. There was a touch of the magician about him. People dead half a century came to life as he spoke. With gusto he recreated for me the great house built in the Scandinavian style in Finland, the blazing fire-places and huge tiled stoves throughout the house, the polar bear rugs on the floors, the massive carved furniture. He told of the distinguished houseguests who arrived from St. Petersburg on weekends and of the festive hospitality, for Andreyev, who had been very poor in his youth, loved to share his affluence with his family and friends. Chukovsky described my great-grandmother Anastasya, nicknamed Businka, Andreyev's mother and his close friend and confidante, a gifted storyteller herself. And he spoke of my grandmother, Andreyev's beloved first wife, called Lady Shura. Especially, though, Chukovsky was intent on recapturing Andreyev's warmth, his gift for compassion partly hidden by the trappings of fame and wealth.

An episode during a visit to Chukovsky's house is suggestive of his uncanny ability to bring Leonid Andreyev to life. One afternoon he had a special surprise for me, one that joined past and present in a way I would never forget.

Andreyev's mother, nicknamed Businka.

He had called me out into the garden, where a drab gray truck, like a closed delivery van, was parked under the trees. Two young men stood by the truck. With the authority of a theatrical director, Chukovsky set them in motion. One opened the back of the truck, and I saw that it was filled with electronic recording equipment. It was a sound truck from a Moscow TV station, which was making a filmed interview with my host. Chukovsky climbed inside. Both young men disappeared after him. Soon Chukovsky summoned me into the crowded interior and handed me a pair of earphones. I put them on and heard a lot of crackling, some coughing and wheezing noises, then a male voice, strangely enthusiastic, slightly breathless. It resembled my brother's voice. It was youthful, aware of its own effect, and a bit tentative because of this. I realized that the man speaking was my grandfather. He was addressing a political rally more than half a century ago; he would have been about my age then, or younger. When the recording ended I took off the earphones with wonder. Chukovsky was nodding in delight. "This is the live Andreyev—Andreyev's live voice," he said.*

---

* Olga Carlisle. *Solzhenitsyn and the Secret Circle*, Holt, Rinehart and Winston, New York, 1978, pp. 66–67.

Leonid Andreyev was born on August 9, 1871, in the town of Orel in the central Russian woodlands, a region that had been the birthplace of many writers, including Turgenev and Tolstoy. His father, a land surveyor of legendary strength and drinking ability, was the son of a local landowner and a serf girl. His mother, née Packowska, was a descendant of an aristocratic Polish family that generations before had become Russified and impoverished. Leonid was the first of six children. He was a bright, energetic child who learned to read at an early age, tried to run away to America after reading James Fenimore Cooper, and in school resisted the strict rules and regulations and all studies that failed to enchant him. Very early his imagination had been stirred by the vivid fantasies related by his mother and by the theater. He developed a passion for reading, but his earliest artistic expression was not writing but drawing and painting, for which he had shown a talent almost from infancy.

But very early, too, the dark side of his nature appeared. Everything we know about Leonid Andreyev suggests that even as an adolescent he was manic-depressive, though in those years that illness had not been identified. Throughout his life he experienced deep depressions followed by periods of feverish intellectual activity. His heavy drinking (which was to stop in 1902 when he married Alexandra Mihailovna) dramatically intensified these depressions. As a very young man he had several unhappy love affairs and made more or less determined attempts to take his life. There was a streak of wildness in him, a need to touch at the limits of experience in life, as he would later do in literature. Gorki relates that on their very first encounter, Andreyev told him how, in order to test his nerves, he had thrown himself under a speeding freight train, fortunately falling between the rails so that the train passed over, only stunning him.

During his university years Andreyev was possessed by the philosophical questions of the times. The 1880s and 1890s were a period of strenuous intellectual repression in Czarist Russia, but early on he had become acquainted with forbidden editions of Dmitri Pisarev and Tolstoy and—most important—with the works of Schopenhauer. He also came under the influence of *Thus Spake Zarathustra*, but he soon rejected the then-fashionable Nietzscheanism. Though not a churchgoer, he was fascinated by issues of good and evil, and his values were shaped by the Russian Orthodox tradition. Many of his stories, including "Darkness," are inspired by themes out of the Scriptures. Dostoyevski was his favorite author, though he also passionately admired Tolstoy, to whom he dedicated his "Seven Who Were Hanged."

In 1889 his father died, leaving the family in severe need. Andreyev helped his mother support and educate his brothers and sisters, notably by painting portraits. In 1890 he entered law school in St. Petersburg, and in 1894 he transferred to the University of Moscow, where his family joined him, giving him a measure of stability.

Andreyev wrote his first stories when he was still a student. In 1895 some of these appeared in the *Orel Herald*, one of the most progressive Russian newspapers of that time. More stories came out in 1896, the year he met Alexandra Mihailovna, who was then only sixteen. Little by little the young woman to whom Gorki would give the name Lady Shura became for Andreyev a symbol of light and survival in a life marked by horrendous periods of self-doubt.

After his graduation in 1897, he worked in a law office. There he was asked to contribute journalistic accounts of cases to a smaller newspaper, the *Moscow Herald*, and then to the more important *Courier*. An Easter story, "Bergamot and Garaska," inspired by daily life in Orel, came to the attention of Gorki, then at the height of his fame and the leader of a loosely linked group of realistic writers. It was then that the intense, stormy friendship between Andreyev and Gorki began. On Gorki's recommendation, Andreyev was invited to participate in the Moscow "Wednesdays," at which young realists with liberal political views read and criticized one another's works and occasionally played host to well-known artists and musicians.

Andreyev's first volume of stories, published in 1901 by Gorki's publishing house, Znanie, was well received. Reprinted in 1902 in an enlarged edition, it became very successful. In early 1902 Andreyev married Alexandra Mihailovna. Until her death from puerperal fever in 1906, he lived out the happiest, most inspired four years of his life. Veresayev, one of the members of the Wednesday group, described Alexandra Mihailovna's role as a critic: "She had a vast, intuitive understanding of what her artist-husband wanted and could give, and in this respect she was the living embodiment of his artistic conscience."*

Two stories published in 1902, "The Abyss" and "In the Fog," made Andreyev famous overnight. They dealt with adolescent sexuality in a repressive society and had an enormous effect on the Russian reading public. That effect was amplified by the strident denunciations of Andreyev's immorality that appeared in the conservative press. Most remarkable was the Countess Tolstoy's letter. Leo Tolstoy's wife publicly accused Andreyev of inviting unsuspecting Russian readers "to see and examine the decomposed corpse of human degradation and to close their eyes to God's wonderful spacious world." But there were also letters in fervent support of Andreyev's denunciation of social hypocrisy, as well as considerable critical praise. Chekhov, for instance, thought that because of its absurdity, the countess's letter could only be a forgery. "In the Fog" had made a powerful impression on him. The publication of the two stories marked an important moment for those within the Russian intelligentsia who believed that the function of literature was to press society into reexamining its moral foundations. Another, very short story from the same period, "At the Station" shows Andreyev moving in that direction. Indeed it seems to predict the positive turn towards the openness of the Gorbachev era.

Published at the end of the previous year, 1902, "The Thought"

---

*All quotations in this introduction not marked otherwise are from James B. Woodward, *Leonid Andreyev, A Study*, Clarendon Press, Oxford, 1969.

shocked and fascinated readers. The story is the confession of a man who murders his friend in cold blood, then simulates madness to escape punishment, losing his mind in the process. "The Thought" provoked debate not only among readers but also in psychiatric circles. In the story—inspired in part by the allegorical structure of Edgar Allen Poe's "The Fall of the House of Usher"—Andreyev indicted society's misplaced confidence in human intellect, a theme that absorbed him all his life. Years later he turned the story into one of his most forceful plays. The deranged protagonist is so convincing that some of Andreyev's detractors maintained that he himself had spent time in a psychiatric ward. Andreyev's impatience with critics began then.

He longed for responsive criticism. Because he wrote under extreme emotional stress and because he searched relentlessly for the most evasive artistic and philosophical truths, his stories are often cryptic, their messages ambiguous. Andreyev asked questions without providing answers. Overcome by the urgency of his own questioning, he sought out criticism that would throw light on aspects of his work that were enigmatic even to him. Understandably such criticism was seldom forthcoming—except from the two people who played crucial roles in his life, Lady Shura and Gorki, next to his mother his closest friends. Both were eventually to desert him—his wife through death, his friend through political passion. In Gorki especially, Andreyev recognized an outstanding critic; yet as his friend became more and more involved with Marxist ideology, the differences between their artistic judgments widened.

"The Red Laugh," Andreyev's response to the Russo-Japanese War, was published in late 1904 in a volume of Znanie miscellany. Sixty thousand copies were sold, a huge sale for those times. The story was written in only nine days and nights. Andreyev's intensity of feeling was such that Alexandra Mihailovna spent long nights in his study wrapped in her shawl, helping him with her presence and silence. In "The Red Laugh," Andreyev's ability to project the emotions of his characters as if they were his own is at its strongest, yet Gorki found this somewhat stylized novella less terrible than the facts. So did Tolstoy, and yet readers today find in the work a warning, an intimation of what the ultimate war, different from all others, might be. About "The Red Laugh" Veresayev remarked, "Omitted from view is the most salutary attribute of man—his ability to accustom himself to everything." Yet that is precisely what is so striking in this story: the revelation of man's inability to adapt to that final conflict, of which the Russo-Japanese War was but one of many rehearsals. Still, some of Andreyev's contemporaries recognized the encoded prophecy in "The Red Laugh." The Symbolist Andrei Bely wrote: "Chaos within appears to us in the form of madness—in the form of the atomization of life into a countless number of separate channels. It is the same in the field of learning: clumsy specialization produces a multitude of engineers and technicians with the mask of learning on their faces and with the chaotic madness of amorality in their hearts. The unprincipled application of learning is creating the horrors of the present war with Japan—a war in which we see before us the symbol of rising chaos."

Written the same year, "The Thief," a seemingly realistic story about a trivial daily event, echoes the sense of despair that is to be found in "The Red Laugh." This story as well won the admiration of the Symbolists, the writers with modern metaphysical sensibilities whose audience was rapidly growing in Russia. Alexander Blok said of "The Thief," "There is nothing here but wild horror, for suddenly all masks are torn off." Of all Andreyev's works it was the favorite of another, younger Symbolist, Alexei Remizov.

Shortly before the outbreak of the 1905 revolution, in February, Andreyev, who though a committed liberal was distrustful of all groupings and never belonged to a political party, was arrested and imprisoned. He had allowed the Central Committee of the Social Democratic Workers' party (the Bolsheviks) to hold a meeting at his apartment in Moscow. Gorki was a member of that party. Andreyev was released soon afterward but was now counted among the polit-

Self-portrait.

ical enemies of the state, even though at this period, as a writer, he was separating himself from the engaged realists and activists and was increasingly attracted to the Symbolists, whom Gorki considered decadent. As always in Andreyev's work, the basic questions of existence took precedence over political ones.

However, Andreyev's friendship with Gorki prevailed for some years. It was with Gorki, then living in exile on Capri, that Andreyev spent the first agonizing months following the death of his wife. It was there in 1906 that he experienced a rebirth of inspiration and wrote in rapid succession some of his most arresting works, the play *The Black Masks* and the stories "Judas Iscariot" and "Darkness." Eventually he left Znanie in favor of Shipovnik, a St. Petersburg house that published Blok, Bely, and Remizov.

"Darkness" was inspired by the experience of a Socialist Revolutionary, Peter Rutenberg, whom Andreyev met at Gorki's on Capri.

Gorki was never to forgive his friend for (as he saw it) misusing Rutenberg's story and thus slandering a worthy revolutionary: Rutenberg had been the organizer of the assassination of Father Gapon, the agent provocateur who had instigated the tragic "bloody Sunday" massacre, which triggered the revolutionary events of 1905. In fact, however, in this tale—which was to remain Andreyev's favorite of all his "offspring"—he likened the young revolutionary to Christ. Far from portraying, as Gorki maintained, "the cattle and darkness over the human," he had tried to show the victory of the spirit over the darkness of everyday life; of genuine self-sacrifice over the moral complacency of terroristic tactics.

Earlier, in 1903, Gorki had written to Andreyev, "The situation is such that the Russian writer must be a political worker, now more than ever." Andreyev would not conform. In 1906 he wrote: "It is true that the nature of my literary activity makes me a revolutionary, but this is not the revolutionism that is required by the moment." Yet one of his most memorable longer stories, "The Governor," was directly based on a revolutionary act committed in February 1905, a few days after bloody Sunday. In a letter to Veresayev, Andreyev set forth the facts behind the tale: "The motive of the murder of the grand duke [the governor of Moscow] was the beating of demonstrators in the streets of Moscow on December 5 and 6; it was then that the Socialist Revolutionaries 'sentenced' him and Trepov [the Moscow chief of police] to death, announcing the fact to everyone in proclamations. Everyone, even S.A. [Grand Duke Sergei Alexandrovich] himself, waited expectantly; the execution was duly carried out."

"The Governor" was first called "The God of Vengeance," after Schopenhauer's variation of the biblical phrase "Vengeance is mine; I will repay, saith the Lord," which Tolstoy had used as the epigraph of *Anna Karenina*. The mystical idea of retribution against one who has violated the natural order—in this case by killing forty-eight innocent strikers—is at the heart of the story. Once again

1 8

Andreyev was possessed by his theme: "There were various thoughts and there were various words, but there was a single feeling—a huge, dominating, all-penetrating, all-conquering feeling, which in its power and indifference to words resembled death."

The Social Democrats were outraged; they considered Andreyev decadent. "We have before us a vivid example of the replacement of social psychology with social mysticism," wrote Anatoly Lunacharsky, the future Bolshevik people's commissar of enlightenment. In 1907 Andreyev's treatment of revolutionary themes in the play *Czar Hunger*, published by Shipovnik, caused Lunacharsky to declare that Andreyev had "the mind of a petty bourgeois, an artist perhaps, but still a hopeless petty bourgeois." In fact, in those years Andreyev was beginning to mourn the fateful conflict between humanistic values and the revolution.

The following year, 1908, Andreyev published what is perhaps his finest work. *The Seven Who Were Hanged* is, on the surface at least, a realistic novella. It too was inspired by current events—the ruthless governmental repressions that followed the 1905 revolution. It was dictated in part by Andreyev's urge to denounce the death penalty, as Tolstoy, to whom it is dedicated, was also doing at that time. In 1909, when the story was republished, Andreyev donated the income from it to the inmates of the Schlüsselburg fortress, where many political prisoners were then detained.

In *The Seven Who Were Hanged*, Andreyev came to terms with death more convincingly than in any other of his works. Chukovsky said of it: "Andreyev rejects one world in order to find another at once—herein lies his strength and his greatness." The psychological portraits of the seven convicts—two common criminals and five revolutionaries—are masterful. One of them, that of Werner, clearly embodies Andreyev's own search for transcendence over both death and self-absorption. The coldness of the intellectual is overcome in a moment of ecstasy: "It was as if he were walking along a very high mountain ridge, narrow as the edge of a knife blade; on one side he could see life, and on the other death, like two deep, beautiful, glittering seas that merged on the horizon into a single, infinitely wide expanse."

The same year, *The Seven Who Were Hanged* was translated into English by Herman Bernstein, a *New York Times* correspondent who, until Andreyev's death, provided a link between the writer and the United States. Andreyev's introduction to the American edition, a work that was reissued time and again, struck a chord with American readers, in particular with those thousands of immigrants from eastern Europe who were then becoming a growing part of the American reading public. The introduction begins:

> I am very glad that "The Seven Who Were Hanged" will be read in English. The misfortune of us all is that we know so little, even nothing, about one another—neither about the soul, nor the life, the sufferings, the habits, the inclinations, the aspirations of one another. Literature, which I have the honor to serve, is dear to me just because the noblest task it sets before itself is that of wiping out boundaries and distances.
>
> As in a hard shell, every human being is enclosed in a cover of body, dress, and life. Who is man? We may only conjecture. What constitutes his joy or his sorrow? We may guess only by his acts, which are ofttimes enigmatic; by his laughter and by his tears, which are often entirely incomprehensible to us. And if we, Russians, who live so closely together in constant misery, understand one another so poorly that we mercilessly put to death those who should be pitied or even rewarded, and reward those who should be punished by contempt and anger—how much more difficult is it for you Americans to understand distant Russia? But then, it is just as difficult for us Russians to understand distant America, of which we dream in our youth and over which we ponder so deeply in our years of maturity.
>
> The Jewish massacres and famine; a Parliament and executions; pillage and the greatest heroism; "The Black Hundred," and Leo Tolstoy—what a mixture of figures and conceptions, what

a fruitful source for all kinds of misunderstandings! The truth of life stands aghast in silence, and its brazen falsehood is loudly shouting, uttering pressing, painful questions: "With whom shall I sympathize? Whom shall I trust? Whom shall I love?"

In the story of "The Seven Who Were Hanged" I attempted to give sincere and unprejudiced answer to some of these questions.*

By 1908 Andreyev was withdrawing from the literary worlds of both Moscow and St Petersburg, where he had lived on and off since Lady Shura's death. In February he wrote Gorki, "I will leave this detestable city with its wretched bustle and once and for all come face to face with nature, with the sea, the sky, the snow, face to face with pure human thought." It was in that year that he commissioned a disciple of the elder Saarinen to build him the sumptuous country house I remember seeing as the wooden castle in the faded photographs. It stood in a secluded spot near Vammelsu—in Russian, "Black River"—about forty miles west of St. Petersburg. My father, who spent most of his childhood there, remembered it as "heavy, magnificent, and beautiful. A tall square tower rose fifty feet from the ground. The vast slate roof with its many pitches, the gigantic square white chimneys—each the size of a watchtower—the geometric pattern of the beams and the stout shingles, everything without exception was truly magnificent."† Andreyev, who had remarried in the spring of 1908, was to make his home here until his death. Though he made several trips to Europe and visited St. Petersburg, he preferred to live in the country. There he wrote and practiced the other arts for which he had a passion, painting and photography. As he had written to Gorki, he deeply loved nature. Each year he took time off from writing to savor the brief,

---

* From the introduction to *The Seven Who Were Hanged*. The World Publishing Company, Cleveland, Ohio, 1941.

† Vadim Andreyev, *Detstvo*, Moscow, 1963.

*Andreyev and his second wife in exile in Finland.
The children are peeking out from the rear.*

bright northern summer. In the winter he skied and worked daily—
or rather nightly, drinking glass after glass of strong tea.

After the publication of "Darkness" he never regained the critical
acclaim of his early years, yet until the revolution he remained
enormously popular with the Russian public, whom he reached
through his stories and through the stage. Since his first play, *To
the Stars*, written in 1906, Andreyev remained deeply involved with
that medium. His plays, though they vary greatly in style, deal with
the same existential and political themes as do his stories. Several
of them were forbidden by the censors for political or religious reasons. One, *The Life of Man*, a symbolist drama finished shortly after
Alexandra Mihailovna's death, became for a time a household word
in Russia. Its impact on the public can only be compared to that of
"The Abyss" and "In the Fog." It was staged in February 1907 in

In costume.

St. Petersburg, in Vera Komissarzhevskaya's theater, directed by Vsevolod Meyerhold, Russia's great experimental director. The same year, in December, *The Life of Man* was presented in the realistically oriented Moscow Art Theater, where Constantin Stanislavsky had once worked with Chekhov.

Since its invention Andreyev had been fascinated by the possibilities of the cinema. In 1910, long after the furor over "The Abyss" had died down, he visited Leo Tolstoy and was warmly received by him and the countess. Among other subjects Andreyev and Tolstoy discussed the tantalizing future of the new art form. A member of Tolstoy's entourage wrote: "At tea [Leonid Andreyev] told Lev Nikolayevich about the critic Kornei Chukovsky, who had raised the question of a special dramatic literature for the cinema. Andreyev himself was very enthusiastic about this. Lev Nikolayevich listened rather skeptically at first, but gradually he seemed to become more interested: 'I shall certainly write for the cinema,' he announced at the end of the discussion." The next day as he was leaving, "Andreyev thanked him with emotion. Lev Nikolayevich asked him to come again: 'We shall be closer,' he said. 'Let me embrace you.' " The same evening Tolstoy "said at the table that he had been thinking all night about what should be written for the cinema: 'You see,' he said, 'this can be understood by great masses of people, and by all nations.' " *

Self-portrait with Tolstoy.

Leo Tolstoy.

In 1916 one of Andreyev's plays was made into a movie in Moscow. *He Who Gets Slapped*, a lyrical drama that unfolds against a circus background, had first been successful on the stage in both Moscow and St. Petersburg. At the premiere in St. Petersburg, the play and its author received fourteen curtain calls. *He Who Gets*

* V. F. Bulgakov. *The Last Year of Leo Tolstoy*, The Dial Press, New York, 1971.

Slapped is the only play of Andreyev's that has become a part of the American repertory. Produced first in New York by the Theater Guild in the twenties, with the beautiful Margolo Guilmore as Consuello, the play was warmly received. At about that time, it also inspired a marvelous, if somewhat mysterious, Hollywood production starring Lon Chaney, which surely would have delighted Andreyev. Since then the play has often been revived—in the fifties at the Circle in the Square, with Robert Culp in the role of He; at the Guthrie Theater in Minneapolis in the seventies; at the Berkeley Repertory in the eighties; and it is frequently staged on American campuses. In 1956 Robert Ward, an American composer, used the play as the subject of his opera *Pantaloon*. And in the sixties in Paris Sasha Pitoëff, the son of the émigré theatrical family that staged Andreyev in the twenties, created a radio play of *He Who Gets Slapped*.

At the outbreak of World War I, despite his antipathy toward the czarist regime and his horror of war, Andreyev assumed a patriotic stand. He worked as an editorial writer for newspapers that supported the war effort. He loathed German militarism. He hoped that the conflagration would lead to progressive changes within the czarist government. He welcomed the democratic reforms heralded by the February Revolution, but the October coup d'état horrified him—his editorials about it are masterpieces of political invective. Andreyev viewed the Bolshevik takeover as a catastrophe for Russia. The use they made of terror he saw as absolute evil. This was why in SOS he appealed to the Western powers to come to his country's aid, to avert the cataclysm that his merciless vision revealed to him. As the Bolsheviks triumphed, Andreyev became an outcast, an exile in his own house, which now lay beyond the Soviet border. He found it difficult to write and experienced a deep sense of isolation. In 1918, deploring his inability to fight against the evil that had befallen his country, he tried to analyze his own motives for isolating himself at Vammelsu:

In building this enormous house in the desert, as if on the edge of the land of Canaan, I wanted to create a beautiful life severely devoted to tragedy. To be outside of society, of routine—and I found myself outside of life as well, throwing my writings into life once in a while, like a boy throwing stones over a fence into a stranger's garden. . . . Peter the Great did me in. He cut a window open onto the sea, and I sat near it to admire the view from the shore, and now I drift away. Finland! Why am I in Finland?*

Overtaken by poverty, hunger, and sorrow, Andreyev died of a heart attack less than a year later. Shortly before his death, Gorki, whom Lenin had entrusted with the task of saving Russian writers from starvation while bringing them into the fold of Soviet literature, sent an emissary to Andreyev. Gorki offered two million rubles for the rights to Andreyev's books and for his support for the Bolsheviks' literary work. Andreyev angrily refused. According to Chukovsky, when the news of Andreyev's death reached Gorki, he wept. "However strange it may seem, he was my only friend," he said. "Yes, the only one."

Once again, years after the deaths of both men, Gorki, who had launched Andreyev's career, was to play another benevolent role in his friend's destiny. Throughout the Stalinist years, Leonid Andreyev was not republished in the Soviet Union. Had it not been for his friendship with Gorki, it would have been easier to erase him from the Soviet version of Russian literary history, as has happened, for instance, to Nikolai Gumilyov and Alexei Remizov, major voices long silenced in the Soviet Union. In the relatively tolerant Khrushchev era, it was simpler to acknowledge his existence and his relationship with Gorki than to exclude him altogether. Officially he was presented as a minor figure corrupted by early fame and by

---

* As told to OAC by Vadim Andreyev. Cited in *Voices in the Snow*, Random House, New York, 1971.

Later years.

decadent ideas, a writer who had failed time and again to heed Gorki's advice not to stray from the path of realism.

Gorki had indeed been critical of "The Red Laugh" for the abstract way in which it depicted war. He had seen "Darkness" as a slander against revolutionary idealism. These criticisms are still echoed by contemporary critics, sometimes, it seems, without benefit of a return to the works themselves. Yet the popularity of Andreyev's writings in the USSR in the post-Stalinist era speaks for itself. The fact that he dealt boldly and compassionately with the great themes of modern literature—the depersonalization of man in modern society, the impossibility of a just revolution, the prospect of a forthcoming holocaust—was a revelation to Soviet readers force-fed a diet of socialist realist trivia for so many years.

A selection of Andreyev's stories was published in Moscow in 1956, followed in 1959 by a volume of plays. More complete versions of the stories were reissued in the seventies and again in the eighties. For decades Andreyev's plays had not been staged. In 1967 one of his early dramas, *The Days of Our Life*, was produced in Leningrad. Other productions followed, though Andreyev's plays with political overtones, such as *Savva* and *Czar Hunger*, and existential themes, like *The Black Masks*, are not performed in the Soviet Union.

An important contribution to the revival of Andreyev in the USSR was made by Kornei Chukovsky, who in the sixties, owing to his venerable age and fame as a children's author, had gained a measure of authority. In 1958 he published a volume of literary recollections that included a lengthy portrait of Andreyev. Then in 1965, the irrepressible scholar-collector Ilya Zilberstein was able to bring out a selection of the Gorki-Andreyev correspondence in a volume of the outstanding archival series Literary Legacy. This volume included most, but not all, of the letters that had been preserved. Despite Zilberstein's admirable persistence, some materials—for example, those dealing with Andreyev and Gorki's joint efforts in protesting the Czarist government's anti-Semitic policies—were omitted on the censors' orders.

As for Andreyev's own works, each printing, no matter how large, has always immediately sold out, not only in the Soviet Union but in other Eastern European countries as well. Today he is especially appreciated in Italy, Spain, Latin America, and Czechoslovakia.

Only now, in the eighties, is it possible for me to hear clearly the voice of Andreyev. I have lost my fear of the devils in the storeroom. His contemporaries often accuse him of a lack of taste, of naiveté, of affectation. Some of this criticism is quite justified; yet his best works are filled with a very modern, raw power. He had a rare gift for embodying emotional states and philosophical concepts into original, vivid fictional characters.

Andreyev's gift of prophecy, in particular of the imminence of universal cataclysm, was extraordinary. His reckless, deep-diving sensibility resonates with our times. He has served as an inspiration for a number of contemporary writers, for Pavel Kohout in his *Poor Murderer*, produced on Broadway in the seventies, and for Camus in his play *Les Justes*. (Before he died Camus was planning an adaptation of Andreyev's *Anathema*, a symbolist play about good and evil—for which Andreyev was anathematized by the bishop of Saratov, an early supporter of Rasputin.) "Andreyev, an old friend, a friend of my childhood. A huge writer," said Milan Kundera when I met him in 1985, and we discussed his favorites—notably "Darkness"—among the stories.

The stories collected here I read as tales of our own times as well as of Andreyev's. In addition to the "live Andreyev" of my father's and Chukovsky's recollections, I have heard him resound on the stage, in He's speech about immortal love in *He Who Gets Slapped* and, in Paris in 1962, when Laurent Terzieff played Kerzhentsev in *The Thought*, doing full justice to the mesmerizing complexities of this play. I hear his voice in the tales of terrorism as experienced by both the perpetrators and the victims, in the words of those who are about to be put to death lawfully, and in the tales of the dark side of sex. And especially I hear it in that solemn refusal to accept the inevitability of death that distinguishes Russian writers from all others.

THE THOUGHT

On the eleventh of December, 1900, Anton Ignatyevich Kerzhentsev, a medical doctor, committed a murder. The evidence presented in connection with the crime, as well as certain circumstances
that preceded it, gave rise to the suspicion that Kerzhentsev's mental faculties were not normal.

Committed for tests at the Elizavetinskaya Psychiatric Hospital,
Kerzhentsev was subjected to a severe and attentive examination by
several experienced psychiatrists, one of whom was Professor Drezhembitsky, recently deceased. What follows is an account of what
happened, written by Dr. Kerzhentsev himself a month after the
tests began. Along with other materials obtained by the examiners,
this report served as the basis for the judicial evaluation.

I

Learned gentlemen, I have been concealing the truth, but now circumstances compel me to reveal it. Upon hearing it you will understand that this truth is not so simple a matter as it might appear to
the uninitiated: a question either of the straitjacket or of shackles.
For there is a third possibility: neither one nor the other but more
dreadful than the two combined.

Alexis Konstantinovich Savelov, whom I killed, was my classmate
in high school and at the university, though we followed different
professions: I as you know am a doctor, while he graduated from
law school. It cannot be said that I disliked the deceased; I always
did like him, and I have never had a closer friend than he. Yet
despite all his attractive features, he was not among those who in-
spire me with respect. The astonishing softness and pliancy of his

nature, his strange inconstancy in the spheres of thought and feeling, the extremity and groundlessness of his ever-changing judgments forced me to regard him as a child or a woman. People close to him, often suffering from his outbursts, and who because of the illogic of human nature loved him very much, tried to find a justification for his defects and for their own feeling and declared him an "artist." Indeed it appeared that this meaningless word explained him perfectly and that what to any normal person would appear objectionable thus became tolerable or even good. Such was the strength of this contrived word that even I at one time succumbed to the general mood and willingly forgave Alexis his minor shortcomings. Minor because he was incapable of important ones, as he was incapable of anything important. His literary works provide sufficient evidence of this. Everything in them is minor and unimportant, regardless of what might be said by myopic critics dedicated to the discovery of new talents. His works are charming and insignificant, and he himself was charming and insignificant.

When Alexis died he was thirty-one years old, younger than I by a little more than a year.

Alexis was married. If you saw his wife now, after his death, dressed in mourning, you could not imagine how beautiful she once was, she looks so terrible now. Her cheeks are gray and the skin of her face is so flabby—old, old, like a worn glove. And she has wrinkles. Now they are wrinkles, but in another year they will be deep furrows and grooves. She loved him so very much! Now her eyes no longer sparkle and laugh, as they always did before, even when they should have been weeping. I saw her only for a minute, having met her by accident at the investigator's office, and I was astounded by the change. She could not even glare at me in anger. She was so pitiful!

Only three people—Alexis, I, and Tatiana—knew that five years ago, two years before she married Alexis, I had proposed to Tatiana Nikolayevna and was rejected. Of course that only the three of us knew is only a supposition, for Tatiana Nikolayevna has a dozen friends who may well have been told in detail how once Dr. Kerzhentsev dreamed of marriage and received a humiliating rejection. I do not know whether she remembers that she then burst out laughing. Most likely she does not remember—she laughed so often. So you might remind her: *On the fifth of September she laughed.* If she denies it—and she will deny it—remind her how it happened. I, the strong man who had never wept, who had never been frightened of anything, I stood before her and trembled. I trembled and saw how she was biting her lip, and I had already reached out to embrace her when she raised her eyes and there was laughter in them. My arms remained outstretched and she laughed and laughed for a long time, as long as she pleased. Later she did apologize.

"Please excuse me," she said, but her eyes still laughed.

I, too, smiled, and even if I could have forgiven her laughter, I could never forgive myself for this smile. This was the fifth of September at six in the evening, St. Petersburg time. I mention the time because we were then standing on a railroad platform, and even now I clearly see the big white face of the clock with the black hands straight up and down. Alexis Konstantinovich was also killed at exactly six o'clock—a strange coincidence, which might be revealing to a perspicacious person.

One of the reasons I was confined here was the absence of motive for the crime. Now you plainly see that a motive existed. Of course it was not jealousy. Jealousy presupposes a fiery temperament and inferior mental capacities—that is, the exact opposite of what I am—a cold, rational creature. Revenge? Yes, that might be it, if it is necessary to use an old word for a new and unknown emotion. The fact is that Tatiana Nikolayevna caused me to make a mistake, and this always angered me.

Knowing Alexis well, I was certain that Tatiana Nikolayevna, married to him, would be very unhappy and would regret having refused me; and this was why I so insisted that Alexis, who was simply enamored, should marry her. Only a month before his tragic death he said to me, "It's to you that I owe my happiness. Isn't this true, Tanya?"

She looked at me and answered, "It is." And her eyes smiled.

Later we all burst out laughing as he embraced Tatiana Nikolay-evna (they felt no restraint in my presence) and added, "Yes, my friend, you lost out, didn't you?"

This inappropriate, tactless joke shortened his life by a full week. I had originally intended to kill him on the eighteenth of December.

Yes, their marriage turned out to be a happy one, particularly for her. He did not love Tatiana Nikolayevna passionately because he was incapable of deep love. He had his beloved occupation—litera-ture—which led his interests beyond the confines of the bedroom. She, on the other hand, loved only him, and lived only through him. Moreover, he was unwell. Frequent headaches, insomnia, and these indispositions caused him distress. But for her to nurse him and gratify his whims was bliss. A woman in love becomes irresponsible.

And so day after day I saw her smiling face, her happy face, young, beautiful, carefree. And I thought, this is my doing; I wanted to give her a worthless husband and deprive her of myself, but in-stead I gave her a husband whom she loves, and I am still around. You will understand this oddity: She is brighter than her husband and loved to converse with me, but when the conversation was over she would go off to sleep with him and be happy.

I cannot recall when the thought of killing Alexis first came to me. It came imperceptibly; but from the very first moment the thought became old, as if I had been born with it. I know that I wanted to make Tatiana Nikolayevna unhappy, and at first I devised many other schemes less fatal to Alexis—I have always been an enemy of unnecessary cruelty. Taking advantage of my influence over Alexis, I had thought of arranging for him to fall in love with another woman or turning him into a drunkard (he had an inclination in that direc-tion), but none of these plans was right. The point is that Tatiana Nikolayevna would have managed to remain happy, even while giving him to another woman, listening to his drunken raving, or receiving his drunken caresses. What she needed was for this man to live, so that she might serve him in one way or another. Such slavish natures exist. And like slaves, they cannot understand or appraise the strength of others besides their masters. The world has seen intelligent women and talented women, but it has yet to see a just woman.

I must frankly admit—and not so as to elicit your indulgence, which I don't need, but in order to demonstrate the correct and normal course by which my resolution was reached—that I had to struggle for a rather long time with my compassion for a man whom I had condemned to death. I pitied him for the moment of terror before death and for those seconds of suffering while his skull was being bashed in. I had pity—I don't know whether you will understand this—for the skull itself. There is a special beauty in a harmoniously functioning living organism, and death, like disease, like old age, is, above all, grotesque. I remember how long ago, when I had just graduated from the university, I had got hold of a beautiful young dog with strong, graceful limbs, and it was very hard for me to skin it, as the experiment required. For a long time I found it distasteful to think of the poor animal.

If Alexis had not been so sickly and fragile—I don't know, perhaps I might not have killed him. To this day I am sorry for his beautiful head. Please convey this to Tatiana Nikolayevna. It was a beautiful, very beautiful head. Only the eyes were wrong. They were pale, without fire or energy.

I might also not have killed Alexis had the critics been right in attributing to him a major literary gift. There is so much that is dark in life, there is such need for great talents to light the way that each must be treasured like a rare diamond, a talent who justifies the existence in the world of thousands of scoundrels and vulgarians. *But Alexis was not such a talent.*

This is no place for literary criticism, but should you read attentively the most acclaimed works of the deceased, you will see that they were not necessary to life. They were necessary and interesting to hundreds of overfed readers in need of diversion, but they were not necessary to life, or to those of us engaged in solving its riddles. While a writer, using the power of thought and talent, should create new life, Savelov was content to describe the old, making no effort to solve life's secret. The only story of his that I like, approaching as it does the realm of the unexplored, is "The Secret"— that is the only exception. The worst was that Alexis was beginning to show signs of having written himself out, and as a result of his happy existence, he had lost the last teeth he had with which to sink into life and gnaw on it. He himself often shared his doubts with me, and I saw that they were well founded. I extracted from him the precise and detailed plans of his future works—let his grieving admirers be comforted: there was nothing new or great in them. Of those near to Alexis, only his wife failed to observe the decline of his talent, nor would she ever have noticed it. Do you know why? She did not always read her husband's works. Yet when I once tried to open her eyes even slightly, she took me for a wretch.

Having made sure that we were alone, she said, "There is something else you can't forgive him."

"What is that?"

"That he is my husband, and I love him. If Alexis were not so crazy about . . ."

She faltered, and I readily finished her thought: "You'd drive me out."

Laughter shone in her eyes. And, smiling innocently, she said slowly, "No, I'd keep you."

And I, who had never let any word or gesture show that I still loved her, thought at that moment: so much the better if she is on to it.

In itself, the taking of a man's life never bothered me. I knew that it is a crime sternly punished by law, but then, almost everything that we do is a crime. Only a blind man will not see that. To those who believe in God this is a crime before Him; for others, a crime before humanity; for some like me, a crime before myself. It would have been a great crime if, having recognized the necessity to kill Alexis, I had failed to carry out my resolve. The fact that people divide crimes into major and minor ones and consider murder a major crime has always seemed to me to be a common, shameful lie before one's conscience—an effort to hide behind one's own back.

I was not afraid of myself—that was more important than anything else. For a murderer the most terrifying thing is not the police or the trial, but the criminal himself, his nerves, the powerful protest of his whole body, trained in familiar traditions. Remember Raskolnikov, who perished so pitifully and so absurdly, and all those multitudes like him.

I gave much time and much thought to this question, trying to imagine what I would be like after the murder. I cannot say that I was fully confident of my future composure—no thinking man, aware of every possibility, could be. But having carefully gathered all the facts of my past, taking into account the strength of my will, the solidity of my yet-untaxed nervous system, my deep contempt of prevailing morality, I could maintain a certain confidence in a favorable outcome of my undertaking. It would not be out of place here to relate an interesting fact of my life.

Once, when I was still a student of the fifth semester, I stole fifteen rubles from money entrusted to me by a friend, claiming that the cashier had made a mistake in his accounting, and everyone believed me. It was more than a simple theft, when someone in need steals from a rich man: here was a breach of trust, the taking of money by a man of means from someone deprived, who was moreover a comrade and a student—this was why they believed me. It may well be that this act seems to you more revolting than the murder of my friend. Isn't this true? But I remember that I was delighted to have done this so well and so adroitly, and I looked into the eyes, straight into the eyes of those to whom I so boldly and freely lied. My eyes are dark, beautiful, frank—and they were believed. Above all, I was proud of the fact that I felt no remorse whatever, that I did not need to justify myself in my own eyes. To this day I remember with special pleasure the menu of the unnecessarily lavish meal to which I treated myself with the stolen money and ate with appetite.

Do I feel remorse now, regret for what I have done? None at all.

I feel weighed down. I feel dreadfully weighed down, more than anyone else on earth; and my hair is turning gray, but that is something else. *Something else.* Something terrifying, unexpected, incredible in its fearsome simplicity.

II

My task was as follows: I had to kill Alexis. I had to have Tatiana Nikolayevna see that it was I who had killed him, while I remained out of reach of the law. Not to mention the fact that my punishment would provide Tatiana Nikolayevna with another occasion to laugh, I myself wanted to avoid hard labor. I love life.

I love it when a golden wine plays in fine crystal. I love it when weary I can stretch out in a fresh bed. In the spring I love to breathe the clean air, to watch beautiful sunsets, to read interesting and clever books. I love myself, the strength of my muscles, the strength of my thought, clear and precise. I love the fact that I am alone, that no inquisitive glance will penetrate the depths of my soul with its dark caves and abysses, on the brink of which my head grows dizzy. Never did I understand or experience what people call ennui. Life interests me, and I love it for the great mystery it contains. I love it even for its cruelty, for its fierce vengeance, and for the satanic gaiety with which it toys with people and events.

I was the only person whom I respected—how could I risk dispatching this person to hard labor, where he would be deprived of enjoying the varied, complete, and far-reaching existence that he required? Even from your own point of view, I was right in wishing to escape hard labor. I am a very successful practitioner. Because I am well off, I treat a great many impecunious patients. I am useful, surely more so than the murdered Savelov.

It would have been easy to escape punishment. There are a thousand ways to kill a man surreptitiously, and I, as a medical doctor, could have used any one of them with particular ease. Among the schemes I rejected, I considered this one for a long time: to inject Alexis with a loathsome, incurable disease. The shortcomings of this plan were obvious: lengthy suffering inflicted on the victim, something ugly about it, something deep, something too stupid. Then Tatiana Nikolayevna would have found happiness for herself in her husband's illness. My task was particularly complicated by the fact that Tatiana Nikolayevna had to know whose hand had struck her husband. But then, only cowards are afraid of obstacles—people like myself seek them out.

Chance, that great ally of intelligent men, came to my rescue. Learned gentlemen, I take the liberty of bringing to your attention the following detail: it was *definitely* chance, insofar as something external, independent of me, served as a motivation for what happened. In a newspaper I stumbled upon an item about a cashier, or perhaps a clerk (the clipping might be at my house or perhaps at the investigator's office) who feigned an attack of epilepsy during which he lost a sum of money, while in fact he, of course, had stolen it. This clerk turned out to be a coward and confessed, even disclosing where the money was hidden. And yet the thought wasn't bad at all and easy enough to carry out. To feign madness and kill Alexis is a state of supposed aberration, then to recover—this was the plan that I conceived in a single instant yet one that had cost a great deal of time and effort for it to acquire its full and final form. At that time I was only superficially acquainted with psychiatry, like any medical doctor who had not specialized in it. I spent almost a year reading various sources and pondering them. At the end of that time I became convinced that my plan was quite feasible.

The first thing the experts will have to address themselves to is heredity. To my great joy mine turned out to be completely suitable.

My father was an alcoholic; his brother, my uncle, ended his days in an insane asylum, while my only sister, now dead, suffered from epilepsy. It is true that everyone on my mother's side was bursting with health. But then, one drop of insanity is enough to poison many generations. I owed to my mother my excellent health, yet I did suffer from innocuous eccentricities that could be of use to me. My relative unsociability—the sign of a healthy mind, inclined toward spending time in the company of oneself and of books instead of in empty, futile conversation—could pass for pathological misanthropy. My cold temperament, contemptuous of gross sensual pleasures, might pass for a sign of degeneracy. My very insistence in reaching the goal I had set for myself (many such instances could be found in the course of my rich life) would, in the language of you learned experts, be given the terrifying name of monomania, the domination of obsessive ideas.

Therefore, the grounds for simulation were extraordinarily favorable—the statics of insanity were present; only its dynamics were lacking. To the inadvertent natural image, one had to add two or three successful brushstrokes and the picture of insanity would be there. I imagined vividly how it would be, not in terms of rational thought but of lively imagery. Though I do not write stupid stories, I am far from lacking in artistic intuition and fantasy.

I saw then that I would be able to enact my role. An inclination toward dissimulation has always been part of my character and was one of the forms whereby I strove for inner freedom. When I was still in high school, I often simulated friendship. As true friends do, I often walked along the corridors arm in arm. I artfully imitated conversations full of friendly candor, while imperceptibly probing my companion. Then, when the softened comrade revealed himself entirely, I would reject his puny soul and walk away with a proud awareness of my strength and inner freedom. I displayed the same duality at home; just as Old Believers keep separate plates for strangers, I maintained my apartness from other people: for them I had a special smile, special conversations and confidences. I perceived that people do much that is stupid, harmful to themselves, and futile. It seemed to me that if I would tell the truth about myself, I would become like everyone else, and I would become possessed by all this stupidity and futility.

I have always enjoyed being respectful toward people whom I despised and kissing those whom I hated, which has made me free and a lord over others. On the other hand, I have never lied to myself, which is the most widespread and the lowliest form of human enslavement. And the more I lied to people, the more mercilessly truthful I became with myself—a merit that few could claim.

Altogether it seemed to me that an exceptional actor was hidden within me, one capable of combining a naturalness of performance, which at times led to a complete identification with the character portrayed, with a relentless, cold control of the mind. Even when reading a book I would enter fully into the psyche of a character. Would you believe it, even as an adult I wept bitter tears over *Uncle Tom's Cabin*. This is the divine capacity of a supple, exceedingly cultivated mind—that of reincarnation! You live through a thousand lives, descending into the darkness of hell and then reaching the clear mountain heights, embracing the infinite in one glance. If man is destined to become God, his throne shall be a book.

Yes. This is so. Incidentally, I want to complain to you about the regulations here. They put me to bed when I want to write, *when I must write*. Or else the door is left open and I have to listen to a madman's howling. He howls on and on; it is quite unbearable. This is one way of driving one mad, to be able to say later that he was mad from the beginning. Is it possible that they haven't an extra candle so that I don't ruin my eyes with electric light?

Well then. At one time I had even considered going on the stage, but I abandoned this silly idea: deception, when everyone knows it's deception, loses its value. The cheap laurels of the hack repertory actor held little attraction for me. As to the quality of my own art, you may judge it by the fact that many fools consider me even now to be the most sincere and truthful of men. I said "fools" in haste:

the strange thing is that I have, in fact, been most successful with intelligent people. On the other hand, two categories of the lower orders have never accorded me their trust—women and dogs.

Do you know that the esteemed Tatiana Nikolayevna never believed in my love and does not believe in it now, not even after I have killed her husband? According to her logic, I did not love her but killed Alexis because she loved him. And this nonsense seems reasonable and convincing to her. And she is a clever woman.

The role of a madman did not strike me as being difficult to play. Part of the necessary directions I got from books; part I created myself, as any actor in a real role would do; the rest had to be filled in by the public itself, whose sensibilities had been honed by books and theater, which have trained it to recreate living characters from two or three vague traits. Of course, inevitably there would be certain gaps, and this would be hazardous in view of the expert scientific investigation to which I would be subjected, but even this presented no serious danger. The vast realm of psychopathology has still been so little explored, there is so much in it that is dark and accidental, fantasizing and subjectivity play so great a part in it, that I boldy entrusted my fate into your hands, learned gentlemen. I hope I have not offended you. I am not trying to undermine your scientific authority, and I am sure that you will agree with me, as men accustomed to conscientious scientific thought.

Ah, that fellow who's been howling has finally stopped. It's simply unbearable.

At the time when my scheme was being conceived, I had a thought that would hardly have entered the head of a madman. *The thought was about the terrifying danger of my experiment.* Do you understand what I'm saying? Madness is a fire that is dangerous to play with. A bonfire in a powder magazine is less threatening than the first inkling of madness. And I knew this, I knew—but what is danger to a brave man?

And did I not sense my thought as being firm and clear, forged of steel, fully subservient to me? Like a finely sharpened rapier, it bent, it stung, it bit, it rent the fabric of events; like a serpent it glided noiselessly into unexplored, dark depths forever sealed from the light of day; I held its hilt in my hand, the iron hand of a skilled and experienced fencer. How obedient, how efficient and swift was my thought, and how I loved it, my slave, my terrifying strength, my sole treasure!

There! He's howling again, and I can't write any more. How awful it is when a man howls. I have heard many dreadful sounds, but this is the worst. It is like nothing else—the voice of a wild animal passing through a human throat. It is both ferocious and craven; free and yet pitiful to the point of abjectness. The mouth twists to one side; the face muscles strain like ropes; the teeth are bared, doglike; and from the dark opening of the mouth comes this repulsive sound, at once roaring, hissing, laughing, wailing.

Yes, yes. Such was my thought. By the way, you will of course notice my handwriting, and I ask you not to ascribe any importance to the fact that it sometimes wavers and seems to change. I haven't written anything in a long time, recent events and insomnia have greatly weakened me, and now my hand trembles. *This happened to me before . . .*

III

Now you understand something about that frightful fit that overcame me that evening at the Kurganovs. This was my first experiment, and it succeeded even beyond my expectations. It was as if everyone knew ahead of time what would happen to me, as if the sudden madness of a perfectly healthy person appeared quite natural to them, something to be expected. No one was surprised, everyone vied to interpret my performance through the prism of his own fantasy. Rare is the director who can assemble such a magnificent troupe as these naive, stupid, credulous people. Did they tell you how pale and awful I looked? How cold—yes, actually *cold*—sweat covered my brow? How my dark eyes burned with insane fire? When they shared all these observations with me I appeared morose and depressed, while my whole being trembled with pride, happiness, and derision.

Tatiana Nikolayevna and her husband had not been there that evening—I do not know whether you had taken note of that. It was not an accident; I did not want to frighten Tatiana Nikolayevna or, what would be worse, to arouse her suspicion. If there were anyone who could have seen through my game, it would have been she.

All in all there was nothing accidental about any of this. On the contrary, every detail, no matter how small, had been carefully thought through. I chose the middle of dinner to have my fit because everyone would be present and somewhat affected by wine. I sat at the end of the table, far from the candelabra, as I had no intention of starting a fire or of burning my nose. I sat next to Pavel Petrovich Pospelov, that fat pig on whom I had for a long time wanted to play a nasty prank. He is particularly repugnant when he is eating. When I first saw him thus occupied, it struck me that eating is an immoral business. Everything was fitting together nicely. Surely no one noticed that the plate that I shattered with my fist was covered with a napkin so that I would not cut my hand.

The trick itself was amazingly crude, even stupid, but that was precisely what I was counting on. They would not have understood anything more subtle. First I waved my arms around and spoke "animatedly" with Pavel Petrovich, until he started to stare at me, his beady eyes wide with amazement. I then fell into a state of "deep meditation," awaiting a question from the solicitous Irina Pavlovna: "What is the matter with you, Anton Ignatyevich? Why are you so sad?"

When all eyes converged on me I smiled tragically.

"Are you ill?"

"Yes, a little. A bit dizzy. But please don't concern yourself. It will soon pass."

The hostess was reassured, while Pavel Petrovich eyed me with suspicion and disapproval. But in the next moment, when he blissfully brought a glass of port to his lips, I first struck the glass from under his nose and then crashed my fist down on the plate. Now the fragments are flying, Pavel Petrovich flounders and grunts, the ladies are shrieking, while I, baring my teeth, am pulling down the tablecloth with everything on it—that was an entertaining tableau!

Yes, but then I was surrounded and held. Someone fetched water, others propped me up in an armchair, while I roared like a tiger in the zoo and rolled my eyes. And all this was so absurd and all of them so idiotic, that I, savoring the advantage of my situation, actually felt like smashing their faces in. Yet of course I abstained.

Later the scene I was enacting grew calmer. I heaved my chest, raised my eyes, gnashed my teeth, and feebly inquired, "Where am I? What is the matter with me?"

Even this absurd French phrase, *"Où suis-je?"* had great success with this crowd, and no fewer than three imbeciles duly reported, "You're at the Kurganovs." (Then sweetly:) "You know of course, dear doctor, who Irina Pavlovna Kurganova is?"

They were decidedly not up to playing a good game.

A day later—I gave rumors time to reach the Savelovs—there was a conversation with Tatiana Nikolayevna and Alexis. The latter somehow did not grasp what had happened and simply asked, "What was that row you stirred up at the Kurganovs?"

Having said this he went off to work in his study, and from this I knew that had I really lost my mind, it would have been all the same to him and of course it would have been insincere. And here— not that I regretted what had been set afoot—the thought simply struck me: Is it worth it?

"You really love your husband?" I asked Tatiana Nikolayevna, who was following Alexis with her eyes. She turned abruptly.

"Yes. Why do you ask?"

"Oh, for no reason." And after a moment's silence, which was cautious and full of unexpressed thoughts, I added, "Why don't you trust me?"

She looked sharply into my eyes without answering. At that

moment I forgot that once, long ago, she had laughed, and now I was not angry with her, and what I was undertaking seemed unnecessary and strange. This was fatigue, natural after a time of heightened nervous energy, and it lasted only a moment. After a long silence Tatiana Nikolayevna said, "But can one trust you?"

"Of course not," I answered jestingly, while a fire that had been extinguished flared up within me. I felt a strength, a daring, and invincible determination. Proud of the success I had already achieved, I boldly resolved to go to the end. Struggle is the joy of life.

The second attack occurred a month later. This time it all had not been so well thought out, but such care was unnecessary since there was an overall plan. I had no intention to stage it on that particular evening, but since circumstances turned out to be so favorable, it would have been stupid not to take advantage of them. I remember vividly how it all happened. We were sitting in a drawing room chatting when I suddenly felt very sad. I had a clear vision— of a rare kind—about how alien I was to these people and how alone in the world, forever imprisoned in my head, in this jail. At that moment they filled me with revulsion. In rage I brought down my fist and shouted something coarse and was delighted to see fear in their pallid faces.

"Scoundrels!" I was shouting. "Rotten, self-satisfied scoundrels! Liars! Hypocrites! Vicious hypocrites! I loathe you!"

And it is true that I wrestled with them, and then with the lackeys and grooms. But then, I knew that I was wrestling and that I was doing it deliberately. I simply enjoyed beating them up, telling them the truth about themselves. Is everyone who speaks the truth crazy? I assure you, learned gentlemen, that I was aware of everything, that as I struck, I felt under my fist a living body in pain. At home alone I laughed and rejoiced in what an astounding, magnificent actor I was. Then I went to bed and read—I can even tell you what I read: Guy de Maupassant, taking pleasure in him, as always. Then I fell asleep like a child. I ask you, do madmen read books and take pleasure in them? Do they sleep like children?

Madmen do not sleep, they suffer, and everything is murky in their heads. Yes, murky and swirling. They want to howl, to lacerate themselves. They want to get down on all fours and crawl around quietly and then to leap up and shout, "Aaah!"

They want to laugh and to howl. To raise their heads slowly, slowly, little by little, so, so pitifully.

Yes, yes.

But I slept like a child. I ask you, do madmen sleep like children?

IV

Last night nurse Masha asked me, "Anton Ignatyevich, do you ever pray to God?"

She spoke in earnest and believed that I would answer her sincerely and seriously. And I replied without a smile, as she wished me to, "No, Masha, I never do. But if it makes you happy, you may bless me."

And just as seriously, she made the sign of the cross three times over me, and I was happy to have caused this excellent woman a moment's pleasure. Like all those who are free and occupy high positions, you, gentlemen experts, do not pay attention to servants, but we prisoners and madmen see them at close quarters and occasionally make surprising discoveries. It may never have occurred to you, for instance, that nurse Masha, appointed by you to watch over the insane, is in fact *insane herself.* This is how it is.

Observe her walk—silent, gliding, somewhat timed and extraordinarily guarded and deft—as if she were walking between invisible drawn swords. Look into her face—but when she is unaware of your presence. When one of you comes in, Masha's face turns grave, yet she smiles indulgently—that very expression, gentlemen, which your faces display at this moment. The fact is that Masha possesses the strange and significant faculty of reflecting in her face the expressions of those around her. Sometimes she looks at me and smiles. It is a pale, mimetic smile, not her own. Then I understand that I was smiling when she first looked at me. Sometimes Masha's face shows suffering and sadness; she knits her brow, and the corners of her mouth fall; her whole face ages by ten years and darkens, as my own face must do sometimes. Sometimes my eyes frighten her: You know how unsettling and even scary the eyes of a man in deep thought are. Then Masha's eyes widen; her pupils turn dark. She raises her arms and comes up to me and does something friendly and unexpected—smoothes my hair, straightens my robe. "Your belt will come loose," she says, her face still showing fear.

But sometimes I see her alone. And when she is alone there is a strange absence of expression on her face, which is then as pale, beautiful, and enigmatic as the face of a dead woman. If one should call out to her, "Masha!" she will quickly turn and smile *her own* smile, tender and timorous, and she will ask, "Can I get you anything?"

She is always serving something, and if there is nothing to serve or to clear away, she becomes visibly worried. She never makes a sound. I have never seen her drop or knock anything. I have tried to talk to her about life, but she is indifferent to everything, even to murders, fires, and other horrors, which usually so impress simplehearted people.

"Do you realize they are being wounded, killed, and they leave small hungry children at home?" I was telling her about the war.

"Yes, I understand," she said and asked distractedly, "Would you like some milk? You haven't eaten much today." I laugh and she answers with an anxious laugh.

She has never been to the theater, she is not aware that Russia is a country and that there are other countries, she is illiterate, and knows only those parts of the New Testament that are read in church. Every evening she goes down on her knees and prays for a long time.

I used to consider her a stunted person, born for slavery, but a certain event forced me to change my view. You might have been informed that I had a bad moment here, one that of course was caused only by fatigue and a temporary loss of energy. *It was the towel incident.*

Of course I am stronger than Masha, and I might have killed her. We were alone, and had she screamed or touched my hand . . . But she did nothing of the sort. She only said, "Don't, my dear."

Since then I have often thought about this "don't," and I cannot understand its surprising power, which I feel even now. It is not in the word itself, which is senseless and empty; rather, it lies within the depths of Masha's unknown, inaccessible soul. She knows something. Yes, she knows, but she cannot or will not tell about it. Later I often tried to get Masha to explain this "don't," but she could not.

"Do you think that suicide is a sin? That God has forbidden it?"

"No."

"Why, then, the 'don't'?"

"Just don't," she said with a smile, and asked, "May I get you something?"

She is obviously insane but quiet and useful, like so many insane people. And you must not touch her, learned gentlemen.

Here I shall indulge in a digression, since what Masha did yesterday has plunged me into memories of my childhood. I don't remember my mother, but I had an aunt called Anphisa, who made the sign of the cross over me every night. She was a taciturn spinster with pimples on her face, and she was greatly embarrassed when my father joked about suitors. I was still a youngster, about eleven, when she strangled herself in the small shed where we kept our coal. Afterward she kept appearing before my father, and this cheerful atheist ordered regular services to be said for her soul.

My father was very intelligent and talented, and his speeches in court caused not only nervous ladies but serious and well-balanced people to weep. I alone did not weep when I listened to him, because I knew him, and I knew that he understood nothing of what he was saying. He possessed considerable knowledge, many thoughts,

and even more words; and his words and his ideas and his knowledge often combined felicitously and beautifully, but he himself
understood nothing of this. *I often wondered whether he even existed*—he seemed to have no inner core but to be all sounds and
gestures, and it seemed to me that he was not a person but a flickering cinematographic image, connected to a gramophone. He did
not understand that he was a man who was alive and destined to
die, and he sought nothing. And when he went to bed and ceased
to move and fell asleep, he surely dreamed no dreams and stopped
existing. He was an attorney and with his tongue he earned thirty
thousand a year, and not once did he ever reflect upon this circumstance. I remember having gone with him to visit an estate he had
just bought, and I had said, pointing out the trees on the grounds,
"Clients?"

Flattered, he smiled complacently and said, "Yes, my friend, talent is a great thing."

He drank heavily, and his intoxication expressed itself only in
that his whole behavior became manic and accelerated and then
slowed abruptly as he dropped off to sleep. Everyone considered him
exceptionally gifted, while he simply declared that had he not become a famous lawyer, he would have been a famous artist or writer.
Unfortunately, this was true.

He understood me least of all. There came a time when we were
threatened with the loss of everything we had. To me this was horrifying. Nowadays, when only wealth provides freedom, I cannot
conceive what would have become of me if fate had placed me in
the ranks of the proletariat. Even today I cannot imagine without
anger anyone daring to restrict me, to compel me to do things that
I don't want to do, purchasing for a few pennies my labor, my blood,
my nerves, my life. This horror I experienced only for one moment,
because the next minute I realized that people like myself are never
poor. My father did not understand this. He saw me as a dull young
man and viewed my helplessness with apprehension.

"Oh, Anton, Anton, what will become of you?" he would say. He himself had become quite depressed. His long, unkempt hair fell over his forehead; his face was yellow.

I replied, "Papa, don't worry about me. Since I am without talent, I'll kill a Rothschild or rob a bank."

He became angry because he took my answer as a flat, ill-considered joke. He saw my face, he heard my voice—and still he took it to be a joke. Wretched pasteboard clown, who through a misunderstanding is called a man!

He did not know my soul, but the whole outward order of my life filled him with indignation because he could not comprehend it. I was a good student in high school, and this distressed him. When guests came—lawyers, literary people, and artists—he would point his finger at me and say, "My son is first in his class. Why is the Lord punishing me?"

And they all laughed at me, and I laughed at them. But my conduct and my attire upset him even more than my successes. He would come to my room for the express purpose of moving my books around (in a way that I would not notice) and creating disorder. My neat hair caused him to lose his appetite.

"The superintendent makes us cut our hair short," I would tell him gravely and respectfully.

He would swear vehemently, while I was shaking with contemptuous inner laughter, and I divided the world into plain superintendents and antisuperintendents—all after my head: some to cut my hair, others to stretch it.

The worst of all for my father were my notebooks. Drunk, he would examine them with a hopeless and comic despair.

"Have you ever in your life made an ink spot?"

"Yes, I have, papa. The day before yesterday I made an ink spot on my trigonometry."

"Did you lick it off?"

"What do you mean?"

"Did you lick off the spot?"

"No, I blotted it."

With a drunken gesture my father waved me off and growled as he rose to his feet, "No, you are no son of mine. No! No!"

Among those notebooks that he hated, there was one that none-theless might have given him pleasure. It contained no crooked line, no ink spot, no erasure. It contained these lines: *"My father is a drunk, a thief, and a coward."*

This was followed by certain details, which out of respect for my father's memory and out of respect as well for the law, I shall not repeat here.

Here I remember a certain fact that I had forgotten, one that, as I see it, will be of great interest to you, learned gentlemen. I am very pleased that I have remembered it, very pleased indeed. How could I have forgotten?

We had a chambermaid called Katya, who was my father's mistress and mine as well. She loved my father because he gave her money, and me because I was young, had beautiful dark eyes, and gave her no money. The night my father's corpse lay in the parlor, I went to Katya's room. Her room was nearby. I could clearly hear the voice of the deacon.

I am certain that the immortal spirit of my father was duly satisfied.

This is indeed fascinating, and I do not understand how I could have forgotten it. You, gentlemen experts, might consider it a boy's prank, a child's meaningless defiance, but this is not so. This, learned gentlemen, was a hard struggle, a victory that cost me dearly. What was at stake was my life. Had I backed off, been incapable of loving, I could have killed myself. *I remember that I had made up my mind about this.*

What I was doing was not easy for someone of my age. Now I know that I was battling windmills, but at the time I saw it in another light. It is hard for me now to summon the past, but I remember having had the feeling that in a single act I had broken all laws, human and divine. And I was very apprehensive, to a ridiculous degree; but I controlled myself, and when I entered Katya's room I was prepared for her kisses, like Romeo.

Yet, it seems that in those days I was still a romantic. Happy times, how distant they are! Learned gentlemen, I remember that coming out of Katya's room, I stopped before my father's corpse. I crossed my arms on my chest like Napoleon and gazed at it with inane pride. And then I jumped, startled when the shroud stirred. Happy, distant times!

I hate to say it, but it seems I never stopped being a romantic. I may even have once been an idealist. I believed in human thought and its boundless power. The whole history of mankind appeared to me as the march of one triumphant thought—and not so long ago. It is terrible for me to realize that my entire life has been a lie, that all my life I was insane, like that demented actor whom I see in the next ward. He collected pieces of colored paper and declared that each was worth a million. He implored visitors to give bits of paper to him and stole paper from the toilet, to the great amusement of the staff, to whom it afforded an opportunity for vulgar jokes. He utterly despised these people, but he liked me and as a parting gift gave me a million.

"It's only a million," he said, "but you must forgive me; I have such expenses, such dreadful expenses right now." And taking me aside, he explained in a whisper, "I am getting ready for Italy. I want to banish the pope and introduce this new money. Later, on Sunday, I shall proclaim myself a saint. The Italians will be delighted: they are always happy when they have a new saint."

Have I not lived all along with a million?

I hate to think that my books—my companions and friends—still stand on their shelves and silently preserve what I considered to be the wisdom of the world, its hope and its happiness. I know, learned gentlemen, that whether I am crazy or not, from your point of view I am a scoundrel. You should see this scoundrel when he enters his library!

Learned gentlemen, do go and examine my apartment; you will find it instructive. In the upper left drawer of my desk, you will find a detailed catalog of the books, pictures, and objects I have collected: there you will find the keys to my bookcases. You are men of science, and I trust that you will treat my things with due respect and care. *I must also request that you make sure that the lamps do not smoke.* There is nothing worse than soot. It penetrates everywhere, and it is extremely hard to get rid of.

[Note on a scrap of paper.]

Just now the intern Petrov has refused to give me chloralamide in the dose I require. First, I am a doctor and I know what I am doing, and so if it is denied to me, I shall take measures. I have not slept two nights and have no desire to go mad. I demand that chloralamide be given me. I demand it. It is *dishonorable* to drive a man mad.

V

After my second attack people began to be frightened of me. In many houses doors would be slammed shut in my face. Acquaintances whom I met by chance would bristle at my approach, smile maliciously, and inquire pointedly, "Well, my dear friend, how is your health?"

The situation was such that I could commit any kind of lawless act and not lose the respect of those around me. I looked at people and thought to myself: If I wanted to, I could kill this one or that one, and nothing would happen to me. And what I experienced then was something new, pleasant, and a little frightening. Human beings ceased to be inviolable creatures whom we fear to touch. It was as if they had shed a skin, were naked, and to kill them was easy and even appealing.

Fear, like a thick wall, protected me from probing eyes, so there was no need for a third preparatory attack. Only in this respect did I vary from my plan. A great talent is measured by the fact that while it builds structures for itself, it knows how to change as circumstances change, thereby altering the entire course of battle. But a formal absolution of sins, past and future, was still needed—a medical certification of my illness.

At this time a happy concurrence of events made it possible for me to go to a psychiatrist, with the visit seeming to be no more than chance or even necessity. This was perhaps an excessive refinement in the perfecting of my role. Tatiana Nikolayevna and her husband themselves sent me to the psychiatrist.

"Dear Anton Ignatyevich, please do go to the doctor," said Tatiana Nikolayevna. She had never before called me "dear." I had to appear insane to receive this small endearment.

"All right, Tatiana Nikolayevna, I will," I replied meekly. The three of us—Alexis was there—were sitting in the study where the murder was to take place.

"Yes, Anton, you must go," Alexis said with authority. "Otherwise you'll get into trouble."

"How could I get in trouble?" I was timidly justifying myself before my demanding friend.

"Who knows? You might bash somebody's head in."

I was turning in my hands a heavy cast-iron paperweight. I looked first at it and then at Alexis and asked, "Head? You said somebody's head?"

"Yes, head. Hit it with something like this, and that will be that."

It was becoming interesting. *It was precisely what I meant to do, crush the head with this object, but now this very head was discussing how it would happen.* It discussed and smiled blithely. Yet there are people who believe in premonitions—that death sends before it invisible heralds. What nonsense!

"One couldn't do much with this," I said. "It's too light."

"What do you mean, too light?" Alexis said indignantly, grabbing the paperweight out of my hands and swinging it around a few times by its thin handle. "Try it."

"Yes, I know—"

"No, take it and see for yourself."

Reluctant, smiling, I took the heavy object, but here Tatiana Nikolayevna intervened. Pale, her lips quivering, she said, or rather shrieked, "Stop it, Alexis!"

"What is this, Tanya," he asked in surprise. "What is the matter with you?"

"Stop it! You know how I hate this kind of joke."

We laughed and the paperweight went back on the table.

At Professor T.'s everything happened as I expected. He was very cautious, expressed himself with restraint, and was extremely serious. He asked whether I had relatives who might take care of me; he advised me to stay home, to rest, and to calm down. Invoking my position as a medical doctor, I had a slight argument with him. And if he still had any doubt, at this time, when I dared disagree with him, he definitively consigned me to the ranks of the insane. Learned gentlemen, you will of course not give any weight to this harmless joke, played upon one of our colleagues. There is no doubt that as a scientist, Professor T. deserves respect and honors.

The next few days were among the happiest of my life. I received sympathy as an acknowledged invalid; I received visits. People addressed me in an absurdly indulgent manner. Only I knew that I was as healthy as anyone, and I took delight in the precise, powerful workings of my thought. Of all that is astounding and incredible that makes life rich, nothing is more so than human thought. There is divinity in it, a promise of immortality, a boundless power. People are seized with exhilaration and wonderment when they behold the snowy peaks of great mountains. If they could only understand themselves they would be astounded more by their ability to think than by mountains and all the marvels and beauties of the world.

The simple thinking of a laborer about how to place one brick on top of another in the right way—here is the greatest miracle and the deepest mystery.

I was exulting in my thought. Innocent in her beauty, she gave herself to me with passion, like a lover; she served me like a slave and sustained me like a friend. Don't imagine that in all those days spent at home between four walls, I was thinking only about my plan. No, as far as that was concerned, everything was clear and thought through. I pondered everything. I and my thought seemed to play with life and death, and we soared above them, high above them.

By the way, in those days I solved two very interesting chess problems, over which I had struggled for a long time unsuccessfully. You, of course, know that about three years ago I participated in an international chess tournament and I came in second after Lasker. Were I not an enemy of publicity and had I continued to participate in tournaments, Lasker would have had to cede his place.

From the moment that Alexis's life was put in my hands, I felt especially drawn to him. It pleased me to think that he was living, eating and drinking, taking delight in life—and all this because I allowed it. It was not unlike what a father feels for his son. If anything worried me it was his health. Despite his frail condition, he was unforgivably careless: he refused to wear a sweater, and in the foulest weather he went out without galoshes.

Tatiana Nikolayevna would reassure me. She stopped by my house and assured me that Alexis was in good health and was even sleeping well, which was unusual for him. Delighted, I asked Tatiana Nikolayevna to pass on a book to Alexis—a rare volume that I had acquired by accident and that Alexis had admired for a long time. It is possible that from the standpoint of my plan, this gift was a mistake. I could be accused of hatching a scheme, but I so wanted to please Alexis that I decided to take a small risk. I even disregarded the fact that from the standpoint of the artistic perfection of my performance, the sending of this gift was excessive.

On this occasion I was very nice to Tatiana Nikolayevna and made a good impression on her. Neither she nor Alexis had witnessed my attacks, and evidently it was hard and even impossible for them to imagine that I was insane.

"Do come to see us," said Tatiana Nikolayevna as we parted.

"I can't," I said with a smile. "The doctor forbids it."

"What nonsense! You can come to us. It's just like home. And Alexis misses you."

I promised to come and no promise was ever given with as much assurance of fulfillment as this one. Does it not seem to you, learned gentlemen, considering all these happy coincidences, that it was not I alone who condemned Alexis to death, but *someone else, too?* Yet in fact, there was no one else, and nothing could be more simple or logical.

The cast-iron paperweight stood at its usual place when, on the eleventh of December at 5:00 P.M., I came into Alexis's study. Before dinner—they dined at seven—Alexis and Tatiana Nikolayevna were in the habit of taking a rest. Nonetheless they were very pleased that I had come.

"Thank you for the book, my friend," said Alexis, shaking my hand. "I was about to call on you, but Tanya said that you were quite recovered. We are off to the theater. Will you come with us?"

We fell into conversation. That day I had decided not to dissemble (and this lack of dissembling was its own subtle dissembling), and being still under the effect of exalted thought, I spoke at length and interestingly. If the admirers of Savelov's talent knew how many of "his" best thoughts were born and nurtured in the head of obscure Dr. Kerzhentsev!

I spoke clearly, precisely, honing my sentences. At the same time I was watching the hands of the clock, and I thought that when they reached six, I would become a murderer. I said something amusing and they laughed. I tried to capture the feelings of a man who was not yet a murderer but who would soon become one. I now understood Alexis's life process not in any abstract way but directly:

the beating of his heart, the pulse of blood in his temples, the silent vibration of his brain; and I understood how this process would stop, the heart no longer circulating the blood, the brain arrested.

What would be its last thought?

At no time had the clarity of my consciousness reached such height and power; never did I possess such a full, many-sided awareness of a harmoniously functioning "I." Like God: not seeing, I saw; not hearing, I heard; not thinking, I understood.

Seven minutes remained, when Alexis lazily arose from the sofa, stretched, and went out.

"I'll be right back," he said.

I did not want to look at Tatiana Nikolayevna, and I went over to the window, opened the curtains, and stood there. Without turning around I felt that Tatiana Nikolayevna had hastily crossed the room and stood next to me. I heard her breathing and realized that she was not looking out the window but at me. I remained silent.

"How beautifully the snow shines," said Tatiana Nikolayevna, but I did not respond. Her breathing became more rapid, then seemed to cease.

"Anton Ignatyevich!" she said, then broke off.

I remained silent.

"Anton Ignatyevich!" she repeated in a voice so uncertain that I glanced at her. She quickly drew back and almost fell, as if she had been struck by the terrible force of that glance. She drew back and rushed toward her husband, who was entering the room.

"Alexis!" she said. "Alexis, he—"

"What about him?"

Without smiling, but with a trace of jest, I said, "She thinks that I want to kill you with this thing."

And very calmly, making no effort at concealment, I picked up the paperweight, held it in my hand, and quietly approached Alexis.

He, without blinking, gazed at me with his pale eyes and repeated, "She thinks—"

"Yes, she thinks that."

Slowly, leisurely, I raised my arm, and just as slowly Alexis raised his, while keeping his eyes on me.

"Wait!" I said sternly.

Alexis's arm remained suspended, and, still keeping his eyes on me, he smiled incredulously with his lips alone. Tatiana Nikolay-evna screamed something wildly, but it was too late. I struck him on the side of the head with the sharp edge. And when he fell, I leaned down and struck him two more times. The investigator told me that I had struck him repeatedly, because his head was all battered, but this is untrue. I struck him only *three times*: once when he was standing and twice when he was on the floor.

It is true that the blows were very hard ones, but there were only three. This I remember for certain—*three blows*.

VI

Don't try to read what is crossed out at the end of page 4. And don't attach undue importance to my revisions or take them to be signs of deranged thinking. In the strange position in which I found myself, I had to be extraordinarily careful, a fact that I do not deny and that you will well understand.

The dark of night always strongly affects a strained nervous system, and this is why terrifying thoughts so often come at night. That evening, the first after the murder, my nerves were, of course, under particular strain. No matter how self-possessed I was, it is no joke to kill a man. At tea, having put myself in order, scrubbed my nails, and changed clothes, I invited Maria Vasilyevna to sit with me. She is my housekeeper and in some respects my wife. It seems she has a lover on the side but she is a beautiful woman, gentle and not greedy, and I easily made my peace with this small fault, which is all but inevitable when a person must trade love for money. And this stupid woman was the first to strike a blow against me.

"Kiss me," I said.

She smiled stupidly and froze in her chair.

"Come on!"

She shivered, flushed, and with frightened eyes leaned toward me imploringly across the table, saying, "Anton Ignatyevich, my dear, go to the doctor!"

"What's this all about?" I demanded angrily.

"Oh, please don't shout. You frighten me! My darling, my angel."

Yet she knew nothing about my attacks or about the murder, and I had always been kind and even-tempered with her. Which is to say that there was something singular in me that was frightening. This thought flickered through my mind and disappeared at once, leaving a strange chill in my legs and back. I gathered that Maria Vasilyevna had somehow learned something, either from a servant or by having found my stained clothing, so that her fear would have a natural explanation.

"You may go," I told her.

Then I lay down on the sofa in my library. I didn't feel like reading. My entire body was weary; I felt like an actor who has just performed his role brilliantly. It pleased me to look over my books; it pleased me to think that someday I would be reading them. My apartment also pleased me, and the sofa, and Maria Vasilyevna. Fragments of lines from my role passed through my head; in my mind I repeated some of the gestures I had made, and occasionally a criticism drifted by: at this or that point it could have been done better. However, I was very pleased by my improvised command, "Wait!" Indeed, this was a rare and, for those who have not experienced it themselves, an unbelievable instance of the power of suggestion.

"Wait!" I repeated, closing my eyes, and I smiled. My eyelids became heavy, and I began to feel sleepy, when languidly, simply, like all the others, a new thought entered my head, a new thought possessing all the characteristics of *my* thought: clarity, accuracy, and simplicity. It came languidly and stopped. Here it is literally, just as it came to me, in the third person:

"It is quite possible that Dr. Kerzhentsev is really insane. He thought that he was simulating madness, but he is really insane. He is insane now."

This thought returned three or four times, but I was still smiling, not understanding: *"He thought that he was simulating madness, but he is really insane. He is insane now."*

But when I understood—At first I thought that Maria Vasilyevna had said this, because it seemed to me that there had been a voice that sounded like hers. Then I thought of Alexis. Yes, of Alexis, who was dead. Then I understood that it was I who had thought this—and this was dreadful. Clutching at my hair, I found myself standing in the middle of the room, saying, "So it's all over. The very thing I feared has happened. I came too close to the borderline, and now there is only one thing before me—madness."

When they came to arrest me I was, according to them, in a terrible state: disheveled, my clothes torn, pale, frightening to behold. But good Lord! To survive such a night and not go mad—does that not mean that one's brain is indestructible? In fact, I had only torn my clothes and broken a mirror. By the way, let me give you a piece of advice. Should one of you ever have to live through what I did that night, make sure to cover the mirrors in the room where you will be thrashing around. Do cover them!

I find it terrifying to write about this. I fear the very thing that I must remember and express. But it can be postponed no longer, and it may well be that with my halting words, I only heighten the terror.

That evening!

Imagine a drunken snake—yes, yes, a drunken snake: it has lost none of its malice; its agility and swiftness have increased, and its fangs are as sharp and as venomous as ever. And it is drunk, and it is in a closed room filled with people trembling with horror. Coldly ferocious, it slithers among them, coils around their legs, sinks its fangs into their very faces, their lips, and then it coils upon itself and bites its own body. And it seems that there is not one but a thousand writhing snakes biting and devouring themselves. Such was my thought—that very thought in which I believed—and it was in the sharpness and venomousness of its fangs that I saw my salvation and my protection.

One thought splintered into a thousand thoughts, and each of them was strong, and all were hostile. They swirled in a wild dance to the music of a monstrous voice, sonorous as a trumpet, arising from depths unknown to me. *This was a thought on the run, the most terrifying of all snakes, hiding in darkness.* From within my head, where I was clutching it tightly, it escaped into secret reaches of my body, into its black, uncharted depths. And from there it cried out, like someone lost, like a fugitive slave, insolent and bold, fully aware of its impunity.

"You thought that you were pretending, but in fact you were insane. You are puny, you are nasty, you are stupid, you are Dr. Kerzhentsev. Some Dr. Kerzhentsev! The mad Dr. Kerzhentsev!"

So it cried out, and I did not know where its monstrous voice was coming from. I do not even know who it was; I call it "the thought," but perhaps it was not that. Thoughts are what swirl in the head as birds swirl over flames, while this was calling out from below, from above, from the sides, where I could not see it or catch it.

The most frightening thing that I experienced was the realization that I do not know myself, and never did. As long as my "I" was to be found within my brightly lighted head, where everything moves and lives in regulated order, I understood and knew myself, and reflecting on my character and plans, it seemed to me that I was the master. Now I saw that I was not the master but the slave, wretched and powerless. Imagine that you live in a house with many rooms. You occupy only one room while thinking that you own the whole house. And suddenly you learn that in the other rooms there are occupants. *Yes, occupants.* Enigmatic creatures, people perhaps, but maybe not, and the house belongs to them. You would like to know who they are, but the door is closed. And behind it there is no voice or sound. At the same time you know that right there, behind that silent door, your fate is being decided.

I came up to the mirror—Cover the mirrors! Cover them!

From that moment I remember nothing until the police and the court authorities arrived. I asked what time it was and was told that it was nine o'clock. For a long time I found it difficult to realize that only two hours had passed since my return home, only three since the moment of the murder of Alexis.

Forgive me, learned gentlemen, for describing in such a general and imprecise way this moment so important to your work—my dreadful state after the murder. But this is all that I can remember and can express in human terms. For instance, I cannot express in human terms the horror that I constantly felt at that time. More-over, I cannot say with absolute certainty that all that I have so feebly suggested happened in reality. Perhaps it never happened and something else happened instead. Only one thing do I remember clearly—this thought or voice, or perhaps something else: *"Dr. Ker-zhentsev thought that he was simulating madness, but he is really insane."*

Right now I am taking my pulse: 180! And that at the mere rec-ollection of it!

VII

The last time, I wrote a great deal of unnecessary and pathetic nonsense, and unfortunately you have by now received it and read it. I fear that it will give you a false notion of my personality and of the actual state of my mental faculties. However, learned gentle-men, I have faith in your knowledge and in your clear intellects.

You understand that only serious reasons could have forced me, Dr. Kerzhentsev, to reveal the whole truth about Savelov's murder. And you will easily understand and appreciate these reasons when I say that even now, I don't know whether I pretended to be insane so as to be able to kill with impunity or whether I killed because I was in fact insane; and I probably shall never know. The nightmare of that evening has passed, but it has left a fiery mark. I have no unfounded fears, but I have the dread of a man who has lost everything, who has a cold awareness of a fall, destruction, duplicity, and entrapment.

You, who are scientists, will argue about me. Some of you will say that I am insane; others will prove that I am sound and will only admit to certain limitations due to degeneracy. But with all your knowledge you will not prove as clearly as I will whether I am insane or whether I am not. My thought has come back to me, and as you will see, it lacks neither strength nor sharpness. Excellent, energetic thought—for enemies, too, must be given their due!

I am insane. Shall I tell you why?

First of all, I am condemned by my heredity, the very heredity that pleased me so when I was conceiving my plan. The attacks that I had in childhood . . . I plead guilty, gentlemen. I wanted to hide from you this detail, about the attacks, and wrote that as a child I was bursting with health. Not that I saw a danger to myself in these trifling, short-lived fits. I simply did not want to encumber my narrative with unnecessary details. Now this detail is useful to me for a strictly logical line of thinking, and as you see, I give it to you freely.

Here it is. My heredity and my attacks testify to my predisposition to psychic illness. And, unnoticed by me, it began a long time before I contrived the plan of the murder. But, possessing, *like all madmen*, an unconscious cunning and an ability to accommodate my insane actions to the norms of various modes of thinking, I began to deceive not others, as I had thought, but myself. Led on by an alien force, I pretended that I was proceeding on my own. The rest of the argument can be shaped as easily as wax. Is this not so?

It is easy enough to prove that I did not love Tatiana Nikolayevna and that there were no real motives for the murder but only imaginary ones. In the strangeness of my plan and the cold-bloodedness with which I carried it out, in my attention to small details, it is easy enough to observe the same insane will. Even the very keenness and exhilaration of my thought before the murder testify to my abnormality.

> So, in the circus, mortally wounded,
> I acted out the death of a gladiator.

I did not leave a single detail of my life unexplored. I examined it fully. Each of my steps, each of my thoughts I put to the test of madness, and it fit in every instance. It turned out—and this was what was most astonishing—that even before that night the thought had already occurred to me: am I not really insane? But I would somehow dismiss this thought and forget it.

And having proved that I am insane, do you know what I discovered? That *I am not insane*—this is what I discovered. Please hear me out.

The main thing my heredity and my fits point to is degeneracy. I am one of those who is degenerating, of whom many can be found if one were to look a bit attentively, even among you, learned gentlemen. This provides a splendid key to everything else. My moral views you may attribute not to conscious reflection but to degeneracy. Indeed, moral instincts are buried so deeply that only by some deviation from the normal can one completely free oneself from them. And science, still too bold in its generalizations, attributes such deviations to degeneracy, even if a man were built like an Apollo and be idiotically healthy. But be this as it may, I have nothing against degeneracy—it puts me in excellent company.

Nor will I stand by my motive for the crime. I tell you truthfully that Tatiana Nikolayevna really did offend me with her laughter, and I deeply concealed the outrage, as happens with secretive, solitary natures such as mine. But let's suppose that this is not true. Let's even suppose that I did not love her. Is it not possible to allow that by killing Alexis I wanted simply to test my powers? Do you not freely admit to the existence of people who at the risk of their lives climb inaccessible mountains only because they are inaccessible, without calling such people mad? You would not dare call Nansen, that great man of the past century, mad. Moral life, too, has its poles, and I wanted to reach one of them.

You are dismayed by the lack of jealousy, vengefulness, greed, and other truly stupid motives, which you have become used to considering as the only ones that are real and sound. But then, you men of science will condemn Nansen, along with the fools and ignoramuses who regard his enterprise as madness.

My plan. It is unusual, it is original and daring to the point of insolence—yet is it not reasonable from the point of view of the goal I set for myself? And it was precisely my inclination toward dissimulation, which I have quite reasonably explained to you, that suggested this plan to me. Exhilaration? Is genius, then, really insanity? Cold-bloodedness—but why must a murderer always tremble, turn pale, and hesitate? Cowards always tremble, even when embracing chambermaids. And then is bravery insanity?

How easy it is to explain my own doubts about my health! Like a true artist I went too far in my role. I for a time identified myself with an imaginary character, and briefly I lost my sense of who I am. Will you say that even among the lawyers who playact every day, there are not those who, enacting Othello, experience the urge to kill?

Isn't it all quite convincing, gentlemen of science? Yet do you not observe one strange thing: when I prove that I am out of my mind, it seems to you that I am sound, and when I am proving that I am sound, you hear a madman speaking.

Yes. This is because you don't believe me. But then, I don't believe myself either, because I don't know *who* in myself to believe. Should I believe the base, insignificant thought, the deceitful lackey who will serve anyone? It is only capable of blacking boots, and I have befriended it and made it my god. Down from your throne, wretched, impotent thought!

And so, learned gentlemen, insane or not?

Masha, dear woman, you know something that I don't. Tell me, whom should I ask for help?

I know your answer, Masha, and *it is not right*. You are a good, kind woman, Masha, but you know neither physics nor chemistry, you have never been to the theater, and you do not know that the earth on which you live, serve, clean, accept actually turns. But it does turn, Masha, and we all turn with it. You are a child, Masha; you are a dumb creature; you are almost a plant—and I greatly envy you, almost as much as I despise you.

No, Masha, it is not you who will answer me. And you know nothing. It is not true! In one of the dark chambers of your humble house dwells someone very useful to you, but in my house that room is vacant. He who lived there died long ago, and I have erected a sumptuous monument on his grave. *He is dead, Masha, dead, and shall not be resurrected.*

So who am I, learned gentlemen, a madman or not? Forgive me for the rude insistence with which I press you with this question, but then, you are "men of science," as my father called you when he wanted to flatter you. You have books, and you command clear, precise, and infallible human thought. Of course, half of you will hold to one opinion, the other half to another; but I will believe you, learned gentlemen, believe the first half and the second as well. Tell me then . . . And to assist your enlightened minds, I shall disclose an interesting, a very interesting, little fact.

During one of those quiet, peaceful evenings that I spent between these white walls, I observed that each time I looked at Masha's face I saw an expression of horror, dismay, and submission to some powerful dread. Then she left, and I sat on the made-up bed and continued to think about what I wanted. I wanted to do strange things. I, Dr. Kerzhentsev, wanted to howl. Not to shout but to howl, like that other inmate. I wanted to tear my clothes and claw myself with my nails. I wanted to grab my shirt at the collar, pull at it a little at first and then rip it apart. I, Dr. Kerzhentsev, wanted to get down on all fours and crawl. It was quiet all around, and the snow beat at the window, and somewhere nearby Masha was silently praying. And I was thinking long and hard about what to do. If I should howl the noise would cause a scandal. If I were to tear my shirt they would notice it in the morning. Quite reasonably I elected the third choice: to crawl. No one would hear me, and if they were to see me, I would say that I was looking for a lost button.

While I was choosing and deciding all was well—not dreadful at all but rather pleasant, so much so that, as I remember, I was swinging my foot. But then I thought to myself, "But why crawl? Am I really insane?"

I was seized with terror and now I wanted to do everything at once: to crawl, to howl, and to claw. I became angry.

"So you want to crawl?" I asked. But there was no answer, no urge.

"Don't you want to crawl?" I insisted. No answer.

"Well, crawl then!"

And so, rolling up my sleeves I got down on the floor and started to crawl. I had not yet crossed half the room when I became so amused by the absurdity of it that I sat there and laughed and laughed.

With my customary and still-unquenched faith that one could know something, I thought that I had found the source of my insane desires. Evidently the urge to crawl and the rest of it were the result of autosuggestion. The persistent thought that I was insane had given birth to insane desires, and as soon as I began to gratify them, it turned out that they did not exist and that I therefore was not insane. A quite simple, logical argument, as you see. But . . .

But then I was crawling, wasn't I? What was I—a madman trying to justify himself or a sane man driving himself mad?

Help me, you learned men! Let your authoritative words tip the scales in this or that direction and so resolve this wild, dreadful dilemma. And so—I am waiting!

I am waiting in vain. Oh, my dear blockheads, are you not as I?

Doesn't the same base human thought, forever deceiving, forever changing, phantomlike, work in your bald heads as it does in mine? In what way is my thought any worse than yours? If you should try to prove me mad, I shall prove to you that I am normal; if you try to prove me normal, I shall prove to you that I am mad. You will say that one must not steal, kill, or lie because it is immoral and criminal, and I will show that one may kill and lie and that it is highly moral. You will think and say your piece, and I will think and say my piece, and we shall all be right, and none of us shall be right. Where is the judge who can decide between us and find the truth?

You have one enormous advantage, which grants to you alone the knowledge of the truth: you have not committed a crime, you are not under indictment, and you have been invited to explore my psychic condition for a substantial fee. This is why I am insane. On the other hand, if it were you who were confined here, Professor Drezhembitsky, and I who had been invited to observe you, then you would be the madman and I the king of the roost—the expert, the liar, who differs from other liars only in that he lies under oath.

It is true that you have not killed anyone, have not stolen for the sake of stealing, and when you hire a cab you feel obliged to haggle over a small coin in order to demonstrate your mental health. However, something surprising might just take place . . .

Suddenly, the very next day, right now, this minute, when you read these lines, you will have an extremely stupid, extremely imprudent thought: Am I not insane? Who will you be then, Herr Professor? Such a stupid, frivolous thought—for why should you be losing your mind? But just try to get rid of it. You were drinking milk believing that it was whole until someone told you that it was cut with water. And so of course: no more whole milk.

You are insane. Don't you want to crawl on all fours? Of course you don't. Who in his right mind would want to do that? But then, are you sure? Don't you have a slight urge, the very slightest, just a trifling one you can even laugh at, to slip down from your chair and crawl around a little? Of course not. Why should such an idea occur to a man who has just been taking tea and conversing with his wife? And yet do you not feel something in your legs that you did not feel before? Doesn't it seem that something strange is happening to your knees: a heavy numbness fighting a desire to bend, and then . . . *For indeed, Professor Drezhembitsky, how can anyone stop you if you want to crawl around a bit?*

No one.

But don't crawl just yet. I still need you. My battle is not over yet.

VIII

One of the paradoxical manifestations of my nature is that I like children very much, very small children, when they just begin to talk and resemble small animals, puppies, kittens, small snakes. Even snakes are attractive in their childhood. On a serene sunny day this past fall, I observed the following scene: a tiny girl, in a padded coat with a hood, under which one could see only pink cheeks and a tiny nose, wanted to approach a small, thin-legged, slender-headed dog, standing fearfully with its tail between its legs. And suddenly she became frightened, turned, and, without an outcry or a tear, hid her face in her nurse's lap. The tiny dog blinked. The nurse had a kind, simple face.

"Don't be frightened," the nurse said, smiling at me.

I do not know why, but I often remembered this little girl when I was free, preparing my plan for Savelov's murder; and I also do here. Looking upon this lovely group under the bright autumn sun, I had the strange feeling that here was the answer to my riddle and that the murder I had conceived was a cold lie from out of another, different world. The girl and the dog were so small, and they were so frightened of each other, and the sun was so warm—all this was so uncomplicated and full of gentle wisdom that the mystery of the world was contained in this moment. Such was my feeling. And I said to myself, "I must think this through." But I never did.

I don't remember now what that was all about, and I try my best to understand, but I cannot. And I don't even know why I am telling you this ridiculous, pointless story when there is still so much I have to say that is serious and important. *Now I must end.*

Let us leave the dead in peace. Alexis is dead, he started to rot a long time ago, he is no more—the hell with him! There is something rather nice about being dead.

Let us not speak of Tatiana Nikolayevna, either. She is unhappy, and I join in the general commiseration. Yet what is her unhappiness and all the unhappiness in the world compared to what I, Dr. Kerzhentsev, am living through now! Many wives lose beloved husbands, and many husbands remain to be lost. Leave them alone; let them weep.

But right here, inside my head . . .

Learned gentlemen, you must understand how terribly it has all turned out. I loved no one in the world except myself, not my lowly body, loved by vulgarians, but my human thought, my freedom. I have never known anything that surpassed my thought, I worshiped it—and did it not deserve it? Did it not, like a giant, wrestle with the whole world and its delusions? It lifted me to the peak of a high mountain, and I saw, far below me, little people swarming with petty animal passions, with their eternal fears in the face of life and of death, with their churches, liturgies, prayers.

How mighty I felt—how free, how happy! Like a medieval baron in his eagle's nest in an impregnable castle, proudly and imperiously surveying the valleys below, so was I, unconquered and proud, in my castle, within the bones of my skull. Lord of myself, I was also lord of the world.

I have been betrayed. Basely, treacherously, the way women and slaves betray, and the way thoughts do as well. My castle became my prison. Enemies attacked me in my castle—where is salvation?

Within my impregnable castle, within the thickness of its walls, lies my doom. My voice cannot be heard outside. Who is so strong as to save me? No one. For there is no one stronger than I, and I am the sole enemy of my "I."

My wretched thought has betrayed me, I who so believed in it and loved it. It is as good as ever; it is as luminous, sharp, and resilient as the blade of a rapier. But its hilt is no longer in my hand. And it is killing me, its creator and master, with the same dull indifference with which I used it to kill others.

Night is coming and I am seized with unspeakable terror. Once I was strong and stood solidly on this earth, but now I am thrown into the void of boundless space. Great and terrible is my solitude, in which I, who live, feel, think and am unique, find myself—so small, insignificant, and weak and ready to be snuffed out at any moment. It is the threatening solitude in which I am a tiny fragment surrounded and choked by a dismal silence filled with mysterious enemies. Wherever I go I carry them within me; alone in the void of the universe, I am no friend to myself. Wild solitude in which I do not know who I am, in which my lips, my thought, my voice, belong to these enemies.

I cannot live this way. Yet the world is sleeping quietly, husbands are kissing their wives, scholars are giving lectures, and the beggar rejoices in the penny thrown his way. Oh, insane world, happy in your madness, terrible will be your awakening!

Who will be strong and help me? No one. No one. Where will I find the eternal to which my pitiful, powerless, fearfully lonely self might cleave? Nowhere. Oh, dear little girl, why is it toward you that my bloodstained hands reach now? For you, too, are human and insignificant and alone and vulnerable to death. Is it that I pity you or that I court your pity, wishing to hide behind your helpless body from the hopeless void of time and space? But no, this, too, is all a lie!

Learned gentlemen, I want to ask you for a great favor, and if you have the slightest human decency, you will not refuse me. I hope that we understand each other well enough not to believe each other. And if I should ask you to say at the trial that I am sound, I will be the last to believe you. You may decide for yourselves, but no one will decide this question for me:

Did I simulate madness in order to kill, or did I kill because I was mad?

But the judges will believe me and will give me what I want: hard labor. Please do not put a false construction on my intentions. I do not repent my killing Savelov; I am not seeking redemption through punishment, and if I must kill someone—say, to rob him, in order to demonstrate my sanity—I shall oblige with pleasure. In hard labor I am looking for something else. I don't know what it is myself.

A vague hope draws me toward these people who have broken your laws, who have killed and robbed; perhaps among them I shall find new life forces and will again become reconciled with myself. Oh, I know you! You are cowards and hypocrites; you love your peace of mind above all else. You will cheerfully shut up in an insane asylum a thief who has stolen a loaf of bread; you would rather call the whole world and yourselves insane than question your pet fantasies. I know you. The criminal and the crime—these are forever your anxieties: the horrendous voice of the uncharted void, the implacable condemnation of all your measured, moral lives; and no matter how you shut your ears, that voice comes through! I want to join the ranks of the criminals. I, Dr. Kerzhentsev, will join the ranks of that dreaded army, as an eternal reproach, as one who asks for and awaits an answer.

I do not beg but demand that you declare me sane. Lie, if you do not believe it. But if you should cravenly wash your hands and commit me to the insane asylum—or free me—I warn you in a friendly way: I will cause you serious trouble.

I acknowledge no judge, no law, no interdictions. Everything is permitted. Can you imagine a world in which there would be no law of gravity, no up and down, in which everything depends on whim and chance? I, Dr. Kerzhentsev, am this new world. Everything is permitted. And I, Dr. Kerzhentsev, will prove it to you. I shall pretend to be well, I shall attain freedom, I shall devote the rest of my life to study, I shall surround myself with your books, I shall wrest from you the might of your knowledge, of which you are so proud, and I shall find the one thing that has long been needed. *It will be explosive matter.* So powerful that no one has ever seen anything like it; more powerful than dynamite, more powerful than nitroglycerin, more powerful than the very thought of it. I have genius. I have persistence, I shall find it. *And when I find it I will blow up your accursed earth, which has so many gods and no one, eternal God.*

At his trial Dr. Kerzhentsev was very quiet, and he maintained the same listless attitude throughout the proceedings. He responded to questions impassively and with indifference, sometimes requesting that they be repeated. On one occasion he amused the public which packed the courtroom in large numbers. The presiding judge addressed an order to the clerk, and the distracted defendant, evidently not having heard, rose and asked loudly, "What? Must I go?"

"Go where?" asked the judge in surprise.

"I don't know. I thought you said something."

The crowd laughed, and the judge explained to Kerzhentsev what had happened.

Four psychiatrists were called to the stand. Their opinions were divided equally. After the prosecutor's speech the judge turned to the defendant, who had refused the services of an attorney. "What does the accused have to say in his defense?"

Dr. Kerzhentsev stood up. With dull, unseeing eyes he gazed for a long time at the judge, then looked at the public. And those on

whom this heavy, sightless stare fell experienced a strange and painful sensation, as if out of hollow sockets death itself, indifferent and
mute, had gazed upon them.

"Nothing," said the defendant.

And once again he stared at the people assembled to judge him
and repeated, "Nothing."

1902

—Translated by Henry and Olga Carlisle

THE
RED LAUGH

Fragments of a
Manuscript

PART I

First Fragment

. . . madness and horror.

I first became aware of it when we were marching along the road to N.—ten hours without a break, without slowing down, without picking up those who collapsed but leaving them to the enemy, who was following us in a compact mass that in three or four hours would obliterate our footprints with its own. The heat was horrendous. I don't know what the reading was—forty, fifty degrees, perhaps more. I do know that it never let up but remained penetrating. The sun was enormous, fierce, as if the earth had moved near it and would soon burn up.

My eyes would not stay open. Their pupils, shrunken to the size of poppy seeds, searched in vain for shade beneath the cover of lowered eyelids. It felt better if I shut my eyes. I walked like that for a long time, for several hours, conscious only of the movement of the crowd around me, of the heavy, uneven tramp of men's feet and horses' hooves, of the grinding of iron wheels crushing gravel.

No words were spoken. We were an army of mutes. When someone fell, he fell silently. I myself stumbled and fell several times, and then, involuntarily, I would open my eyes. What I saw was fantastic, the leaden ravings of a world gone mad. The burning air quivered, and the stones, too, quivered in silence. They seemed to be on the point of melting. Far ahead, where the road began to turn, the rows of men, guns, and horses seemed to be wavering soundlessly in the air, as if they were not living people but an army of disembodied shadows.

Then suddenly I thought about home: a corner of my room, a patch of pale blue wallpaper, and the dusty carafe of water untouched on my small desk—my desk, with its one leg shorter than the others, a wedge of folded paper steadying it. My wife and my son were in the next room, though I did not see them. Had I been able to cry out I would have done so: this simple and peaceful picture, this patch of pale blue wallpaper, the untouched dusty carafe were so extraordinary.

I recall that I stopped, raising my arms, but someone pushed me from behind; I walked ahead quickly, forcing my way through the crowd, hurrying, no longer noticing the heat or my fatigue, until the question of what I was doing, where I was hurrying brought me to a stop. Just as hurriedly I turned and made my way into the open, over a gully; I sat down cautiously on a rock, as though that rough, hot stone had been the goal of all my exertions.

That was when I first became clearly aware of the men marching silently in the glare of the heat, swaying and collapsing, and I saw that they were madmen. They did not know where they were going or why the sun was burning them—they did not know anything. A horse with insane red eyes raised its head above the crowd, its mouth wide open; yet its strange, terrifying cry was inaudible. It reared, then fell to the ground. For a moment the crowd closed in, then stopped; hoarse, hollow voices were heard; a sharp shot rang out, then the endless, silent movement resumed. I sat on that rock for an hour.

Close to me a man was lying face down. I could tell he was dead by the indifferent way his face pressed against a jagged, hot rock, by the white palm of his upturned hand, but his back was just like a live man's, and only a slight yellowish tinge, such as can be seen on smoked meat, spoke of death. I wanted to move away but did not have the strength. From the throbbing in my head I realized that I was about to succumb to sunstroke, but I waited calmly, as in a dream in which death is only one stage in a journey of wonderful, confused visions.

Then I saw a soldier detach himself from the crowd and move straight toward me. For a moment he disappeared in the gully; when he scrambled out and walked on, his steps were unsteady. There was something desperate about his attempts to coordinate his thrashing limbs. He was coming toward me so intently that fear cut through the heavy drowsiness in my brain, and I asked, "What do you want?"

He stopped, as if all he had been waiting for were spoken words, and he stood there, huge and bearded, his collar torn open. He did not have a rifle; his trousers were held up by one button; his white flesh showed through his fly. His arms and legs were flailing about. He was trying in vain to control them. Again and again he brought his arms together, but they kept flying apart.

"What are you doing? Sit down!" I said. But he stood there silently, trying vainly to compose himself, staring at me. Against my will I got up. Staggering up to him I looked into his eyes and saw in them a dark, horrifying void. Instead of contracting, his pupils dilated, filling his eyes. What a sea of fire he must have seen through those huge black windows! Perhaps I was just imagining it, and it was only death looking at me—but no, I was not mistaken: in those black, bottomless pupils, edged with a thin orange ring like birds' eyes, there was more than death and the horror of it.

"Get away!" I yelled, backing off. "Get away!"

As if all he had been waiting for was someone to speak out, he collapsed upon me, knocking me off my feet, still as huge, sprawling, and mute as before. Shuddering, I freed my legs from under his weight, leapt up, and was about to run away, toward the sun-drenched, deserted, wavering distance, when there was a blast to the left beyond a hill, followed by two more in quick succession, like echoes. Somewhere above, a shell flew past with a joyful, many-voiced whine, screaming and howling.

They had outflanked us!

The lethal heat and my fear and exhaustion vanished. My thoughts were clear, my comprehension sharp. As I ran toward the ranks, which were drawing up, I saw faces lit up; they seemed joyous; and I heard hoarse, loud voices trading orders and jokes. As the sun climbed higher it turned dimmer and duller and again a shell sliced through the air with a joyful screech, like a witch.

I drew nearer.

Second Fragment

. . . . gone were most of the horses and gunners. The same in the Eighth Battery. In ours, the twelfth, by the end of the third day, only three guns were left, six men, and one officer—myself. We had not slept or eaten for twenty hours. Hellish thunder and screeching had shrouded us in madness for three whole days, cutting us off from the earth, the sky, our own men—those of us still alive, stumbling around like lunatics. The dead lay there peacefully while we moved about, did our job, talked, and even laughed—like lunatics. Our movements were sure and swift, our orders precise; they were carried out accurately, but had any one of us been asked who he was, he would not have been likely to find an answer in his darkening mind. As in a dream, faces seemed to be those of old friends; everything that was happening seemed familiar, natural, a repetition of previous events. Yet when I looked closely at one or another of the faces around me or at a gun or listened to the roaring, it all struck me as being novel and infinitely mysterious. Night fell imperceptibly. We hardly had time to realize that it had come, when the sun was again blazing above us. We only learned from newcomers to our battery that the battle had entered its third day, and we soon forgot all about it: to us it felt like a single day, without beginning or end, now dark, now bright, equally incomprehensible and blind. And none of us feared death, because none of us understood what death was.

On the third or fourth night (I do not remember which) I lay down for a minute against a parapet, and as soon as I shut my eyes, the same familiar, extraordinary vision was before me: a patch of pale blue wallpaper and the untouched dusty carafe on my table.

And my wife and my son were in the next room, though I could not see them. Only this time, on the table, the lamp with the green shade was lit: it had to be late evening or night. This vision persisted. Calmly, attentively, I was able to watch the light playing on the facets of the carafe. I studied the wallpaper and wondered why my son was not asleep: it was already night; he should have been in bed. Then I examined the wallpaper again: all those tendrils and silvery flowers, those trellises and trumpets—I had no idea that I knew my room so well. Once in a while I opened my eyes and saw the black sky with beautiful, fiery streaks. Then I closed them again and studied the wallpaper, the sparkling carafe, wondering why my son was not asleep: it was already night; he should have been in bed. Once a shell exploded nearby; my legs rocked; there was a loud scream, louder than the explosion itself, and I thought, "Someone's been killed!" But I did not sit up or tear my eyes away from the lovely pale blue wallpaper and the carafe.

Later on I got up, walked about, gave orders, looked into people's faces, adjusted the gunsight, still wondering, why wasn't my son asleep yet? Once I asked the driver about it, and he gave me a long, detailed explanation and we both nodded. He was laughing, his left eyebrow twitching as he winked slyly at someone behind me, yet there was nothing there but the soles of someone's feet.

It was daytime then and suddenly a drop of rain fell. Rain like our own, the most ordinary droplets of water. Yet it was so unexpected, so weird, that we were all seized with panic. We abandoned our guns, stopped firing, and sought shelter wherever we could. The driver I had just been talking to crawled under the gun carriage and curled up there, even though he could have been crushed at any moment. A fat sergeant began undressing a corpse, while I rushed around the battery looking for a raincoat or an umbrella. At once a strange silence descended upon the vast area where rain was falling. A tardy shell passed overhead and burst, and everything became silent—so silent that one could hear the fat sergeant breathing heavily and the raindrops drumming on the stones and the guns. This gentle steady patter, reminiscent of autumn, the smell of the freshly moistened earth, the silence seemed for a moment to cut short the bloody, savage nightmare. When I glanced at the wet, glistening gun, it, oddly, made me think of something dear and kind—my childhood, perhaps, or my first love. But another loud explosion thundered out far away, and the brief, enchanted stillness ended; people crawled out of their shelters as suddenly as they had taken cover; the fat sergeant shouted at someone; a gun boomed, followed by another; once more a solid, bloody fog filled our heads. No one noticed when the rain stopped; I only remembered water running down the flabby, yellow face of the dead sergeant. The rain must have lasted quite a while. . .

. . . Before me stood a very young officer, a volunteer. Saluting, he reported that the general was asking us to hold out for another two hours, when the reinforcements would arrive. I wondered why my son was not yet asleep and said that I could hold on for as long as was necessary. Then I became intrigued by the man's face, no doubt because it was so unusually, startlingly pale. I had never seen anything paler than that face: even the dead have more color than this young, beardless fellow. Surely on his way to us he had been very frightened and had found it hard to hold himself together. He was saluting in order to control his fear by this simple, familiar gesture.

"Are you afraid?" I asked, touching him on the elbow. But his elbow was as stiff as a piece of wood, while he only smiled gently and silently. Or, rather, his lips twitched into a smile; his eyes showed only his youth and his fear, nothing else. "Are you afraid?" I repeated softly.

Again his lips twitched. He was trying to speak, and then something incomprehensible, monstrous, supernatural happened. I felt a blast of warm air on my right cheek and swayed violently, and now, instead of that pale face before me, there was something short, blunt, and red. Blood poured from it as if it were one of those uncorked bottles on a cheap billboard. A kind of smile was lingering on that blunt, red stump pouring blood, a toothless laugh—the red laugh.

I recognized it. I had looked for it and now had found it: the red laugh. That was what was in all those strange, mutilated, mangled bodies. The red laugh. It was in the sky, in the sun; soon it would engulf the whole earth.

But they, calmly, deliberately, like lunatics . . .

Third Fragment

. . . madness and horror.

They say that a lot of men suffering from mental illness have appeared in our army and in the enemy's as well. Four psychiatric wards have been set up on our side. When I was at headquarters, one of the adjutants showed me around . . .

Fourth Fragment

. . . entwined like snakes. He had seen the barbed wire, cut loose at one end, slice through the air and wrap around three soldiers. The barbs tore through their uniforms, stuck into their flesh, and the screaming soldiers spun around in a frenzy, two of them dragging the third, who was already dead. Then only one was alive, and he kept trying to free himself from the others' corpses, but they dragged and rolled over him, and suddenly they all stopped moving.

He said that at least two thousand men had died in that one place. While they were cutting the wire and becoming entangled in its snake's coils, a hail of fire rained on them. He said that it had been very frightening and that the attack would have ended in a panic-stricken flight had the soldiers known in what direction to run. But the struggle with ten or twelve rows of barbed wire and a labyrinth of deep holes filled with sharp stakes had completely dis-oriented them.

Some, temporarily blinded, had plunged into the funnel-shaped holes and were impaled on the stakes; they jerked and danced like puppets. New bodies pressed down on them, and soon the whole pit up to its rim had become a heaving mass of blood-soaked live bodies and corpses. Hands were reaching in all directions from under-neath, fingers were contracting convulsively as they seized at any-thing they could cling to. Caught in these traps men were unable to climb out again: hundreds of fingers, strong and blind as claws, gripped their legs, clutched at their clothes, dragged them down into the pit and poked at their eyes. Many, like drunkards, had run straight onto the wire; they hung on it and screamed until a bullet killed them.

In fact, they all seemed drunk to him: some were swearing fear-somely, others roared with laughter as the wire grabbed them and they died on the spot. He himself had felt very strange, though he had not touched anything all day: his head was spinning, and for minutes on end, his fear became wild ecstasy—the euphoria of fear. When someone nearby started to sing, he joined in the song, and soon there had been a whole choir singing harmoniously. He did not remember what they had sung, but it had been something merry, a dancing tune. They were singing while everything around them was blood red. The sky itself was red, as if a cosmic catastrophe had taken place, causing strange changes in colors. Blue and green and other soft shades had disappeared, while the sun burned like a red firework.

"Red laugh," I said.

He did not understand.

"Yes, they did laugh, as I said. Like drunkards. They may well also have danced. Certainly the movements of those three were like dancing."

He remembered clearly: when he was shot through the chest and had fallen down, for a time, until he lost consciousness, his feet had jerked as if keeping step in a dance. Now he recollected that attack with an odd feeling—part fear, part a wish to relive the experience.

"You want another bullet in your chest?" I asked.

"Well, not every time," he said. "But wouldn't it be good to get a medal for bravery?"

He was lying on his back, yellow, sharp nosed, with high cheekbones and sunken eyes, looking like a corpse and still dreaming of receiving a medal. His wound was festering, he was running a fever; in two or three days he would be thrown into the pit with the other dead, and yet he was lying there, smiling dreamily, talking about a medal.

"Have you sent a telegram to your mother?" I asked.

He was scared. He looked up at me sternly, angrily, and said nothing. I too was silent. The groans and ravings of the wounded could now be heard clearly. When I stood up to leave he grasped my hand in his hot, still-powerful grasp, fixing his sunken, burning eyes on me in longing and anguish.

"What is all this? Please tell me," he asked with shy insistence.

"What do you mean?"

"I mean, all of this. My country. But my girl is waiting for me to return. How can I make her understand about my country?"

"Tell her about the red laugh," I said.

"You're joking. I'm trying to be serious. I have to make her understand, but how? If you knew what she writes! Her words are turning gray like her hair. But then . . ." He looked at me with curiosity, pointed his finger, and said with a sudden laugh, "You're getting bald. Didn't you know?"

"There're no mirrors here."

"People around here are growing gray and bald. Quick, give me a mirror! I can feel white hair growing out of my scalp! Quick, give me a mirror!"

As I left the hospital he was growing delirious, crying and yelling.

That evening we organized a party—a strange, sorrowful party at which the shadows of the dead mingled with the guests. We decided to meet in the evening to have tea, just as we do outside, just as we do at home, and we got hold of a samovar and even found a lemon and some glasses. We sat down under a tree, just as we do at home. Singly or in couples or groups of three, we gathered and talked—joking, full of anticipation—but soon we fell silent and averted our eyes: there was something oppressive in this gathering of survivors. Ragged, emaciated, filthy, scratching ourselves as if we suffered from a virulent rash, no longer ourselves, we saw one another and were terrified. Vainly I searched for a familiar face in that crowd of confused men. Restless, hurried, moving about with spasmodic lurches, glancing over their shoulders, gesticulating wildly—these were strangers. Their voices, too, sounded different, abrupt, hesitating. They started shouting or laughed senselessly, irrepressibly at the slightest provocation. Everything was strange to me now: the trees, the sunset, and even the water, whose smell and taste were peculiar. It was as if we had departed this earth like the dead, moving into some other world full of enigmatic events and malevolent, sad ghosts. The sunset was yellow, icy; above it loomed heavy black, immobile clouds. No light shone on them. The earth below was black. Our faces appeared yellow, like the faces of the dead. The samovar had gone out. The brass reflected the yellow menace of the sunset.

"Where are we?" someone asked in an anxious voice.

Someone else sighed, another convulsively cracked his fingers and laughed, while yet another jumped to his feet and quickly circled the table. It was common now for people to suddenly start racing around, either in silence or muttering weirdly.

"We are at war, that's where," said the man who had been laughing, and again he burst into a long, hollow laugh, as if he was choking.

"Why are you laughing?" someone exclaimed indignantly. "Please stop it!"

The other man choked once again, giggled, fell silent. The black cloud was settling on the earth. We could hardly make out one another's sallow faces. Someone asked, "By the way, where is Bootsy?"

Bootsy was what we called one of our comrades, a diminutive officer who wore huge rubber boots.

"He was here a minute ago. Where are you, Bootsy?"

"Stop hiding, Bootsy. We can smell your boots."

Everyone burst out laughing, until a harsh voice from the darkness interrupted, "Stop it. You ought to be ashamed of yourselves. Bootsy was killed this morning while he was on reconnaissance."

"There must be some mistake; he was here just now."

"No, he wasn't. You there in charge of the samovar, pass me a slice of lemon."

"I want some too."

"It's all gone."

"That's not fair," said a quiet, resentful voice full of longing, almost on the verge of tears. "I only came because of the lemon."

Someone again burst into hollow laughter, but this time no one tried to stop him. He snickered, then fell silent. A man said, "To-morrow we go on the offensive."

Several voices yelled angrily, "On the offensive! What do you mean?"

"But of course you know . . ."

"Can't you talk about something else? Give us a break!"

The sun had set, the black cloud climbed higher, the sky became lighter, the faces looked familiar again. The man who had been circling around us returned to his seat, calmed down.

"What's happening at home now?" he asked vaguely. A kind of apologetic irony could be heard in his voice.

And again, fear and confusion seized us, an overwhelming sense of alienation. We all began talking at once, clanging our glasses, shouting, racing around, slapping one another's backs, arms, knees. Then we all fell silent at once, overcome by anguish.

"At home?" someone shouted in the dark. His voice shook with emotion, with fear and anger. He stumbled over certain words, as if he had lost the habit of using them. "At home? What home? Does such a thing exist somewhere? Don't interrupt me or I'll start firing. At home, every day I took a bath—do you understand what I'm saying?—a bath with water, water right up to the edge of the tub. Now I don't even wash every day, I have scabs on my head, my whole body itches, things are crawling all over my body, I'm going crazy with the filth—and you say 'home'! I'm an animal. I despise myself; I no longer know who I am. Death is not all so terrible. They're tearing my brain to shreds with their shrapnel. No matter where they're shooting from, it always hits my brain—and you say 'home'! What home? Streets, windows, people—I wouldn't go out into the street now. I'm ashamed! When you brought out that samovar, I was ashamed to look at it."

That obsessive laughter began again. Someone yelled, "This is terrible; I'm going home!"

"Home?"

"You don't know what home is!"

"Home—listen to him: he wants to go home!"

A wave of laughter and eerie shouting arose, then everyone fell silent, overcome by anguish in the presence of the irrational. Not I alone but all of us became aware of *it*. It was coming at us from the barren black ravines where those who had been abandoned were perhaps still dying among the rocks; it poured down from the extraordinary alien sky. Petrified we stood around the cold samovar while the gigantic shapeless shadow that had risen over the world looked down on us fixedly and quietly from the sky. Suddenly, next to us, probably at the regimental commander's quarters, a band began to play, and the frantically merry, deafening sounds were like flares in the night. The music was full of mad gaiety and defiance; it rushed ahead, discordant, loud. Players and listeners both saw that enormous shapeless shadow that had risen over the world.

The trumpet player was already possessed by it; it filled his brain, his ears. The jerky, cracked sound thrashed about and ran away, lonely, trembling, demented. The other sounds were searching for that trumpet. Awkwardly, ragged, stumbling, much too close to the black ravines where men were perhaps still dying among the rocks.

We stood in silence around that cold samovar for a long time.

Fifth Fragment

. . . had fallen asleep when the doctor woke me, prodding me lightly. I woke up screaming, as we all did whenever anyone woke us, and I rushed to get out of the tent. The doctor held me firmly by the arm, apologizing. "I frightened you; I'm sorry. I know you need sleep."

"Five days . . ." I mumbled drowsily and fell back asleep, and slept for a long time, or so it seemed, until the doctor spoke again, prodding my side and legs gingerly.

"It's very important; it really is. There are still many wounded out there."

"What wounded? You've been bringing them in all day long. Leave me alone. It's not fair. I haven't slept for five days."

"Don't be angry, my good fellow," the doctor murmured, awkwardly putting my cap on my head. "Everyone's asleep. I can't rouse anyone. I have an engine and seven cars ready, and I need extra hands. Of course, I understand—please, my dear fellow. Everyone's asleep; they all refuse to get up. I'm afraid of falling asleep myself. I don't remember when I last slept. I'm beginning to hallucinate. Come on, put your feet on the ground. There, that's it."

The doctor's face was ashen, and he swayed on his feet. It was clear that should he lie down he would sleep for several days on end. My legs kept buckling; I started to walk, dozing on my feet. Then unexpectedly, out of nowhere, the black silhouettes of the train appeared before us. Barely visible in the darkness, people were wandering around, slowly, silently. There was no light anywhere. Only the closed firebox cast a faint reddish light on the track.

"What is this?" I asked, backing away.

"We're about to leave. Surely you haven't forgotten? We're leaving," said the doctor.

The night was cold, and he was shivering. Watching him I felt the same tingling shiver run over my body as well.

"The hell with you!" I yelled. "Couldn't you have gotten someone else?"

"Quiet, please!" The doctor held my arm.

From out of the darkness a man said, "If you fired a salvo right now, no one would stir. They're all asleep. We could tie them all up in their sleep. I just passed the sentry: he didn't say a word, didn't budge. He was sleeping too. Why in hell didn't he fall down?"

The speaker yawned and stretched; his clothing rustled. I put my trunk on the floor of the car, tried to climb in, and was instantly asleep. Someone lifted me up from behind and shoved me inside. For some reason I tried to kick him. Again I fell asleep, hearing fragments of conversation as if in a dream:

"At the seventh verst."

"You have the lights?"

"No, he refused to come."

"Over here. Back it up a bit. That's it."

The cars jolted and rattled. Gradually my drowsiness was driven away by these sounds and by my all-too-comfortable position. The doctor had fallen asleep. When I took his hand it was limp and heavy like a dead man's. The train was moving slowly, cautiously, vibrating slightly, as if it was feeling its way along the track.

A student who served as an orderly lit the candle in one of the lamps, illuminating the sides of the car and the black hole at the open door. He said with displeasure, "What the hell! What can we do for them now, anyway! By the way, be sure to wake him up before he really falls asleep. Otherwise you won't be able to. I know from experience."

We shook the doctor awake and he sat up blinking and bewildered. He wanted to lie down again, but we didn't let him.

"Right now a drop of vodka would be a good idea," said the orderly.

We each took a swallow, and that woke us up. The big black square of the doorway began to turn pink, then red. An enormous silent glow appeared beyond a range of hills, as if the sun were rising in the middle of the night.

"That's far away, at least twenty versts!"

"I'm cold," said the doctor, his teeth chattering.

The student glanced out the door and gestured to me. I looked out. Along the horizon a silent chain of red, motionless fires smoldered, as if dozens of suns were rising at the same time. It was no longer very dark. The hills stood black and dense in the distance, bathed in a gentle, still light. I glanced at the student: his face was that same ghostly red, the color of blood turned to air and light.

"Are there many wounded?" I asked.

He waved his hand dismissively.

"There're more madmen than wounded."

"You mean real madmen?"

"What other kind is there?"

He was looking at me, and in his eyes there was that same fixed, wild look of cold terror that I had seen in the eyes of the soldier who had died of sunstroke.

"Please stop it," I said, turning away.

"The doctor's mad, too. Take a look at him."

The doctor was not listening. He was squatting on his haunches, swaying, his lips and fingertips moving noiselessly. In his eyes I saw that same fixed, dumbfounded, stunned look.

"I'm cold," he said and smiled.

"To hell with all of you!" I shouted, retreating into a corner of the car. "Why did you have to bring me along?"

No one answered. The orderly was looking out at the slowly spreading glow. The back of his head with its curls was that of a very young man. Whenever I looked at his head I kept seeing a woman's slender fingers running through those curls, and this image was so distasteful that I began to hate the orderly and could not look at him without revulsion. "How old are you?" I asked, but he did not turn or answer.

The doctor was rocking back and forth. "I'm cold," he said.

"When I think—" said the orderly, without turning around. "When I think that somewhere there are streets, houses, universities—"

He broke off, as if he had said all there was to say, and fell silent. The train stopped abruptly, and I was thrown against the side of the car. We heard voices as we jumped out.

Something was lying on the tracks in front of the engine, a bundle with a leg sticking out of it.

"Wounded?"

"Dead. Head blown off. If you don't mind I'll put the headlight on now. Otherwise we'll be running over them, too."

The bundle with the leg sticking out of it was thrown aside; for a second the leg jerked upward as if it wanted to run through the air, then it was all swallowed up by the black ditch. The headlight came on. The engine loomed darker than before.

"Listen!" someone whispered in quiet terror.

How had we not noticed it before? From all around us we heard moaning. It was unlike anything we had ever heard. We could not make out anything on the dim, reddish surface of the plain. It was as if the earth itself were moaning, or perhaps the sky, illuminated by a yet-invisible sun.

"We're at the fifth verst," said the engineer.

"It comes from out there," the doctor waved ahead.

The orderly shuddered. Slowly he turned toward us. "What is it? It's unbearable."

"No, we must go!"

We set off on foot in front of the engine, which cast a long, continuous shadow onto the tracks—not a black shadow but red, because of that gentle crimson light at the edges of the sky. With each step we took, that wild, incredible moaning swelled, as if the red air was moaning, as if the earth and the sky was moaning. Its regularity and strange indifference made me think of cicadas chirping in a meadow, in a summer meadow. Now there were more and more bodies. We examined them perfunctorily and tossed them off the tracks—the indifferent, still, limp bodies that left dark, oily stains from the blood that had soaked into the earth. At first we counted them, but soon we gave up. There were too many of them, too many for that sinister night, whose breath was cold and which moaned with every particle of its being.

Suddenly the doctor was shouting and threatening with his fist. "How can this be? Listen! Listen!"

We were nearing the sixth verst. The moaning grew more distinct, sharper; we could almost make out the twisted mouths uttering the sound. We were peering into the deceptive pink haze, when next to us by the tracks, there was a loud, imploring, tearful cry. We found him at once, that wounded soldier whose face was nothing but a pair of eyes; they looked immense as the light fell on him. He stopped groaning and looked at each of us in turn, at the lamps we held over him. In his eyes we saw mad joy at seeing people and lights, and mad fear that they would suddenly vanish like a mirage. Perhaps he had already dreamed of people with lamps bending over him who had then been swallowed up by his bloody, confused nightmare.

We moved on. Almost at once we came across more wounded. One was lying on the track; the other was weeping in the ditch. While they were being picked up, the doctor said to me, trembling with rage, "Well, what do you say?"

A few steps ahead we met a lightly wounded soldier cradling an arm in his hand. He was coming straight at us with his head thrown back. He did not seem to notice when we stepped aside to make way for him. He did not seem to see us. He stopped for a moment by the engine, walked around it, and went on past the cars.

"Climb in," the doctor called out, but there was no reply.

Those were the first we found, and they horrified us. But more and more of them turned up right on the track and on either side of it. Then the whole plain, bathed in the motionless reflection of distant fires, began to heave as if it were alive, to reverberate with loud cries, screams, curses, and moans. Dark lumps started to move, to crawl like drowsy crayfish let out of a basket—contorted, weird, not at all human, with their brisk, indefinite movements and their leaden stillness. Some were mute and docile; others howled and swore at us. They hated us, their rescuers, as if we had created that blood-soaked, indifferent night and their lonely vigil among the corpses and their hideous wounds. There was no room left in the cars. Our clothes were soaked, as if we had stood for a long time under a rain of blood. Still more wounded were brought in. The plain around us continued to heave in that same live, demented way.

A few crawled up to us; others managed to walk, staggering and falling as they came. One soldier was running. His face was smashed in; he had only one eye, which shone wildly. He was almost naked, as if he had just come from the baths. Shoving me aside, he found the doctor with his one good eye and seized him by his collar with one hand.

"I'll punch your face in!" he yelled, and shook the doctor, with a stream of vicious obscenities. "I'll punch your face in, you bastard!"

The doctor tore himself free and, stuttering with fury, shouted, "I'll have you court-martialed, you swine! I'll have you arrested. You're interfering with my work! You swine! You animal!"

We pulled them apart, but the soldier kept shouting for a long time, "You bastards! I'll punch your faces in!"

I was exhausted and went off for a smoke. From the caked blood my hands looked as if I were wearing black gloves. I could barely bend my fingers and kept dropping cigarettes and matches. When I had lit up, the smoke tasted different; it had a peculiar flavor that I have never tasted any other time. At that moment the young orderly came up to me, the one who had ridden with me in the car. Though I had the impression that I had met him many years before, for the life of me I could not remember where. He was marching, as if on parade. He looked through me and into the distance, into the sky.

"They're asleep," he said. He seemed completely calm.

I was stung, as if the reproach was directed at me personally. "They've been fighting like lions for ten days."

"But they're asleep," he said again, looking through me and into the distance. Then he leaned toward me and shook his finger at me, saying dryly and calmly, "I must tell you something. I must."

"What is it?" I asked.

He drew closer to me, shaking his finger meaningfully and repeating his words as if they expressed a coherent thought: "I must tell you something. I must. You'll pass it on to them."

Still looking at me in the same stern way, he shook his finger again, then took out his revolver and shot himself through the temple. I was neither surprised nor frightened. Shifting my cigarette to my left hand, I felt his wound with my finger. Then I walked back to the train.

"That orderly has just shot himself," I told the doctor. "I think he's still alive."

He clutched his head and wailed, "Oh, the hell with him! The train is full. That one over there is threatening to shoot himself, too," Then he screamed threateningly, "And I swear, I will too! Yes, I will! And if you don't mind, you'll go back on foot. The train is full. You can file a complaint if you wish."

Still yelling he turned his back to me, and I went up to the man who had said he would shoot himself next. He, too, was an orderly, a student. His forehead pressed to the side of a car, he was sobbing, his shoulders heaving.

"Don't," I said, touching his shoulder.

But he did not turn around and went on crying. The back of his head looked youthful like the other's and just as frightening, and he stood there bent over against the car like a drunk vomiting. His neck was covered with blood—he must have smeared it on with his hands.

"Well?" I said impatiently.

He lurched away from the car, his head still bent; hunched like an old man he walked into the darkness, away from us all. I don't know why, but I followed him. We walked like that for a long time, away from the train. I think he was still crying; I began to feel miserable and soon wanted to cry myself.

"Stop!" I called to him, coming to a halt.

But he shuffled on, hunched down, his shoulders drawn together. Then he disappeared into the reddish haze, which looked like light but did not illuminate anything. I was alone.

On my left, a long way away, a string of flickering lights floated by: the train was leaving. I was alone among the dead and the dying. How many were there here who were still alive? Everything around me was still, but in the distance the plain still pulsated as if it were living—or did it only seem that way because I was alone? But the moaning had not died down. It was still hanging over the earth—thin, hopeless, like a child crying or like the whimpering of a thousand abandoned, freezing puppies. It entered my brain like a sharp, icy needle and moved slowly back and forth . . .

Sixth Fragment

. . . they were on our side. In the midst of the strange confusion that had disrupted the operations of both our army and the enemy's in the past month, upsetting plans and orders, we had become convinced that the enemy—his fourth division, to be exact—was advancing toward us. We were prepared for the attack when through binoculars we saw that the attackers were wearing our uniform. Ten minutes later it became a joyous certainty: they *were* from our side! Evidently they, too, had recognized us: they were moving toward us perfectly calmly, and we sensed in their approach the same happy anticipation of an unexpected encounter that we ourselves felt.

When they began firing on us, for a time we could not understand what was happening, and we went on smiling under a great hail of shrapnel and bullets that cut down hundreds of men. Someone yelled that there had been a mistake, and—I remember very clearly—we realized at last that it really was the enemy before us, wearing their own uniforms, not ours, and we immediately returned their fire. After about fifteen minutes of this strange battle, both my legs were blown off. I only regained consciousness in the field hospital, after the amputation.

When I asked how the battle had ended, I received evasive, reassuring answers, from which I understood that we had been defeated. Then I was filled with joy at the thought that now that I had no legs I would be sent home, that I was, after all, still alive, with years before me—an eternity. However, only a week later I discovered certain details that aroused fresh doubts and a new fear that I had never experienced before.

Yes, it appears that they were from our side, that it was one of our own shells, fired from one of our cannons by one of our soldiers that had torn off my legs. No one could explain it. Something unaccountable had happened; something had blurred our vision, and two regiments of the same army, a half mile from each other, had spent a full hour almost destroying each other, fully convinced that they were fighting the enemy. Afterward people were reluctant to speak of this incident, referring to it by hints and allusions; and, most amazing of all, many of those who did speak of it still had not accepted the fact that there had been a mistake. Or, rather, they acknowledged it but thought that at first we really had been fighting the enemy, who had then somehow slipped away in the general confusion, leaving us firing on our own forces. Some talked openly about this, with precise explanations that to them seemed plausible and clear. I myself still cannot comprehend how this strange misunderstanding occurred, because I first had seen our scarlet uniforms and later the enemy's orange ones. Soon everyone forgot the episode and only referred to it as an authentic battle; and many reports were written about it in that vein, with complete sincerity, and sent to the newspapers; I read them when I got home. At first those of us who had been wounded in this battle were treated in a strange fashion: it seemed that we were less to be pitied than the other wounded; but soon that, too, was forgotten. And only the recurrence of cases like the one I have described—for instance, the fact that two detachments of the enemy's forces nearly wiped each other out one night in hand-to-hand combat—led me to believe that there really had been a mistake.

Our doctor, the one who had amputated my legs, a gaunt old man who stank of iodoform, tobacco smoke, and carbolic acid and was always smiling through his sparse yellow-gray mustache, said to me with his eyes squinted, "You're lucky to be going home. Something's wrong here."

"What do you mean?"

"Just what I said. Wrong. Things were simpler in the old days."

Almost a quarter of a century ago he had taken part in the last European war, and he often spoke of it with satisfaction, but he did not understand this present war and, as far as I could see, was afraid of it.

"Yes, very wrong." He sighed and frowned, disappearing behind a cloud of tobacco smoke. "I'd get out myself if I could."

Then, leaning toward me he whispered through his yellow, smoke-stained mustache, "There'll soon come a time when no one will get out of here. Yes. Not me or anyone else."

And in his old eyes so close to mine, I saw that same vacant, stunned look. And something horrible, unbearable, like the collapse of a thousand buildings at once, flashed through my brain, and turning cold with fear I whispered, "The red laugh."

He was the first to understand me. He quickly nodded his head in agreement.

"Yes. The red laugh."

He drew his chair up close to my bedside and, looking around cautiously, began talking in a fast whisper, moving his pointed little beard up and down as old men do.

"You're leaving soon; so I'll tell you. Have you ever seen a fight in an insane asylum? No? Well, I have. Lunatics fight exactly like sane people. Understand? Just like sane people."

"So?" I asked, whispering, too, frightened.

"That's it—exactly like sane people!"

"The red laugh," I said.

"They had to flood them with water."

I remembered the rain that had frightened us so and grew angry. "You're out of your mind, doctor!"

"No more than you. In any case, no more than you."

He clutched his sharp, old-man's knees with both hands and snickered as he squinted at me over his shoulder; with that unexpected, painful smile still imprinted on his dried-up lips, he winked at me slyly, several times, as if the two of us were sharing something hilarious that no one else knew about. With the solemnity of a magician performing a trick, he raised one hand high in the air and lowered it again very slowly, until two of his fingers gently touched the blanket where my legs would have been if they had not been cut off.

"Do you understand this?" he asked mysteriously. Then, with a solemn and significant gesture, he pointed to the rows of beds where wounded men were lying and demanded, "Can you explain this?"

"They are the wounded," I said. "The wounded."

"The wounded," he repeated like an echo. "The wounded. Without legs, without arms, with holes blown through their stomachs, crushed chests, eyes gouged out. You can understand that? I'm very glad. Does that mean you'll understand this, too?"

With an agility that I would never have suspected in someone his age, he bent over and suddenly stood on his hands, balancing his legs in the air. His white gown dropped around him, blood rushed to his face, and, fixing me with a strange, upside-down gaze, he spoke with difficulty, gasping out his words: "And this . . . you understand . . . this, too?"

"Stop it!" I hissed in alarm. "Stop it or I'll scream."

He stood up and resumed his normal position, sat again by my bedside, and, catching his breath, said in a sententious tone, "No one can understand that."

"There was shooting again yesterday," I said.

"There was shooting again yesterday. And there was shooting the day before," he said nodding his head in agreement.

"I want to go home!" I said with longing. "Doctor, my dear friend, I want to go home. I can't stay here, where I can't believe any more that there is a home where everything is all right."

He was thinking about something else and did not answer. I started to cry.

"My God, I have no legs! I so used to love riding a bicycle, walking, running, and now my legs have gone. My son used to ride on my knee; he would laugh—and now . . . Damn them! Why should I go home? I'm only thirty years old. Damn you all!"

And I sobbed and sobbed, thinking of my dear legs, my quick, strong legs. Who had taken them from me? Who had dared?

"Listen," the doctor said without looking at me. "Yesterday I saw a soldier who had gone mad. An enemy soldier who had come up to our lines. He was almost naked, bruised and scratched all over, starving like an animal. His hair was shaggy like all of ours. He looked like a savage, a primitive creature, an ape. He was waving his arms, making faces, singing and shouting, and looking for a fight. We fed him and then chased him away, out onto the plain. What else can you do with them? Night and day they wander all over the hills, like threatening phantoms, back and forth in all directions, going nowhere. They wave their arms; they laugh and shout and sing. When they meet each other, they fight or just pass each other by. What do they eat? Probably nothing at all, or perhaps the corpses, which they share with the animals, with those fat, well-fed dogs that run wild and fight all night long and howl in the hills. At night, like birds raised by a storm, like misshapen moths, they are attracted to light, and whenever a bonfire is lit against the cold, a half hour later a dozen noisy, ragged silhouettes like shivering apes loom around it. The soldiers shoot at them, sometimes by mistake, sometimes on purpose, exasperated by their wild and frightening shouts—"

"I want to go home!" I screamed, covering my ears.

But as if through cotton, more horrible words assailed my exhausted brain.

". . . There are many of them. They die by the hundreds in deep ravines, in traps prepared for those of sound mind and body, caught on barbed wired, impaled on stakes; they take part in regular, reasonable battles, and they fight like heroes, always up front, always fearless, though often they attack their own side. I like them. At this moment I still am slowly losing my mind—and this is why I'm sitting here talking to you—but when my mind finally goes, I'll walk out onto the plain, onto the plain, and I'll call out, I'll call out and gather these brave men around me, these intrepid knights, and I'll declare war on the whole world. In a joyous throng, with music and singing we'll enter towns and villages, and wherever we go everything will turn red, everything will twirl and dance like fire. Those who do not die will join us, and our valorous army will grow like an avalanche and purify the entire world. Who said that it was wrong to kill, burn, and plunder? . . ."

Now he was shouting, this crazy doctor, and his shouts awakened the dormant pain of those whose chests and stomachs had been torn open, whose eyes had been gouged out, whose legs had been hacked off. Loud, tearful groaning now filled the ward, and from all sides pallid, yellow, haggard faces turned toward us, some with no eyes, some so monstrously deformed that it seemed they had returned from hell. And they groaned and listened, and at the open door the great black shadow that was rising over the world cautiously looked in, and the crazy old man went on ranting with his arms outstretched.

"Who said that it was wrong to kill, burn, and plunder? We shall kill, we shall burn, and we shall plunder. Our merry, carefree band of brave spirits will destroy everything: their buildings, their universities, their museums. Our merry lads full of blazing laughter will dance on the ruins. I shall declare the country our madhouse; and all who have not gone mad, our enemies and madmen themselves. And when I shall reign over the world as its sovereign, mighty, invincible, joyous, what glad laughter shall ring through the universe!"

"The red laugh!" I cried out. "Help! I hear the red laugh again!"

"My friends!" the doctor went on, addressing the groaning, mutilated shadows. "My friends, we'll have a red moon and a red sun, and the animals will have jolly red fur, and we'll flay the skin off anyone who's too white—Have you ever tried drinking blood? It's a little sticky, a little warm, but it's red and has such a merry red laugh!"

Seventh Fragment

. . . it was a sacrilege, it was illegal. The Red Cross is respected all over the world as inviolable, and they saw that the train was not carrying combatants but harmless casualties, and they should have warned about the mine. Poor souls. They were already dreaming of home . . .

Eighth Fragment

. . . around a samovar, around a real samovar, steaming like a locomotive, giving off so much steam that even the glass of the lamp was misted. And the cups were the same pretty little cups, blue outside, white inside, that had been a wedding present from my wife's sister, a charming and excellent woman.

"Are they still all in one piece?" I asked in disbelief as I stirred the tea with a well-polished little silver spoon.

"One got broken," replied my wife absentmindedly as she opened the samovar tap, letting the hot water run gracefully and lightly.

I burst out laughing.

"What's so funny?" demanded my brother.

"Nothing. Will you take me back to my study just one more time? Will you do that for the hero? You could loaf while I was gone; now I'm going to make you shape up." And I began to sing, as a joke of course, "Make haste, friends, onward to do battle with the foe."

They understood the joke and smiled, except my wife, who kept her head lowered and went on wiping the cups with a clean, embroidered tea cloth. In my study I saw once again the pale blue wallpaper and the lamp with its green shade at my little desk and the carafe of water standing on it. The carafe was rather dusty.

"Give me some water from the carafe, will you?" I said cheerfully.

"You've just had tea."

"Never mind. Give me the water. And you," I said to my wife, "please take the boy into the other room for a while."

In little sips, savoring it, I drank the water, while my wife and my son sat in the next room where I could not see them.

"All right. Very good. Now come back in. But why is the boy up so late?"

"He's glad to have you home. Darling, go to your father."

But the child burst into tears and buried his face in his mother's skirt.

"Why is he crying?" I asked in bewilderment and looked around at the others. "Why are you all so pale and silent? Why are you following me like shadows?"

My brother gave a loud laugh and said, "We aren't at all silent."

My sister said, "We have been speaking the whole time."

"I'll see to the dinner," said my mother and hurriedly left the room.

"No, you haven't," I said with unexpected insistence. "I haven't heard a word from you all day long. I'm the only one who's been chattering and laughing, enjoying myself. Aren't you glad to see me back? Why do you avoid looking at me? Have I changed that much? Yes, that must be it. I see no mirrors around. Have you put them away? Give me a mirror!"

"I'll get one," my wife said. She stayed away for a long time. It was the maid who brought me a small mirror. I looked into it. I had already seen my reflection in train windows and at the station. Now I saw my face, a bit older perhaps, but perfectly normal. My family had apparently thought that I would scream and faint. They were so relieved when I inquired calmly, "Is there anything wrong with my appearance?"

My sister was seized by a fit of laughter and ran out of the room. My brother said calmly, "No, you haven't changed much. Got a bit bald perhaps."

"Be thankful I still have a head at all," I replied in a detached tone. "But where are they all running off to, one after the other? Take me through the rooms again, will you? What a comfortable wheelchair. Makes no noise at all. How much did you pay for it? Anyway, money doesn't matter to me now. I'm going to buy myself such a pair of legs—even better . . ."

Then I saw my bicycle. It was hanging on the wall, almost new; only its tires needed air. There was some mud dried on the back one, from the last time I had used it. My brother did not say anything and stopped pushing my wheelchair. I understood his silence and indecision.

"In our regiment only four officers are still alive," I said morosely. "I'm very lucky. You'd better have the bike. You can pick it up tomorrow."

"All right, I'll do that," my brother agreed. "Yes, you are lucky. Half the town is in mourning. As for your legs—well, that . . ."

"Of course. I'm not a mailman."

My brother suddenly asked, "Why does your head shake?"

"It's nothing. It will pass. The doctor said so."

"And your hands?"

"Yes, yes. My hands too. It will all pass. Please, let's go on. I'm tired of being in one place."

They had annoyed me, these discontented people, but my joy returned when they began making my bed—a real bed, a fine bed that I had bought just before my wedding four years before. They spread the clean sheets, fluffed the pillows and tucked in the blanket, while I watched the whole ceremony with tears of laughter in my eyes.

"Now you can undress me and put me to bed," I said to my wife. "How nice."

"Yes, my dearest."

"Come on, then! What are you waiting for?"

"Yes, dearest."

She was standing behind me by the dressing table. I twisted my head trying to catch sight of her. Suddenly she screamed, the way I had only heard people scream in the war.

"It's not true!"

She rushed to me, embraced me, flung herself beside me, and pressed her head against the stumps of my legs, drew back in horror and then pressed herself against them, kissing my poor stumps and weeping.

"What have they done to you? You were so young and handsome. It can't be true. How cruel people are! Why, why this? What good has it done anybody? My poor, good, sweet darling!"

Then they all came running in to see why she was screaming, my mother, my sister, my old nurse, and they were all crying and trying to speak as they fell down by my legs and cried their eyes out. And my brother stood in the doorway, pale, completely white, and his jaw trembled as he shrieked, "You're driving me mad! Stark raving mad!"

My mother was crawling around my wheelchair, no longer screaming but wheezing and banging her head against the wheels.

And there was my bed, fresh and clean, with its pillows fluffed and its blanket tucked in, the bed I had bought four years before, just before my wedding . . .

Ninth Fragment

. . . I was taking a hot bath while my brother hovered around restlessly in the little room, sitting down, getting up again, picking up the soap, the bath towel, bringing them close to his myopic eyes then putting them back again. Then he turned to the wall and, scratching at the plaster with one finger, talked on heatedly:

"Judge for yourself: you can't teach people compassion, reason, logic for centuries with impunity—developing their awareness. That's it—their awareness. It's easy to become hardened, lose your sensitivity, get used to the sight of blood and tears and suffering—like butchers and some doctors and the military; but how is it possible to deny the truth once you have seen it? In my opinion it's quite impossible. From early childhood I was taught to be kind to animals, to be compassionate. Every book I read taught this, and I'm filled with pity for those who suffer in your damned war. But with time I am beginning to get used to all the deaths, the suffering, the bloodshed. I feel that in everyday life I am becoming less sensitive, less responsive, that I only react to powerful excitation; yet I still cannot get used to the fact of war. My mind refuses to conceive what is fundamentally insane. A million men assembled in a certain place to kill one another systematically, and they all suffer, and they all are miserable. What is that if not madness?"

My brother fixed his naive, nearsighted eyes on me inquiringly.

"The red laugh," I said lightly, splashing myself.

"To tell you the truth," began my brother, trustingly placing his cold hand on my wet shoulder and quickly drawing it back. "To tell you the truth, I am very afraid of going mad. I don't understand

what's happening. I don't understand, and that appalls me. If someone could only explain all this to me, but no one can. You were
there; you saw it. Explain it to me."

"Go to hell!" I said in jest, splashing myself again.

"You too," said my brother sadly. No one will help me. It's terrible. I'm beginning to lose track of what's permitted and what's
forbidden, what's rational and what's insane. If I were to take you
by the throat, lightly at first as if caressing you, and then strangle
you—what would that be?"

"You're talking nonsense. No one does things like that."

My brother rubbed his cold hands together, smiled gently, and
went on. "While you were still there, there were nights when I
couldn't sleep. I had strange thoughts: I wanted to take an ax and
kill them all—our mother and sister, the maid, the dog. Of course
they were only thoughts, and I'd never do anything of the sort."

"I hope not," I said, splashing myself.

"I'm also afraid of knives, of anything sharp and glistening. I have
the feeling that were I to pick up a knife, I would certainly cut
someone's throat. Why not, after all, if the knife is sharp enough?"

"A good enough reason. What a strange fellow you are! Let's have
a little more hot water."

My brother turned on the faucet and continued:

"Another thing is that I'm afraid of crowds, of too many people
together. In the evening if I hear noise in the street, loud shouting,
I shudder and imagine that the slaughter has begun. When I see a
few people facing one another and I don't hear what they're talking
about, I begin to think that at any moment they'll start screaming,
rush at one another, that the killing will begin. And you know"—
mysteriously he leaned close to my ear—"the papers are full of news
of murders, of all kinds of strange murders. It isn't true that there're
as many minds as there are people; humanity has only one mind,
and it is beginning to cloud over. Feel how hot my head is. It's
burning. Sometimes it grows cold and everything in it freezes

111

becomes numb, turns into terrible, deathly ice. I must go mad—
don't laugh, brother—I must go mad. That's fifteen minutes; it's
time to get out of your bath."

"A little longer, one more minute."

It felt so good to sit in that bath, like I used to do, listening to
my brother's familiar voice, not paying much attention to what he
was saying, looking at everyday objects—the slightly tarnished brass
faucets, the pattern on the wall, the photographic equipment neatly
arranged on the shelves. I would take up photography again, take
pictures of peaceful landscapes, of my son walking, laughing, playing. I could do that without legs. And I would start writing again,
about learned books, about the latest achievements of the human
intellect, about beauty and peace.

I burst out laughing, splashing myself.

"What's the matter?" asked my brother, turning pale with fright.

"Nothing. I'm glad to be home."

He smiled at me as if I were a child, a younger brother, though
I was three years older; and he became thoughtful again, like an
adult, an old man whose thoughts were vast, ponderous, and ancient.

"You can't get away from it," he said, shrugging his shoulders.
"Every day at about the same time, the newspapers close the elec-
trical circuit and the whole world jumps. These simultaneous sensations, thoughts, this suffering and horror sweep the ground from
under my feet, and I feel like a chip of wood tossed on the waves,
a speck of dust in a whirlwind. I am torn violently from my everyday
existence, and every morning there is a terrible moment when I am
suspended over the black abyss of madness. And I will fall into it; I
must fall into it. You still don't know everything, brother. You don't
read the papers; you're in the dark about a lot of things. You still
don't know everything, my friend."

I considered what he was saying to be a rather morbid joke, part
of the craziness of those who look closely into the madness of war

and try to issue warnings. Yes, I took it for a joke, as if at that moment, splashing in the hot water, I had forgotten everything that I had seen.

"Well, let them keep me in the dark, but now I've got to get out of this tub," I said flippantly. My brother smiled and called the servant, and together they lifted me out and dressed me. I drank some aromatic tea from a favorite faceted glass and reflected that life was perfectly possible without legs. Then they wheeled me up to my desk in the study, and I got ready to work.

Before the war I had often reviewed foreign literature, and now a pile of wonderful books in their dear yellow, blue, and brown covers lay within reach. My joy was so overwhelming, my pleasure so profound that I could not bring myself to start reading at once but first leafed through them and ran my fingers over them. I could feel myself breaking into a smile—a very stupid smile no doubt, but I could not hold it back, lost as I was in admiration of the typefaces and vignettes, the severe, beautiful simplicity of their design. How much intelligence and love of beauty had gone into their making! How many people had had to strive, how much talent and taste had been expended on the creation of this one letter alone, so harmonious and eloquent in its interlacing strokes.

"And now to work!" I said seriously, filled with respect for my labor.

I took up a pen to write the title, and like a frog tied to a string, my hand jumped all over the paper. The pen jabbed, squeaked, leapt, slid uncontrollably, tracing lines that were jagged, crooked, completely meaningless. I did not cry out or so much as move a muscle. I froze as I began to suspect the terrible truth. My hand still leapt about on the brightly lit paper, and each finger trembled with mad horror, as if they were still there at the front, seeing the glow of fires and the blood, hearing the groans and screams of unspeakable pain. They had separated from me and were living a life of their own; they had become their own ears and eyes, these madly trembling fingers. And growing colder, lacking the strength to cry out or to move, I followed their wild dance across the sparkling white sheet of paper.

It was quiet. They thought that I was working and had closed all the doors so as not to distrub me. Alone, unable to move, I sat in my room and dutifully watched my hands shake.

"It's nothing," I said aloud, and in the peace and solitude of my study, my voice sounded hoarse and unpleasant, like the voice of a madman. "It's nothing; I'll dictate instead. After all, Milton was blind when he wrote *Paradise Regained*. I can still think. That's all that matters."

And I proceeded to compose a long, clever sentence about the blind Milton, but the words got confused or omitted, as when type is set badly, and by the time I was near the end of my sentence I had forgotten its beginning. I tried to recall how it all had started, why I was composing this strange meaningless sentence about someone called Milton—and I could not.

Paradise Regained, Paradise Regained, I repeated over and over and could not understand what I was saying.

Then I suddenly realized that I was forgetting many things, that I had become absentminded and often could not identify familiar faces. Even in a simple conversation, words would escape me, or else I could not, for the life of me, remember the meaning of a word. I had a clear picture of my days: they were strange, short, chopped off like my legs, with mysterious empty spaces, long hours when I was unconscious or insensible, of which I remembered nothing.

I wanted to call my wife, but I had forgotten her name. This neither surprised nor frightened me. Gently I whispered, "Wife!"

This awkward and unusual salutation sounded softly and died away without response. It was quiet. They were afraid of disturbing my work by making noise, and all was still: a true scholar's study, cozy, quiet, conducive to contemplation and creativity. "What dears to take such good care of me!" I thought, quite touched.

Then inspiration, blessed inspiration, visited me. The sun caught fire in my head, and its ardent, creative rays burst over the whole world, scattering flowers and songs. And all night I wrote, oblivious of fatigue, soaring freely on the wings of mighty, blessed inspiration. I was writing something great, something immortal—about flowers and songs. Flowers and songs . . .

PART II

Tenth Fragment

. . . fortunately, he died last week, on Friday. I must say it again—
it was the best thing for my brother. A legless cripple, shaking all
over, his soul shattered, he was frightening and pitiful in his last
insane, creative ecstasy. After that first night he wrote steadily for
two months without leaving his wheelchair, refusing to eat, weeping and cursing whenever, even for a minute, we took him away
from his desk. He moved his inkless pen across the paper at incredible speed, throwing aside one blank sheet after another, always
writing, writing. He no longer slept. Twice, thanks to heavy doses
of narcotics, we managed to put him to bed for a few hours, but
after that, even drugs were powerless to overcome his creative fever.
He insisted that the curtains be drawn and the lamp lit all day, to
give the illusion of permanent night. He smoked cigarette after cigarette and wrote. He appeared to be happy, and I have never seen
a sane person with such an inspired face, that of a prophet or a
great poet. He had become emaciated, having the waxen appearance
of a corpse or an ascetic, and his hair had turned completely gray.
When he began his mad endeavor, he was still youthful; at the end
he was an old man. Sometimes he forced himself to write more than
usual, and his pen would jab the paper and break, but he never
noticed. At such times it was impossible to go near him: at the
slightest touch he would have a fit of weeping or of laughter. Once
in a great while he would relax, blissfully, and would chat with me
in a benevolent way, always asking the same questions: Who was I?
What was my name? How long had I been involved with literature?
Then, complacently, always in exactly the same words, he would
tell me about his ridiculous fear of having lost his memory and of
no longer being able to work—and with what brilliance he had dis-

proved this outlandish notion by proceeding with his great, immortal work about flowers and songs.

"Of course, I don't expect to be recognized by my contemporaries," he would say with a mixture of pride and modesty, placing his trembling hand on the pile of blank pages, "but posterity—posterity will understand the value of my idea."

Not once did he refer to the war or to his wife and son. His huge illusory task absorbed him so completely that he was unaware of anything else. We could walk about and talk in his presence without his noticing us; nor did his face ever lose its terribly intense, inspired look. In the silence of the night, when everyone was asleep and he alone tirelessly spun the endless thread of his madness, he was especially forbidding, and I and our mother were the only ones who could bring ourselves to go near him. Once I tried to give him a pencil in place of his dry pen, thinking that perhaps he was really forming words, but all that appeared on the paper were ugly, jagged, meaningless lines.

He died at night, at his work. I knew my brother well, and his madness did not surprise me. The passionate yearning for work, which came through in his letters from the front, became the center of his life when he returned, a compulsion certain to clash with the impotence of his tormented, exhausted brain and bring on a catastrophe. I think that I have reconstructed accurately the sequence of sensations that led fatefully to his death. In general, everything I have recorded here about the war is based on my brother's words, which were often confused and incoherent. Only certain isolated scenes were so deeply etched in his brain that I can quote them almost word for word as he described them.

I loved my brother, and his death weighs on me like a stone, oppressing my brain with its senselessness. It has added another knot to the net of incomprehension drawn tight around my head like a shroud. The family has gone away to live with relatives in the country, and I am completely alone in the house, in this little house that my brother loved. The servants were let go. Sometimes the janitor from next door comes over to light the stoves in the morning, but the rest of the time I am alone. Like a fly trapped between the panes of a double window, I rush around striking transparent, impenetrable barriers. And I feel—I know that I shall never escape from this house. Now that I am alone, the war possesses me completely; it stands before me like a terrible enigma that I cannot clothe in flesh. I see it in all possible forms: a headless skeleton on horseback, a shadow born in storm clouds, silently enveloping the earth; but no image gives me the answer I seek or dispels the cold, constant dread that possesses me.

I do not understand war, and I am bound to go mad, like my brother, like thousands of others who have been brought back from it. This does not frighten me. The death of my reason will be as honorable as the death of a sentry at his post. But waiting for it— this slow, inexorable approach of madness, this impression of something enormous falling into an abyss—this is what my thought cannot bear. My heart is numb; it has died and it will never revive; only thought is still alive, still battling, once as strong as Samson but now defenseless and weak as a child. My poor thought! I feel so sorry for it. There are times when I can no longer bear the torment of the iron bands that squeeze my brain. I have an irresistible urge to rush out into the street, into the square where there are people, and to shout, "Stop the war at once, or else . . ."

Or else what? Do words exist that could make them see reason, words that could not be answered by other, equally loud, false words? Or should I fall to my knees before them and weep? But hundreds of thousands are filling the world with their tears, and what good does it do? Or should I kill myself before their eyes? Kill myself! Thousands are dying every day, and what good does it do?

And when I sense my own impotence, I feel a wild frenzy, the frenzy of the war that I hate. Like the doctor, I want to burn their houses with their treasures, their women and children, to poison the water they drink, to raise the dead from their graves and throw the corpses into their contaminated dwellings, onto their beds. Let them sleep with them like their wives, like their mistresses.

Oh, if I were only the Devil! I would bring to the earth the horror that hell breathes; I would become the monarch of their dreams, and when, with a smile on their lips, they had made the sign of the cross over their children, I would rise up before them—black . . .

Yes, I must lose my mind; let it only be soon, soon . . .

Eleventh Fragment

. . . prisoners of war, a bunch of trembling, frightened men. As they were led out of the railroad car, the crowd howled like a huge vicious dog on a short, flimsy chain. They howled, then fell silent, breathing heavily, as the prisoners walked along close together, their hands in their pockets, ingratiating smiles on their pale lips. They walked as if at any moment they expected to be struck on the backs of their knees with a long stick. But one of them, who kept a little apart from the others, was calm, stern, unsmiling, and when his black eyes met mine, I read open hatred in them. I saw clearly that he despised me and was prepared for anything I might do to him. Had I suddenly set about to kill him, unarmed as he was, he would not have cried out, nor would he have defended himself or protested. He was prepared for anything I might do to him.

I ran along with the crowd, trying to meet his eyes again, and just as the prisoners were entering a building, I did. He was the last, stepping aside to let his comrades pass, and he glanced at me again. Then I saw in his large black, pupilless eyes such torment, such depths of horror and madness that I felt I was looking into the most unhappy soul in the world.

"Who is the man with the strange eyes?" I asked one of the guards.

"An officer. Insane. There're lots like that."

"What's his name?"

"He doesn't speak, won't give his name. The others don't know who he is. He must have strayed in with them. He's already tried to hang himself once, so what can you say?" With a dismissive wave of his hand, the guard disappeared into the building.

Now it is evening, and I think about this man. He is alone among enemies, who he believes are capable of doing anything at all to him, and with his own people, who don't know him. He remains silent, waiting patiently to leave this world for good. I do not believe that he is insane, nor that he is a coward. He was the only one with dignity among those trembling, frightened men, whom he clearly does not recognize as his own. What is he thinking about? What despair there must be in the soul of a man who won't even give his own name before dying! But then, why should he? He is finished with life and with people; he has understood their true worth, and no one exists for him—neither his people nor the strangers, for all their shouts, their rages, and their threats. I asked more questions about him. He had been captured in that last, terrible battle, in which tens of thousands had been killed. He offered no resistance when he was seized; for some reason he was unarmed, and when a soldier who was still unaware of this struck him with his saber, he did not move or raise his arms in defense. But, unfortunately for him, his wound was light.

So perhaps he really is insane? The guard said there were lots like that . . .

Twelfth Fragment

. . . is beginning. . . . Last night when I went into my brother's study, he was sitting in his chair at his desk piled high with books. As soon as I lit the candle the hallucination vanished, but it was a long time before I could bring myself to sit in that chair. It was frightening at first—empty rooms that rustle and creak give rise to horror—but soon I even began to enjoy it: better to see my brother than anyone else. Still, that whole evening I did not leave the chair. I felt that should I get up he would immediately take his old place again. When I left the room I did so quickly, without looking back. Lamps should be lit in all the rooms—but is that a good idea? It would be worse if I saw things in the light. At least this way, there's a doubt.

Today I went in with a candle, and no one was sitting in the chair. Obviously it had been only a passing shadow. I had been to the station again—I go there every morning now—and I saw a whole car full of insane soldiers from our army. The doors were kept locked, and the car was being shunted to another track, but I had time to make out several faces through the windows. They were horrifying. One in particular. Exceptionally long, bright yellow like a lemon, with an open black mouth and motionless eyes, it was so like a mask of horror that I could not tear my eyes away. It looked at me, directly at me, motionless; then it slid away as the train began to move. If I should see it now in this dark doorway, I would not be able to bear it. I made inquiries: there were twenty-two mad-men in that car. The epidemic is spreading. The newspapers keep quiet about it. Nor do things look so good here in town. Tightly sealed black coaches have been appearing in the streets. Just today I counted six of them in different parts of town. I shall probably be taken off in one of them myself.

Yet every day the newspapers call for fresh troops and fresh blood, and I understand less and less what it all means. Yesterday I read a very dubious article that claimed that there are many spies, rene-gades, and traitors among us, that we ought to be watchful, that the nation's wrath would ferret out the culprits. What culprits? What had they done? In the streetcar coming home from the sta-tion, I overheard a bizarre conversation:

"They ought to be lynched," one man said after scrutinizing everyone around him, including me. "Yes, traitors ought to be lynched."

"Without mercy!" another man agreed. "We've been too lenient with them as it is."

I jumped off the streetcar. Here everyone is grieving over the war—these men, too, in their way—and what does it all mean? A bloody mist is settling over the earth, clouding our vision, and I am beginning to think that universal catastrophe is at hand. Madness is coming from out there, from those fields red with blood. I am a strong, healthy man; I do not suffer from debilitating diseases that might affect my brain. Yet I can see the infection spreading to me as well, and already half my thoughts no longer belong to me. This is worse than a plague with all its horrors. At least you could hide somewhere from the plague, protect yourself somehow; but how can you escape thoughts, which know no barriers in time or space?

During the day I can still fight it off, but at night, like everyone else, I become the slave of my dreams, and my dreams are full of horror and madness . . .

Thirteenth Fragment

. . . violence everywhere, mindless and bloody. The slightest clash leads to savage reprisals, and out come knives, stones, logs, and it no longer matters who gets killed. The red blood cries out to be spilled, and it flows freely and abundantly.

There were six of them, peasants, led by three soldiers with rifles at the ready. In their rustic dress, with their claylike faces and hair like tangled fur, led by the soldiers through the streets of the wealthy city, they looked like slaves out of antiquity. They were being led to the war, prodded by bayonets, innocent and slow-witted as oxen being led to slaughter. First came a young boy, tall, beardless, a small, immobile head atop a neck as long as a goose's. His whole body was bent forward like a dry stick, and he was staring at the ground before him so intently that he seemed to be looking to the very center of the earth. Last came an older man, stocky and bearded;

he showed no will to resist, and no thought showed in his eyes, but the earth seemed to seize his feet, clinging to them, and he walked as if a strong wind were blowing him backward. The soldier behind him prodded him with the butt of his rifle, and one of his feet would come unstuck and snap forward while the other remained fixed to the ground. The soldiers looked bored and malicious. They all had been walking like this for a long time, and by the way they carried their rifles, one could sense how tired and indifferent they were, marching out of step, peasants themselves. It was as if the silent, stubborn, senseless resistance of their six charges had clouded their disciplined minds, and they no longer knew where they were going or why.

"Where are you taking them?" I asked the nearest soldier. He gave a start and fixed me with a glance that felt like a bayonet plunged into my chest.

"Keep away!" he said. "Keep away, or—"

The older man chose this moment to run away, trotting over the railing along the boulevard, where he squatted as if he were trying to hide. No animal would have acted so stupidly. The soldier flew into a rage. I saw him go up to the peasant, lean over, switch his rifle to his left hand and strike the soft, flat body with his right. He struck him again and again. A crowd gathered. I heard laughter, shouting . . .

Fourteenth Fragment

. . . in the eleventh row of the orchestra. On both sides elbows were pressing against me, and all around I could see immobile heads in the semidarkness tinged with red by the light from the stage. And I was gradually seized with terror at the thought of so many people enclosed in so restricted a space. Each of them was listening in silence to what was being said on stage or perhaps thinking his own thoughts, but together they made more noise than the actors with their loud voices. They coughed, blew their noses, rustled their clothes, and shuffled their feet. I could distinctly hear their deep, uneven breathing, which was warming the air. They were frightening because each could so easily turn into a corpse, and each carried madness in his head. From the calm of these well-groomed heads resting securely on starched white collars, I sensed a hurricane of insanity ready to burst out at any second.

My hands went cold as I realized how many of them there were, how frightening they were, and how far I was from the exit. They were calm, but if someone shouted, "Fire!" . . . And to my horror I felt a passionate urge to do just that, an urge that I cannot recall without my hands going cold again. Who would stop me from shouting, "Fire! Run for your lives! Fire!"?

A convulsion of madness would grip their calm limbs. Men would leap up, yelling, howling like animals; they would forget wives, sisters, mothers; they would rush in all directions as if stricken with sudden blindness; and in their sudden madness they would throttle one another with their white, perfumed hands. The lights would go up; a man with a pallid face would shout from the stage that everything was all right, that there was no fire; and the orchestra would strike up with tremulous, savagely merry music; but they would not hear and would go on strangling and trampling, bashing women's intricate coiffures. They would tear off ears and bite off noses, and they would rip off their clothes and in their madness shamelessly show themselves naked. And their beautiful, beloved, sensitive wives would squeal and thrash about helplessly at their feet, still trusting in their nobility, but the men would viciously strike their upturned faces and fight their way to the door. For they will always be murderers, and their calm, their nobility are those of well-fed beasts who feel out of danger.

And when half of them lie as corpses and the rest cower in a trembling, ragged group at the exit, I shall come out on the stage, smiling falsely, and say to them with a laugh; "That is for killing my brother."

I must have whispered something out loud, because my neighbor on my right shifted in his seat and said angrily, "Be quiet! I'm trying to hear."

That amused me and I became playful. With a stiff look of concern I leaned toward him.

"What's the matter?" he asked suspiciously. "Why are you looking at me like that?"

"Please be quiet," I whispered softly. "Don't you smell burning? The theater is on fire."

He had sufficient willpower and presence of mind not to cry out. His face turned pale and his eyes bulged out over his huge cheeks, which were as big as bulls' bladders, but he did not cry out. He got up quietly, without so much as a thank-you, and walked toward the exit, swaying and forcing himself convulsively to walk slowly. He was afraid that others would realize that there was a fire and block his escape, he being the only one who deserved to live.

I felt disgusted and I, too, left the theater. Moreover, I did not want to reveal myself too soon. Out in the street I glanced up at the sky toward where the war was raging. Everything was calm. The night clouds, tinted yellow by the streetlights, floated slowly by. "Perhaps this is all a dream and there's no war at all," I thought, lulled by the calm of the sky and the city.

Just then a boy came dashing around the corner, shouting joyfully; "Crushing defeat! Huge losses! Extra! Night extra!"

I read it under a streetlight. Four thousand killed. In the theater there had probably been no more than a thousand in the audience. And all the way home I was thinking: four thousand bodies.

Now I am afraid of entering my empty house. As I put the key in the lock and look at the mute surface of the door, I became aware of the dark, empty rooms through which a man in a hat will soon pass, glancing over his shoulder. Inside I can easily find my way up the stairs, but I keep striking matches until I find a candle to light. I no longer go into my brother's study, and I keep it locked. I sleep in the dining room, the only room I use now. It is more peaceful there, and the air seems to have preserved traces of conversations, laughter, the merry chatter of dishes. Sometimes I can clearly hear the scratching of an inkless pen, and when I go to bed . . .

Fifteenth Fragment

. . . this stupid and terrifying dream. It is as if the top of my skull has been removed, exposing my brain, which, defenseless, submissively, greedily drinks in all the horrors of these mad and bloody days. I lie there curled up in a four-foot space, yet my thoughts embrace the planet. I see through everyone's eyes and hear through their ears. I die with those who are killed; I weep in anguish with the wounded and abandoned; when blood flows from someone's body, I feel the pain of the wound and I suffer. What never was and what is far away I see as clearly as what was and what is near. There is no limit to the suffering of my naked brain.

And the children, the innocent little children! I saw them in the street, playing war and chasing one another, and one of them was crying in his thin childish voice, and I shuddered with horror and disgust. I went back home, night fell, and in my burning dreams that blazed in the middle of the night, these little innocent children became a horde of infant murderers.

Something malevolent was burning with a broad red flame, and in the smoke swarmed freakish children with the heads of adult killers. They were leaping around lightly and nimbly, like gamboling lambs, but their breathing was heavy and sickly. Their mouths were like the maws of toads opening and closing convulsively. Red blood coursed sullenly under the transparent skin of their bare bodies, and they were killing one another as they played. They were worse than anything I had ever seen, because they were so small and could go everywhere.

I looked out the window, and a little boy saw me, smiled, and asked with a look whether he could come in. "I want to come in," he said.

"You'll kill me."

"I want to come in," he said and suddenly turned frightfully pale and began to claw his way up the white wall, like a rat, like a starving rat. He lost his grip several times and squeaked, and darted across the wall so quickly that I could not follow his sudden, jerky movements.

"He might crawl in under the door," I thought in horror, and as if guessing my thoughts he became long and swiftly crawled through the dark slit under the front door, the tip of his tail wagging. I had time to hide under a blanket and listened as the little creature searched for me in the dark rooms, treading cautiously with his tiny bare feet. Very slowly, with frequent hesitations, he approached my room and came in; for a long time I heard nothing more, not a movement, not a rustle, as if there were no one at all at my bedside. Then a little hand began to raise the edge of my blanket, the cold air of the room touched my face and chest. I tried to hold onto the blanket, but it was being pulled off me from all sides, and suddenly my legs felt cold, as if they had been plunged into water. They lay there defenseless in the icy darkness while he looked at them.

Outside, in the courtyard beyond the walls of the house, a dog barked and fell silent, and I heard it rattling its chain as it retreated into its doghouse. And the creature was looking at my naked legs in silence. I knew he was there. I knew by the horror that like death held me with the stony rigidity of the grave. Had I been able to scream, I would have awakened the whole city, the whole world; but my voice had died inside me, and without stirring I submitted to the touch of his cold little hands making their way up my body toward my throat.

"No!" I moaned and woke up for a moment, panting; and I saw the watchful, living darkness of the night, and I must have fallen asleep again.

"Calm yourself," said my brother as he sat down on my bed,

making it creak, he was so heavy in death. "Calm yourself: you're dreaming. You only imagined you were being strangled; you are actually sound asleep in the dark rooms where there's no one, and I'm in my study writing. None of you understood what I was writing; you mocked me and called me a madman—but now I'll let you in on a secret. I'm writing about the red laugh. See it?"

Something enormous, red, and bloody, was standing over me and laughing toothlessly.

"That's the red laugh. When the world goes mad it laughs like that. You do know, don't you, that the world's gone mad? There are no flowers left, no songs; it has become round and smooth and red, like a head with the skin torn off. Can you see it?"

"Yes, I see it. It's laughing."

"Look what's happening to its brain. It's red like bloody mush."

"It's screaming."

"It's in pain. It has no more flowers or songs. Now let me lie on you."

"I'm miserable. I'm frightened."

"We the dead lie down on the living. Are you warm?"

"Yes."

"Do you feel better?"

"I'm dying."

"Wake up and shout. Wake up and shout. I'm leaving you . . ."

Sixteenth Fragment

. . . the battle had been raging for more than a week. It began the Friday before last. Saturday, Sunday, Monday, Tuesday, Wednesday, Thursday passed, then Friday again, and it, too, passed and the battle is still going on. The two armies, hundreds of thousands of men, are facing each other, neither giving ground, ceaselessly firing explosive shells; and every minute living men are turned into corpses. The din, the constant detonations in the air make the sky itself shudder and black storm clouds gather—but they face each other, neither giving ground, and go on killing. Three days without sleep and a man falls ill; he loses his memory. They have not slept for more than a week, and they are all insane. This is why they feel no pain, why they give no ground, why they will fight until the last man is dead. It is reported that when certain units ran out of ammunition, the men fought on with stones, with their bare hands, biting like dogs. Should any of those men ever return home, they will have fangs like wolves—but none of them will. They have gone mad and will fight to the end. Everything is turned upside down in their heads. They don't understand anything: if they were suddenly turned around, they would start firing on their own side, believing they were shooting at the enemy.

Strange rumors circulate. They are passed on in whispers, as faces turn pale with horror and wild forebodings. Listen, brother, listen to what they're saying about the red laugh! It seems that ghostly detachments have appeared, phantom hordes, identical to living armies. They appear suddenly at night, when the crazed men have dropped off for a moment's sleep, or else at the height of a battle, when even the brightest day becomes spectral; and they start firing phantom guns, filling the air with phantom thunder, while the men—the living, insane men, stunned by surprise—fight to the death against the phantom enemy, losing their last vestige of sanity with horror, turning gray on the spot and dying. The phantoms disappear as suddenly as they came; silence falls, and there are freshly mutilated bodies on the ground. Who killed them? Do you know, brother? Who killed them?

When there is a lull between battles and the enemy is far away and a lonely shot rings out in the depths of the night, men leap to their feet and start shooting into the darkness. Who do they see there? What dreadful being shows his silent face breathing madness and horror? You know, brother, and I know too. Others still do not know, but they already begin to feel something, and they ask, turning ashen, "Why are there so many madmen? There were never that many before."

They would like to believe that things are the same as they used to be, that the universal violence against reason will not affect their own weak little minds.

"Men have been fighting since the beginning of time; yet nothing like this has ever happened before, has it? Anyway, struggle is the law of life," they say confidently, calmly. Yet they themselves turn pale, look around for a doctor, call out: "Water! Quickly, a glass of water!"

They would willingly become idiots, these people, if that would only help them stop hearing how their reason rocks and breaks up in its mismatched struggle with the absurd. On days when out there men were continually being turned into corpses, I could not find peace anywhere and rushed around visiting people. I heard a lot of conversations like that, and I saw a lot of people with false smiles, maintaining that the war was far away and had nothing to do with them. But I encountered even more raw, true horror and bitter tears and frenzied despair, as mighty reason itself strained to scream out through man its final plea, its final curse, "When will this insane war ever end?"

Visiting friends whom I had not seen for several years, I happened to meet an insane officer who had been sent back from the front. We had been school friends, but I did not recognize him. Neither, for that matter, did his own mother—had he lain in the grave for a year, he would have looked more like himself than he did now. His hair was completely white; his features had not altered that much, but as he never spoke—was always straining to listen—his face bore such a menacing mask of remoteness and alienation that one didn't dare engage him in conversation. According to his family this is what happened: His regiment had been waiting in reserve, while the one next to it was sent ahead on a bayonet attack. Men were running past, shouting "hurrah" so loudly that they almost drowned out the shooting—and then suddenly everything stopped, the shooting and the hurrahs, and it was silent as the grave. The bayonet fighting had begun. That silence his reason could not endure.

Now he is calm as long as people around him are talking and making noise; he listens and waits; but as soon as there is a moment's silence he clutches his head and throws himself against the walls and furniture in fits that resemble epileptic seizures. Members of his large family take turns watching him, surrounding him with sounds, but there are still the long silent nights, and this is when his father, white haired and a little mad himself, takes things into his own hands. He has filled his son's room with clocks that tick loudly and strike almost continuously at different times. He is building a wheel for him that produces a steady rattle. None of the family has lost hope that he will recover—he is only twenty-seven—and it is even rather merry at their house nowadays. They dress him smartly, in civilian clothes, see that he is clean and neat, and with his white hair and young, thoughtful face, his weary, noble movements, he is even rather handsome.

When I heard this story I went up to him and kissed his hand—his pale, limp hand that would never be raised to strike another blow—and no one was particularly surprised. His young sister did smile at me with her eyes and afterward paid such attention to me that I might have been her fiancé, someone she loved more than anyone in the world. Indeed, she was so attentive to me that from the depths of my abject heart that never loses hope, I almost told her about my dark and empty rooms, where I am worse than alone. She saw to it that we were left by ourselves.

"How pale you are," she said with kindness. "You have circles under your eyes. Are you ill? Are you grieving for your brother?"

"I'm grieving for everyone. And I am a bit unwell."

"I know why you kissed his hand. The others didn't understand, but I did. It was because he's mad, wasn't it?"

"Yes, that was why."

She became thoughtful, looking just like her brother, only much younger.

"And me," she said, hesitating and blushing but without lowering her gaze. "Will you let me kiss your hand?"

I dropped to my knees in front of her and said; "Give me your blessing."

She drew back, turning pale, and, barely moving her lips, whispered, "I am not a believer."

"Neither am I."

For a moment her hands touched my head; then that moment passed.

"Do you know that I'm going out there?" she asked.

"Go. But you won't be able to stand it."

"Perhaps not. But they need help, too—as you do, as my brother does. It's not their fault. Will you remember me?"

"Yes. Good-bye."

"Farewell."

I felt calm, lighthearted, as if I'd already gone through the worst of death and madness. Yesterday for the first time I entered my house without fear. I opened my brother's study and sat at his desk for a long time. When I suddenly awoke in the middle of the night, as if I had been shaken awake, I heard the scratching of a dry pen on paper. I was not frightened and almost smiled as I thought:

"Work away, brother, work away! Your pen is not dry; it is dipped in living blood. Your pages may appear blank, but their menacing emptiness says more about war and human reason than anything written by the cleverest of men. Work away, brother, work away!"

This morning I read that the battle is still raging, and again I am seized by anxiety and a sense of something falling inside my brain. It is coming, it is near, it is already at the threshold of these bright, empty rooms. Remember, remember me, my dear girl. I am going mad. Thirty thousand dead. Thirty thousand dead . . .

Seventeenth Fragment

. . . some sort of slaughter in town. Dark, dreadful rumors . . .

Eighteenth Fragment

While looking through the endless list of the dead in this morning's paper, I came across the name of someone I knew. My sister's fiancé had been killed, an officer called up at the same time as my dead brother. An hour later the postman handed me a letter addressed to my brother, and I recognized the handwriting on the envelope as being that of the man who had just been killed. One dead man was writing to another—though that was, of course, better than when the dead write to the living. I was told that a mother kept getting letters from her son a month after reading in detail in the papers about his ghastly death—he was blown to pieces by a shell. He was a loving son; each of his letters was full of comforting words, of young, naive hope for future happiness. He was dead; yet every day he wrote about life with infernal regularity, and his mother stopped believing in his death. And when one day went by without a letter, then a second and a third, and the endless silence of death closed around her, she took her son's large old revolver in both her hands and shot herself in the chest. Apparently she did not die. I don't know; I did not hear.

I looked at that envelope for a long time, reflecting that he had held it in his hands, had bought it somewhere or given his orderly money to buy it at a shop; he had sealed it and probably mailed it himself. And then the complicated mechanism of the post had gone to work. The letter had sailed forth, past forests, fields, towns, passing from one pair of hands to another, onward toward its destination. He had put on his boots that last morning while the letter sailed on. He was killed and still it sailed on. He was thrown into a pit and covered with other corpses and with earth while the letter sailed on past forests, fields, towns—a living ghost in its gray envelope covered with postmarks. And now I am holding it in my hands.

This is what the letter says. It is written in pencil on scraps of paper and is not finished. Something interrupted him.

". . . It is only now that I understand the great joy of war, the primordial pleasure of killing people—intelligent people, artful, cunning, infinitely more intelligent than the most vicious beasts of prey. Taking life away forever is just as fine as playing lawn tennis with planets and stars. My poor friend, it is such a pity you are no longer here with us but are condemned to the stale boredom of everyday banality. In this atmosphere of death, you would have found what your restless, noble heart has always sought—a feast of blood. This hackneyed image conceals a deep truth. We wade up to our knees in blood, and our heads spin from this red wine, as my brave men jokingly call it. To drink your enemy's blood is far from being the senseless custom we thought it was. Our ancestors knew what they were doing . . .

". . . The carrion crows are cawing. Do you hear them? They blacken the sky. They perch next to us, fearless; they follow us everywhere, and they are always overhead, covering us with a black lace umbrella, a moving tree with black leaves. One came up close to my face and was about to peck me—he must have thought I was dead. The carrion crows are cawing, and it worries me a little. Where have so many come from?

". . . Last night we cut the throats of our enemies as they lay asleep. We crept up to them silently, like hunters. We crawled so cunningly that we didn't brush against a single corpse, didn't frighten off a single crow. We crept like shadows, and the night concealed us. I killed the sentry myself. I knocked him to the ground and strangled him first, before he could cry out. You understand? The slightest outcry and all would be lost. But he didn't cry out. I don't think he even realized that he was being killed.

"They were all asleep around smoldering campfires, sleeping as peacefully as if they had been at home in their own beds. We spent over an hour killing them; only a few awoke before our knives struck. They squealed and begged for mercy; they defended themselves with their teeth. One of them bit a finger off my left hand, which carelessly I was using to hold down his head. He bit my finger off, and I twisted his head off. What do you think? Are we even? Why didn't they wake up? You could hear the bones cracking and the flesh being hacked off. Then we stripped them naked and shared their clothes among us. Don't take offense at that silly detail. With your scruples, you'll say it smacks of marauding, but we ourselves were almost naked, our clothes in shreds. I'd been wearing a woman's jacket for a long time and looked more like a camp follower than an officer of a victorious army.

"Of course, I understand you're married now, and perhaps you're not comfortable reading such things. But you do understand? Women. Hell, I am young and I crave love! By the way, didn't you once have a fiancée? Didn't you show me a snapshot of a young girl and tell me it was your fiancée? There was something so very sad written on it. You cried. That was a long time ago; I barely remember. There's no time for such feelings in war. You cried. What were you crying about? What was written there that was so sad, so melancholy, like a little flower? And you cried and cried. You, an officer—you should be ashamed to cry.

"The carrion crows are cawing. Do you hear them, my friend? The carrion crows are cawing. What do they want?"

Then the penciled lines faded out, and the signature could not be read.

And strangely enough, I did not feel the least bit sorry for the dead man. I had a clear image of his face, soft and delicate as a woman's: the coloring of his cheeks, the clarity of his eyes, his little beard that was so downy and delicate that it, too, was quite feminine. He loved books, flowers, music; he hated everything that was coarse. He wrote poetry. My brother, speaking as a critic, said that it was very good. And I could not connect anything of what I knew and remembered about him with the cawing of the crows nor the bloody slaughter nor with death.

. . . The carrion crows are cawing . . .

And suddenly, for one wild, unspeakably happy moment, it seemed clear to me that the whole thing was a lie. There was no war: there were no dead, no corpses, nor was there the horror of our stricken, helpless reason. I was sleeping on my back, having a terrible dream, as in childhood: the silent, empty rooms, devastated by death and fear, and I holding some kind of crazy letter in my hand. My brother was alive, and they were all sitting there at tea. And I could hear the clinking of the china.

. . . The carrion crows are cawing . . .

But, no, it is all true. Unhappy planet! It is all true, and the crows really are cawing. It is not the invention of an idle scribbler seeking cheap effects, nor is it the fantasy of a madman. The crows are cawing. Where is my brother? He was gentle and noble and wished no one harm. Where is he? I am asking you, you damned murderers! Before the whole world I am asking you—murderers, crows perched on carrion, wretched, imbecile beasts! Beasts! Why did you murder my brother? If you had faces I would slap them, but you don't have faces: you have the snouts of wild beasts. You pretend to be human, but under your gloves I see your claws; under your hats I see the flattened skulls of beasts: behind your clever speeches I hear hidden madness rattling its rusty chains. And with all the strength of my grief, of my anguish, of my defiled thoughts, I curse you, wretched, imbecile beasts!

Final Fragment

. . . and through you, life will be reborn!

The orator was shouting and struggling to keep upright on a barrier post, waving a banner over whose folds crawled the inscription "Down with War!"

"You are young; you have your whole lives ahead of you. You must save yourselves and future generations from this horror, this madness. We have no strength to go on; blood rises up to our eyes, the sky is falling around our heads, the earth is opening under our feet. Good people . . ."

An enigmatic humming rose from the crowd, and at times the speaker's voice was drowned out by this threatening noise.

"I may be mad, but I'm speaking the truth. My father and my brother are rotting out there like carrion. You must light bonfires, dig pits, destroy and bury all the weapons. Demolish the barracks. Rip off the soldiers' bright garments of madness. We cannot go on. People are dying—"

A tall man struck the speaker and knocked him off the post. The banner rose once more, then fell. I did not have time to see the attacker's face; at once it all became a nightmare. Everything started to move and to howl; stones and logs flew through the air; fists were raised above heads and came crashing down on people. Like a live, roaring wave, the crowd lifted me up and carried me to the side, throwing me hard against a fence, then it took me up again and bore me off in another direction, until I was shoved against a stack of logs that was tottering forward and threatening to tumble on our heads. Something rattled and clicked sharply into the logs. There was a momentary lull—and again the roaring started, immense, full-throated, elemental. Then again the sharp rattle. Next to me someone fell, and blood began to pour from a red hole where his eye had been. A log came spinning through the air, catching me in the face. I fell and started to crawl among trampling feet, trying to make my way out into the open. I climbed over fences, breaking my fingernails, and clambered onto piles of firewood. One collapsed under me, and I slid down in an avalanche of knocking logs. Later I barely managed to escape from a square courtyard. Behind me, getting closer all the time, there was still thundering, roaring, howling, rattling.

A bell was ringing; something came crashing down, like a four-story house collapsing. The twilight seemed to be lingering on to prevent night from falling, as if the shots from that direction were tinged with red and were driving off the darkness. Jumping down from the last fence, I found myself in a narrow twisting alley, a corridor between two blank walls, and I ran down it for a long time, but the alley was blocked off by still another fence, beyond which loomed black mountains of firewood and timber. Again I clambered over them, falling into pockets where it was silent and smelled of damp wood, and as I scrambled into the open, I did not dare look back. I could tell what was happening there by the reddish glow that spread over the black logs and made them look like slain giants. My battered face went numb and felt like a plaster mask, and my pain died away. I think I must have fainted in one of the black holes, but I am not sure. My only clear memory is of running and running.

Later I ran along dark, unfamiliar streets between black, dead-looking houses. I could not find my way out of the mute labyrinth they formed. I should have stopped to try to orient myself, but I couldn't. The roaring was getting closer all the time; sometimes as I came around a corner, it would hit me in the face: red, wrapped in clouds of crimson, swirling smoke. I would turn back until it was behind me again. On one street corner I saw a strip of light that was extinguished as I approached; a shop was being shut hastily. Through a crack, just before it all sank into silent, expectant gloom, I caught a glimpse of a counter and a barrel. Then a man was running toward me. We almost bumped into each other in the darkness. He stopped a couple of steps away. I did not know who he was; all I could make out was his dark, watchful silhouette.

"Where are you coming from?" he asked.

"Back there."

"And where are you going?"

"Home."

"Ah! Home?"

He was silent for an instant; then he suddenly threw himself at me and tried to knock me down. His cold fingers felt greedily for my throat, but they got tangled in my clothes. I bit his hand, tore myself free, and ran away. For a long time he chased me down those deserted streets, his boots clattering loudly; then he dropped back— perhaps my bite had caused him pain.

I do not know how I found my street. The lamps were off here, too, and the houses stood without a single light, as if they were dead. I would have gone by without recognizing anything had I not happened to glance up just then and see my own house. I hesitated: the house where I had lived for so many years looked alien on that strange, dead street, which echoed sadly and oddly with the sound of my heavy breathing. Then I was struck with a frenzy of fear at the thought that I had lost my key. I had great difficulty finding it, though it was right there in my outside pocket. When the lock clicked, the sound echoed so loudly that it seemed as if the doors of all the dead houses along the street had opened at once.

I hid in the cellar at first but soon became uneasy and bored. Something began flickering before my eyes, and I crept quietly up the stairs. Feeling my way in the dark, I locked the doors of all the rooms and decided to barricade them, but the sound of furniture being dragged through those empty rooms was terribly loud, and it alarmed me.

"I'll await death like this. It doesn't matter now," I decided.

There was still warm water in the washbasin, and, groping, I washed myself and dried my face. Where it had been smashed it stung, and I decided to have a look at myself in the mirror. I struck a match, and in the weak, uneven light that flared up, I saw something so hideous looking at me out of the darkness that I threw the match to the floor. My nose must have been broken.

"Doesn't matter now," I thought. "It doesn't matter to anyone."

I felt elated. Striking postures and making faces as if I were on stage playing a burglar, I headed for the sideboard and looked for food. I was aware of how absurd my contortions were, but I was enjoying myself. I went on making faces while eating, playing at being a glutton.

But the silence and darkness frightened me. I opened the window into the yard and listened. At first, because there was no street traffic, I thought that it was completely still. No one was shooting. But I soon began to hear a rumbling of distant voices, shouts, the crash of falling objects, roars of laughter. The sound grew louder. I looked up at the sky: it was crimson and racing swiftly overhead. The shed across the way, the cobbles of the yard, the doghouse all glowed red. I called quietly down to the dog, "Neptune!"

Nothing stirred in the doghouse, and next to it I made out the gleam of a broken chain. The distant shouting and crashing were getting louder and louder. I shut the window.

"They're coming this way!" I thought and began looking for a place to hide. I opened the stoves, felt around the fireplace, looked inside the oven, but nothing would do. I went through all the rooms, except the study, which I did not wish to enter. I knew that he would be sitting in his chair at his desk piled high with books, and I would have found the sight of him unpleasant just then.

Gradually I began to get the impression that I was not alone. Others were silently moving around me in the darkness. They almost touched me, and once someone's breath turned the back of my neck to ice.

"Who's there?" I asked in a whisper, but no one answered.

But when I started moving again, they walked behind me, silent and terrifying. I knew that I was imagining they were there because I was ill, running a fever, but I could not overcome the fear that was making my whole body shiver as if I had a chill. I felt my forehead: it was burning hot.

"Perhaps I'd better go in after all," I thought. "At least he's not a stranger."

He was sitting in his chair at his desk piled high with books, and this time he did not vanish. Reddish light penetrated the drawn curtains, but it did not light the room; I could barely see him. I sat to one side of him, on the sofa, and waited. It was quiet in the room, but the rumbling, the crashing and shouts were getting nearer. The crimson light was growing brighter, and I could now see him in his chair, his black, cast-iron profile thinly outlined in red.

"Brother!" I said.

But he made no sound, immobile and black, like a monument. The floor creaked in the next room, and suddenly it became unusually silent, as in the domain of the dead. All sounds died away, and even the crimson light dimmed to the shade of deathliness and silence. I thought that this silence was emanating from my brother and I told him so.

"No, it doesn't come from me," he said. "Look out the window."

I drew open the curtains and shrank back.

"So that's what it is!" I said.

"Call my wife," my brother told me. "She's never seen it before."

She was sitting in the dining room sewing. When she saw my face she got up obediently, stuck her needle into her work, and followed me. I opened the curtains at all the windows and the crimson light streamed in, but somehow it did not make the room brighter; only the large red squares of the windows burned with immobile fire.

We went to the window. The even, fiery red sky, cloudless, starless, sunless, stretched from the eaves of the house to the horizon and beyond. Beneath it stretched an equally even, dark-red plain, and it was covered with corpses. They were all naked, lying with their feet toward us, so that all we could see were the soles of their feet and the triangles of their chins. It was silent. They were all dead; no one had been forgotten on that endless plain.

"There're more and more of them," my brother said.

He, too, was standing at the window. Now everyone was there: our mother and sister and all the others who lived in our house. I could not see their faces but recognized them by their voices.

"You're imagining it," my sister said.

"No, it's true. Look."

It was true; there were more bodies. We looked carefully to find out why, and we saw that wherever there had been an empty space near a body another would appear—the earth was expelling them. All the spaces were being filled, and soon the whole earth was bright with pale pink bodies in rows, with the soles of their feet toward us. The room, too, grew brighter with a dead, pale pink light.

"Look: there's no more room for them," my brother said.

Our mother answered, "There is one in here."

We turned. On the floor behind us lay a naked, pale pink body, its head thrown back. At once a second appeared next to it, then a third. The earth was expelling them one after another, and soon rows of pale pink dead bodies filled all the rooms.

"They're in the nursery, too," the nanny said. "I've seen them."

"We must leave," our sister said.

"But there's no way out," replied my brother. "Look."

It was true. Their bare feet were already touching us as they lay there shoulder to shoulder. And then they all stirred and shuddered and rose a little higher in their neat rows: new bodies were rising out of the earth and forcing them up.

"They'll smother us!" I said. "Let's escape through the window."

"Impossible!" said my brother. "We can't go there. Look what's out there!"

Out the window, in the still, crimson light, stood the red laugh.

NOVEMBER 8, 1904
—Translated by Henry and Olga Carlisle

AT THE
STATION

It was early spring when I went for a stay in the country. The paths were still covered with last year's dark leaves. I had come alone, and alone I wandered among the empty houses whose windows reflected the April sun. I ascended their broad, open verandas, wondering who would be living there under the green tents of birches and oaks. Whenever I closed my eyes, I seemed to hear cheerful steps, young voices singing, and the ring of women's laughter.

I often went to the station to meet the passenger trains. Not that I was expecting anyone—no one would be visiting me—but I love those broad-shouldered iron giants as they rush by, swaying along the tracks with their weight and power, carrying off people I do not know but who are dear to me. To me they are alive and extraordinary. In their speed I sense the vastness of the earth and the strength of man, and when they cry out so imperiously and freely, I think, "This is how they cry out in America, in Asia, in fiery Africa."

The station was small, with two short sidings, and after the train had left, it became quiet and empty; the woods and sunbeams took over the low platform and the tracks, flooding them with silence and light. Along the sidings, under a slumbering railway car, chickens were hard at work around the cast-iron wheels, and as I watched their quiet, meticulous industry, I could not believe that there really was an America, an Asia, a fiery Africa.

Within a week I got to know all the inhabitants of that little neighborhood, and I nodded to them as to acquaintances, the watchmen with their blue workmen's shirts, the silent switchmen with their colorless faces and their brass horns sparkling in the sun.

And every day I saw a gendarme at the station. He was a strapping, robust fellow, as they all are, with a broad back tightly molded by his dark blue uniform, with enormous hands and a youthful face, in which the blue-eyed innocence of the countryside could still be glimpsed under the somber self-importance of the official. At first his eyes searched me grimly and suspiciously, his face set severely, inaccessibly; and whenever he walked by me, the click of his spurs was pointedly sharp, eloquent. Soon however he became used to me, as he had become used to the posts that support the roof over the platform, to the tracks of the siding, and to the abandoned railway car under which the chickens were occupied. In such quiet places habits are quickly established.

When he stopped noticing me, I realized that this man was bored, as bored as anyone on earth—bored by the station, by the absence of thought, by the devouring power of idleness, and by his own exceptional position, lost as it was in limbo between the inaccessible authorities of the station and their subordinates, who were unworthy of him. His soul thrived on the disruption of order, but in this small station no one provided any, and each time a passenger train departed without the slightest adventure, disappointment and the annoyance of someone who has been tricked could be seen in his face. Lost in uncertainty, he would stand there for a few moments and then, aimlessly with an idle step, stroll to the other end of the platform. On his way he might stop for a second near a woman waiting for the next train, but a woman is only a woman, and frowning, the gendarme would walk on. Then he would sit heavily, listlessly, as if exhausted, and he would feel how soft and limp his arms were under the uniform, how his whole strong body, created for work, was lost in painful, enervating idleness. Some are bored just in the head, but he was bored throughout, from head to toe. Even his cap, which he pushed back on his head, looked bored, its cockiness useless, and his spurs clinked dissonantly, as if they were tone-deaf. Then he would start yawning. How he yawned! His mouth was distended from ear to ear: it widened and took over his whole face; it seemed that in another second, one would be able to see all of him through this growing chasm, down to his belly full of groats and cabbage soup. How he yawned!

I would leave then in a hurry, but I, too, would start yawning, my temples throbbing, my eyes watering, the trees along the way all distorted by my tears.

Once a passenger without a ticket was thrown off a mail train, and that was a holiday for the bored gendarme. He pulled himself up; his spurs clicked distinctly and menacingly; his face showed concentration and anger. His happiness was short-lived, however. With curses and a clattering of coins, the passenger paid his fare and quickly climbed back on the coach, while behind him the great, listless body of the gendarme loomed idly again. I was truly worried for him when he began yawning.

For some days now near the station, workmen had been busy clearing a space. When I returned after two days in the city, bricklayers were putting up a third course of bricks; a new building was going up to serve as a station. Several of the bricklayers there worked quickly and well. It was wonderful to see how a straight, graceful wall was growing directly out of the earth. Having mortared one course, they were laying the next, making sure that the bricks fit as they set them in a pattern—broad side, then narrow side, out— measuring them so that the corners were neat. They thought things through, and though they knew what they were doing—a well-defined, easy task—their thoughts were clear, and that made their work pleasing and interesting for the eye to follow. I was watching them with delight when the voice of authority sang out next to me.

"Listen, you! What are you doing? Not that one!"

It was the gendarme speaking. Leaning over the metal fence that separated the workmen from the asphalted platform, he was pointing insistently at a brick.

"I'm speaking to you, you with the beard. That half brick should go there!"

The workman, whose beard was spattered with mortar here and

there, silently turned around—the gendarme was stern and impe-
rious—then silently followed the pointed finger with his eyes, picked
up the half brick, tried it, then dropped it back on the pile. The
gendarme looked darkly at me and walked away, but the seduction
of the work in progress was stronger than propriety: having paced
the platform twice, he again stopped before the workman, striking
a scornful, detached pose. But there was no more boredom in his
face.

I went off into the woods. When I returned home through the
station, it was one o'clock, and the workmen were resting. The
place was deserted as usual, but someone was hovering around the
unfinished wall. It was the gendarme. He was picking up bricks
and finishing the wall's fifth course. I could only see his broad back
clad in tight cloth, but it expressed concentration and indecision.
The work was turning out to be more complicated than he had anticipated. His untrained eye was playing tricks on him. He leaned
back, shaking his head, picking up another brick as his sword rattled against the ground. Once he raised a finger in the air with the
classic gesture of a man who has solved a problem—the one Ar-
chimedes must have used—and his back was straighter, firmer, more
self-assured. Still, his whole body had a certain furtiveness to it,
like that of a child fearing to be caught.

Imprudently I struck a match to light a cigarette, and the gendarme turned around startled. At a loss for a second, he looked at
me, and suddenly his young face was illuminated with a tender,
pleading, trusting smile. But the next moment he again looked inaccessible and severe, and his hand reached up to his thin mustache—his hand, unfortunately, still holding a brick. I could see
how painfully ashamed he was of the brick and of his own un-
guarded smile, which had betrayed him. Most likely he was incapable of blushing; otherwise he would have turned the very color of
the brick he was holding in his hand.

Now the wall is half done, and from the platform one can no
longer see what the skilled bricklayers are doing on their scaffold-

ing. Again, down on the platform, the gendarme languishes, and he yawns. When he passes me by, turning away, I feel that he is embarrassed and that he hates me. I look at his strong arms, moving idly in their sleeves; at his spurs, which strike a discordant note; at his sword hanging aimlessly; and it seems to me that all of this is unreal—that the scabbard holds no sword that could cut a man to pieces, that the holster holds no revolver with which to shoot a man dead. Even his uniform is not real but a weird costume in which he is deliberately masquerading, in broad daylight, in the full, revealing April sun, among simplehearted working men and the busy chickens who are collecting seeds under the slumbering railway car. But at times—at times I am afraid . . . and it is a terrible fear. The man is too bored.

SEPTEMBER 1904
—Translated by Henry and Olga Carlisle

THE
THIEF

I

Fyodor Yurasov, a thief who had served three sentences, set out to visit his former mistress, a prostitute who lived about seventy miles out of Moscow. At the station he sat in the first-class restaurant eating pies and drinking beer, waited on by a man in a black jacket. Later, when everyone began to move toward the train, he mingled with the crowd, and, somewhat inadvertently, taking advantage of the general commotion, he stole a wallet from the pocket of an old gentleman who happened to be near him. Yurasov was in no need of money—he had plenty of it, in fact—and this casual, unplanned theft could only do him harm, as it eventually did. The gentleman must have suspected the theft; he stared curiously and fixedly at Yurasov, and though he did not stop he turned several times to look back at him.

The next time Yurasov saw the gentleman was from the train window. Looking upset and perplexed, the man was walking quickly along the platform, hat in hand, staring up into people's faces, searching for someone on the train. Fortunately, the final signal was given, and the train started. Yurasov looked out cautiously: The gentleman, hat still in hand, was standing at the end of the platform, carefully peering into the passing cars as if he were counting them; even in his fat, awkward legs there was bewilderment. He stood there; yet it must have seemed to him that he was walking, his legs were spread in such a funny position.

Yurasov drew himself up, tightened his knees, and felt that he was taller and straighter than usual, a smart fellow indeed. Tenderly, confidently, he stroked his mustache with both hands; it was long, fair, beautiful, hanging down the sides of his face. While his fingers enjoyed the pleasant sensation of soft, thick hair, his gray eyes gazed down with aimless, naive severity at the winding rails of the adjoining tracks. With their metallic sparkle and silent twisting they looked like snakes swiftly escaping.

Counting the stolen money in the lavatory—it amounted to some twenty-four rubles—Yurasov squeamishly turned the purse over in his hands. It was old and greasy, it did not close well, and it smelled of perfume, as though it had been in the possession of a woman. This odor, stale but exciting, reminded Yurasov pleasantly of his forthcoming visit. Smiling, gay, carefree, ready for friendly conversation, he went into a compartment determined to be like the other passengers—polite, formal, unassuming. He wore a coat made of real English cloth, shoes of yellow leather, and he believed in his coat and in his boots. He was convinced that he would be taken for a young German clerk from a sound commercial house. He always followed the financial news in the papers, knew the current prices of stocks and could talk about business matters. It sometimes seemed to him that he was not the peasant Fyodor Yurasov, a thief who had served three sentences, but a respectable German, Heinrich Walter by name. The woman to whom he was going called him Heinrich, and his friends called him "the German."

"Is this seat taken?" he asked politely, though it could be seen at a glance that the seat was free, since there were only two other passengers in the compartment—an old, retired officer and a lady who was obviously returning to the country from a day of shopping. Neither replied. With affected agility he dropped onto the soft, springy seat, carefully stretched out his long legs, showing his yellow shoes, and took off his hat. Then, with a friendly glance at the old officer and at the lady, he placed his broad white hand on his knee so that the ring on his finger with its large stone could be plainly seen. The stone was a fake diamond and shone ostentatiously. The passengers noticed it but said nothing; they neither smiled nor became more friendly. The old gentleman turned the page of his paper, and the lady, young and beautiful, stared out the window. With a vague feeling that he was found out again, that he was not taken for a young German, Yurasov quietly withdrew his hand, which now seemed to him too large and too white, and asked in a deferential voice, "Are you returning to your country house?"

The lady, pretending not to hear, assumed a reflective air. Yurasov was familiar with this expression, when people became distant, annoyingly distant. Turning to the old man he asked, "Would you be good enough to look in your paper and see where Ribinsky shares are. I can't remember."

Slowly the old man put his paper down, pressed his lips together sternly, and, with his weak eyes, gazed at him with an offended air. "What was that? I didn't hear."

Yurasov repeated his question, pronouncing his words distinctly, while the old man stared at him disapprovingly, as at a grandson who has gotten into trouble or a neglectful soldier. Gradually he became irritated: the skin on his head under his thin gray hair grew red; his chin trembled. "I don't know," he grumbled. "I don't know. There's nothing of the kind in the paper. The questions some people ask!"

And he returned to his paper, lowering it once in a while to peer disapprovingly at the annoying man. It seemed to Yurasov that everyone in the compartment was ill natured and remote, and he felt that it was strange to be sitting in a second-class compartment on a soft, springy seat. With dull despair and anger in his heart, he recalled how everywhere among respectable people, he met with this sometimes hidden, but often open, hostility. He wore a coat of real English cloth, yellow shoes, and a costly ring, but they did not seem to notice these things and instead saw something else, something he himself failed to see when he looked at himself in the mirror or into his consciousness. In the mirror he looked like other people, only perhaps better; it was not written on his face that he was the peasant Fyodor Yurasov, a thief who had served three sentences, and not a young German named Heinrich Walter. As usual, this incomprehensible, treacherous something that was apparent to all except himself aroused in him dull despair and fear. He wanted to run away, and looking around sharply and suspiciously—not at all like an honest German clerk—he stalked out of the compartment with long, hard strides.

II

It was early June; everything before his eyes all the way to the distant, unmoving stretches of woodland was young and strong and green. The grass was green; the seedlings in the still-bare vegetable gardens were green; everything was so wrapped up in itself, so deeply immersed in silent, creative meditation, that if the grass and the trees had been human, their faces would have been turned to the earth, preoccupied and distant, their lips pursed in deep silence. Yurasov—sad, pale, standing alone on the cramped, rocking open platform—anxiously felt this in a vague, troubled way. The beautiful, silent, enigmatic fields were just as cold and withdrawn as the people in the car. High above the fields, the sky was self-contained; somewhere behind him the sun was setting, its straight broad rays spreading over the earth; yet no one was looking at him in this deserted place; no one thought about him; no one cared. In the town where Yurasov was born and had grown up, the houses and streets had eyes; they looked at people. Some were unfriendly and malicious, others were kind—but here no one noticed him, no one knew him. The coaches, too, seemed lost in thought; the one in which he was traveling was racing along, leaning and rocking with an angry motion; the one behind ran at the same speed yet quite independently, as if it were alone, and it, too, seemed to be gazing at the earth and listening. Beneath the cars there was a many-voiced rumbling—now a song, now music, now some strange, incomprehensible conversation, distant and alien. People could be seen, appearing small in the green wilderness, working, looking fearful—or were they joyous? Once in a while the fragments of a song could be heard, drowned in the sounds of the wheels. There were tiny houses scattered about, and their windows looked straight out into the fields.

If at night you were to look out from these windows, you would see the fields—the open, free, dark fields. Every day and every night, trains passed here, and there were always those quiet fields with diminutive people and houses. The day before at that hour, Yurasov had been sitting in the Progress restaurant without a thought to fields, yet they had been here—just as quiet, beautiful, and pensive. Over there stood a grove of large old birches with rooks' nests in their green tops. While he had been at the restaurant drinking vodka with friends, looking at the aquarium with its sleepless fish, the birches had stood here just as quietly and calmly, with the same darkness all around them.

With the odd feeling that only the city was real and that all of this was an illusion (that one had only to close one's eyes and open them again to find it gone), Yurasov shut his eyes tightly and stood perfectly still. Instantly such a pleasant, unusual sensation came over him that he did not wish to open them again. Doubt and thought and relentless, dull despair vanished; his body swayed involuntarily and pleasantly with the motion of the train, and a warm, soft, gentle breeze from the fields caressed his face and his thick mustache. There was a ringing in his ears; from beneath came the rhythmic murmur of the wheels, which sounded like music, like a song, like a distant conversation, sad and sweet. He vaguely imagined that from his bowed head to his feet he could feel the vibration of an all-embracing void; that a blue-green space filled with gentle, secret caresses stretched before him; that unexpectedly, somewhere in the distance, a quiet, warm rain was falling.

The train slowed down and stopped for a single minute. At once Yurasov was enveloped by an immense stillness, as though it were not one minute that the train would stand still but a year, a decade, an eternity. All was quiet—the dark, oily stone of the roadbed, the corner of the low red roof over the deserted platform, the grass on the bank. There was an odor of birch leaves, of meadows, of fresh manure, and these, too, seemed invested with immense stillness. Awkwardly a passenger jumped from an adjoining car and walked away. He seemed like a bird that had always flown and now was walking. The path was long and obscure; his steps were short—he moved his feet absurdly in this immense stillness.

Gently, as though ashamed of its own noise, the train moved on, and only a full mile farther on did all the parts of its iron body get into swing. Yurasov—tall, thin, supple—paced the little platform in agitation. Unconsciously twirling his mustache, he gazed up with sparkling eyes, clinging eagerly to the iron bar on the side of the car where the large red sun was disappearing below the horizon. He had just found out something that had escaped him all his life, something that had made him like that uncouth, clumsy passenger who had walked away instead of flying like a bird.

"Yes, yes," he said to himself, resolutely shaking his head; "of course it is so; of course." And the wheels echoed in chorus, "Of course it is so, of course."

Indeed, it seemed to him that now he must not speak but sing, and Yurasov began to sing—softly at first, then louder and louder, until the sound of his voice joined with the rumbling of the wheels. The rhythm of his song was the rhythm of the wheels, the melody a clear, pliant wave of sound. But there were no words, there was no form; distant and vague and terribly vast like the fields, the song ran off with mad swiftness, and the human voice followed it freely and lightly. High, then low, it spread over the earth—soaring over the meadows, darting through the woods, and lightly losing itself in the limitless sky. So should a bird fly when spring calls it, without aim or path, trying to embrace the whole ringing breadth of the vast heavens. So, no doubt, the green fields themselves would have sung, had they been endowed with voices. So do the little people sing in the green distance on summer evenings.

Yurasov sang on, and the crimson reflection of the setting sun lit up his face, his coat of English cloth, his yellow shoes. He sang, saying good-bye to the sun, and his song grew sadder and sadder, like a bird that, feeling the vastness of the heavens, trembles with an unknown despair and calls out to it knows not whom.

The sun had set, and a gray web lay over the still earth and the quiet sky. The gray web lay over his face, erasing the last reflections of sunset and making it look deathly. Come to me! Why don't you come? The sun had set, and the fields were growing dark. It was lonely and painful for the solitary heart. So lonely. Come to me. The sun had set. The fields were growing dark. So come to me, come!

His soul wept and the fields grew darker. Only the sky over the setting sun grew brighter and deeper, like a beautiful face turned toward someone beloved who is ever so quietly disappearing.

III

The conductor came through, and in passing he said roughly to Yurasov, "No standing on the platform. Go inside."

He went off, slamming the door angrily. Just as roughly Yurasov called after him, "You fool!"

It seemed to him that the coarse words, the slamming of the door were all the doing of the respectable people in the car. Becoming again the German Heinrich Walter, he shrugged his shoulders with an irritable, offended air and said to an imaginary respectable gentleman, "How rude! People always stand on the platform, and he says you can't. How devilishly rude!"

Then there was a halt, with its sudden, powerful stillness. In the night the grass and the woods smelled stronger, and the people walking about did not seem so out of place. The transparent twilight gave them wings; two women in light dresses seemed not to be walking but floating like swans. Again he felt both happy and sad and wanted to sing, but his voice would not obey; his tongue formed dull, commonplace words, and the song would not come. He wanted to dream, to weep sweetly and inconsolably, but instead his attention was drawn to an imposing gentleman to whom he remarked ponderously, "Have you noticed how Sormovsky has been rising?"

And again the dark, moving fields became aloof and cold. The sounds of the wheels were dissonant and unintelligible. It seemed that they were wrangling and hindering one another's progress. Something was knocking; there was rusty squeaking and scraping: it sounded like a drunken, foolish crowd. Then it broke up into groups; dissolute voices burst into a *café chantant* chorus: "Malania, my round-eyed girl . . ."

With such disgusting clarity did Yurasov recall this song that was sung in all the public gardens—and that he and his friends had sung—that he tried to ward it off with his hand as if it were a stone flung at him. And such was the cruel power in these painfully senseless words, persistent and insolent, that the whole train, the hundreds of rolling wheels, took them up: "Malania, my round-eyed girl . . ."

Repulsive and clinging, this song attached itself to Yurasov with a thousand thick lips and kissed him with impure, wet kisses. A thousand throats roared. The wheels were like hideous round faces, borne along in that whirlwind, and each hammered, "Malania, my round-eyed girl . . ."

Only the fields were silent. Cool and calm, absorbed in pure reflection, they knew nothing of the distant stone cities where men lived or of their disturbing, stupefying thoughts. The train was bearing Yurasov forward, but this senseless song was calling him back to the city, tugging at him roughly and cruelly—a poor runaway prisoner caught at the prison gates. He was stretching out his hands to the unknown, happy vastness, but his fate, the cruel bondage amid stone walls and iron railings, stood before him. The indifference of the fields, their aloofness, filled him with utter loneliness. The feeling of being discarded from life like a dead man terrified him. Had he been asleep for a thousand years and awakened in a new world among new people, he could not have felt lonelier than now. He wanted to recall something dear to him, but there was nothing to recall. The shameless song roared in his tired brain, giving birth to painful reflections, casting a shadow over his entire life. He saw the garden where they had sung that song. He had stolen something there, and they had hunted for him. They had all been drunk, both he and those who hunted him with shrieks and shouts. He had hidden in a dark corner, and they had lost him. He had sat there for a long time, near some old planks full of nails, beside a barrel of quicklime. He had felt the freshness and fragrance of the earth and the strong smell of young poplars. Along the nearby paths festively dressed people had strolled, and a band had played. A gray cat had gone by, pensive, indifferent to the voices and the music. He had called it. The cat had come up and purred and rubbed against his knees. It had let him kiss its furry muzzle, which smelled of herring. He had made it sneeze, and it had gone off, majestic and indifferent like a society lady. Then he had come out of his hiding place and had been caught.

On that night there had at least been a cat to comfort him, but now there was nothing but the complacent fields. Yurasov began to hate them with all the power of his loneliness. Had he had the strength, he would have stoned them; he would have assembled thousands of people and ordered them to stamp out the soft, treacherous green that brought joy to all but him, that drained the last drop of blood from his heart. Why had he left the city? Had he not come, he would have been sitting in the Progress drinking wine, talking, and laughing. He began to hate the woman to whom he was going, the wretched partner of his wretched life. She was rich now; she kept two young girls for sale. She loved him and gave him as much money as he wanted. When he got there he would beat her until blood flowed, and she would squeal. Then he would get drunk and cry and clutch his throat. Sobbing he would sing, "Malania, my round-eyed girl . . ."

The wheels no longer sang with him. Like sick children they grumbled plaintively and pressed against one another as though seeking caresses and consolation. From above, the austere, starry sky looked down on him; the severe, virgin darkness of the fields surrounded him. Scattered lights were like tears on a beautiful, pensive face. In the distance the red lights of a station twinkled.

The warm fresh night air carried the sweet strains of music. The unsettling dream was gone. With the lightheartedness of a man who has no place on earth, Yurasov forgot it at once. He listened excitedly, trying to catch the familiar melody.

"They're dancing!" he said, smiling, exhilarated, his laughing eyes peering around. He rubbed his hands. "They're dancing. Damned if they aren't dancing!"

He braced his shoulders, unconsciously swaying to the familiar tune, feeling its rhythm. He was very fond of dancing, and when he danced he was kind and gentle—no longer either the German Heinrich Walter or Fyodor Yurasov, the thief who had served three sentences, but a third person about whom he himself knew nothing. When gusts of wind carried the sounds away over the fields, he was ready to weep, fearing that the music was gone forever. But the whirling sounds returned, louder and more joyful, as though they had gathered strength from the dark fields.

"They're dancing! Damned if they aren't dancing!"

IV

They were dancing near the station. The summer people had organized a dance; they had hired a band. Along the wooden platform they had hung red and blue lanterns, which had chased the darkness to the very tops of the trees. Youths, girls in light dresses, students, a young officer wearing spurs—so young that he looked as if he had put on a fancy dress uniform—all were turning smoothly on the broad platform. Dresses blew out with the wind and rose beneath their feet. In the dim, mysterious light of the lanterns, everyone seemed beautiful, and the dancers looked ethereal and touching in their purity. Around them was night and they were dancing; ten steps out of the circle, the vast, all-powerful darkness would swallow them—and they were dancing. The band played for them pensively, softly, sweetly.

The train stopped for five minutes, and Yurasov mingled with the onlookers. In a dark, colorless ring they surrounded the platform, holding onto the wire fence—dim and superfluous. Some smiled guardedly; others were sad, with that peculiar, wan sadness of people watching the gaiety of others. But Yurasov was full of cheer; he appraised the dancers with the enthusiastic eye of an expert, tapping his foot lightly. Then suddenly he decided, "I won't go on. I'll stay and dance."

From the circle, making their way haughtily through the crowd, came a couple, a girl in white and a youth almost as tall as Yurasov. Past the sleepy cars at the end of the wooden platform, where darkness stood like a sentinel, they walked, beautiful and seeming to carry with them some of the light. To Yurasov it seemed that the girl shone, so white was her dress, so dark the brows of her pale face. With the confidence of a good dancer, he caught up with them and asked, "Can you please tell me where I can get a ticket for the dance?"

With a stern glance over his shoulder, the beardless youth said, "It's a private dance."

"I'm a stranger passing through. My name is Heinrich Walter."

"I told you, it's a private dance."

"My name is Heinrich Walter. Heinrich Walter."

"Look here!" the youth began threateningly, but the girl pulled him on. If she had only looked at Heinrich Walter! But she did not, and like a cloud lit by the moon, she shone white in the darkness and then dissolved into it.

"I don't care!" Yurasov whispered proudly after them, but his soul grew white and cold as if snow had fallen—pure, white, dead snow. For some reason the train was still standing there, and Yurasov paced up and down past the railway cars, so handsome, solemn, and majestic in his cold despair that no one would have taken him for a thief who had served three sentences in prison. He was calm; he saw and understood everything, except that his feet—as though they were made of rubber—did not feel the ground, and in his soul something was dying, quietly, without pain, without a flutter. Then it was quite dead.

The music was still playing, and mingled with it he heard a disquieting conversation:

"Conductor, why doesn't the train leave?"

Yurasov slowed his steps and listened carefully. Behind him the conductor replied indifferently, "There must be a reason. Perhaps the engineer has gone to the dance."

The passenger laughed, and Yurasov walked on. On his way back he overheard two conductors talking:

"They say he's on this train."

"Who saw him?"

"No one saw him. The gendarme said so."

"Your gendarme is full of lies. Thinks he knows everything."

The bell rang. Yurasov hesitated. From the dance the girl in white came by on someone's arm, and he jumped onto the open platform of the coach and went to the far side of it. Then he no longer saw the girl in white or the dancers, but the music burst out for a moment in waves of rich sound, then died away in the darkness and stillness of the night. He was alone on the rocking platform, amid the vague shadows of the night; everything was moving, everything had its own ghostly destination, which eluded him. Everything was passing him by—vast and ghostly like figures in a dream.

V

Pushing Yurasov with the door, without noticing him, the conductor quickly crossed the platform, a lantern in his hand, and disappeared. Neither his footsteps nor the slam of the door could be heard over the noise of the train, but his aggressive movements were like a sudden shriek. Yurasov froze. Like fire a thought possessed him: "They're looking for me." They had telegraphed, he had been recognized, now they were hunting him down. The "he" about whom

the conductor had spoken so enigmatically was Yurasov. How frightening it was to be that impersonal "he," spoken of by strangers.

Even now they were talking about "him," looking for "him." In-
stinctively he could feel them coming for him from the other end of
the train. Three or four, with lanterns. They looked at the passengers, peered into dark corners, awakened those who had dozed off.
They whispered among themselves, and step by step they were coming closer to Yurasov, to the man on the platform who listened tensely.
The train rushed fiercely on, and the wheels no longer talked; they
screamed with iron tongues, whispered austerely, then shrieked in
a wild frenzy of rage—a pack of maddened dogs.

Yurasov clenched his teeth and stood motionless thinking. To jump
off the train at this speed was impossible. The next station was still
a long way ahead. He had to get to the front of the train and wait
there. While they were hunting through the other cars, something
might happen—a stop or a slackening of speed—and he would jump
out. He went through the first door with an affected, polite *pardon*
ready, to avoid suspicion, but in the dark third-class coach, it was
so crowded, there was such a chaos of bundles, trunks, and projecting limbs, that he lost hope of reaching the door at the far end,
and he felt a new terror: how was he to get through? The passengers were asleep, their legs stuck out in the aisle barring his way.
They projected from below; they hung down from above, knocking
against his head and shoulders; they moved about sleepily from one
seat to another, strangely assertive in their efforts to get back to
their old places and positions. Like springs they bent and unbent,
knocking against him with their dead weight. At last he was at the
door, but barring it like two iron bolts were two legs in a huge pair
of knee boots, and when he shoved them aside, they sprang back
obstinately, pressing against the door, bending as though they were
boneless. Finally he managed to squeeze through a narrow crack.
He thought he had reached the platform, but it was only another
part of the coach, with similar stacks of bundles and random limbs.
When he managed to force his way to the platform, his eyes had

the vacant look of a bull, and the dark terror of a hunted animal at bay seized him. Breathing heavily he listened for the sound of steps in the roaring of the wheels. Then, conquering his animal fear, he reached the dark, silent door. Again there was a long struggle against hostile human legs.

In a first-class compartment he came across a group of passengers who were not asleep. They all knew one another and had gathered in the narrow corridor by an open window. A young lady with curled hair was looking out the window. The wind blew the curtain back, moving the lady's ringlets, and it seemed to Yurasov that the air was laden with the scent of costly perfume from the city.

"Pardon!" he said in despair. *"Pardon!"*

The men moved away, slowly, reluctantly, staring at him with animosity. The lady at the window had not heard him. At last, another young woman, repressing her laughter, reached out and touched her rounded, tightly clad shoulder. The lady turned and, before stepping aside, looked at him for a long time—at his yellow shoes, at his coat of real English cloth. In her eyes he saw the darkness of night; she half closed them as though deliberating whether to let him pass or not.

"Pardon!" he appealed, and the lady in her rustling silk skirt unwillingly backed away.

Then came more third-class coaches. It seemed as if he had passed through dozens, hundreds of them—open platforms, stubborn doors, and hostile, tenacious legs. Finally he reached the last platform and beyond it the dark, blank wall of the baggage car. Again he froze: something rushed by him, roaring; the floor beneath his trembling legs was shaking.

Suddenly the cold, hard wall he was leaning against was pushing him away. Softly and determinedly it pushed and pushed, cautiously, like a living enemy afraid to come out into the open. All Yurasov could sense now was this huge, merciless hunt. It seemed to him that the whole world, once so aloof, had now risen up and, enraged, was pursuing him—the complacent fields, the pensive lady by the window, the massed, lifeless, obstinate legs. Those legs had been limp and sleepy, but now they were chasing him, stampeding him, dancing, jumping, crushing everything in their path. He was alone, and they were thousands, millions, the whole world. They surrounded him; he could not escape.

The coaches rushed on, rocking madly from side to side, mad iron monsters chasing one another on their short legs, shrewdly pressing against the earth. It was dark on the platform, nowhere a glimmer of light; one could see only shadows on elongated legs that walked backward, phantoms that came right up to the train and then disappeared into the limitless darkness. The green fields and woods were dead: only their ominous ghosts hung over the thundering train. And these others—slowly, stealthily—were searching a few cars away, perhaps only one. Three or four of them, with lanterns, examining the passengers, exchanging glances, whispering together— and with absurd, barbarous thoroughness they were moving toward him. Now they were opening a door, now another . . .

With a last effort Yurasov got hold of himself. Looking around carefully he tried to climb up on the roof of the coach. He stood up on the narrow iron bar that bolted the baggage car door and, twisting, lifted himself up, his legs flailing in the icy air. His hands slid on the slippery iron roof; he caught hold of a gutter, but it crumpled like paper; his yellow shoes, hard as wood, slid down hopelessly. He was falling but, wriggling in the air like a cat, he was able to land on the platform. He felt pain in his knees; there was a sound of tearing cloth: his coat had caught on a projection as he fell. He examined the tear as though it were of the greatest importance and shook his head sadly.

Yurasov was exhausted; he wanted to lie down on the floor, to cry and say, "Take me." He had chosen the spot where he would lie down, when he remembered the coaches and the tangle of legs, and he heard clearly those three or four men coming toward him. Again animal fear possessed him and hurled him around the platform like a ball, from one side to the other. Again he tried to climb up on the roof—when a hoarse, fiery howl, unlike anything he had ever heard before, assailed his ears and stunned his mind. It was the whistle of the locomotive over his head, signaling an approaching train, but to Yurasov in his terror, it seemed horrible and irrevocable, as if the world had caught up with him at last and its multitudinous voices were joined in one enormous cry of satisfaction.

And then, as out of the darkness ahead came the ever-growing, ever-nearing roar and the light of the oncoming postal train lay on the opposite tracks, he threw aside the iron barrier and jumped down where, quite near, the lighted rails shone like snakes. He hit hard with his teeth, rolled over several times, and when he raised his face with its toothless mouth and crumpled mustache, lights of some kind were suspended over him, three dull lamps behind convex lenses.

He did not understand their meaning.

1904
—Translated by Henry and Olga Carlisle

THE
ABYSS

I

The day was coming to an end, but the young pair continued to walk and talk, observing neither the time nor where they were going. Before them, in the shadow of a hillock, loomed the dark mass of a small grove, and between the branches of the trees, the sun blazed like glowing embers, igniting the air and transforming it into flaming golden dust. So near and luminous did the sun appear that everything else seemed to have vanished; it alone remained. It painted the road with its fiery tints. It hurt the strollers' eyes; they turned back, and all at once everything within their vision was extinguished, became peaceful and clear, small and distinct. Somewhere afar, a mile away, the red sunset seized the tall trunk of a fir, which blazed among the green like a candle in a dark room. The ruddy glow of the road stretched before them, and every stone cast its long black shadow; and the girl's hair shone as a golden-red aureole. A stray, thin hair, wandering from the rest, wavered in the air like a golden spider's thread.

The darkness ahead did not break or change the course of their talk. It continued as before, intimately and quietly; it flowed along tranquilly on the same theme: the strength, the beauty, and the immortality of love. They were both very young: the girl was seventeen, Nemovetsky four years older. They wore students' uniforms: she the modest brown dress of a pupil of a girls' school, he the handsome attire of a technological student. And like their conversation, everything about them was young, beautiful, and pure. Their bodies were erect and flexible and seemed to be made of air; their step was light and springy, their voices fresh, even as they uttered simple words filled with thoughtful tenderness, words that

sounded like a rivulet on a calm spring night when the snow has
not yet wholly thawed from the dark meadows.

They walked on, turning as the unknown road turned, and their
lengthening shadows, with absurdly small heads, now advanced sep-
arately, now merged into one long, narrow strip, like the shadow of
a poplar. But they did not see the shadows, for they were too absorbed in their talk. While talking, the young man kept his eyes
fixed on the girl's handsome face, upon which the sunset had left
some of its delicate tints. She, on the other hand, was looking down
at the path, brushing aside tiny pebbles with her umbrella, observing how first one then the other tip of her shoe showed from under
her dark dress.

The path was intersected by a ditch with edges of dust showing
the impress of feet. For an instant they paused. Zinotchka raised
her head, looked up with a vague gaze, and asked, "Do you know
where we are? I've never been here before."

He looked around carelessly. "Yes, I know. The town is there
behind the hill. Give me your hand. I'll help you across."

He reached out his hand, white and slender like a woman's and
which had not known hard work. Zinotchka felt happy. She wanted
to jump over the ditch all by herself, to run away and shout, "Catch
me!" But she restrained herself, with decorous gratitude nodded
slightly; timidly she reached out her hand, which still retained its
childish plumpness. He badly wanted to squeeze tightly this trembling little hand, but he also restrained himself, and with a half
bow he deferentially took it and modestly turned away when, in
crossing, the girl showed her ankle. And once more they walked
and talked, but their minds were on the momentary contact of their
hands. She still felt the dry heat of his palms and his strong fingers;
she felt pleasure and slight embarrassment, while he was conscious
of the yielding softness of her tiny hand and saw the black silhouette of her foot and the small slipper that tenderly embraced it.
There was something poignant, something perturbing in this persistent appearance of the narrow hem of white petticoats and of the

slender foot; with an unconscious effort of will, he crushed this feeling. Then he felt more cheerful, and his heart was so full and free that he wanted to sing, to reach to the sky, to shout: "Run! I want to catch you!"—that ancient expression of primitive love among the woods and thundering waterfalls.

And he was close to tears from all these desires.

The long, absurd shadows vanished, and the dust of the path became gray and cold, but they did not notice this and went on chatting. Both had read many good books, and the radiant images of men and women who had loved, suffered, and perished for pure love swirled before their eyes. They recalled fragments of verse that love dressed in mellow harmony and sweet sadness.

"Do you remember where this comes from?" asked Nemovetsky, recalling, "once more she is with me, she whom I love; she from whom I have hidden all my sadness, my tenderness, my love . . ."

"No," said Zinotchka, and repeated thoughtfully, "all my sadness, my tenderness, my love."

"All my love," echoed Nemovetsky involuntarily.

Other memories returned to them. They remembered those girls, pure like white lilies, who, attired in the black garments of nuns, sat apart from one another in the park, grieving among the dead leaves yet happy in their grief. They also remembered the men, proud, energetic, yet suffering and yearning for love and the delicate compassion of women. The images they evoked were sad, but in that sadness love shone all the more radiant and pure. As immense as the world, as bright as the sun, it arose fabulously beautiful before their eyes, and there was nothing mightier or more beautiful on the earth.

"Could you die for the one you love?" Zinotchka asked, as she looked at her childish hand.

"Yes, I could," Nemovetsky replied with conviction, and he looked at her frankly. "And you?"

"Yes, I could too." She grew pensive. "It's bliss to die for the one you love. I'd like to very much."

Their eyes met, clear, calm, saying good things while their lips were smiling. Zinotchka paused. "Wait a moment," she said. "You have a thread on your coat."

And trustfully she raised her hand to his shoulder and with two fingers carefully removed the thread.

"There!" she said and, becoming serious, asked, "Why are you so thin and pale? You study a lot, don't you? You mustn't overdo it, you know."

"You have blue eyes with bright sparks," he replied, searching her eyes.

"And yours are black. No, dark, warm brown. And in them—"

She turned away. Her face slowly flushed, her eyes became embarrassed and timid, while her lips involuntarily smiled. Without waiting for Nemovetsky, who was smiling with secret pleasure, she moved forward but soon paused.

"Look, the sun has set!" she exclaimed with grieved astonishment.

"Yes, it has," he responded with sudden sorrow.

The light was gone, the shadows had died: everything became pale, still, lifeless. On the horizon where earlier the sun had blazed, dark masses of cloud now crept in silence and, step by step, consumed the light blue spaces. The clouds swirled and collided, slowly and ponderously assuming the shapes of awakened monsters; they reluctantly advanced, as if driven against their will by some terrible, implacable force. Tearing itself away from the rest, one tiny luminous cloud drifted on alone—a frail, frightened fugitive.

II

Zinotchka's cheeks grew pale; her lips turned blood red. The pupils of her eyes widened and darkened. She whispered, "I'm frightened. It's so quiet here. Have we lost our way?"

Nemovetsky frowned and looked around.

Now the sun had set, and the night breeze had arisen; the surroundings seemed cold and uninviting. A gray field spread out all around them, covered with trampled grass, clay gullies, hillocks, and holes. There were many holes; some were deep and sheer, others were small and overgrown with grass. The silent dusk had crept into them, and because there had been people here who had labored and left, the place appeared all the more desolate. Here and there, like the coagulations of cold lilac mist, groves and thickets loomed, as if harkening to the abandoned holes.

Nemovetsky stifled a heavy feeling of anxiety and said, "No, we haven't lost our way. I know the road. First to the left, then through that tiny wood. Are you afraid?"

She smiled bravely and said, "No, not now. But we must get home soon and have tea."

They walked on but soon slowed down again. They looked straight ahead but they felt the hostility of the dug-up field, which surrounded them with a thousand dim, motionless eyes, and what they felt drew them together and evoked memories of childhood. These memories were luminous, full of sunlight, of green foliage, of love and laughter. It was as if all that had not been life at all, but an immense, gentle song in which they themselves had been sounds, two little notes: one as pure and clear as ringing crystal, the other somewhat deeper yet more animated, like a small bell.

Now they saw people. Two women were sitting at the edge of a deep clay pit. One sat cross-legged and stared down into it; the kerchief she wore had shifted, showing her tangled hair. Her rounded back was half covered by a dirty blouse with a pattern of flowers as big as apples, its strings undone. She did not look at the passersby. When they had passed, she began to sing in a thick, masculine voice:

> For you alone, my adored one,
> Like a flower I did bloom . . .

"Varka, did you hear that?" She turned to her companion and, receiving no answer, broke into loud, coarse laughter.

Nemovetsky had known such women, repulsive even when they wore expensive, elegant gowns. He was used to them, and now they glided away from his glance and vanished, leaving no trace. But Zinotchka, who nearly brushed them with her modest brown dress, felt something hostile, pitiful, and evil, which for an instant entered her soul. In a few moments the impression was obliterated, like the shadow of a cloud running across a sunny meadow. So when two people passed them—a man wearing a jacket and a cap but barefoot, with a woman as filthy as the other two—Zinotchka gave no thought to them. Unconsciously for a second she followed the woman with her eyes, surprised to see that her dress was so light that it clung to her legs as if it were wet; caked mud formed a broad border at the hem of her skirt. She felt something disquieting, something desperate about the swirl of this light, dirty cloth.

They walked on and continued to talk, followed by a dark cloud that moved lazily, carefully, casting a transparent shadow. It was marked with brassy yellow spots, stripes of light boiling silently within its dark, heavy mass. Stealthily the darkness thickened. It was as if, imperceptibly, ailing daylight were dying. Now they talked about those terrifying thoughts and feelings that visit people when they cannot sleep at night, when they are not diverted by noise and conversation, when darkness, which is an immense, many-eyed life, presses their faces.

"Can you imagine infinity?" Zinotchka asked him, putting her small, rounded hand to her forehead and closing her eyes tightly.

"Infinity? No . . ." answered Nemovetsky, also shutting his eyes.

"Sometimes I imagine it. I saw it first when I was quite young, as if I were seeing a huge number of carts. One, two, three—carts without end, an infinity of carts . . . It's terrifying!" Zinotchka shivered.

"But why carts?" Nemovetsky smiled, though he felt uncomfortable.

"I don't know. But I did see carts. One, then another—endlessly."

Stealthily the darkness thickened. The cloud was now ahead of them, as if it were looking into their lowered, paling faces. Dark figures of ragged, dirty women appeared more often; it was as if the deep holes, dug for some unknown purpose, had cast them up to the surface. Sometimes alone, sometimes two or three together they appeared, and their voices sounded loud and strangely bleak in the still air.

"Who are these women? Where do they all come from?" Zinotchka asked in a low, timorous voice. Nemovetsky knew who the women were. He felt terrified at having ventured into this evil and dangerous neighborhood, but he answered calmly, "I don't know. It's nothing. Let's not talk about them. It won't be long now; we have only to pass through this little wood, and we'll reach the gate and the town. It's too bad we started so late."

She thought his words absurd. How could he call it late when they started out at four o'clock? She looked at him and smiled. But his brows did not relax, and in order to calm and comfort him, she said, "Let's walk faster. I want tea. And the wood's quite near now."

"Yes, let's walk faster."

When they entered the wood and the silent trees joined in an arch over their heads, it became very dark but also very snug and quiet.

"Give me your hand," said Nemovetsky.

Unsure, she gave him her hand, and the light touch seemed to lighten the darkness. Their hands barely touched, and Zinotchka drew away from him slightly. But their whole minds were concentrated on the place where their hands met. And again they wanted to speak about the beauty and the mysterious power of love—but to talk without breaking the silence, to talk not with words but with their eyes. They wanted to look at each other, but didn't quite dare.

"And here are more people!" said Zinotchka lightly.

III

In a clearing where there was more light, three men sat in silence around an empty bottle. They stared at the newcomers. One of them, who, being beardless, resembled an actor, laughed and whistled suggestively.

Nemovetsky's heart sank, and he was seized by great fear. As if pushed from behind, he walked straight toward the men sitting by the path. They were waiting; three pairs of eyes—unwavering, dark, terrifying—watched the strollers. And, hoping to gain the good will of these somber, ragged men, whose silence was threatening, and to gain their sympathy for his helplessness, he asked, "Is this the way to the gate?"

They did not reply. The beardless one whistled something vaguely mocking, while the other two remained silent and looked at them with heavy, malevolent concentration. They were drunk, angry, and they were hungry for love and destruction. One of them, who was fat and ruddy, slowly and unsteadily rose to his feet like a bear, sighing heavily. His companions glanced at him, then once again fixed their eyes on Zinotchka.

"I'm afraid," she said inaudibly.

Nemovetsky did not hear her, but he understood her from the pressure of her arm. And, trying to appear calm yet feeling the irrevocable certainty of what was about to happen, he walked on with measured firmness. Three pairs of eyes neared, gleamed, and were left behind. "We must run," thought Nemovetsky; then he said to himself, "No, we'd better not."

"The fellow's a weakling. What a shame," said the third, a bald-headed man with a thin red beard. "But the little girl's just fine. She'd make anyone happy."

All three gave a forced laugh.

"Wait, mister! I want a word with you!" said the tall man in a thick bass voice, and he glanced at his friends. They rose.

Nemovetsky walked on without turning around.

"You ought to stop when you're asked," said the red-haired man. "And if you don't, you're likely to get something you ain't counting on!"

"Do you hear?" growled the tall man, and in two leaps he caught up with the strollers.

A massive hand fell on Nemovetsky's shoulder and sent him reeling. He turned and met his assailant's bulging, terrifying eyes. They were so near that it was as if he were looking at them through a magnifying glass, and he clearly saw small red veins on the whites and yellowish pus on the lids. He dropped Zinotchka's numb hand, and reaching into his pocket, he murmured: "Money? I'll gladly give you some."

The bulging eyes grew rounder and gleamed. And when Nemovetsky averted his gaze, the tall man stepped slightly back and, with a short jab, struck Nemovetsky's chin from below. Nemovetsky's head shot backward, his teeth clicked, his cap fell from his forehead; arms flailing he fell on his back. Silently, without a cry, Zinotchka turned and ran as fast as she could. The beardless man uttered a long, strange shout. Still shouting he ran after her.

Nemovetsky jumped up reeling, but before he could stand straight, a blow on the neck knocked him down again. Two of them were beating him, and he was frail and unused to fighting. Nonetheless he struggled for a long time, scratched with his fingernails like a woman, bit, and sobbed in despair. When he was too weak to do more, they lifted him up and carried him away. He still resisted, but there was a din in his head; he no longer understood what was happening, and he slumped helplessly in the arms that bore him. The last thing he saw was the red beard, which almost touched his mouth, and beyond it the darkness of the wood and the light-colored blouse of the running girl. She ran swiftly and silently, as she had run just a few days before when they were playing tag, and behind her, overtaking her, raced the beardless one. Then Nemovetsky felt an emptiness around him; his heart stopped as he plunged downward, then struck the ground and lost consciousness.

The tall man and the red-haired one, having thrown Nemovetsky into a pit, stopped for a few moments to listen to what was happening at the bottom. But now their eyes were turned toward the direction taken by Zinotchka. From there came a shrill, stifled woman's cry that quickly died. The tall man exclaimed angrily, "The swine!"

Then he started running in a straight line, breaking twigs on the way like a bear.

"Me too! Me too!" cried his red-haired companion in a thin voice, running after him. He was weak and he panted; in the struggle his knee was hurt, and he felt bad because he had thought about the girl first, and he would get her last. He paused to rub his knee, then, blowing his nose with one finger, once more began to run, shouting plaintively: "Me too! Me too!"

The dark cloud had spread across the sky, and a still night had fallen. The darkness soon swallowed the short figure of the red-haired man, but for some time there could be heard the uneven fall of his feet, the rustle of the disturbed leaves, and the shrill, plaintive cry: "Me too, brothers! Me too!"

IV

Earth got into Nemovetsky's mouth and ground between his teeth. As he regained consciousness, his first strong sensation was the thick, reassuring smell of the soil. His head felt dull, as if lead had been poured into it; he found it hard to move. His whole body ached, he had an intense pain in his shoulder, but no bones were broken. He sat up, and for a long time he stared upward, not thinking or remembering anything. Directly above him there was a bush with broad black leaves, and clear sky was visible between them. The storm cloud had passed over without a drop of rain, leaving the air dry and light. In the middle of the sky the moon appeared, encircled by a transparent ring. It was waning, and its light was cold and melancholy. Wisps of cloud raced high in the sky where the wind was strong; they did not obscure the moon but seemed to be avoiding it. In the loneliness of the moon, in the careful shifting of the high, light clouds, in the imperceptible breathing of the wind below, one felt the mysterious depth of the night that reigned over the earth.

Nemovetsky remembered what had happened and could not believe it. It was all so terrifying and so improbable. Could reality be so horrible? He too, as he sat there in the night gazing up at the moon and the racing clouds, seemed strange to himself—not himself. And he began to think that it was only a nightmare. The women they had met were also a part of this dream.

"It can't be!" he said with conviction and weakly shook his heavy head. "It can't be!"

He reached out his hand and began to feel for his cap. When he did not find it, everything became clear to him; he understood that what had happened had not been a dream but a dreadful reality. The next moment, again possessed by terror, he scrambled up, but the earth gave way, and he clutched at an overhanging bush.

Once out of the pit he began to run, aimlessly, without choosing a direction. He ran for a long time, circling among the trees. Then suddenly he ran off in another direction. Branches scratched his face, and again everything seemed like a dream. And it appeared to Nemovetsky that something like this had happened to him before: darkness, invisible branches, while he had been running with his eyes closed, thinking that it was a dream. He paused, then sat down clumsily on the flat ground. Again he thought of his cap, and he said to himself: "This is me. I must kill myself. Yes, I must kill myself, even if this is a dream."

He sprang to his feet and started running, then collected himself and slowed to a walk, trying to remember the place where they had been attacked. It was quite dark in the woods, but sometimes a stray, bewildering ray of moonlight broke through; it lighted up the white tree trunks, and the wood seemed to be full of motionless and mysteriously silent people. All this, too, seemed as if it had happened before, and it was like a dream.

"Zinaida Nikolayevna!" called Nemovetsky, pronouncing the first word loudly, the second more quietly, as if, with the loss of his voice, he had also lost hope of a response. No one answered.

Then he found the path and recognized it at once. He reached the clearing. There he understood that it all had been real. In terror he ran, shouting, "Zinaida Nikolayevna! It's me! It's me!"

No one answered. He turned in the direction where he thought the town was and called out distinctly, "Help!"

Again he ran around, muttering, searching the bushes. A vague white shape appeared directly before him. It was the prostrate body of Zinotchka.

"Oh, my God!" said Nemovetsky with dry eyes but in a voice that sobbed. He dropped to his knees and touched the girl lying there.

His hand fell upon her bared body—smooth, firm, and cold, but not dead. Shuddering he drew back his hand.

"Darling, sweetheart, it's me," he whispered, seeking her face in the darkness. Then he reached out his hand in another direction and again touched the naked body, and wherever he put his hand, he touched this woman's body, which was smooth and resilient and seemed to grow warm under his hand. Sometimes he snatched his hand away quickly, and again he let it rest; and just as, all tattered and without his cap, he did not appear real to himself, so it was with this bared body: he could not associate it with Zinotchka. All that had happened here, all that the men had done with this mute woman's body appeared to him in all its loathsome clarity, and he found a strange, intensely eloquent response throughout his own body. He reached forward in a way that made his joints crack; dully fixed his eyes on the white shape; frowned as if in deep thought. The horror at what had happened weighed on him like a stone, leaving him powerless and alienated.

"Oh, my God!" he repeated, but the words rang false, as if they were forced. He felt her heart: it beat faintly but evenly, and when he bent toward her face, he became aware that she was breathing faintly, as if she were simply sleeping. Softly he said to her, "Zinotchka, it's me!"

But he felt then that it might be better if she did not awaken for a long time. He held his breath, glanced quickly around him, then cautiously caressed her cheek; first he kissed her closed eyes, then her lips, whose softness yielded under his strong kiss. Fearing that she might awaken, he drew back and froze. But the body was motionless and mute, and in its helplessness and vulnerability, there was something pitiful, exasperating, and yet attractive. With deep tenderness and the caution of a thief, Nemovetsky tried to cover her with the shreds of her dress, and this double sensation of fabric and flesh was as sharp as a knife and as incomprehensible as madness. He was both defender and aggressor. He was hoping for help from the surrounding woods and darkness, but they gave him no comfort. Here was the advent of animals, and suddenly, beyond ordinary, intelligible human life, he smelled the burning lust that filled the air.

"What is this?" he cried out loudly and wildly and sprang up, appalled at himself.

Zinotchka's face flashed before him and vanished. He tried to believe that this body was Zinotchka, with whom he had lately walked and who had spoken of infinity, but he could not. He tried to feel the horror of what had happened, but the horror was too great for comprehension.

"Zinaida Nikolayevna!" he shouted imploringly. "What is this? Zinaida Nikolayevna!"

But the ravaged body remained mute, and continuing his mad monologue, Nemovetsky dropped to his knees. He begged, threatened, said that he would kill himself, and he shook the prostrate body, lifting it, pressing it to him, and almost gouging it with his nails. The now-warmed body softly yielded, obediently following his motions, and all this was so terrible, so incomprehensible and savage, that Nemovetsky once more leapt to his feet and shouted, "Help!" But this cry too sounded false, as if it were forced. And once more he threw himself on the unresisting body with kisses and tears, feeling the presence of an abyss, a dark, terrible, enticing abyss.

Nemovetsky was no more; he had stayed behind, and the other who had replaced him was now passionately and cruelly mauling the hot, submissive body and, with the sly smile of a madman, was repeating, "Answer me! Or don't you want to? I love you! I love you!"

With the same smile he brought his widened eyes close to Zinotchka's face and whispered, "I love you! You don't want to speak, but you are smiling, I can see that. I love you! I love you! I love you!"

He pressed the soft, will-less body harder to him. Its lifeless submission awakened a savage desire. He wrung his hands. His only human trait now being an ability to lie, he whispered, "I love you! We'll tell no one, and no one will know. I'll marry you—tomorrow, whenever you like. I love you. I'll kiss you, and you'll respond. All right, Zinotchka?"

Forcefully he pressed his lips to hers and was aware of his teeth entering her flesh. In the force and anguish of the kiss he lost the last sparks of reason. It seemed to him that the girl's lips quivered. For a single instant flaming horror illuminated his mind, revealing before him a black abyss.

And the black abyss swallowed him.

JANUARY 1902
—Translated by Henry and Olga Carlisle

DARKNESS

I

It usually happened that good luck was with him in everything that
he did, but in the last three days circumstances developed unfavor-
ably and even hostilely. As a man whose short life resembled an
immense, dangerous, extremely risky game, he had experience with
sudden changes of fortune and knew how to deal with them. Life
itself was at stake—his and the lives of others—and that fact alone
had accustomed him to concentration, quick-wittedness, and cold,
hard calculation.

Now he again had to use his wits. An accident, one of those small
accidents that cannot be predicted, had put the police on his trail.
It had now been two days that he, a well-known terrorist, a bomb
thrower, had been hunted by detectives, who were driving him relentlessly into an ever-narrowing circle. One after the other, safe
houses were closed to him. Certain streets were still open, certain
boulevards and restaurants, but stress and extreme fatigue (due to
two nights of insomnia) presented other dangers: he might fall asleep
on a bench on the boulevard or even in a cab, and, absurdly, he
would then be taken to the police station as a drunk. This was
Tuesday. On Thursday an important terrorist act was planned. Their
entire small organization had for a long time been involved in setting
up the murder, and the honor of throwing the last, decisive bomb
had been assigned to him. No matter what, he had to carry on.

On that October evening, standing at the crossing of two busy
streets, he decided to go to that house of prostitution in ——Lane.
He would have taken this somewhat questionable step sooner had
there not been a complicating circumstance. Although he was twenty-
six years old, he was a virgin, did not know women, and had never
been to a brothel. At one time he had had to struggle with his

rebellious flesh, but little by little abstinence had become a habit, and he developed a calm, indifferent attitude toward women. Now, placed in a position of confronting a woman who practiced love as a profession, perhaps facing the prospect of seeing her naked, he foresaw a whole series of peculiar and extremely unpleasant embarrassments. He had made up his mind that in the last extremity, if it became necessary, he would come together with a prostitute, because now that his flesh was no longer rebellious and he was facing such a huge and important step, virginity and the fight for it had lost their value. Nonetheless, it was unpleasant, as a minor, disagreeable obstacle can sometimes be. Once in the execution of a terrorist act—in which he was involved in the role of alternate assassin—he saw a dead horse with its hindquarters torn apart and its entrails spilling out, and this filthy, revolting, unnecessary, and yet unavoidable detail had given him then a feeling that was more painful than a comrade's death in the same explosion. And while the prospect of Thursday, when he would probably have to die, filled him with calm, serenity, and even happiness, the thought of a night with a prostitute, with a woman who practiced love as a profession, seemed absurd to him, senseless—the incarnation of a small, confused, unclean chaos.

But there was no choice. And already he was swaying with fatigue.

II

It was still quite early when he arrived, about ten o'clock, but the large white parlor with the gilded chairs and mirrors was ready for guests, and all the lights were burning. At the piano with its raised lid sat the piano player, a quite presentable young man in a black frock coat—the house was an expensive one. He was smoking, carefully tapping the ashes of his cigarette so as not to dirty his coat, while leafing through sheet music. In the corner nearest the darkened drawing room sat three young women on three chairs side by side, conversing softly.

When he came in with the madam, two of the young women stood up while the third remained seated. The two who stood wore deep décolletage, while the third wore a black, high-necked dress. The two were looking at him directly, with indifferent, weary expressions, while the third had turned away and sat calmly in profile, as would any proper young lady lost in thought. Apparently it was she who had been telling a story to her two friends who had been listening, and now she went on thinking about it, silently continuing it in her mind. And because she was silent and thoughtful, and because she did not look at him, and because she alone had the appearance of a respectable woman, he chose her. He had never before been in a house of prostitution and did not know that in every well-appointed house, there are one or perhaps two such women. They are usually dressed in black, like nuns or young widows; their faces are pale without color, and even severe; and their task is to give the illusion of propriety to those who seek it. But when they go off to a bedroom with a man and become intoxicated, they are like all the others and sometimes even worse: they create scenes and break china; sometimes they dance naked and run out into the parlor naked—and even beat up overinsistent men. These are the women with whom drunken students fall in love and whom they try to persuade to start a new and virtuous life.

But he did not know this. When she stood up reluctantly and sullenly, glancing at him with annoyance, with her made-up eyes, and brusquely showed her pale, matte face, he once again thought, "How very respectable she is!"—and felt relief. But maintaining that perpetual and necessary dissimulation that split his life in two and turned it into an act, he rocked back and forth on his feet in a fatuous manner; he snapped his fingers and spoke to the young woman in the uninhibited voice of a confirmed *débauché*.

"So, how is my little chick. Shall we go to your room? Where is your little nest?"

"Now?" said the young woman in surprise, and she raised her brows. He laughed suggestively, flushed deeply, and, showing his large, even white teeth, said, "Of course. Why should we waste precious time?"

"There'll be music here. We're going to dance."

"But what is dancing, my precious? Empty twirling, chasing one's tail. As for the music, we'll hear it from there."

She looked at him and smiled. "You hear it a little."

He was beginning to appeal to her. His face was broad, with high cheekbones. He was clean shaven; his cheeks and the narrow space over his firmly drawn mouth were ever so slightly turning blue, as happens to very darkhaired men who shave regularly. His dark eyes were beautiful, although there was something too fixed about their gaze, and they moved slowly and heavily as if sweeping over a great distance. But though he was shaven and his manners were free and easy, he did not resemble an actor but rather a foreigner who had spent time in Russia.

"Aren't you German?" asked the young woman.

"Partly. I'm more English. Do you like Englishmen?"

"But you speak Russian so well. One wouldn't know."

He remembered his English passport, the affected accent that he had used lately, and the fact that he had now forgotten to pretend, as he should have, and blushed again. And frowning slightly, in a dry, businesslike manner in which exhaustion could be detected, he took the young woman by the elbow and swiftly led her away.

"I'm Russian. Russian! Well, where are we going? Show me where."

In the large mirror that reached to the floor, the two were sharply reflected. She, in black, was pale and looked beautiful at a distance, while he was very tall, broad shouldered, also in black, as pale as she. His brow and full cheeks appeared especially pallid in the electric light from the fixture above. In place of eyes both had black, somewhat mysterious yet beautiful spaces. And the black, stern couple they formed amid the white walls, within the broad gilded mirror frame, caused him to think in surprise of a bride and groom. However, probably because of his insomnia and state of exhaustion, he was confused, and his thoughts were unexpected, incongruous. In the next minute, glancing at the black, stern, mourning pair, he thought of a funeral. Both notions were equally disagreeable.

Apparently his feeling was communicated to the young woman. In silent wonderment she gazed at him and at herself. She narrowed her eyes, but the mirror did not respond to this slight movement, and it still continued to outline as heavily and relentlessly the same immobile couple. Perhaps it looked beautiful to the young woman, or perhaps it recalled a melancholy memory of her own — she smiled softly and lightly squeezed his hard, bent arm.

"What a pair!" she said, and suddenly the heavy black arrows of her lashes with their finely curled tips became visible in the mirror.

But he did not respond and resolutely went on, taking the young woman with him, and her high French heels clicked on the parquet floor. As usual the hallway was dark; the shallow rooms had their doors open. They went into one of them, marked "Luba" in an uneven hand.

"Here we are, Luba," he said, looking around and rubbing his hands in a habitual movement, as if he were carefully washing them. "Now let's have some wine and—what else—some fruit perhaps?"

"The fruit here is expensive."

"That's all right. Do you drink wine?"

He forgot himself and used the formal "you," and though he noticed it, he did not correct himself: there was something about the way she had touched him that made him unwilling to address her informally, to be charming and to pretend. It seemed that she shared his feeling. She looked at him intently and, hesitating, replied with a note of uncertainty in her voice, which her choice of words belied, "Yes, I do. Wait a moment. I'll ask for only two pears and two apples. Will that be enough for you?"

She, too, was now using the formal "you," and in the manner in which she pronounced it, there was the same uncertainty, a slight hesitation, a question. But he did not notice this and, left alone, proceeded to make a quick, thorough survey of the room. He tried the door, which locked securely with a hook and also a key. He went to the double window, opening both. The room was high up, on the third floor, and overlooked the courtyard. Uneasy, he frowned and shook his head. Then he checked the lights. There were two bulbs, and when the upper one went off, the red-shaded one by the bed went on, as in any good hotel.

But the bed!

He hunched his shoulders and grinned, but he did not laugh; he had that urge to change facial expressions that possesses secretive people and those with something to hide, when they are finally left alone.

The bed!

He walked around it; he touched the quilted comforter, which was turned back; and with sudden mischievousness, pleased as he was with the idea of sleep, he cocked his head in a boyish manner, thrust out his lip, and widened his eyes, thus expressing his amazement. But he soon turned serious and sat down, and in a state of fatigue, he waited for Luba. He wanted to think about Thursday, about the fact that he was now in a brothel—actually in a brothel!—but his thoughts disobeyed him; they bristled and ran into one another. This state of affairs was beginning to interfere with his sleep, the prospect of which had seemed so sweet out in the street. He no longer gently stroked the stubble of his face but now twisted his arms and his legs, stretching his body as if he wanted to tear it apart. Suddenly he began to yawn in earnest, to the point of tears. He took his pistol and the three extra clips and angrily blew into the muzzle—everything was in good order, and he was insufferably sleepy.

When the wine and fruit were brought in and Luba arrived, delayed for some reason, he locked the door, at first with just the latch, and he said, "Well, here—drink, Luba. Please."

"And you?" asked the young woman, with a swift, oblique glance.

"I will, later. You see, I've been celebrating two nights in a row and haven't slept at all, and now . . ." He yawned extravagantly, stretching his jaw.

"Well?"

"I won't be long. I'll sleep for an hour—I won't be long. But you drink, go ahead. And have some fruit, too. Why did you order so little?"

"May I go down to the parlor? The music is about to begin."

This was not right. They would start to talk, to speculate about the strange visitor who had gone to bed; this would not be right at all. And stifling his yawn, he asked in a restrained and serious manner, "No, Luba; I'll ask you to stay here. You see, I don't like to sleep in a room alone. It's a quirk—you'll have to forgive me."

"Well, why not? Since you've paid."

"Yes, yes." He blushed. "Of course. But that's not the point. And if you want, you can lie down too. I'll make room for you. But please lie by the wall. Do you mind?"

"I'm not sleepy. I'll sit up."

"Why don't you read?"

"There's no book here."

"Would you like today's paper? I have it here. There're interesting things in it."

"No, I don't want it."

"Well, as you wish; you know best. But if you don't mind, I . . ." He double-locked the door and put the key in his pocket. He did not notice that the young woman was following him with an odd look. And this polite, correct conversation, so crazy in this unhappy place, where the very air was thick with curses and the fumes of wine, seemed to him simple and natural and quite convincing. With the same sort of politeness, as if he were on a boating party with young ladies, he touched at the lapels of his jacket and asked, "Do you mind if I take off my coat?"

The young woman frowned slightly.

"Please do. After all, you . . ." She did not finish.

"What about my waistcoat? It's very tight."

The young woman did not answer and lightly shrugged.

"Here is my wallet, my money. Please put it away for me."

"You should have left it at the office. Here everything is left at the office."

"Why is that?" He glanced at the young woman, then averted his eyes in embarrassment. "Oh, yes, yes. Well, what nonsense."

"Do you know how much money you have here? Some don't, and then . . ."

"Of course I do. And you mustn't . . ."

He stretched out, leaving room by the wall. And enraptured sleep placed its woolly cheek against his own, softly embraced him, tickled his knees, and quietly put its soft fluffy head on his chest. He burst out laughing.

"Why are you laughing?" the young woman asked, smiling reluctantly.

"Just like that. It's so good. Your pillows are soft. Now we can talk a little. Why don't you drink?"

"May I take off my blouse? Do you mind? I'll have to sit here for a long time." There was light mockery in her voice. But meeting his trusting eyes and hearing his considerate "Of course, go ahead," she explained seriously and simply, "I have a very tight corset. It leaves marks."

"Of course, of course. Go ahead."

He turned away slightly and flushed again. And whether it was because insomnia confused his thoughts or because, at twenty-six, he was actually naive, this "may I" appeared natural to him in a house where everything was allowed and no one asked permission from anyone.

He heard the silk crackle and the snaps open. Then she asked, "Are you a writer?"

"What do you mean, a writer? No, I'm not. Why? Do you like writers?"

"No, I don't."

"Why not? They're people . . ." He yawned slowly and pleasure-ably. "They're all right."

"What is your name?"

After a silence he replied sleepily, "Call me—Peter. Why not?"

Then she asked, "What are you, then? Who are you?"

She asked softly but so carefully and firmly that her voice gave the impression that she was moving with her whole body toward him. He no longer heard her, however, he was falling asleep. His fading consciousness flared up for one instant, creating a single im-age in which time and space merged into a varicolored mass of shad-ows, of darkness and light, of movement and stillness, of people and endless streets, endless wheels—the visual imagery of these two wild days and nights of flight. Suddenly all this grew calm, faded, and disappeared, and in the soft half-light, in the deepest quiet, he saw one of the rooms of the picture gallery, where yesterday, for two full hours, he had found refuge from the detectives. He was sitting on an extraordinarily soft red-velvet couch, gazing steadily at a large black painting, and such serenity flowed from this old crack-led picture, such rest for the eyes, such an easing of the mind, that for a few minutes, as he was beginning to doze, he fought against sleep, vaguely frightened of it as of an unknown threat.

But the music started in the parlor—rapid, bouncing beats—and he thought, "Now I can sleep," and at once he fell into a deep slumber. Solemnly, dear fluffy sleep embraced him warmly, and to-gether, in deep silence, holding their breaths, they sped off into the transparent, melting depths.

He slept a couple of hours on his back, in the perfectly correct position that he had assumed before falling asleep, his right hand in the pocket that contained the key and the revolver. The young woman with her bare arms and neck sat across from him, smoking, slowly drinking her brandy, and staring at him. Sometimes, in order to examine him more closely, she craned her long neck, and when she did so, two deep furrows showed at the corners of her mouth. He had forgotten to turn off the overhead light, and under its harsh

glare he was neither young nor old, strange nor familiar, but altogether unknown: his cheeks, his beaklike nose were unknown, as
was his strong, even breathing. His thick, dark hair had been cropped
close like a soldier's, and on his left temple there was a small white
scar from some old wound. He did not wear a cross around his neck.

Down in the salon the music would die down and then burst
forth again—the piano, the fiddle, the singing, the hammering of
dancing feet—while she sat smoking cigarette after cigarette and
studying the sleeping young man. She craned her neck in order to
examine his left hand, which was resting on his chest. It had a
broad palm with large fingers. At rest it gave a feeling of uncomfortable weight. Carefully the young woman lifted it and placed it
beside his body. Then she got up noisily and with a violent movement turned off the switch as if she wanted to break it, putting on
the bedside light with its red shade.

But he still did not move, and his face, which was now pink,
kept its disquieting calm. Turning away, the young woman embraced her knees with her bare, rose-colored arms and threw her
head back, gazing up at the ceiling with her black, unblinking eyes.
Frozen between her teeth was a burned-out cigarette.

III

Something threatening and unexpected had taken place. Something
very important had occurred while he slept. He perceived it at once,
even before he awoke, as he first heard a strange, hoarse voice. He
sensed it with the refined awareness of danger that for him and his
comrades had become a sixth sense. Quickly he swung his legs to
the floor and sat up, tightly clenching the revolver in his pocket,
while his eyes keenly searched the pink smoke. When he saw her
still in the same position, with her translucent pink shoulders and
breasts, and the mysterious, dark, immobile eyes, he thought: "She
has betrayed me!" He looked more attentively, took a deep breath,
and corrected himself: "She hasn't yet, but she will."

Bad!

He sighed again and asked gently, "Well?"

But she was silent. She smiled triumphantly and maliciously. She looked at him and was silent, as if she considered that he was already hers, and, at leisure, unhurriedly, she wanted to savor her power.

"What did you just say?" he asked with a frown.

"What did I say? 'Get up' was what I said. Enough. You've slept enough. Enough of all this. This is not a flophouse, my dear!"

"Turn on that light!" he ordered.

"I won't."

He turned it on himself. And under the white light he saw the infinitely angry, black, made-up eyes and mouth, drawn with anger and contempt. He saw the bare arms. And all of her, alien, determined, ready for something irreversible. This prostitute appeared repulsive to him.

"What's the matter with you? Are you drunk?" he asked earnestly, reaching for his starched collar. But she anticipated his movement, seized the collar, and without looking flung it behind the dresser.

"I won't give it to you!"

"What's this?" He repressed a shout and seized her arm in a hold that was like an iron band, and the fingers of her slender hand weakly opened.

"Let go—you're hurting me!" said the young woman, and he eased his grip but did not release her.

"Be careful!" he said.

"What is this, my dear? Do you want to shoot me? What do you have in your pocket—a revolver? Well then, why not shoot me? Show me how you do it. Well, just look at him. He comes to a woman and lies down and goes to sleep. 'Drink,' he says, 'while I take a snooze.' With his fresh haircut and his shave so that no one will recognize him. And what about the police? Do you want to go to the police, my dear?"

She laughed loudly and gaily, and with a sense of horror he saw in her face an expression of wild, desperate joy. As if she were losing her mind. And at the thought that all would be lost so absurdly, that he would now have to commit this stupid, cruel, and totally unnecessary murder and still probably die himself, he felt even more horror. Very pale but still calm in appearance, he looked at her even more intently, following her every movement and word and calculating.

"Well, why are you silent? Has fear got your tongue?"

If he seized her supple, snakelike neck and squeezed, she wouldn't have time to cry out, of course. And why shouldn't he? Right now, while he was pinning her arm down, she thrashed her head like a snake. And why not—but downstairs . . .

"Luba, do you know who I am?"

"I do. You are—" She firmly and solemnly stressed the syllables. "—you are a revolutionary. That's who you are."

"And how do you know?"

She smiled ironically. "We don't live in the sticks."

"All right, let's admit—"

"Yes, let's. Let go of my arm. You people know how to show off your strength to women. Let go!"

He released her arm and sat down, gazing at her with a heavy thoughtfulness. A little ball of anxiety was racing in his brain, but his face remained calm, serious, and somehow melancholy. And again, with this thoughtfulness and sadness he looked alien and, one would assume, like a perfectly decent man.

"What are you staring at?" the young woman shouted rudely, and to her own surprise she added a cynical curse. He raised his brows but continued to stare, and he spoke calmly in a somewhat muffled, remote voice, as from very far away.

"All right, Luba. Of course you can turn me in, and not just you but anyone in this house, almost anyone in the street. They would shout, 'Stop him! Seize him!' And at once there would be dozens, hundreds who would grab me and perhaps kill me. Why? Because

I've done nothing to anyone, because I've given my life to these people. You understand what it means to give one's life?"

"No, I don't," the young woman said sharply. But she was listening carefully.

"Some will hound me out of stupidity; others, out of deliberate meanness. Because evil people can't stand good people; they can't."

"Why should they?"

"Don't think that I'm bragging. Look, Luba, what has my life been? I've been in and out of jail since I was fourteen. I was thrown out of school, turned out of the house—my parents did that. Once I was almost shot; only a miracle saved me from the firing squad. Think of it, my whole life has been for others. Nothing for myself, nothing."

"And just why are you so virtuous?" asked the young woman mockingly. But he answered in all seriousness.

"I don't know. I must have been born that way."

"Well, as for me, I was born bad. I walked the same path you did—straight ahead! Come off it!"

But he seemed not to hear. Looking inward into his past, which, as he spoke, stood before him unexpectedly and clearly heroic, he went on.

"Just think: I'm twenty-six, my hair is turning gray, yet I'm still . . ." He hesitated slightly, then went on firmly, even defiantly. "I've never had a woman. Do you understand? Never. You're the first I've ever seen like this. And the fact is, your bareness makes me uncomfortable."

Again the music burst forth wildly, and the stamping of feet in the salon shook the floor slightly. Someone, drunk, whooped frantically as if driving a herd of crazed horses. Yet the room was calm, and the tobacco smoke swirled in a pink mist and disappeared.

"So that's what my life has been!" And lost in thought he sternly lowered his eyes, overwhelmed by the recollection of his pure and painfully beautiful life. She said nothing. She got up and threw a shawl around her shoulders. Then, meeting his surprised and rather grateful glance, she laughed derisively and flung it off again and opened her camisole in such a way that one tender, translucent, pink breast was exposed. He turned away and shrugged his shoulders.

"Drink up!" said the young woman. "Enough clowning."

"I don't drink."

"You don't? Well, I do!" And again she laughed nastily.

"If you had a cigarette I'd take it."

"Mine are no good."

"It doesn't matter."

And when he took the cigarette, he saw with pleasure that Luba had fastened her camisole—there was still hope that everything would be all right. He smoked clumsily, without inhaling, and held his cigarette like a woman, between two tense outstretched fingers.

"You don't even know how to smoke!" said the young woman angrily, and rudely she snatched the cigarette away. "Enough of that."

"Now you're angry again."

"Yes, I am."

"But why, Luba? Think: I haven't slept for two nights in a row and I have run around the city like a hounded wolf. If you denounce me they'll take me away. What satisfaction will that be for you? Look here, Luba, I'm still alive and won't give myself up." He fell silent.

"Will you use your gun?"

"Yes, I will."

The music stopped abruptly, but that wild man, crazed with drink, continued his whooping. It sounded as if someone else, as a joke or in earnest, were trying to stop his mouth with his hand, and the sound was all the more desperate and frightening for being muffled by fingers. The room smelled of perfume or perhaps of cheap toilet soap, and the smell was heavy, moist, lewd; and a crumpled blouse and some kind of skirt were hanging in full sight on a peg on one wall. And all of this was so revolting, and it was so strange to think that this, too, was life and that people could lead such lives always, that the young man drew his shoulders together in bewilderment and once again gazed around the room.

"This room is so . . ." he said meditatively and settled his eyes on Luba.

"This room is so—*what?*" she said curtly. And looking at her, the way she was standing, he understood that he should feel sorry for her. As soon as he understood this, he did feel sorry for her in all sincerity.

"Poor Luba."

"Why 'poor Luba'?"

"Give me your hand."

And carefully demonstrating his attitude toward the young woman as a human being, he took her hand and respectfully drew it to his lips.

"This, for me?" she asked.

"Yes, Luba, for you."

And very softly, as if she were thanking him, the young woman said, "Out! Get out, you idiot!"

He did not understand at first. "What?"

"Leave! Get out of here. Out."

Silently, with a long stride, she crossed the room, retrieved the white collar from a corner, and threw it at him with an expression on her face that said it was a filthy rag. Just as silently, with an air of arrogance, without so much as a glance at the young woman, he began slowly and calmly to put on his collar, but within an instant, shrieking wildly, Luba struck him violently on the cheek. The collar rolled on the floor. He staggered but did not fall. Exceedingly pale, almost blue, but still silent, with the same look of bewildered superiority, he fixed his eyes on Luba. She was breathing rapidly and looking at him in terror.

"What now?" she breathed. He stared at her without speaking, and driven quite mad by this arrogant lack of responsiveness, terrified, irrational, as if confronting a stone wall, the young woman grabbed him by the shoulders and violently sat him down on the bed. She leaned very close to him, eye to eye. "Well, why don't you say something? What are you doing to me, you bastard? Kissing my hand! You have come here to show off! To show how wonderful you are! What are you doing to me? Making the most of my wretchedness?" She shook him by the shoulders, and unconsciously opening and closing her slender fingers like a cat's claws, she scratched him through his shirt.

"So you've never had a woman, have you? And you dare tell me this, me who all men—Where is your conscience? What are you doing to me? You won't give yourself up alive, will you? But I am dead; do you understand, bastard? I am dead. Well, I spit in your face, living bastard. Now, get out! Go now. Go!"

With a rage he could no longer contain, he shoved her away and she hit her head against the wall. Apparently he was no longer thinking straight, because his next, equally swift and determined movement was to draw his revolver—and a black toothless mouth was smiling. But the young woman did not see his bespattered face, which was distorted by wild anger, or the black revolver. Covering her face with her hands, as if she wanted to drive them into the depths of her skull, she walked around him in quick long strides and threw herself face down on the bed. Silently she began to sob.

Nothing was happening as he had expected. Nonsense and absurdity prevailed; hysteria and chaos were showing their ravaged, drunken face. He put away the useless revolver and began to pace the room. The young woman was crying. He walked back and forth. She went on crying. He stood over her, hands in his pockets, and studied her. Still lying face downward, she was sobbing violently, suffering as only people do over their wasted lives, over something irretrievable. Her bare shoulder blades writhed as if she were lying on a bed of hot coals. At times she seemed to be withdrawing, embracing her sadness and her misery. The music started up again with a mazurka. There was a clicking of spurs. The officers had arrived.

He had never witnessed such weeping, and he was troubled. He removed his hands from his pockets and said quietly, "Luba."

She went on sobbing.

"What's the matter, Luba?"

The young woman answered something, but so softly that he did not hear it. He sat next to her on the bed, lowered his close-cropped head, and put his hands on her shoulders. His hands quivered wildly in response to the woman's pitiful bareness.

"I can't hear you, Luba. Luba!"

In a muffled voice choked with tears, she said, "Don't go yet. The officers have come. They might—Oh, God, what is happening?"

Swiftly she sat up on the bed and froze there clasping her hands, gazing straight ahead in terror. It was a frightening look that lasted only a moment. Again she lay face down and wept. Downstairs the spurs clicked rhythmically, and the piano player, overexcited or perhaps intimidated, struggled to keep up with the fast beat.

"Have some water, Luba dear. Aren't you thirsty?" he whispered, bending close to her. Her hair covered her ear, and wanting to be heard, he carefully pushed away the black, frizzy strands, which had been damaged by curling irons, exposing the small reddish shell of her ear. "Please let me get you some water."

"No, I don't need any. It will pass by itself."

She was quieting down. Her weeping ended with a couple of long, muffled sobs, and her shoulders stopped quaking. He was caressing her softly from her neck to the lacy edge of her camisole.

"Are you better, Luba? Dear Luba?"

She didn't answer, and with a long sigh she turned around and cast a quick, gentle glance at him. Then she sat up next to him, looked at him again, and she touched his face and eyes with strands of her hair. She sighed again and gently and spontaneously put her head on his shoulder. And he, just as gently and naturally, embraced her lightly. The fact that his fingers touched her bare shoulders no longer disturbed him. They sat this way for a long time in silence, their dark, rounded eyes gazing straight ahead. Together they sighed.

Suddenly there was the sound of voices and steps in the hallway, the dainty clicking that young officers' spurs make. These sounds grew louder and stopped at their door. The young man quickly stood up, as someone started rapping at the door with his knuckles, then pounded with his fist, and a woman's muffled voice called out, "Lubka, open the door."

IV

He watched her and waited.

"Give me your handkerchief!" she said, holding out her hand without looking at him. She rubbed her face, blew her nose hard, threw the handkerchief on his knees, and crossed to the door. He watched and waited. On the way she turned off the light. They were plunged into darkness, and he heard his own heavy breathing. He sat down on the bed, which creaked lightly.

"Well, what is it? What do you want?" demanded Luba through the door. Her voice was slightly annoyed but calm.

At once, several female voices rang out, interrupting one another. Just as suddenly they stopped, and a strangely respectful male voice asked her to come out.

"No, I won't."

Again the voices sounded, and again, cutting them off as scissors snip thread, the man's voice spoke out, youthful and persuasive. He had to be a man who had solid white teeth and a mustache and who clicked his heels and bowed from the waist. Unexpectedly Luba laughed.

"No, no, I won't come out. It's all very well but I won't."

Once again there was banging on the door, laughter, swearing, the clicking of spurs, which then moved away from the door and disappeared down the corridor. In the darkness Luba found the young man's knee and sat next to him on the bed but did not put her head on his shoulder. She explained tersely, "As I told you, the officers are giving a ball. They're inviting everyone. They'll be dancing a cotillion."

"Luba, turn on the light, please," he asked gently. "Don't be angry."

She got up in silence and switched on the light. Now she returned to her chair. She did not smile, but she was polite, like a hostess who has to sit through a long, disagreeable visit.

"You're not angry with me, Luba?"

"No—why should I be?"

"I was surprised just now, hearing you laugh so happily. How can you?"

She laughed without looking at him.

"I am happy and I laugh. But you mustn't go now. You'll have to wait for the officers to leave. They will soon."

"All right; I'll wait. Thank you, Luba."

She laughed again. "What are you thanking me for? How polite you are."

"Do you like me to be?"

"Not very much. Who were your people?"

"My father was an army doctor. His father was a peasant. We're Old Believers."

Luba looked at him with some interest. "Really! You don't wear a cross around your neck."

"No, I don't," he laughed. "We carry our crosses on our backs."

The young woman looked unhappy.

"You're sleepy. Why don't you lie down instead of wasting your time like this."

"No, I'm not sleepy now."

"As you wish."

There was a long, embarrassed silence. Luba looked down and played with a small ring on her finger. The young man was surveying the room but avoided looking at her, focusing instead on the small, half-empty glass of cognac. Suddenly, with extraordinary clarity, he felt that he had seen all this before: the amber-colored liquor in the glass, the young woman twirling her ring, and he himself—not quite the same person but someone different, someone strange. The music would have stopped, just as it had at this moment, and there would have been a light clicking of spurs. As if he had already experienced this—perhaps not in this house but in a place very similar to it, where he had taken some decisive action around which other events had clustered.

This bizarre feeling was so strong that he shook his head in dismay. It faded quickly but not completely: what remained was a light, indelible trace of troubled memories about things that had never occurred. Later in the course of this remarkable night, as he caught himself staring at an object or a face, he would try to recall them from the depths of the past or perhaps even from the realm of things that had never been. Were he not so certain that it had never happened, he would have said that he had been in this room before—it had at moments all seemed so familiar. It was an unpleasant sensation, one that alienated him slightly from himself and his comrades and, curiously, drew him closer to the brothel and its wild, detestable life.

The silence was becoming heavy. He asked, "Why don't you drink?"

She was startled. "What?"

"You should drink, Luba. Why don't you drink?"

"I don't alone."

"Unfortunately, I don't drink."

"I don't alone."

"I'd rather have a pear."

"Please do. That's why we ordered them."

"Would you like one?"

The young woman didn't answer and turned away. She caught him looking at her bare, pink shoulders and covered them with her gray knitted shawl.

"It's cold," she said sharply.

"Yes, it is," he agreed, though he found the small room hot. Again there was a long, tense silence. From downstairs a loud, insistent refrain could be heard.

"They're dancing," he said.

"They're dancing."

"Luba, why were you so angry with me? Why did you hit me?"

"I had to; so I did. Why do you ask? I didn't kill you, did I?" She laughed nastily.

The young woman had said, "I had to." She had looked at him directly with her black, made-up eyes, and, with a pallid yet determined smile, said, "I had to." She had a cleft chin. It was hard to believe that this head, which was now so mean and pale, had rested on his shoulder a moment before. That he had caressed her.

"So that's how it is," he said grimly. He paced the room, stopping just short of the young woman. When he sat down again, his expression was remote, stern, and rather arrogant. He was silent. He looked up at the ceiling where a spot of light with pink edges was playing. Something small and black was crawling there, probably a fly from last autumn that had come back to life in the warmth. Awake in the middle of the night, lost, doomed to die soon. He sighed. The young woman burst into loud laughter.

"Why are you so happy?" he asked, looking at her coldly. He turned away.

"You remind me of a writer I know. You're not offended? He feels sorry for me, too, and then gets angry because I don't worship him like an icon. He's so easily offended. If he were God he would claim every last candle." She laughed again.

"How do you happen to know a writer? You don't read anything."

"There's one who comes around," Luba said curtly.

He fell into thought, fixing the young woman with his heavy, altogether-too-probing gaze. As one who had spent his life in revolt, he vaguely recognized in her a rebellious soul, and this moved him and impelled him to try to guess why her wrath was directed at him. The fact that she had, had to do with a writer with whom she probably had conversed; the fact that she could sometimes behave with such calm and dignity, and then to speak so nastily—involuntarily raised her in his esteem and lent to the blow that she had dealt him more meaning and importance than a simple hysterical outburst on the part of a half-clad prostitute in her cups. At first he had been angered, not offended, but now, little by little he was beginning to take offense—and not only in his mind but in the deepest part of his being.

"Why did you hit me, Luba? If you strike someone in the face, you have to tell him why." He pressed his earlier question somberly and insistently. In his prominent cheekbones and heavy brows there was the obstinacy of stone.

"I don't know why I hit you," Luba answered with equal obstinacy but avoiding his eyes.

She offered no explanation. He shifted his shoulders and again examined the young woman intently, trying to understand. Ordinarily his thinking was slow and deliberate. However, once he began to think, he was as persistent as a hydraulic press that slowly and indifferently crushes rocks and girders and people. He pursued his thinking with an intractable hardness verging on cruelty. His thoughts moved in a straight line, untouched by sophistry, half answers, or nuances, until they either evaporated or reached their extreme logical conclusion, beyond which lay mystery and void. He was inseparable from his own thinking, as if he thought with his whole body, and each step immediately became real to him—as happens only to very healthy, spontaneous people who have not yet turned their thinking into a toy.

And now, in a state of exaltation, disoriented, like a great steam engine derailed in the middle of the night that still plows forward through stumps and hillocks, he was looking for a path; he wanted to find it at all costs. But the young woman remained silent and seemed unwilling to talk.

"Luba! Let us speak calmly. We must—"

"I don't want to speak calmly."

"Listen, Luba: you hit me. I can't just leave it like that."

The young woman laughed. "Is that so? What will you do to me? Will you report me?"

"No, but I'll come here until you explain it to me."

"You're most welcome. The house will profit."

"I'll be here tomorrow. I will."

And suddenly, almost simultaneously with the thought that he would not be coming either tomorrow or the day after, he understood with almost complete certainty why the young woman had acted as she did. He felt relieved.

"Oh, now I see! You hit me because I felt sorry for you; I offended you with my compassion, isn't that it? Yes, it was stupid. I didn't mean it, but then, perhaps it really was offensive. Since you're as much of a person as I am . . ."

"As much?" she said with a laugh.

"Well, enough of this. Give me your hand. Let's make peace."

Luba turned pale. "Do you want another smack in the face?"

"Why not give me your hand in friendship? In friendship!" he breathed in a tone of sincerity. But Luba got up and walked away, then said, "Do you know what? Either you're a complete fool or you haven't been knocked around enough."

Then she looked at him and burst into loud laughter. "Well, by God, you're like my writer! Exactly like my writer! You're set up to be kicked around, my dear!"

Apparently in her language the word *writer* was particularly insulting, and she gave it a special twist. And with absolute contempt, treating him like an object, like a total idiot or a drunkard, she strode across the room, hurling in passing, "Why are you still whimpering? Did I hit you all that hard?"

He said nothing.

"My writer says I know how to fight. But it might be that he has a classier face. As for your peasant mug, it feels nothing, no matter how hard you hit it. I've smacked a lot of men in the face, but I never felt sorrier for anyone than I did for my writer. 'Hit me,' he'd say, 'hit me; that's what I deserve.' He's drunk and drooling, and it's disgusting even to hit him. Such a swine. As for your puss, I hurt my hand just hitting it. Here—kiss it and make it well."

She thrust her hand to his lips then started pacing again. Her excitement mounted, and it seemed at moments as if she were choking in a fiery space: she rubbed her chest, she took deep breaths through her wide-open mouth, and in passing she tugged on the window curtains. Twice she stopped to pour cognac and drank it. The second time he said darkly, "And you didn't want to drink alone."

"I have no character, my dear," she told him. "And besides, I'm already poisoned. If I don't drink for a while, I start choking. That's what will kill me."

And suddenly, as if she had only then noticed his presence, she widened her eyes in surprise and burst into laughter.

"And here you are! You're still here; you haven't gone away. Stay awhile." And with a wild gesture she threw off her knitted shawl, and again her shoulders and her delicate hands shone pink.

"And why am I covering myself up? It's hot here and I—I was thinking of him, as I'm supposed to. Listen: why don't you take off your trousers? That's the way it is here; one can go around without pants. Maybe you have dirty underwear. If you like I can lend you mine. Is it all right if they're cut like a woman's? Please put them on! Here, little one, darling; what do you care?"

She was laughing uproariously, choking with laughter, pleading with him with her arms outstretched. Then she quickly slithered to the floor. She knelt, and catching his hands, she begged him, "Please, little one, darling; I'll kiss your hands!"

He moved away and with deep sadness said, "Why are you doing this to me, Luba? What have I done to you? I like you. Why do you do this to me? Why? Have I offended you? If I have, forgive me. Because in all this, I don't know my way around here."

Luba shrugged her shoulders, got up supplely, and sat down again. She breathed heavily.

"So you won't put them on. Too bad. I would have liked to have seen you."

He started to say something, stumbled, and continued hesitantly. "Listen, Luba. Of course, I—all this is nothing. And if you wanted, the light could be turned off. Turn off the light, Luba."

"What?" The young woman opened her eyes wide.

"What I mean is, you are a woman and I—of course I was wrong. Don't think that it's pity, Luba, not at all. I—Luba, turn off the light."

Smiling with embarrassment, he reached for her with the clumsy tenderness of a man who has never had anything to do with women. He saw that she, raising her clasped fingers to her mouth, was holding a huge breath. Her eyes had become enormous, and she was looking with dread, with sorrow, with intractable contempt.

"What is it, Luba?" he said, drawing away. And with cold dread, almost softly, without unclasping her fingers, she said, "You worthless bastard! My God, what a worthless bastard you are!"

And red with humiliation, rejected, shamed because he had offended her, he stamped his foot and hurled these short crude words into her rounded eyes, which were filled with bottomless dread and sorrow: "Whore! Trash! Shut up!"

She gently shook her head and repeated, "My God! What a worthless bastard you are!"

"Shut up, trash! You're drunk. You're out of your mind. You think I want your foul body. You think I was keeping myself for someone like you. Trash, you should be beaten!" He raised his hand as if to strike her.

"My God! My God!"

"And they expect pity! They should be destroyed, these filthy creatures. And the scoundrels who hang around with them. And you dared think this of me!" He grabbed her hands hard and sat her down in a chair.

"You're good, are you? You're good?" she laughed in delight, as if something cheered her immensely.

"Yes, I am good! I have been honest all my life! I have been pure! And you? What kind of a miserable beast are you?"

"Yes, good!" she said, savoring the words with enthusiasm.

"Yes, good. The day after tomorrow I will give my life for the people. And you? And you? You will sleep with my executioners. Call in your officers. I will throw you to their feet and tell them to take their filthy trash. Call them!"

Luba got up slowly. He was highly agitated, haughty, nostrils flaring, but when he looked at her, he met a glare as haughty as his and even more contemptuous. There was even a glimmer of compassion in the arrogant eyes of the prostitute, who had miraculously ascended the steps of an invisible throne from whose heights one surveys with a cold, stern concentration the wretched, screeching crowd below. She no longer laughed, and her agitation was no longer visible. One's eyes were drawn to the steps on which she stood, so haughtily was she glaring.

"What's the matter?" he asked, drawing back, still haughty but yielding to the power of her calm, proud eyes.

And sternly, with an ominous conviction behind which one recognized a million crushed lives, seas of bitter tears, and the flaming, ceaseless rebellion of an outraged sense of justice, she asked, "What right do you have to be virtuous if I am bad?"

"What?" He didn't understand at once, awed by the black chasm that had suddenly opened at his feet.

"I've been waiting for you for a long time."

"You've been waiting for me?"

"Yes. Waiting for someone good. I've been waiting five years, perhaps more. Everyone who has come here has complained that he's rotten. And indeed they are. My writer said first that he was good, but then he admitted that he, too, was rotten. I don't need that."

"What do you need?"

"I need you, my dear. You. You're just right." She calmly and attentively examined him from head to toe, then nodded her head affirmatively. "Yes. Thank you for coming."

He, who wasn't afraid of anything, suddenly became frightened. "What do you want?" he said, drawing further away.

"I had to hit a truly virtuous man, my dear, someone truly good. Those drooly ones aren't worth it. They only dirty your hands. And so that's what I did, and now I can kiss my hand. Dear hand, who has hit someone good!"

She laughed and actually patted and kissed her own right hand three times. He looked at her in disbelief, and his thoughts, usually so slow, now raced wildly. Like a black cloud, something dreadful and irreparable was approaching, something like death.

"What? What did you say?"

"I said it's shameful to be good. Didn't you know that?"

"I didn't," he murmured, suddenly falling into deep thought, seeming to forget all about her. He sat down.

"Well, you better know it."

She spoke calmly, and her deep agitation, like a thousand stifled screams, was visible only in the movement of her breasts under her camisole.

"Well, do you know it now?"

"What?" he said, coming out of his trance.

"I'm asking you: Do you know it now?"

"Wait!"

"I will, my dear. I've waited five years, why wouldn't I wait another five minutes!"

She sat down on a chair, clasping her hands and closing her eyes as if expecting some extraordinary joy. "Oh, my dear, my dear one!"

"You said it's shameful to be good."

"Yes, darling, it is."

"Is that true?" he said fearfully.

"That's how it is. Are you alarmed? Never mind. It's only frightening in the beginning."

"And afterward?"

"Stay with me and you'll find out what happens afterward."

He didn't understand.

"How could I stay?"

It was the young woman's turn to be surprised. "But now, after this, where could you go? Look here, my dear, you can't fool me. You're not a scoundrel like the others. Since you're a good man, you'll be staying here. You won't go anywhere. I haven't been waiting for you all this time for nothing."

"You're crazy!" he said brusquely.

She glared at him and wagged her finger at him. "Don't! Don't speak like that. Since you've seen the truth, bow down to it; don't say, 'You're crazy.' That's what my writer says—'You're crazy!' That's why he's a bastard. But you—be honest!"

"What if I don't stay?" he laughed, his lips turning pale.

"You'll stay," she said with assurance. "Where would you go now? You have nowhere to go. You're honest. A scoundrel has many paths; an honest man has one. I understood this when you kissed my hand. A fool, I thought, but honest. You're not offended that I thought of you as a fool? It's your fault, anyway. Why did you offer me your innocence? You thought you'd offer me your innocence and I would back off. Ah, you poor little fool! At first I was even offended—he doesn't even consider me human—and then I saw that it all came from your goodness. You had it all figured out: I'll give her my innocence, and then I'll become even more innocent, and it will be like a coin that's never been spent. You give it to a beggar, and he gives it back to you. No, my darling; that trick won't work."

"Won't it?"

"No, my dear," she said. "I'm not a fool. I've seen enough merchants. They steal millions and give kopecks to the church and think they've done right. No, my dear; for me you must build a whole church. Don't give me your innocence; give me what is dearest to your heart. Maybe you're offering your innocence because it's become useless to you and a bit moldy. Do you have a fiancée?"

"No."

"But if you had one and she were waiting for you tomorrow with

flowers and kisses and love, would you be offering me your innocence, or wouldn't you?"

"I don't know," he said thoughtfully.

"There you are. You'd say, 'Take my life but save my honor.'
You're offering what is cheap. That won't do. Give me what is most
valuable. Give me what you can't live without."

"Why would I give you anything? Why?"

"What do you mean, 'Why?' So as not to be ashamed."

"Luba!" he exclaimed in surprise. "You, too, are—"

"—good, you're going to say, aren't you? I've heard that said before, often by my writer. Except that it's not true, my dear. I am
an honest-to-god whore. You'll find that out when you stay."

"But I'm not staying!" he cried out through clenched teeth.

"Don't shout, my dear. You can't shout truth down. Truth is like
death: when it comes, you have to take it. It's hard to face up to
truth; I know from my own experience." And looking straight into
his eyes, she added in a whisper, "God, too, is good."

"And so?"

"That's all. You must understand it yourself. I won't say anything
more. It's been five years since I've set foot in a church. But it is
the truth!"

Truth? What truth? What was this new dread, which he had
never experienced in the face of death, or in life. Truth!

With his defined cheekbones, his massive head, a man who only
understood yes or no, he was sitting with his chin in his hands, and
his eyes roved as if he were studying his life from one end to the
other. And that life was falling apart like a badly glued box in the
rain, and in its broken parts it was impossible to recognize the beautiful whole that had once been the pure reliquary of his soul. He
was remembering the people close to him with whom he had lived
all his life and worked in a wonderful unity of joy and fear. They
seemed alien to him, their lives incomprehensible, the work senseless, as if someone had taken his soul into his powerful hands and

broken it the way one breaks a stick across one's knee and flings away the pieces. He had left them only a few hours ago, he had been here only a few hours, and it seemed to him that he had been here all his life, facing this half-naked woman, listening to distant music and to the clicking of spurs, not going anywhere. Everything was topsy-turvy—he only knew that he was pitted against everything that earlier today had been his life and his soul. It was shameful to be good.

He remembered the books that had taught him how to live and smiled bitterly. Books! Here was a book sitting with bare arms and closed eyes, an ecstatic expression on her pale, drawn face, patiently waiting. It was shameful to be good. And suddenly with sorrow and dread, with unbearable pain, he felt that that other life had for him ended forever, that he could no longer be good. To be good had been his only joy, what kept him going, the only thing that had kept both life and death at bay—and this was gone, and there was nothing in its place. Darkness. And whether he was to stay here or go back to his own people, they were no longer his own. Why had he come to this accursed house! It would have been better to have stayed in the street, to have given himself up to the police, to have gone to prison—prison would have been easy. In prison it still would not have been shameful to be good! But now it was too late for prison.

"Are you crying?" the young woman asked anxiously.

"No!" he said brusquely; "I never cry."

"And you mustn't, my dear. It's all right for us women to cry, but you mustn't. If you were to weep, who would answer to God?"

Yes, she was his. This woman was his now.

"Luba!" he exclaimed in sorrow. "What am I to do?"

"Stay with me. Stay with me: you're mine now."

"And what about the others?"

The young woman frowned. "What others?"

"The people! The people, of course! Those I was working for.

Because it wasn't for myself, for my own pleasure that I was getting
ready to commit a murder!"

"Don't speak to me about the people!" said the young woman
sternly, and her lips trembled. "Better not speak to me about the
people, or I might start fighting again. Do you hear me?"

"What's the matter with you?" he demanded in surprise.

"Do you think that we here are animals? That I'm an animal? Be
careful, my dear! You've hidden long enough behind the people: that's
enough. Don't hide from the truth, my friend; there's no place to
hide from truth! If you like the people and feel sorry for our bitter
tribe — I am, take me. And I, my darling, will take you!"

V

She was sitting with her hands intertwined, lost in a beatific lan-
guor, mad with happiness, as if she had gone out of her mind. Rocking her head, without opening her blithely dreaming eyes, she almost
sang:

"My darling! You and I will drink together. We'll cry together.
Oh, how sweetly we'll cry, my dear darling. I'll cry enough for my
whole life! He has stayed with me; he didn't leave. As soon as I saw
you today in the mirror, I knew at once: here he is, my promised
one, my darling. I don't know whether you're my brother or my
betrothed, but you're all mine, close to me, desired."

He, too, remembered the dark, silent, mournful couple within
the golden frame of the mirror, and his impression then had been
of a funeral. And suddenly it all became so painful, such a nightmare, that he began gnashing his teeth. And remembering, he thought
of the revolver in his pocket, the two-day-long manhunt, the plain
door; how he had searched for a doorbell, and how a bloated lackey
in a dirty shirt had come out, struggling into his jacket; how he had
followed the madam into the white salon and seen the three girls
who had seemed so alien to him.

Now he was feeling freer, and finally he saw that he was the same as always yet completely free—free and able to go wherever he wanted.

Sternly he looked around the unfamiliar room and solemnly, with the conviction of a man who for an instant has come out of a drunken stupor, he appraised himself in this strange environment and said to himself, "What is this? What nonsense! What an absurd dream!"

But the music was still playing. The woman sat there with her entwined hands, and speechless she laughed, weighed down by her insane, unheard-of happiness. It was not a dream.

"What is this? Is this truth?"

"Yes, my dear! You and I are inseparable."

Yes, this was truth. Those flattened, wrinkled skirts hanging on the wall in their ugliness were truth. This bed on which a thousand drunken men had thrashed in spasms of repulsive lust was truth. This stale, moist stench of perfume, which clung to his face and which made life impossible, was truth. The music and the spurs were truth, and so was this woman, with her pale, exhausted face and her piteously happy smile.

He rested his massive head on his hands and looked up with the hunted eyes of a wolf who is either about to be killed or to attack. His thoughts were broken:

This was truth. It meant not leaving, either today or the day after, and everyone would know why I hadn't acted. I stayed with a whore, went on a drunken binge, and I would be called a traitor, a coward, a scoundrel. Some would take my side and try to understand, but it was better not to count on that; it was better this way. If something is over, it's over; if it's darkness, it's darkness. But what next? I don't know. Darkness. Probably some kind of horror, because I don't know their ways. I must learn to be bad. Who will teach me? Will she? No, she's not right; she doesn't know a thing. I'll manage. One must indeed be evil, so that—Oh, something immense will be destroyed! And then? Then sometime I'll come to her, or to a tavern, or to hard labor, and I'll say, "Now I'm not ashamed. Before you I stand guilty of nothing: now I am exactly like you— filthy, fallen, wretched." Or else in my fallen state, I'll come out on a public square, and I'll say: "Look at me! I had everything: intelligence, honor, dignity, and even—frightening to consider— immortality; and I have thrown all of this at the feet of a prostitute, I have given up everything because she was bad." What will they say? Their mouths will fall open; they will call me a fool! Of course I'm a fool. Is it my fault that I'm good? Let her try to be good, let everyone—Distribute the wealth among the needy. But this is shar- ing, and this is Christ, in whom I don't believe. Or else: Who will offer his soul—not his life but his soul—this is the way I want it. But did Christ himself sin along with the sinners, the lechers, the drunks? No, he only forgave them; he loved them. Now I love her, I pardon her, I pity her—but why must I become like her? Yes, but she doesn't go to church. Neither do I. It's not Christ, it's something else, something more frightening.

"Luba, it's frightening!"

"It is frightening, my dear. It is frightening to confront the truth."

Here she's still talking about truth. But why is it all terrifying? What am I afraid of? What do I have to fear, since it's all my choice? Of course there is nothing to fear. In that public square, before those astounded people, will I not be better than they? Naked, filthy, in rags, my face hideous to behold, having given everything away, will I not be proclaiming eternal justice, to which God himself must submit? Otherwise He is not God!

"There is nothing to be afraid of, Luba!"

"Yes, dear, there is. If you are not frightened, all the better, but don't tempt fate. Don't."

"This is how I'll end up. It's not what I expected. Not what I expected for my young, beautiful life. My God, this is madness. I have gone mad! It's not too late. It's not too late. I can still get away!"

"My darling," the woman murmured, clenching her hands. He

looked at her somberly. In her closed eyes, in her errant, happy, senseless smile, there was an insatiable hunger, as if she had already devoured something huge and were ready to go on devouring. He again looked darkly at her thin, delicate hands, at the dark shadows under her arms and got up slowly. With a final effort to save something precious—be it his life or his sanity or his old ways— he started to dress with deliberate care.

"Where is my tie?"

"Where are you going?" the woman said, looking up. She dropped her hands and leaned toward him.

"I'm leaving."

"Leaving?" she repeated. "Where?"

He laughed bitterly.

"You think I've nowhere to go? I'm going to my friends."

"To the good ones. You were tricking me?"

"Yes, to the good ones." He laughed again. Now he was dressed. He straightened his jacket. "Give me my wallet."

She gave it to him.

"And my watch?"

She gave him the watch, too. Both objects had been lying on the bed table.

"Good-bye," he said.

"Are you afraid?"

She had put the question calmly, directly. He glanced at her: a tall, slender woman standing there with fine, almost childlike hands. She was smiling, her lips pale, and she asked, "Are you afraid?"

How curiously she would change: one moment she was strong, even intimidating, the next she was sorrowful and looked more like a young girl than a woman. But what did it matter? He started toward the door.

"But I thought you'd stay."

"Did you?"

"I thought you'd stay. With me."

"Why?"

"Just so I would be better. You have the key. It's in your pocket."

He was unlocking the door.

"Well, then, go on. Go join your good friends, and I'll—"

And just then, in that final moment, when all he had to do was to open the door and find his friends again, a beautiful life, and a heroic death, he did something wild and unaccountable that would cost him his life. Was it the madness that sometimes suddenly seizes the strongest, the steadiest of minds? Or was it that, to the screeching of a drunken fiddle within the walls of a brothel, bewitched by the made-up eyes of a prostitute, he had discovered some last, terrible truth about life, about himself—a truth that others would not understand? But whether it was madness or sanity, whether his new understanding was a lie or a fresh truth, he accepted it firmly and irrevocably, in the same matter-of-fact way that had held his former life to a straight, burning line and gave it the wings of an arrow.

Slowly, very slowly he ran his hand over his short straight hair, and, not bothering to lock the door again, he simply turned back into the room and took his old place. His pale, broad, beardless face appeared strange, like a foreigner's.

"What are you doing? Have you forgotten something?" The woman was surprised; she had no idea what was happening.

"I haven't forgotten anything."

"Then why aren't you going?"

Calmly, with the expression of a stone on which life, with its heavy hand, has carved a new, dreadful last commandment, he said, "I refuse to be virtuous."

The woman was seized with joyous agitation. She undressed him as one would a child. She undid the laces of his shoes, fumbling with the knots. She stroked his head, his knees. Her heart was so full she was afraid to break the spell with laughter. Suddenly, looking at his face, she said anxiously, "You're so pale! Here, have a drink. Is it so hard to stay—you said your name was Peter?"

"I lied to you. My name is Alexei."

"It doesn't matter. Do you want a full glass? But you must be careful if you're not used to drinking."

And with her mouth open, she watched him drink in slow, uncertain swallows. He started coughing.

"It's all right. You'll learn how to drink. I can tell. What a fine fellow; how lucky I am!"

With a screech she jumped at him and started choking him with quick, hard kisses he had no time to respond to. "How ridiculous," he thought, "a stranger kissing like this!" He squeezed her hard in his arms, preventing her from moving, and for a time in silence, immobile himself, he held her this way, as if he were experiencing the force of that moment of quiet, his own strength, and that of the woman. As for her, she nestled happily in his arms.

"Well, all right," he said with a faint sigh.

And again the woman rushed around the room as if set afire by wild happiness. She so filled the room with her movements that there seemed to be several half-crazed women present, talking, darting about, pacing, kissing him. She poured him cognac and was drinking herself. Suddenly she remembered something and clasped her hands.

"The revolver! We've forgotten about the revolver! Give it to me quickly. Let me take it downstairs."

"Why?"

"Because I'm afraid of those things. What if it goes off?"

He laughed and said, "What if it goes off? Yes. What if it does?"

He took out the revolver and slowly, as if weighing the heavy, obedient weapon in his hand, he gave it to the young woman. He gave her the loose cartridges, too.

"Take them."

When he was left alone without the revolver that he had carried for so many years, in that room with the half-open door through which came distant, unknown voices and the soft clicking of spurs, he felt the enormity of what he had taken on. He quietly paced the room then suddenly stopped, and, as if confronting his friends, he said, "Well?"

He stood in this position, crossing his arms, as if looking at them. Much was said in this sharp word. It was a last farewell, a vague challenge, an irreversible, malicious determination to fight everyone, even his own friends. It was also a very small, quiet complaint.

He was still standing there when Luba rushed in, speaking heatedly.

"My darling, you won't be cross? Please don't. I have invited my girlfriends here—a few of them. Do you mind? You understand: I wanted very much to show you off to them, my promised one, my darling. Is it all right? They're very nice. No one has taken them tonight, and they're all alone. The officers have gone off to the rooms. One young one saw your revolver and praised it. He said that it's a very good one. Darling, is it all right?" the young woman asked as she covered him with short, quick, hard kisses.

But now they were already coming in, squealing, mincing, looking for seats next to one another. There were five or six of them, the oldest and least pretty, heavily made-up with painted eyes and heavy bangs falling to their eyebrows. One or two had pretended to be embarrassed and giggled, while the others were simply looking for cognac, and these had stared at the young man squarely and had shaken hands with him as they entered. Apparently they had been preparing for bed, because they were wearing light dressing gowns; but one, who was fat, lazy, and indifferent, had come in in only her skirt, exposing her huge arms and swollen breasts. She and another one, whose mean, birdlike face was covered with makeup that resembled dirty stucco, were quite drunk, while the others were only tipsy. And all these half-dressed, unabashed, giggling women were suddenly all around him, and at once the room smelled unbearably of flesh, beer, cognac, and moist, cheap scent. A sweaty servant wearing a tight jacket rushed in with cognac and stout, and the women in chorus greeted him, "Markusha! Dear Markusha! Markusha!"

It seemed that it was a custom for them to greet him with such outcries, and even the fat, drunken one lazily groaned, "Markusha!"

All this was quite extraordinary. They drank, they clinked glasses; they all spoke at once about their own affairs. The mean one with the birdlike face told in an irritated, shrill way about a guest who had taken her for a time and with whom something had not worked out. They used obscenities but not as men do, in a tone of indifference, but bitingly and provocatively. They called everything by its street name. At first they paid little attention to him, and he remained resolutely silent and observed. The happy Luba sat very quietly next to him on the bed, her arm around his neck. She did not drink much herself but she refilled his glass. Often she whispered into his ear, "My darling!"

He drank a lot but did not become inebriated. Something else was happening to him, which strong, mysterious alcohol sometimes produces in people. It was as if, while he was silently drinking, inside him a huge destructive process were happening, swift and mute. It was as if everything he had learned in the course of his life, everything he had loved and pondered—conversations with comrades, books, dangerous and exciting work—were silently consumed, annihilated without a trace, while he himself was not destroyed but unaccountably grew stronger and harder. As if with each glass he were returning to something primal, to his grandfather, to his great-grandfather, to those elemental, primitive rebels for whom rebellion and religion were one. Like a dye that washes off in water, the bookish wisdom of others was fading, and in its place appeared something peculiar, somber, and wild, like the voice of the dark earth itself. This ultimate dark wisdom of his spoke of untamed distances, boundless, impassable woods, endless fields. In it one could hear the frenzied ringing of bells, the bloody reflection of fires, the clanging of iron shackles, and the frantic praying and the satanic laughter of a thousand gigantic throats—the black cupola of the sky above his uncovered head.

Here he was with his broad, pale face, suddenly so near, so close to these wretched noisy people around him. In his hollow, burned-out soul, and in that world of his that had collapsed, his incandescent will flared with the white sheen of molten metal. Still blind, still aimless, his will crouched hungrily. His body was quietly steeling itself with a feeling of boundless might, the power to create everything and to destroy everything.

Suddenly he struck the table with his fist. "Drink, Lubka!"

Smiling, glowing, she obediently poured herself a drink. He lifted his own and said, "To our brothers!"

"You mean your brothers?" whispered Luba.

"No, I mean ours. To our brothers. To the scoundrels, the shits, the cowards, to those crushed by life. To those who are dying of syphilis."

The woman laughed, but the fat one objected in her lazy way, "Look here, my pet, you're going too far."

"Shut up!" said Luba, turning pale; "he belongs to me."

"—to all who are blind from birth. We who can see must put out our eyes." Again he crashed his fist on the table. "Shame to those with sight who look upon those who are blind from birth. Since our lamps cannot light up all of the darkness, let's put them out and crawl into the darkness. If there's no paradise for everyone, I don't want it either, because it's not paradise, ladies, it's a pigsty. Ladies, let us drink to the extinction of all lights. Drink up: darkness!"

He wavered slightly and drank up. He was speaking with some difficulty but firmly, distinctly, with pauses between each clearly enunciated word. No one understood this wild talk, but everyone liked it. He appealed to them, pale as he was, and because of his remarkable anger. Suddenly Luba spoke rapidly, with her arms outstretched:

"He's my betrothed. He'll stay with me. He was honest, he had comrades, but now he'll stay with me."

"Come and work here. Take Markusha's place," said the fat one lazily.

"Shut up, Manka; I'll bash your face! He'll stay with me. He was honest once."

"We were all honest once," said the mean, old one. Others joined in:

"I was honest till I was four."

"I'm honest now, by God."

Luba was close to tears.

"Shut up, you bitches. Your honesty was taken from you, but he gave his up himself. He took it and gave it up: 'Take my honesty! I don't want it!' You are all here in this place—but he is still innocent."

She caught her breath in a sob. Everyone burst into loud laughter. It was drunkards' laughter filled with uncontained feelings. They laughed as only people do in a small room already so noisy that the laughter becomes deafening. They wept with laughter, falling upon one another and moaning. The fat one squawked in a thin voice and was slipping off her chair. Finally, watching them, he too burst into laughter. As if a whole satanic world had gathered here to inter with laughter one tiny, innocent honesty, and the dead honesty itself was laughing, too. Only Luba did not laugh. Trembling with indignation she wrung her hands, she shouted, and finally she threw herself at the fat woman, who kept her off with her bare arms that were like logs.

"Enough!" he shouted, but no one listened. Finally, little by little, they fell silent.

"Enough!" he shouted again. "Stop it. I have another joke for you."

"Forget about them!" Luba was saying, drying her tears with her fist. "They must all be thrown out."

"Are you scared?" he asked, turning to her, still shaking with laughter. "You wanted decency? Fool, that's all you've been wanting all along! Let me continue!"

And paying no further attention to her, he turned to the others, getting up and raising his hands over his head. "Listen! Wait! I'll show you. Look at my hands."

And in a mood of gaiety and curiosity, they looked at his hands and waited with their mouths open like obedient children.

"Here," he said, shaking his clenched hands, "I hold my life in my hands. Do you see that?"

"We do! Go on!"

"My life was beautiful. It was pure and wonderful. It was like a lovely porcelain vase, and now look, I am smashing it!" He brought his hands down with a moan, and all eyes were then fixed on the floor as if indeed something delicate and fragile were actually lying there in pieces—a beautiful human life.

"Stamp on it, girls. Crush it until not a piece is left." And he, too, stamped his foot.

Like children delighted with a new prank, they got up with shrieks and laughter and stamped their feet on the spot where the invisible, delicate fragments of the vase lay—a beautiful human life. Little by little they were seized by rage. The laughter and shrieking stopped. Only heavy breathing and whimpering could be heard, and the stamping of feet, angry, merciless, irrepressible.

Over her shoulder, like a wounded queen, Luba was looking at him with furious eyes, and suddenly understanding, crazed, with a cry of joy, she threw herself in the middle of the women and started stamping her feet. Were it not for the solemnity of the drunken faces, the anger in the dulled eyes, the anger of the contorted mouths, one might have thought that this was some strange new dance, performed without music or rhythm. Clutching his bristly skull with his fingers, the young man was looking on sternly.

In the darkness two voices could be heard.

Luba's voice was intimate, concerned, responsive, with that slight anxiety that women's voices take on in the dark. His was firm, calm, distant. He spoke with an insistence that betrayed a state of drunkenness that had not quite passed.

"Are your eyes open?" asked the woman.

"Yes."

"Are you thinking about something?"

"Yes."

Silence and darkness, and again the attentive, guarded female voice.

"Tell me about your comrades. Can you?"

"Why not? They were once—"

He used the past tense the way the living speak of the dead—or the dead speak of the living. He spoke calmly, almost indifferently, with funereal music in his evenly flowing voice, like that of an old man telling children a heroic tale about times long past. Before Luba's enchanted eyes, in the boundless darkness of that room, a handful of people appeared, all exceedingly young, all without mothers and fathers, all hopelessly hostile, both to the world as it exists and to the world as it will be. In their dreams they dwell in a distant future, among their brothers yet unborn. They live their short lives like pale, bloody shadows, ghosts, with which people frighten one another. Their lives are extremely short. Before each stands the gallows, hard labor, or madness. They have no other expectations. There are women among them.

Luba gasped and raised herself on her elbow. "Women! What are you saying, my darling?"

"Young, delicate women. Almost adolescent. They follow the men daringly, and courageously go to their deaths."

"To their deaths. Good Lord!" Luba drew in her breath and leaned against his shoulder.

"Why are you distressed?"

"It's nothing, my dear. I'll be all right. Tell me more. I want to hear more." He proceeded with his story. And surprisingly, ice turned to fire, death turned to life. In the funereal tones of this farewell speech, the young woman, her eyes staring in the darkness, heard the promise of a new, happy, vigorous life. Tears came to her eyes and dried again. Moved by rebelliousness, she listened avidly, and each of his words, heavy as hammerblows on red-hot iron, welded a new resonance in her soul. The blows fell relentlessly, and her soul resounded. And suddenly in the airless, reeking room, a new voice was heard, a human voice. "My dear, I too am a woman!"

"What do you want?"

"I too could join them."

He was silent. And because he said nothing, and because he was their comrade and lived with them, he suddenly appeared to her so special and important that she felt embarrassed to be just lying there next to him, embracing him. She moved away slightly and shifted her hand in such a way that her touch would be as light as possible. Forgetting her hatred of those who were virtuous, her tears and her curses, her long years of solitude in this den, conquered by the beauty and selflessness of this other life, she was flushed and near tears at the awesome thought that they might not receive her.

"Darling, will they accept me? Oh, God, do you think they will? Won't they feel disgust for me? Won't they say, 'You can't. You're dirty. You sold yourself.' Tell me, what do you think?"

He was silent a moment, then replied with a message of hope: "They'll accept you. Why wouldn't they?"

"My darling, they are so—"

"Virtuous." He said the word as if he were closing a sentence. And joyously, with a touching sense of trust, the young woman repeated, "Yes, virtuous."

Her smile was so radiant that it could have lighted the darkness itself. New stars were rising for her. She was perceiving a new truth that brought with it not fear but happiness.

In a timid, pleading voice she said, "Let's go to them, my darling! You'll bring me along; you won't be ashamed of me. They will understand how you got here. They'll surely understand. You were a hunted man. Where were you to go? In such circumstances a man would hide in a garbage dump. As for me, I'll do my best. Why are you silent?"

There was heavy silence in which the beating of two hearts could be heard—one quick and anxious, the other calm and distant.

"Are you ashamed to bring someone like me along?"

The heavy silence continued and was now icy and stony.

"I won't go. I refuse to be virtuous."

After another silence he said, "They are the masters." And his voice sounded lonely and strange.

"Who?" asked the young woman in a low voice.

"My former friends."

Again there was a lengthy silence, as if a bird was falling in wide circles, without striking the earth and dying. In the darkness he felt Luba climbing over him, trying to touch him as little as possible.

"What are you doing?"

"I don't want to lie down any more. I want to get dressed."

She must have got dressed and sat down, because the chair creaked slightly. Everything became so quiet that it seemed there was no one in the room. The silence lasted for a long time, until in a calm, serious voice he said, "Luba, there may be some cognac left on the table. Have a glass and come lie down."

VI

When the police arrived it was daybreak and the house was quiet, as any house would be at that hour. After much hesitation and doubts, fears of scandal and of becoming involved, Markusha had been dispatched to the police station with a detailed and accurate report about the strange visitor, along with his revolver and his extra cartridges. There they guessed at once who he was. For the last three days the police had been obsessed by him, sensing his presence nearby. In fact, his trail had been lost precisely in——Lane.

For a moment there had even been a question of searching every brothel in the district, but then a fresh, false trail had been picked up, the search diverted, and the brothels were forgotten.

The telephone had jangled urgently, and in less than a half hour, in the October chill, a huge body of detectives and police was moving in, stamping down the hoarfrost on the empty streets. The district chief walked in front, his whole body projecting his awareness of the sinister threat to his person. He was a very tall, elderly man wearing a loose-fitting uniform. He was yawning, his large red nose nestled in his gray mustache, and he was thinking with cold distress that it would have been better to wait for the soldiers, that it was absurd to go after such a man with only a bunch of sleepy, clumsy town cops who didn't even know how to shoot straight. In his own mind he had already thought of himself several times as a "casualty in the line of duty," and each time he was seized by a fit of yawning.

This old district chief was always slightly drunk. He had been corrupted by the brothels located in his district, which paid him a great deal of money to stay in business. In no way was he prepared to die. When he had gotten up that morning, he had passed his revolver from one sweaty palm to the other, and though there was little time, for some reason he ordered his uniform brushed as if he were going to a review. The day before at the station, the police had among themselves held conversations about the individual with whom the entire police force was obsessed at that time. The district chief, with the cynicism of a canny old drunkard, had called him a hero and declared that he himself was an old police whore. As his aides roared with laughter, he assured them, in all seriousness, that they needed a hero like this, if only to hang him:

"We string him up, and it's fine with him and it's fine with me. He goes straight to the kingdom of heaven, and I have the satisfaction of knowing that brave men still exist in this world. Why are you grinning like that? What I'm telling you is true!"

In fact, he himself was laughing as he said this. He had long ago forgotten the difference between truth and lies in what he said—

the lies that permeated his whole senseless, drunken life like tobacco smoke. But today, in the October morning, proceeding down
the frosty street, he clearly felt that what he had maintained yesterday was indeed a lie and that they were dealing with a scoundrel,
and he was ashamed of his childish words of the day before.

"A hero! In no way! Good Lord, if he so much as moves, I'll kill
him like a dog," thought the district chief almost prayerfully.

And again he wondered why he, an elderly district chief, suffering from gout, wanted so much to go on living. And suddenly he
knew: it was because of the beautiful hoarfrost on the street. He
turned and shouted ferociously, "Get in step! You're walking like
sheep!"

There was a draft under his coat, and his jacket was too loose, as
if he had suddenly lost weight. Despite the cold, the palms of his
hands were sweaty.

They surrounded the house as if it were not one man they were
after but a regiment. Slowly, on tiptoe, they moved inside and up
the stairs and down a dark corridor that led to a terrifying door.
There was desperate banging, shouting, frightened threats to shoot
through the door. When a pack of them finally rushed into the small
room, almost throwing half-naked Luba to the floor, filling the room
with their boots, coats, rifles, this is what they saw: The young man
was sitting on the bed wearing only a shirt, his hairy legs planted
on the floor. He did not speak. There was no bomb nor any other
menacing object. It was an ordinary prostitute's room with a broad,
wrinkled bed, clothes scattered around, a table stained and sticky
with beer—and on the bed sat a beardless man with a broad, sleepy
face and hairy legs, saying nothing.

"Hands up!" shouted the district chief from behind someone's back,
and he clenched the revolver harder in his sweaty palm.

But the man on the bed did not raise his hands and said nothing.

"Search him!" shouted the district chief.

"He has nothing! I've taken away the revolver! Oh, my God!"
shouted Luba, her teeth chattering in fear. She too was wearing

only a wrinkled shirt, and the half-naked man and woman provoked shame, disgust, and pity mingled with revulsion among the uniformed men. They searched his clothes, felt the bedding, looked into corners and into the chest of drawers and found nothing.

"I've taken away the revolver!" Luba repeated senselessly.

"Shut up, Lubka!" the district chief shouted. He knew the young woman well—had spent the night with her two or three times—and he believed what she was now saying. However, this happy outcome was so unexpected that he wanted to shout out in delight, to give orders, to show his power.

"What's your name?" he asked the young man.

"I won't tell you. And I won't answer any of your questions."

"Of course, of course, sir!" replied the district chief ironically, but he was a bit let down. Then he looked at the other's hairy legs, at the whole sordid scene, at the young woman, who was trembling in a corner, and suddenly he had doubts.

He took a detective aside. "Are you sure it's him? Doesn't it all look . . ."

The detective studied the young man's face carefully, then nodded his head. "It's him. It's just that he's shaved his beard. I recognize his cheekbones."

"It's true that they look like a bandit's."

"Look at the eyes, too. I'd spot him out of a thousand from those eyes."

"The eyes, yes. Let me see the picture."

For a long time he examined the matte, unretouched photograph. It showed a very handsome, innocent-looking young man with a broad, Russian-style beard. The eyes might have been the same, but instead of being somber they were calm and clear.

"You can't see the cheekbones."

"Under the beard. If you let your eye feel through . . ."

"That may be, but do you think he looks that way because he goes on drunken binges?"

A tall, thin detective with a yellow face and a sparse beard, himself a drinker, smiled condescendingly. "These people don't go on binges."

"I know they don't. Still . . ." The district chief approached the young man. "Listen, did you take part in the murder of——?" And he respectfully named a very famous and important personage.

The young man said nothing and smiled. He was swinging one foot from side to side.

"You've been asked a question!"

"Leave him alone. He won't answer. Let's wait for the captain and the procurator. They'll make him talk."

The district chief laughed, but he was growing more and more uncomfortable. When they had crawled under the bed, they had spilled something, and the closed room smelled unpleasant. "How revolting!" thought the district chief. Though he was not fastidious, he was staring in disgust at the bare, swinging foot. "How does he dare?" He turned and saw a young, blond policeman with bleached lashes who was looking at Luba and smirking, holding his rifle with both hands like a night watchman.

"Hey, Lubka!" the district chief shouted. "You bitch, why didn't you report at once who was with you?"

"I . . ."

Skillfully the district chief slapped both her cheeks.

"Take that! And that! I'll show you people here!"

The young man raised his brows and stopped swinging his foot.

"Don't like it, young fellow?" said the district chief, feeling more and more contemptuous. "Well, that's the way it is. You kissed this pretty mug, and we slap it around."

He laughed, and the flustered policemen smiled. But the oddest thing of all was that the battered Luba laughed too. She looked amiably at the old district chief as if she was delighted by his humor and his cheerful disposition. Since the police had entered, she had not glanced once at the young man, betraying him openly and na-ively. He was aware of this and smiled the strange smile of a stone in a forest. Now half-dressed women were crowding at the door.

Among them were those who had sat there the night before. They looked on with indifference, with dull curiosity, as if they had never seen him before. It was obvious that they remembered nothing of the previous night. Soon they were chased away.

It was now broad daylight, and the room was dirtier and more revolting than ever. Two officers came in. They were sleeping, their faces creased, but they were neatly dressed. They came up to the young man and examined him from his head to his naked feet. Then they cast glances at Luba, exchanging comments freely.

"You shouldn't come in, gentlemen. No, by God, you shouldn't." said the district chief without conviction, and he glared malevolently at the young man.

"Look at this fine one!" said the younger of the officers, who at a cotillion would be the one to summon the dancers. He had beautiful white teeth, a bushy mustache, tender eyes with the lashes of a young girl. This young officer stared at the man under arrest with disgust and pity, and he screwed up his face as if he might weep. He was particularly revolted by the young man's callused hands and his dirty feet. He shook his head and said with a frown: "How could you do this, sir? How could you?"

The older officer laughed. "So this is how it is, Mr. Anarchist. You sin with the girls just as we do. Could it be that your flesh, too, is weak?"

"Why did you give up your revolver?" demanded the younger officer heatedly. "You could at least have fired some shots. I understand that you might find yourself here. This might happen to anyone—but why did you give up your revolver? That's not a nice thing to do to your comrades." To the older officer he explained, "Do you know what? He had a Browning with three clips. Can you imagine? It's crazy."

The young man was smiling mockingly, full of his own terrible, secret truth. He gazed at the agitated young officer and swung his foot with an air of indifference. He was not embarrassed by the fact that he was half naked and that his legs were hairy and his feet dirty. Had he been led out as he was then into a crowded city square, and had he sat there in full sight, he would have swung his hairy leg in just the same way and smiled as mockingly.

"They don't know what true comradeship is," said the district chief, looking ferociously at the swinging foot. Still without conviction, he admonished the officers, "Conversations are forbidden, gentlemen. By God, they are. You know yourself. Those are the orders."

But other officers came in, looking around, exchanging remarks. One who was acquainted with the district chief shook his hand. Luba was beginning to flirt with them.

"Can you imagine? A Browning with three clips, and he gave it up voluntarily," said the young officer. "I don't understand."

"You'll never understand, Misha."

"But they don't seem to be cowards."

"Misha, you're an idealist. You're still wet behind the ears."

"Samson and Delilah!" a short officer with caved-in nose and a thin mustache said with a nasal twang.

"She's no Delilah, but she did him in anyway."

They all laughed.

The district chief smiled and, rubbing his long red nose, suddenly came up to the young man. He stood there screening him from the officers with his huge coat, and he spoke in a hushed whisper, rolling his eyes wildly:

"You should be ashamed of yourself, sir! Why don't you put your pants on? There're officers here. It's shameful! What a hero! Taking up with a whore. What will your comrades say? You're an animal."

Luba listened, straining her neck to hear. The three were close together: three lives, three truths; the old bribe taker and drunkard, dreaming of heroes; a depraved woman in whose soul the seeds of heroism and abnegation had fallen; and the young man. At the district chief's words he had paled slightly and might have been about to say something, but instead he smiled and again calmly swung his leg.

One by one the officers left. The policemen were growing accustomed to the surroundings, to the two half-naked people, and they stood there with that absence of expression of sleepy sentries everywhere. Leaning forward with his hands on the table, the district chief fell into deep, sorrowful thought—about the fact that he would not be able to go back to sleep today, that he had to go to the police station and attend to business, and other, even more depressing, reflections.

"Can I get dressed?" asked Luba.

"No."

"I'm cold."

"Doesn't matter. Just sit there."

The district chief was not looking at her. Leaning over to the young man, craning her slender neck, she silently moved her lips. He raised his brows questioningly, and this time she whispered, "Darling! My darling!"

He nodded his head and smiled at her tenderly. The fact that he had smiled and therefore forgotten nothing of the night before, the fact that he was so proud and virtuous, naked and dirty as he was and despised by everyone—all this filled her with unbearable love and wild, blind rage. Screeching, she fell to her knees on the damp floor and threw her arms around his cold, hairy legs.

"Get dressed, darling!" she shouted hysterically. "Get dressed!"

"Stop it, Lubka!" The district chief was dragging her away. "He's not worth it!"

"Shut up, you old bastard! He's better than all of you!"

"He's an animal!"

"You're the animal!"

"What's that?" The district chief was suddenly infuriated. "Here, Feodocenko, grab her! Put down your rifle, you idiot."

"Darling! Why did you give up your revolver?" screamed the young woman, fighting off the policeman. "Why didn't you bring a bomb? We would have . . . gotten . . . them all!"

"Shut her mouth!"

Choking, silenced, the young woman was fighting furiously, trying to bite the harsh fingers that were seizing her. Confused, not knowing how to fight with women—now pulling her hair, now seizing her naked breasts—the blond policeman, puffing hard, was throwing her to the floor. Now from the corridor came loud, self-assured voices and the clicking of spurs. A sweet, ingratiating baritone was drawing nearer, as if only now the real opera were beginning.

The district chief straightened his coat.

SEPTEMBER 20, 1907
—Translated by Henry and Olga Carlisle

THE
SEVEN
WHO WERE
HANGED

I
At 1:00 P.M., Your Excellency!

As the minister was a very fat man prone to apoplexy, it was necessary to spare him all agitation; so they took every precaution in warning him that a serious attempt had been planned on his life. When they saw he took the news calmly and even smiled, they told him the details: the attempt was to be made the next day, as he left to make his report. Several terrorists—already given away by a provocateur and now under the watchful eye of police agents—were to meet at 1:00 P.M. near the entrance to the minister's house, armed with bombs and revolvers, and wait for him to come out. There they would be arrested.

"One moment," the minister interrupted in surprise. "How on earth do they know I'll be leaving to make my report at 1:00 P.M., when I only found out myself the day before yesterday?"

The officer in charge of the bodyguard spread his hands in a vague gesture:

"At 1:00 P.M. precisely, Your Excellency."

Astonished but at the same time approving of the measures taken by the police, who had arranged everything so well, the minister shook his head, and a gloomy smile spread across his thick, dark lips. With the same smile, obediently and not wishing to hinder the police any further, he quickly got ready and drove off to spend the night in someone else's hospitable mansion. His wife and two children were taken away too, away from this dangerous house near which the bomb throwers would gather the next day.

While the lights shone in the unfamiliar mansion and the friendly faces greeted him, smiled, and expressed their indignation, the minister felt a pleasant sense of excitement—as if he had just received or was about to receive a great and unexpected decoration. But the

241

people around him went away, the lights were put out, and through the plate glass windows there shone on the walls and ceiling the spectral, filigree light of the electric lamps outside. A light that was alien to this house, with its pictures, statues, and the stillness entering from the street; a light that was itself silent and indeterminate—it provoked disquieting thoughts about the futility of locks, guards, and walls. And then, in the night, amid the silence and solitude of this strange bedroom, the minister began to feel insufferably afraid.

He had something wrong with his kidneys, and whenever he became extremely agitated, his face, arms, and legs filled with fluid and swelled, and this made him seem bigger, fatter, and more massive still. Now, crushing the springs of the bed under his bloated flesh, with the anguish of the sick man he was, he felt his swollen face that seemed to belong to someone else and thought incessantly of the cruel fate being prepared for him. One after another he recalled all the terrible occasions recently when bombs had been thrown at men of his high rank and higher still. The bombs had torn their bodies to shreds, spattering their brains over grimy brick walls and knocking their teeth from their sockets. Because of these recollections, his own obese, sick body spread out on the bed already felt like someone else's that was suffering the fiery blast of an explosion. It seemed as if his arms were being torn from his trunk at the shoulder, as if his teeth were falling out, his brain breaking up into fragments, his legs and feet growing numb and lying submissively on the ground with their toes turned up like those of a corpse. He moved urgently, breathing loudly and coughing so as not to resemble a corpse in any way, surrounding himself with the living sound of creaking springs and rustling bedclothes. To prove he was completely alive, not in the least bit dead—and indeed, like everyone else, far from dead—he said abruptly in a loud, deep voice amid the silence and solitude of the bedroom, "Well done! Well done! Well done!"

He was praising the detectives, the police, and the soldiers, all those who guarded his life and had so opportunely and cleverly prevented his murder. But though he stirred on the bed, praised his protectors, and smiled a wry, forced smile to express his scorn for the stupid terrorists and their miserable failure, he still could not believe he was saved or that life would not suddenly desert him at one fell swoop. It seemed to him that the death people had planned for him—a death that was still only in their minds and their intentions—was already standing there beside him, would continue to do so, and would not go away till those people were arrested, had their bombs taken from them, and were put in a secure prison. Over there in that corner stood death, and it would not go away—could not go away, like an obedient soldier posted on guard at someone else's wish and command.

"At 1:00 P.M., Your Excellency!" came the spoken words, modulated in every tone of voice: first gaily mocking, then angry, then stubbornly obtuse. It was as if a hundred gramophones had been wound up and set going in the bedroom; and all of them, one after the other, with the idiotic diligence of machines, were shouting the words they were ordered to shout: "At 1:00 P.M., Your Excellency!"

This "1:00 P.M." the following day, which until so recently had been in no way distinguishable from any other hour and was merely the steady movement of a hand over the face of his gold watch— this "1:00 P.M." had suddenly acquired an ominous persuasiveness, leapt from the watch face, and began to lead an independent existence, stretching upward like a huge, black pillar that cut his whole life in two. It was as if no other hours existed, either before or after it, and as if it alone, insolent and conceited, possessed the right to some special life of its own.

"Well? What do you want?" asked the minister angrily through his teeth.

And the gramophones blared, "At 1:00 P.M., Your Excellency!" And the black pillar fawned and smirked.

Gritting his teeth, the minister raised himself on the bed and sat up, resting his chin on his palm. He could not possibly sleep on an abominable night like this.

Pressing his face between his plump, scented hands, he imagined with horrifying clarity how he would have got up the next morning knowing nothing about what was in store, would have drunk his coffee, still knowing nothing, and then would have dressed in the anteroom. Neither he nor the hall porter who helped him on with his fur coat, nor the footman who brought him his coffee, would have known that it was utterly senseless to drink coffee and put on a coat when in a few moments all this—the coat, his body, and the coffee inside it—would be obliterated by an explosion and snatched away by death. Now the porter was opening the glass door . . . And it was he—that dear, kind, gentle porter, with his pale blue soldier's eyes and his chest covered with decorations—it was he, who with his own hands was opening that terrible door—opening it because he knew nothing. And everyone was smiling because they knew nothing.

"Oh!" said the minister suddenly in a loud voice, and he slowly took his hands from his face.

Staring far into the darkness before him, his gaze motionless and intent, with the same slow movement, he stretched out his hand, felt for the switch, and turned on the light. Then he stood up and, without putting his shoes on, walked barefoot across the carpet, found another switch on the wall, and turned it on. The room became pleasant and bright, and only the rumpled bed with its quilt that had slipped to the floor told of some horror that was not yet completely over.

Dressed in his nightclothes, his beard disheveled by his restless movements and his eyes full of anger, the minister looked like any cross old man suffering from insomnia and severe breathlessness. It was as if the death being prepared for him had stripped him naked, snatched him from the magnificence and impressive splendor around him—and it was hard to believe that it was he who possessed such

power, that it was his body—such an ordinary, simple, human body—
that was to perish so terribly amid the fire and thunder of a monstrous explosion. Without dressing and not feeling the cold, he sat
down in the nearest armchair, propped his tousled beard on his
hand, and in quiet, profound reverie stared intently at the unfamiliar stucco ceiling.

So that was it! That was why he had felt so afraid and anxious!
That was why death was standing in the corner, why it would not
and could not go away!

"Fools!" he said with weighty contempt.

"Fools!" he said again, only more loudly this time, turning his
head slightly toward the door so those to whom the word referred
could hear. It referred to those whom a short while ago he had
praised so highly and who in an excess of zeal had told him in detail
about the attempt planned on his life.

"Well, of course," he said to himself, his thoughts suddenly res-
olute and fluent, "now they've told me, and I know about it; I feel
frightened, but after all, if they'd not told me, I wouldn't have known
a thing and would have drunk my coffee quite happily. Well, afterward, of course, I'd have been killed, but am I really so afraid of
death? Here I am with bad kidneys, and I'll die someday, I know,
but I'm not afraid because I don't know anything about it. But those
fools said to me, 'At 1:00 P.M., Your Excellency!' They thought I'd
be glad about it, the fools, but instead death has come and stood in
that corner and won't go away. It won't go away because it's me
thinking about it. It's not death that's frightening but knowing about
it, and life would be quite impossible if a man knew with absolute
certainty the day and hour he would die. But those fools go and tell
me in advance, 'At 1:00 P.M., Your Excellency.' "

Everything was so pleasant and easy now, as if someone had told
him he was immortal and would never die. Feeling powerful and
wise again amid this pack of fools, who had intruded so imperti-
nently and senselessly into the mysteries of the future, he began to
think just how blissful ignorance could be, and his thoughts were

the painful thoughts of an ailing old man who had experienced a great deal in his time. No living creature, neither man nor beast, can know the day and hour of its death. Now, not long ago he'd been ill, and the doctors had told him he would die and had suggested he make final arrangements. But he hadn't believed them and had, in fact, remained alive. And in his younger days this had happened: things had been going very badly for him, and he'd decided to do away with himself. He'd gotten the revolver ready, written some letters, and even fixed the time for his suicide, but at the very last minute he'd suddenly thought better of it. Always, at the very last moment, something unexpected might turn up, and for that reason no one can say when he will die.

"At 1:00 P.M., Your Excellency," those obliging asses had told him, and though they had only told him because his death had been averted, simply knowing its possible time had filled him with terror. It was quite possible he would be killed one day, but it would not be tomorrow—it would not be tomorrow—and he could sleep in peace like someone immortal. The fools! They didn't know what great law they had abused, what yawning chasm they had revealed when they had said with that idiotic amiability of theirs, "At 1:00 P.M., Your Excellency."

"No, not at 1:00 P.M., Your Excellency, but no one knows when. No one knows when. What?"

"Nothing," replied the silence. "Nothing."

"No, you said something."

"It's nothing; never mind. I said, 'Tomorrow, at 1:00 P.M.' "

With a sudden feeling of sharp anguish in his heart, he realized he would not know sleep, peace, or joy till this accursed, black hour torn from the watch face had passed. Only the mere shadow of something—something not a single living creature should know—was standing there in the corner, but it was enough to eclipse the light and envelop him in the impenetrable darkness of terror. Once disturbed, the fear of death crept throughout his body, taking root in his bones and thrusting its pallid head from his every pore.

It was no longer tomorrow's assassins that he feared—they had vanished and been forgotten, mingling with the multitude of inimical faces and events surrounding his life—but something sudden and inevitable: an apoplectic stroke, the rupture of some stupid, narrow artery that would suddenly be unable to withstand the pressure of the blood in it and would burst, like a glove pulled tight on plump fingers.

His short, fat neck felt terrible, and it was unbearable to look at his swollen fingers, to feel how short they were, how full of mortal fluid. If earlier, in the darkness, he had been obliged to move so as not to resemble a corpse, then now, in this bright, terrifying, coldly hostile light it seemed terrible, impossible to move, even to reach for a cigarette or ring for someone. His nerves were taut. Each one seemed like a bent wire standing on end, topped by a little head with crazed eyes staring in terror and a gaping mouth choking in silent convulsions. There was no air to breathe.

Suddenly, in the darkness, amid the dust and cobwebs somewhere beneath the ceiling, an electric bell sprang into life. Its little metal clapper beat in spasms of terror against the rim of the gong, fell silent, then shuddered again in incessant, sonorous horror. His Excellency was ringing from his room.

People came running. Here and there, in chandeliers and on walls, lamps flared into life—too few of them for bright light but enough for shadows to appear. They appeared everywhere: rising in the corners and stretching across the ceiling; clinging flickeringly to every projection and running along the walls; and it was hard to see where all these innumerable, misshapen, silent shadows had been before—these mute souls of mute things.

A deep, shaking voice said something loudly. Then they telephoned for a doctor: the minister was ill. His Excellency's wife was sent for, too.

II

Sentenced to Death by Hanging

Things turned out as the police had expected. Four terrorists, three men and a woman, armed with bombs, infernal machines, and re-volvers, were caught right by the entrance to the minister's resi-dence, while a fifth, another woman, was found and arrested in the conspirators' apartment, of which she was the owner. At the same time a great deal of dynamite, many half-finished bombs, and arms were seized there. All those arrested were very young: the eldest of the men was twenty-eight, and the younger of the two women only nineteen. They were tried in the fortress where they had been im-prisoned after their arrest, tried quickly and in a closed court, as was the custom in those merciless days.

At the trial all five were calm, but very grave and thoughtful: so great was their contempt for the judges that none of them wished to emphasize his fearlessness by an unnecessary smile or a feigned expression of gaiety. Their calm was just sufficient to protect their souls and the great, mortal darkness within them from the malevo-lent, hostile eyes of others. Sometimes they would refuse to answer the questions put to them, and at others they would reply—briefly, simply, and precisely, as if they were replying not to their judges but to statisticians filling in special tables of figures. Three of them, two men and one woman, gave their real names, but the other two refused, so their identity remained unknown to the court. Toward everything taking place at the trial they displayed that distant, sub-dued curiosity characteristic of people who are either seriously ill or possessed by a single, vast, all-consuming idea. They shot swift glances around them, took note of an occasional interesting word, then re-turned to their thoughts at the very point where they had left them.

Nearest the judges sat one of the accused who had given his name—Sergei Golovin, the son of a retired colonel and himself a former officer. He was still very young, with fair hair and broad shoulders, and was so robust that neither prison nor the expectation of inevitable death had been able to remove the color from his cheeks and the expression of youthful, happy naiveté from his light blue eyes. He kept on tugging vigorously at his tousled little blond beard, to which he was not yet accustomed, and gazed fixedly at the window, narrowing his eyes and blinking.

The trial was taking place at the end of winter, when, amid snowstorms and leaden frosts, the approaching spring occasionally sent, like a harbinger, one clear, warm, sunny day or even just a single hour, but one that was so springlike, so sparkling and avidly youthful, that the sparrows in the street went mad with joy, and people seemed intoxicated. Now, through the dusty upper window that had not been cleaned since last summer, a strangely beautiful sky could be seen. At first sight it seemed milky gray and smoky, but if you looked at it longer, it turned blue, and the blue grew more and more bright, deep, and boundless. And because the sky was not revealed at once in its entirety but lay chastely hidden in a transparent haze of cloud, it became attractive, like a beloved woman. Sergei Golovin looked at the sky, tugged at his beard, screwed up first one eye, then the other beneath their long, fluffy lashes, and pondered something earnestly. Once he even began to move his fingers quickly, and his face wrinkled up with innocent joy, but he glanced around him, and his joy was extinguished like a spark under someone's foot. Almost at once, almost before it could fade into pallor, the color in his cheeks turned a sallow, deathly blue; and the soft hair torn painfully out by its roots was gripped as in a vice by fingers that had turned white at their tips. But his joy at the spring and at being alive was stronger, and after a few minutes his naive, youthful face was lifted up to the spring sky once more.

The pale young girl whose identity was unknown but whose nickname was Musya gazed into the sky, too. She was younger than Golovin but seemed older, because of her gravity and the blackness of her proud, unflinching eyes. Only her gentle, slender neck and slim, girlish arms told of her age, together with that indefinable quality that is youthfulness itself. That quality sounded clearly with the flawless tone of an expensive instrument in her pure, melodious voice and in every simple word or exclamation that revealed its musical essence. She was very pale, though her pallor was not deathly but that peculiar glowing whiteness seen when a mighty fire seems to burn within a human being, making the body shine translucent like fine Sèvres porcelain. She sat almost motionless and only occasionally, with an imperceptible movement, fingered a deep mark on the middle finger of her right hand—the mark left by a ring she had taken off recently. She looked at the sky not with fond affection or joyful memories but only because in this grimy, official room, that little patch of azure was the most beautiful, unsullied, and honest thing—and unlike the judges, it tried to elicit nothing from her eyes.

The judges felt sorry for Sergei Golovin, but they detested her.

Her neighbor sat motionless too, his hands between his knees in a rather stiff pose. His identity was unknown, but his nickname was Werner. If a face can be locked shut like a heavy door, then he had shut his face like an iron gate and hung an iron padlock on it. He stared fixedly at the dirty plank floor, and it was impossible to tell whether he was calm or desperately agitated, whether he was thinking about something or listening to what the detectives were testifying to the court. He was not tall, but his features were fine and delicate. He was so handsome and gentle that he reminded one of a moonlit night somewhere in the south, on the coast, where cypresses cast their dark shadows, but at the same time he gave the impression of immense, quiet strength, insuperable determination, and cool, audacious courage. The very courtesy with which he made his brief, precise replies seemed dangerous, accompanied as they were by a slight bow; and if on all the others their prisoners' smocks seemed an absurd piece of buffoonery, in his case there was no hint of this whatsoever, so alien did the garment seem to him. Though the other terrorists had been found in possession of bombs and infernal machines, while Werner had only been carrying a black revolver, for some reason the judges regarded him as the leader and addressed him with a certain respect, their words as brief and businesslike as his were to them.

Next to him was Vasily Kashirin, the whole of him consumed by the sheer, intolerable terror of death and by the equally desperate desire to suppress that terror and conceal it from the judges. Since early that morning, as soon as they had been brought to court, he had begun to pant with the racing of his heart. Little drops of sweat kept appearing on his forehead, his hands were clammy and cold, and his shirt, wet with sweat, stuck to his body, hampering his movements. With a superhuman effort of will, he forced his fingers not to shake, while his voice was steady and clear, and his eyes were calm. He saw nothing around him, and the sound of voices reached him as if through a fog, while into that same fog he directed his desperate efforts to answer firmly and loudly. But having answered, he immediately forgot both the question and his reply and wrestled with himself in silent terror once more. So clearly had death laid its hand on him that the judges tried not to look at him. It was as hard to guess his age as it is that of a corpse that has already begun to decompose. According to his papers, though, he was only twenty-three. Once or twice Werner touched him gently on the knee, and each time he answered briefly, "It's all right."

The most terrifying moment for him was when he suddenly felt an irresistible urge to shout—with the desperate, wordless cry of an animal. Then he would touch Werner gently, and without looking up, Werner would reply softly, "It's all right, Vasya. It'll soon be over."

Surveying them all with her solicitous, maternal eye, the fifth terrorist, Tanya Kovalchuk, was tormented by anxiety. She had never had any children and was still very young and red cheeked, but she was like a mother to them all, so full of concern, so infinitely loving were her glance, her smile, her fear. She paid no attention whatsoever to the trial, as if it were something totally incidental, and only listened to the way the others replied: did his voice shake; was he afraid; should she give him some water?

She could not look at Vasya for anguish and only wrung her plump fingers quietly. She gazed at Musya and Werner with pride and admiration, her expression grave and earnest, and she kept trying to catch Sergei's eye with her smile.

"The dear one—he's looking at the sky. Just you look, just you look, my dear one," she said to herself. "But what about Vasya? What on earth's wrong? My God, my God! What am I to do with him? If I say something it'll only make things worse, and what if he starts crying?"

Like a still pool at dawn that reflects the clouds flying by above it, her kind, dear, plump face reflected every swiftly passing feeling, every thought of her four comrades. She paid no attention at all to the fact that she was being tried and would be hanged, too—all that was a source of profound indifference to her. It was in her apartment that a cache of bombs and dynamite had been found, and though it was hard to believe, it was she who had greeted the police with gunfire and wounded one detective in the head.

The trial ended at about eight o'clock, when it was already dark. Before Musya's and Sergei's eyes the blue sky gradually faded, but it did not turn pink and smile softly, as on summer evenings. Instead, it grew dull and gray, then suddenly became cold and wintry. Golovin sighed, stretched, and glanced out of the window once or twice more, but outside the night was already cold and dark. Still tugging at his beard, he began to scrutinize the judges and the soldiers with their rifles as inquisitively as a child and smiled at Tanya Kovalchuk. As for Musya, when the sky grew dim she calmly shifted her gaze, and without lowering her eyes looked into a corner of the room where a cobweb swayed gently in the imperceptible draught from the hot-air heating. And she remained thus till sentence was passed.

After the sentence they bade their defense counsel farewell, avoiding their helplessly dismayed, sorrowfully guilty eyes as they did so. The condemned then found themselves together for a moment in the doorway and exchanged a few brief words.

"It's all right, Vasya. It'll all be over soon," said Werner.

"But I'm all right, old fellow," replied Kashirin loudly in a calm, cheerful voice. And in fact his face had turned a faint pink and no longer resembled that of a rotting corpse.

"To hell with them; they've gone and hanged us after all, you see," said Golovin, and swore.

"It was to be expected," replied Werner calmly.

"Tomorrow they'll pronounce sentence in its final form and then put us all in the same cell," said Tanya, consoling them. "We'll be together right till the execution."

Musya said nothing. Then she stepped forward.

III
You Mustn't Hang Me

A fortnight before the terrorists were tried, the same district military court, but with different judges, had tried and sentenced to death by hanging a peasant called Ivan Yanson.

Yanson had worked as a laborer for a prosperous farmer and had not differed in any particular way from other poor, landless workers like himself. He was an Estonian by birth, from Wesenberg, and gradually, over the course of a few years, by moving from one farm to the next, he had reached the capital itself. He spoke Russian very badly, and as his employer was a Russian—Lazarev by name—and as there were no other Estonians in the vicinity, Yanson did not say a word for almost the whole of his two years on Lazarev's farm. In general, though, he was apparently not inclined to be talkative. He was silent not only with people but with animals, too: he watered the horse in silence; harnessed it in silence as he moved slowly and lazily round it with little shuffling steps; and when the animal, disturbed by his quietness, began to play up and be a nuisance, he beat it with his whip handle in silence. He beat it cruelly, with cold, savage persistence, and if this happened when he had a bad hangover, he would go into a frenzy. Then the sound of the whip could be heard as far away as the farmhouse itself, together with the terrified, abrupt, agonized clatter of hooves on the plank floor of the barn. His master beat Yanson for beating the horse but could not cure him of it, so he gave it up.

Once or twice a month Yanson would get drunk. This usually happened on days when he drove his master to the big railway station where there was a refreshment room. After dropping his master, he would drive half a verst away from the station and, plunging the horse and sleigh off the road into the snow, would wait there until the train had gone. The sleigh lay askew, almost lying on its side, and the bowlegged horse stood up to its belly in the drifts, lowering its muzzle from time to time to lick the soft, feathery snow, while Yanson lay in an awkward, half-sitting position in the sleigh and seemed to doze. The loose earflaps on his shabby fur cap dangled limply like the ears of a setter, and under his small, reddish nose there was a patch of moisture.

Then he would drive back to the station and quickly get drunk.

He would cover the ten versts back to the farm at a gallop. Lashed mercilessly and filled with terror, the jade galloped at top speed like one possessed, as the sleigh swerved from side to side, keeling over and colliding with telegraph poles. Letting go of the reins and almost flying off the sleigh at every moment, Yanson half sang, half yelled something in Estonian in abrupt, indistinct phrases. More often than not, though, he did not sing but silently clenched his teeth in an access of mysterious fury, pain, and ecstasy and hurtled onward like a blind man: he did not see anyone coming toward him, shout to them in warning, or slacken his furious pace, either at bends in the road or when going downhill. How he did not knock anyone down or smash himself to death on one of these wild journeys was beyond comprehension.

He should have been sacked long ago, just as he had been sacked from other jobs, but he was cheap, and other workers were no better, so he stayed two years. Yanson's life was devoid of all events. Once he received a letter in Estonian, but as he was illiterate and those around him knew no Estonian, the letter remained unread. With wild, fanatical indifference, as if he did not understand that it contained news from home, he flung it on the manure heap. Evidently longing for a woman, he even tried to make advances to the cook, but he had no success and was crudely rebuffed and ridiculed: he was short and puny, with a freckled, flabby face and sleepy little eyes that were a dirty bottle-green. He regarded even his failure with indifference, and did not pester the cook any more.

But all the same, Yanson was listening to something the whole time. He listened to the sound of the dismal, snow-covered fields, with their mounds of frozen manure that resembled a line of small graves covered with snow; he listened to the sound of the soft, dark expanse of distance, to the wind moaning in the telegraph wires, and to people's conversation. What the fields and telegraph wires told him, he alone knew, but people's conversation around him was alarming, full of rumors about murder, robbery, and arson. One night the little bell could be heard ringing from the chapel in the neighboring hamlet, its sound so thin and feeble that it resembled the tinkling of a harness bell, and flames crackled against the sky: some strangers had plundered a rich farm, killed the owner and his wife, then set fire to the house.

On their farm, too, life was uneasy: the dogs were let loose not only at night but during the daytime too, and the master kept a gun beside him when he slept. He tried to give Yanson one like it, a single-barreled, old one, but Yanson turned it over and over in his hands, then shook his head, and for some reason refused it. The master could not understand why he did so and cursed him, but the reason was that Yanson had more faith in his Finnish knife than in this rusty old firearm.

"It'll kill me," he said, looking sleepily at his master with glassy eyes.

And the master waved his hand in a gesture of despair.

"Well, you really are a fool, Ivan! What a life it is with workers like you!"

Then one winter's evening, when the other laborer had been sent off to the station, this same Ivan Yanson, who would not trust a gun, made a highly involved attempt at armed robbery, murder, and rape. Somehow he did it with amazing simplicity: he locked the cook in the kitchen; then, with the air of a man who feels extremely sleepy, went lazily up to his master from behind and quickly stabbed him again and again in the back with his knife. The master slumped unconscious to the floor, and his wife began to rush about the room screaming, while Yanson, baring his teeth and brandishing his knife, started ransacking trunks and chests of drawers. He found some money, then noticed the mistress as if for the first time, and without the slightest premeditation flung himself upon her. But because he dropped his knife, she proved to be the stronger and not only resisted him but very nearly strangled him as well. Then the master began to toss about on the floor, the cook started breaking down the kitchen door with the oven fork, and Yanson ran off into the fields. He was caught an hour later, squatting behind a corner of the barn striking one sputtering match after another and trying to set fire to the farm.

A few days later the master died of blood poisoning, and when Yanson's turn came among all the other thieves and murderers, he was tried and sentenced to death. At the trial he was just the same as always: small, puny, and freckled, with sleepy little glassy eyes. It was as if he did not quite understand the meaning of what was happening and were completely indifferent: he blinked his white eyelashes, looked vacantly and without curiosity around the imposing, unfamiliar room, and picked his nose with a stiff, hard, callused finger. Only those who had seen him in church on Sundays might have guessed that he had smartened himself up a little: he had wound a dirty-red, knitted scarf around his neck and moistened his hair here and there. Where his hair was wet, it was dark and smooth, while on the other side of his head it stuck up in light, sparse tufts, like wisps of straw in a bare cornfield flattened by hail.

When sentence was pronounced—death by hanging—Yanson suddenly became agitated. He turned a deep red and began to tie and untie his scarf, as if it were strangling him. Then he began to wave his arms in a confused way and said, addressing the judge who had not pronounced sentence and pointing at the same time to the one who had, "She said I must be hanged."

"Who is 'she'?" asked the president of the court who had read the sentence, his voice a deep bass.

Everyone smiled, concealing their smiles under their mustaches and among their papers, while Yanson pointed at the president with his index finger and replied angrily and distrustfully, "You!"

"Well?"

Yanson again turned his eyes to the silent judge with his restrained smile—someone in whom he detected a friend, someone with no part in the sentence whatsoever—and said again: "She said I must be hanged. You mustn't hang me."

"Take the accused away."

But Yanson managed to say once more in an earnest, forcible tone, "You mustn't hang me."

He looked so absurd, with his outstretched finger and his angry little face, to which he vainly tried to lend an air of gravity, that even the soldier escorting him broke the rules and said to him under his breath as he led him from the room, "Well, old fellow, you really are a fool!"

"You mustn't hang me," repeated Yanson obstinately.

"They'll string you up with my blessing, and you won't even have time to twitch!"

"Come on, keep quiet!" shouted the other escort angrily. But he could not restrain himself either and added: "So you're a thief, too! Why did you go and kill someone, you fool? Now go and hang for it!"

"Might they give him a reprieve?" asked the first soldier, who had begun to feel sorry for Yanson.

"What d'you mean? Reprieve ones like him? . . . Now that'll do; we've done enough talking!"

But Yanson had already fallen silent. Again he was put in the same cell that he had already spent a month in and had had time to grow accustomed to, just as he did to everything else: to beatings, vodka, and the dismal, snow-covered fields strewed with round little mounds like a cemetery. Now he even felt glad when he saw his bed and his barred window, and when they gave him some food— he had not eaten since that morning. The only disagreeable thing was what had happened in court, but he could not think about it and indeed was incapable of doing so. And he could not imagine death by hanging at all.

Though Yanson had been sentenced to death, there were many others like him, and he was not considered an important criminal in the prison. So the warders talked to him without being wary or deferential, just as they would to anyone else not faced with death. It was as if they did not regard his death as death in the real sense. Hearing of the sentence, the warder said to him, "Well then, old fellow! So they've gone and hanged you, have they?"

"But when will they hang me?" asked Yanson mistrustfully.

The warder became thoughtful.

"Well now, you'll have to wait a bit for that, till they've got a batch of you together. To do it first for this one, then for that isn't worth the bother. You'll have to wait till it gets busy."

"Well, when will that be?" Yanson asked insistently.

He was not in the least offended to hear that it was not worth even hanging him by himself, and he did not believe what the warder said, thinking it was an excuse for postponing his execution, then perhaps canceling it altogether. And he felt glad: that imprecise, terrible moment, which he could not think about, retreated into the distance somewhere, becoming wildly improbable and unbelievable, like every death.

"When, when!" The warder was angry now, dim-witted, morose old man that he was. "It's not like hanging a dog, you know: off behind the barn with it, hup! and that's that. But that's how you'd like it to be, isn't it, you fool!"

"I don't want to be hanged!" said Yanson suddenly, his face wrinkling in a cheerful grin. "It was she who said I must be hanged, but I don't want to be!"

And perhaps for the first time in his life Yanson laughed: a rasping, absurd, but terribly joyful, gay laugh. It sounded like a goose cackling: ha-ha-ha! The warder looked at him in astonishment, then frowned sternly. This ridiculous gaiety on the part of a man who was to be executed was an affront to the prison and the execution itself and made them into something very odd. Suddenly, for a single moment, for the very shortest instant, the old warder, who had spent his whole life in the prison, acknowledging its rules as if they were laws of nature, felt that both the prison and all his life in it were a kind of madhouse, in which he himself, the warder, was the chief madman.

"Oh, to hell with you!" he spat in disgust. "What are you grinning for? You're not in an alehouse here, you know!"

"I don't want to be hanged—ha-ha-ha!" laughed Yanson.

"You're Satan himself!" said the warder, feeling the need to cross himself.

No one looked less like Satan than this man, with his small, flabby face, but in his gooselike cackling there was something that destroyed the sanctity and inviolability of the prison. He only had to laugh a little more, it seemed, and the walls would collapse with decay, the bars rusty with moisture would fall from the windows, and the warder himself would lead the prisoners out through the gates: "Please, gentlemen, do have a walk around town—but perhaps some of you might like a trip out into the country instead?" "You're Satan himself!"

But Yanson had already stopped laughing and just narrowed his eyes slyly.

"Well, you'll see!" said the warder in a vaguely threatening tone and walked away, glancing behind him as he did so.

All that evening Yanson was calm and even cheerful. He kept repeating to himself the words he had spoken earlier: "You mustn't hang me," and they were so convincing, so wise, so irrefutable, that it was not worth worrying about a thing. He had forgotten about his crime long ago and only regretted sometimes that he had not succeeded in raping the mistress. But he soon forgot about that, too.

Every morning he would ask when he was going to be hanged, and every morning the warder would reply angrily, "You've still got plenty of time, you Satan! Just you sit there and wait!" And he would walk quickly away, before Yanson had time to burst out laughing.

And because these words were repeated monotonously over and over again, and because every day began, went by, and came to an end just like the most ordinary of days, Yanson finally became convinced that there would be no execution at all. He very soon began to forget about the trial and lay about on his bunk for days on end, dreaming dimly of the dismal, snow-covered fields with their little mounds, of the refreshment room at the station, and of something else that was more distant and bright. He was well fed in prison and very quickly, in just a few days, put on weight and began to give himself airs.

"She'd like me now all right," he once thought, remembering the mistress. "Now I'm a stout fellow, just as good as the master!"

The only thing was that he felt very much like having a drink of vodka, then racing off on the little horse as fast as she could go.

When the terrorists were arrested, the news reached the prison, and one day to Yanson's usual question the warder suddenly gave the unexpected, strange answer, "It'll not be long now."

He looked calmly at Yanson and said meaningfully, "It'll not be long now. About a week, I'd say."

Yanson turned pale and, as if nodding off to sleep, asked with a glassy look in his lackluster eyes, "Are you joking?"

"First you couldn't wait, and now you say I'm joking! We don't joke here. You might like joking, but we don't," said the warder with dignity, and walked away.

Already by the evening of that day Yanson had grown thin. His taut skin, which had been smooth for a while, suddenly puckered into a multitude of little wrinkles and in places even seemed to hang down. His eyes had become completely sleepy, and all his movements had grown very slow and sluggish, as if every turn of his head, movement of his fingers, or step of his foot was an immensely complicated, cumbersome undertaking that had to be considered for a very long time beforehand. That night he lay on his bunk but did not shut his eyes, and though he was sleepy, they remained open until morning.

"Aha!" said the warder with pleasure on seeing him the next day. "You're not in an alehouse here, my lad!"

With the agreeable sense of satisfaction felt by a scientist whose experiment has succeeded yet again, he examined the condemned man attentively and in detail from head to foot. Now everything would proceed as it should. Satan was shamed, the sanctity of prison and execution restored; and with condescension and even genuine pity for Yanson, the old man inquired, "Will you be seeing anyone or not?"

"Why should I see anyone?"

"Well, to say good-bye. Your mother, for instance, or your brother."

"You mustn't hang me," said Yanson quietly, and shot the warder a sidelong glance. "I don't want to be hanged."

The warder looked at him and silently waved his hand in a gesture of hopelessness.

By evening Yanson was a little more calm. The day had been such an ordinary day; the cloudy winter sky had shone in such an ordinary way; footsteps and someone's businesslike conversation had sounded so ordinary out in the corridor; and the cabbage soup made of sauerkraut had smelled so ordinary, natural, and usual—that again he stopped believing in the execution. But by nightfall he was terrified. Formerly he had regarded the night simply as darkness, as a particularly dark time when one had to sleep, but now he felt its mysterious, menacing essence. So as not to believe in death, he had to see and hear ordinary things around him: footsteps, voices, light, and sauerkraut soup, but now everything was unusual, and the silence and darkness themselves already seemed like death.

The longer the night dragged on, the more terrifying it became. With the naiveté of a savage or a child, who thinks everything is possible, Yanson wanted to shout to the sun: shine! and he begged, he implored the sun to shine, but the night steadily dragged her dark hours over the earth, and no force possessed the power to halt her movement. This impossibility, becoming clearly apparent to Yanson's feeble mind for the first time in his life, filled him with terror. Still not daring to perceive it clearly, he now sensed the inevitability of approaching death and, numb with horror, already mounted the first step of the scaffold.

The day reassured him, then the night frightened him again, and so it went on till the night, when he both sensed and realized that death was inevitable and would come in three days' time, at dawn, as the sun was rising.

He had never thought about what death was, and for him it possessed no form; but now he clearly felt it, saw it, and sensed that it had come into his cell and was searching for him. To escape from it, he began to run about the room.

But the cell was so small that it seemed to have not sharp but blunt corners, and they all pushed him back into the middle. And there was nothing to hide behind. And the door was locked. And the cell was light. He collided silently with the walls several times and once banged against the door with a muffled, hollow sound. He ran into something and fell flat on his face, then felt death seize him. Lying on his belly and clinging to the floor, he buried his face in the dark, grimy asphalt and screamed in terror. He lay there yelling at the top of his voice till someone came. Even when they had lifted him from the floor, sat him on his bunk, and poured cold water over his head, Yanson still could not bring himself to open his tightly shut eyes. He would open one a fraction, catch sight of a bright, empty corner of the cell or someone's boot in the wide expanse of the floor, and start shouting again.

But the cold water began to take effect. Things were also helped by the fact that the duty warder, still the same old man as before, hit Yanson across the head a few times by way of a remedy. This sensation of being alive really did drive death away, and Yanson opened his eyes and slept the rest of the night soundly, though with a thick head. He lay on his back with his mouth open, snoring in loud, quavering tones, and between his half-open eyelids, one flat, dead eye gleamed white, its pupil invisible.

From then on everything in the world—night and day, footsteps, voices, and cabbage soup—became sheer horror to him, plunging him into a strange state of incomparable stupefaction. His feeble mind could not connect these two notions that were so monstrously contradictory: the ordinary daylight and the smell and taste of cabbage soup that went with it, and the knowledge that in two days, or perhaps only one day, he must die. He did not think or even count the hours but simply stood in mute horror before this contradiction that tore his brain in two. He turned an even, pale color that was neither red nor white, and appeared calm. But he ate nothing and stopped sleeping altogether: he either sat on his stool all night with his legs drawn up fearfully under him or walked quietly and stealthily around the cell, looking drowsily around him. His mouth was half open the whole time, as if in continual, immense astonishment, and before picking up the most commonplace object, he would examine it vacantly for a long time, then pick it up with mistrust.

Once he had become like this, both the warders and the guard who watched him through the peephole ceased to pay any attention to him. His state was normal for the condemned and, in the opinion of the warder, who had never experienced it, it resembled the condition of a beast at the slaughter, when it is stunned by a blow with an ax butt on the forehead.

"He's dazed now and won't feel a thing right till he dies," said the warder, scrutinizing him with practiced eyes. "Ivan, d'you hear me? Eh, Ivan?"

"You mustn't hang me," answered Yanson in a flat voice, and his lower jaw dropped once more.

"But you shouldn't have killed anybody; then they wouldn't be hanging you," said the chief warder in a didactic tone. Though still a young man, he was very imposing, with decorations on his chest. "But you went and killed someone, and now you don't want to be hanged for it.

"You took it into your head to kill a man for nothing at all. You're stupid, very stupid, but you're a crafty devil as well!"

"I don't want to be hanged," said Yanson.

"All right, my friend; so you don't, but that's your business," said the chief warder indifferently. "Instead of talking nonsense, you'd do better to get your things in order—you must have something, after all."

"He hasn't got anything. Just a shirt and some trousers. Oh, and a fur hat too, the dandy!"

So the time passed until Thursday. On Thursday, at midnight, a lot of people came into Yanson's cell, and a gentleman with shoulder straps said: "Come on, get ready! It's time to go."

Still moving just as slowly and sluggishly as he always did, Yanson put on all the clothes he possessed and tied the dirty-red scarf around his neck. Watching him dress, the gentleman with shoulder straps said to someone as he smoked his cigarette: "How warm it is today! Just like spring!"

Yanson could hardly keep his eyes open and was nodding off, moving so slowly and with such difficulty that the warder shouted at him: "Come on, come on; get a move on! You're half asleep!"

Suddenly Yanson stopped. "I don't want to be hanged," he said limply.

They took him by the arms and led him out, and he stepped forward obediently, squaring his shoulders. Outside he immediately felt a breath of moist spring air, and a wet patch appeared under his nose. Even though it was night, it was thawing more quickly still, and with a ringing sound, merry drops of water fell steadily onto the paving stones. As he waited for the policemen to climb into the unlit black carriage, rattling their swords and stooping as they did so, Yanson idly wiped his wet nose with his finger and adjusted his badly tied scarf.

IV
Us Folk from Orel

During the same session the district military court that had tried Yanson sentenced to death by hanging a peasant from the Elets district of Orel Province, one Mikhail Golubets, nicknamed Mishka the Gypsy, alias the Tatar. His most recent crime, one with precise evidence to prove it, was armed robbery and a triple murder, but before that, his shadowy past was wrapped deep in mystery. There were vague rumors that he had taken part in a whole series of other robberies and murders, and one sensed that the years gone by were full of bloodshed and somber, drunken revelry. With complete frankness and total sincerity, he called himself a robber and referred ironically to those who fashionably styled themselves as "expropriators." He spoke readily and in detail of his last crime, since denying it had gotten him nowhere, but to questions about his past, he only grinned and whistled softly, "Try to find the wind in the fields!"

But when people badgered him with questions, the Gypsy assumed a dignified, serious air. "All us folk from Orel, we're all hotheads," he would say soberly and gravely. "Orel and Kromy, they

2 6 5

say—that's where the best thieves live. Karachev and Livny—they're marvelous for thieves, too. But as for Elets, it's father to all the thieves on earth. There's no doubt about it!"

He was nicknamed the Gypsy because of his looks and his thievish tricks. He was extraordinarily black haired and lean, with yellow patches of burnt skin on his prominent Tatar cheekbones. He rolled the whites of his eyes like a horse and was forever hurrying somewhere. His glance was swift but terrifyingly direct and full of curiosity, and the thing on which it rested seemed to lose something, surrendering part of itself to him and becoming something else. The cigarette he had glanced at was just as difficult and unpleasant to smoke as if it had already been in someone else's mouth. Some perpetually irrepressible force lived within him, first twisting him up like a tightly coiled braid of hair, then flinging him out like a broad sheaf of swirling sparks. And he drank water almost by the bucketful, just like a horse.

To every question at his trial, he leapt up and replied briefly and firmly, apparently even with pleasure, "Correct!"

Sometimes he would emphasize the word: *"Correct!"*

Then quite unexpectedly, when the questions concerned something else, he sprang up and asked the president of the court, "Allow me to whistle!"

"Why do you wish to do that?" asked the judge in astonishment.

"The witnesses say that's how I signaled to my friends, so I'll show you how I did it. It's very interesting, you know."

Rather at a loss, the president agreed. The Gypsy quickly put four fingers in his mouth, two from each hand, rolled his eyes ferociously—and the still air of the courtroom was rent by a real, wild, robber's whistle that deafens horses, makes them twitch their ears and rear, and turns men pale despite themselves. The savage joy of the killer, the mortal anguish of the slain, the sinister shout of warning, the wild cry for help, the darkness of a foul autumn night, and the sound of empty solitude—all this was in that piercing shriek, which seemed to belong to neither man nor beast.

The presiding judge shouted something, then waved his hand at the Gypsy, and the robber obediently fell silent. Like a singer who has triumphantly performed a difficult but always-successful aria, the Gypsy sat down, wiped his wet fingers on his prison smock, and surveyed those present with a self-satisfied expression.

"There's a robber for you!" said one of the judges, rubbing his ear.

But another, with a broad, Russian beard and Tatar eyes like the Gypsy's, gazed somewhere over the thief's head, smiled, and said, "But it really is interesting, you know!"

And with peace in their hearts, without pity or the slightest pang of remorse, the judges sentenced the Gypsy to death.

"Correct!" he said when the sentence was read out. "A good gallows in an open field. Correct!" And turning to the soldier escorting him, he flung out with bravado: "Well let's go, shall we, you ugly devil. And hold on tight to your gun or I'll take it away!"

The soldier glanced at him sternly and warily, caught his fellow escort's eye, and fingered the bolt on his rifle. His companion did the same. And all the way to the prison, the soldiers felt as if they were not walking on the ground but flying through the air. So preoccupied were they by their prisoner that they were unaware of the earth beneath their feet, the time, and their own selves.

Like Yanson, Mishka the Gypsy had to spend seventeen days in prison before his execution. All seventeen days flew by as quickly for him as one, filled as they were with the single, undying thought of escape, freedom, and life. The irresistible force that had hitherto possessed him but was now cramped by the walls, bars, and blind window of his cell channeled all its fury inward and set his mind ablaze, as when a live coal is flung down on a wooden floor. As if in a drunken frenzy, vivid but incomplete images swarmed, collided, and mingled in his head, whirling by in an irrepressible, blinding blizzard, and all were directed toward one thing—escape, freedom, and life. Flaring his nostrils like a horse, the Gypsy would sniff the air for hours on end and imagine he could smell hemp and the pale, pungent smoke of a fire. Then he would spin round his cell like a top, quickly feeling the walls, tapping them with his fingers, planning how to escape, piercing the ceiling with his gaze, and sawing through the bars in his mind's eye. His indefatigability had exhausted the soldier watching him through the peephole, and several times now, in desperation, he had threatened to fire. The Gypsy would make some coarse, derisive retort, and things only ended peaceably because the wrangling between them soon turned into a torrent of ordinary, harmless peasant abuse, amid which talk of shooting seemed impossible and absurd.

At night the Gypsy slept soundly and almost did not stir, lying motionless but alive, just like a temporarily inactive spring. But as soon as he leapt to his feet, he began to circle round and round his cell, feeling the walls and thinking. His hands were constantly hot and dry, but his heart was sometimes filled with sudden cold, just as if a lump of solid ice had been placed in his breast and was sending a slight, chill shiver through his whole body. At these moments the already swarthy Gypsy turned darker still, becoming the dark bluish color of cast iron. He acquired a strange habit: as if he had eaten too much of something that was excessively and unbearably sweet, he kept licking his lips constantly, smacking them and, with a hissing sound, spitting out through his teeth the saliva that constantly filled his mouth. And he could not finish what he was saying; his thoughts were moving so fast that his tongue could not keep up with them.

One afternoon the chief warder came into his cell accompanied by an escort. He looked askance at the floor bespattered with saliva and said gloomily; "Look how filthy you've made it in here!"

The Gypsy retorted swiftly, "You've covered the whole world with filth, you swine, but I haven't said anything to you! What have you come crawling in here for?"

In the same gloomy voice the warder offered him the job of hangman.

"So you can't find anyone, eh? That's smart! Here you are, he says, go and do a bit of hanging, ha-ha! There's necks and ropes all right, but nobody to do the hanging. That's smart; it really is!"

"It'll mean you'll stay alive though."

"I should think so, too! I won't be doing any hanging for you if I'm dead, will I? That's a good one, you fool!"

"What do you say, then? Take it or leave it: yes or no."

"And how do they hang folks here? I bet they strangle 'em on the sly!"

"No, they do it to music," snapped the warder.

"Well, you're a fool all right! Of course you've got to have music! Like this!" And he broke into a rollicking song.

"You've gone right off your head, old fellow," said the warder. "So what do you say, then? Talk sense."

Baring his teeth, the Gypsy grinned: "You're in a hurry! Come back later and I'll tell you."

Into the chaos of vivid but incomplete images overwhelming the Gypsy with their racing torrent, there came bursting a new one: how grand it would be to be the hangman in his red shirt! He vividly imagined the high gallows and the square filled to overflowing with people and how he, the Gypsy, would walk about on the scaffold in his red shirt, carrying his little ax. The sun shines on the heads of the crowd and sparkles merrily on the ax, and everything is so luxuriant and gay that even the man who is about to have his head cut off is smiling too. Beyond the crowd can be seen carts and the muzzles of horses—peasants have driven in from the countryside—and further away still can be seen open fields.

"Ts-akh!" The Gypsy licked his lips, smacked them, and spat out the saliva filling his mouth.

Suddenly it was as if someone had pulled a fur cap over his face and right down over his mouth: everything became dark and airless, and his heart was a lump of solid ice sending a slight, chill shiver through his whole body.

The warder came once or twice more, and each time the Gypsy

said, baring his teeth in a grin: "You're in a hurry! Come back later."

In the end the warder shouted through the peephole in passing: "You've missed your chance, jailbird! They've got somebody else!"

"Oh, to hell with you; do your own hanging," barked the Gypsy. And he stopped dreaming about being a hangman.

But toward the end, the closer the execution came, the racing torrent of broken images became too swift for him to bear. He wanted to stop, plant his feet wide apart, and come to a halt, but the whirling torrent swept him on and there was nothing to grasp hold of: everything was afloat around him. His sleep had already become fitful. New visions appeared, as distinct and weighty as painted wooden blocks, racing by even more swiftly than his thoughts. It was no longer a torrent but an endless cascade hurtling down from a mountain so high that it had no summit—a wildly spinning flight through all the colors in the world. Before his arrest the Gypsy had only sported a rather dandyish mustache, but in prison he had grown a short, black, bristly beard, and it gave him a terrifying, mad look. At times he really did go out of his mind and circled quite senselessly round and round his cell, though he still went on feeling the rough, plastered walls. And he drank water like a horse.

One day toward evening, when the lights had been turned on, the Gypsy got down on all fours in the middle of his cell and began to howl, making the trembling cry of a wolf. He did this particularly earnestly, howling as if carrying out some important and necessary task. He filled his chest with air, then slowly expelled it in a long, quavering howl, narrowing his eyes and listening attentively to the sound he made. The very way his voice shook seemed rather contrived, and he did not howl at random but carefully sounded every note in that wild beast's cry that is so full of unspeakable terror and sorrow.

Then all at once he cut short the howl and without getting up remained silent for a few minutes. Suddenly he began to mutter softly into the floor: "Good friends, dear friends . . . Good friends, dear friends, have pity . . . Good friends! . . . Dear friends! . . ."

And again he seemed to listen to what his words sounded like. He would say a word, then listen.

Then he leapt up and without pausing for breath swore foully for a whole hour.

"Oh, you bastards, to hell with y-y-y-you!" he yelled, rolling his bloodshot eyes wildly. "If I must be hanged, then hang me, instead of . . . Oh, you bastards . . ."

White as a sheet and weeping with anguish and terror, the guard banged on the door with the muzzle of his gun and shouted helplessly: "I'll fire! D'you hear me? I tell you, I'll fire!"

But he did not dare fire; unless there was a real revolt, they never fired on prisoners who were sentenced to death. And the Gypsy ground his teeth, cursed, and spat. Poised on the extremely fine dividing line between life and death, his mind was crumbling like a lump of dry, weathered clay.

When at night they came to his cell to take him to execution, the Gypsy began to bustle about and seemed to revive. The taste in his mouth had become sweeter still, and his saliva streamed down in uncontrollable amounts, but his cheeks had turned faintly pink, and his eyes sparkled with their former, rather fierce slyness. As he was dressing, he asked one of the officials: "Who's doing the hanging, then? The new fellow? He can't be very good at it yet, can he?"

"There's no need to worry about that," replied the official drily.

"But why shouldn't I worry, Your Honor? It's me who's being hanged, you know, not you. Just don't be sparing with that prison soap on the old slipknot!"

"All right, all right, be quiet, please."

"It's him there who's used all your soap up," said the Gypsy, pointing to the warder; "just look how that mug of his shines!"

"Be quiet!"

"Well, don't be sparing with it!"

The Gypsy began to laugh, but the taste in his mouth was growing sweeter and sweeter. Then his legs suddenly began to go strangely numb. All the same, as they went out into the courtyard, he managed to shout, "Carriage for the count of Bengal!"

V
Kiss Him—and Keep Quiet

The sentence on the five terrorists was pronounced in its final form and confirmed the same day. The condemned were not informed when the execution would be, but from the way things were usually done, they knew they would be hanged that same night or, at the very latest, the following night. When they were offered the opportunity of seeing their relatives the next day (that was on Thursday), they realized the execution would be on Friday at dawn.

Tanya Kovalchuk had no close relatives, and what relatives she had were out in the wilds somewhere in the Ukraine and hardly knew about her trial and impending execution. Since Musya and Werner had refused to reveal their identities, they could not see any relatives at all; so only two of the condemned, Sergei Golovin and Vasily Kashirin, were to see their families. Both thought of this meeting with anguish and horror but could not bring themselves to deny their parents a few last words, a last kiss.

Sergei Golovin was particularly worried at the prospect of this meeting. He was very fond of his mother and father, had seen them only a short while ago, and was horrified now at the thought of what the meeting would be like. The execution itself, in all its monstrous singularity, its mind-shattering insanity, was easier to imagine and did not seem as terrible as these few brief, incomprehensible minutes that existed, as it were, outside time, outside life itself. How could he look, what should he think, what should he say? His brain refused to tell him. The most simple and ordinary gesture—taking them by the hand, kissing them, and saying, "Hello, Father"—seemed utterly frightful in its appallingly inhuman, insane falsity.

After sentence had been passed, the condemned were not imprisoned together as Tanya had expected but were each left in solitary confinement. Sergei Golovin spent the whole morning until eleven, when his parents came, furiously pacing his cell, tugging at his beard, screwing up his face pitifully, and muttering something. Occasionally he would stop his pacing, fill his lungs with air, then blow it out like someone who has been under water too long. But he was so full of vigorously youthful life that even at these moments of cruelest suffering, the blood coursed beneath his skin, coloring his cheeks, and his eyes were a bright, innocent blue.

However, everything went much better than he had expected.

The first to enter the room where the meeting took place was his father, Nikolai Sergeyevich Golovin, a retired colonel. Everything about him was white—his face, beard, hair, and hands, as if a snowman had been dressed in human clothes. He was wearing the same little frock coat he always wore, old but well cleaned, with brand-new, crisscrossed shoulder straps and smelling of benzine. He came into the room firmly, as if on parade, his steps brisk and precise, and stretching out his dry, white hand said loudly, "Hello, Sergei!"

Behind him came his mother with her short steps and a strange smile on her face. But she shook his hand, too, and repeated loudly, "Hello, Sergei!"

She kissed him on the lips and sat down without a word. She did not fling herself on his neck, burst into tears, cry out, or do anything terrible as Sergei had expected—she just kissed him and sat down without a word. And she even smoothed her black silk dress with shaking hands.

Sergei did not know that the colonel had spent all the previous night shut away in his little study pondering this ritual with every ounce of strength he possessed. "We must not burden our son's last minutes but make them easier for him," he had resolved, and carefully weighed every possible word, every gesture of the conversation the next day. But sometimes he became confused, forgetting what he had managed to prepare, and wept bitterly on a corner of the oilcloth sofa. But in the morning he had explained to his wife how they should behave during the meeting.

"The main thing is to kiss him—and keep quiet!" he instructed her. "You'll be able to talk later, after a short while, but when you've kissed him, keep quiet. Don't start talking straight after you've kissed him, d'you understand? Or you'll say the wrong thing."

"I understand, Nikolai Sergeyevich," replied the mother, weeping.

"And don't cry. God forbid that you should cry! You'll kill him if you do!"

But why are you crying yourself?"

"Looking at you makes me cry! You mustn't cry, d'you hear?"

"All right, Nikolai Sergeyevich."

In the cab he meant to repeat his instructions once more but forgot. And so, on they rode in silence, both of them bent, old, and gray, thinking their thoughts while the city bustled gaily around them. It was Shrovetide, and the streets were noisy and crowded.

They sat down. The colonel adopted his prepared pose, his right hand behind the lapel of his frock coat. Sergei sat still for a moment, then saw his mother's lined face close beside him and sprang to his feet.

"Sit down, Sergei," begged his mother.

"Sit down, Sergei," said his father, echoing his wife.

No one spoke for a while. The mother was smiling strangely.

"How we've pleaded for you, Sergei!"

"It's no use, Mother . . ."

"We had to try, Sergei, so you wouldn't think your parents had deserted you."

Again no one spoke for a while. It was terrible to utter a word, as if every word in the Russian language had lost its proper meaning and now meant only one thing: death. Sergei looked at his father's clean little frock coat that smelled of benzine and thought: "He's got no orderly these days; so he has to clean it himself. How on earth is it I never noticed him cleaning that coat before? He must do it in the mornings." And suddenly he asked, "How's my sister? Is she well?"

"Ninochka doesn't know a thing about this," replied his mother hastily.

But the colonel stopped her sternly: "Why lie about it? The girl's read the papers! Sergei must know that all . . . his loved ones . . . were thinking and . . ."

He could not go on and stopped. Suddenly, all at once, the mother's face crumpled, quivered, and broke, becoming wild and wet with tears. Her pale eyes stared madly, and her breathing grew more and more loud and rapid.

"Se—Ser—Se—Se—" she said again and again, without moving her lips. "Se—"

"Mother!"

The colonel stepped forward, shaking all over with every fold of his coat and every wrinkle on his face. Without realizing how dreadful he looked himself with his deathly pallor, he said to his wife with desperate, forced firmness: "Keep quiet! Don't torment him! Don't! Don't! He's got to die! Don't!"

Frightened, she had already fallen silent, but he still kept on shaking his clenched fists in a restrained way close to his chest and saying again and again, "Don't torment him!"

Then he stepped back, put one trembling hand behind the lapel of his coat, and, with an expression of forced calm, asked loudly with white lips, "When?"

"Tomorrow morning," replied Sergei, his own lips equally white.

The mother was looking down, biting her lips, and apparently did not hear what was said. And still biting her lips, she uttered the strange, simple words, "Ninochka sends her love, Sergei."

"Give her mine," said Sergei.

"I will. And the Khvostovs send their regards."

"What Khvostovs? Oh, yes!"

The colonel interrupted: "Well, we must go. Get up, Mother, it's time!"

Together the two men lifted the mother, who was weak with sorrow.

"Say good-bye!" ordered the colonel. "Give him your blessing."

She did everything she was told. But as she made the sign of the cross over her son and kissed him with a brief kiss, she shook her head and said senselessly over and over again: "No, that's wrong. No, it's wrong. No, no. What shall I say afterward? What shall I say? No, it's wrong."

"Good-bye, Sergei!" said the father.

They shook hands and kissed briefly but firmly.

"You . . ." Sergei began.

"Well?" asked the father abruptly.

"No, that's wrong. No, no. What shall I say?" said the mother again, shaking her head. She had already managed to sit down again, and the whole of her was rocking to and fro.

"You . . ." Sergei began again.

Suddenly his face crumpled up pitifully like a child's, and his eyes immediately filled with tears. Through their sparkling film, he saw his father's white face close before him with tear-filled eyes just like his own.

"You're a fine man, Father."

"What? What?" said the colonel, startled.

And suddenly, as if collapsing, he fell with his head on his son's shoulder. Once he had been taller than Sergei, but now he had grown shorter, and his soft, dry head lay on his son's shoulder like a small, white bundle. Each avidly kissed the other without saying a word: Sergei, his father's soft, white hair; and the father, his son's prison smock.

"And what about me?" said a loud voice suddenly.

They looked around: the mother stood there with her head flung back, watching them with anger and almost with hatred.

"What did you say, Mother?" shouted the colonel.

"What about me?" she said in an insane voice, tossing her head. "You're kissing each other, but what about me? The men can do it, can they? Well what about me? What about me?"

"Mother!" Sergei threw himself into her arms.

What happened then is something one cannot and should not tell.

The colonel's last words were: "I give you my blessing for your death, Sergei. Die bravely, like an officer."

They left. Somehow they left. One moment they were there, standing and talking, then suddenly they were gone. The mother was sitting here, the father standing there, then suddenly they were gone. Returning to his cell, Sergei lay down on his bunk with his face to the wall so the guards could not see him and wept for a long time. Then, exhausted by weeping, he fell fast asleep.

Only his mother came to see Vasily Kashirin—his father, a wealthy merchant, had not wanted to come. When the old woman came in, Vasily was pacing up and down and shivering with cold, though it was warm and even hot in the room. Their conversation was brief and painful.

"You shouldn't have come, Mother, You'll only torment both yourself and me."

"Why did you do it, Vasya? Why did you do it? My God!"

The old woman burst into tears, wiping her eyes with the ends of her black woolen shawl.

Accustomed like his brothers to shouting at his mother because she was a simple woman, he stopped and, shaking with cold, said angrily: "There we are! I knew it! You don't understand a thing, Mother! Not a thing!"

"Well, all right, all right. What's wrong—are you cold?"

"Yes—" snapped Vasily, and he began pacing the room again, looking at his mother angrily and askance.

"Have you caught a cold, perhaps?"

"Oh, mother, what have colds got to do with it when . . . ."

And he waved his hand in a gesture of despair. The old woman meant to say, "Your dad's been telling me to make some pancakes since last Monday," but she took fright and began to wail:

"I says to him: he's your son after all, you know, so go and give him your blessing. But oh, no, he dug his heels in, the old devil . . ."

"Well, to hell with him! What kind of a father is he to me? He's been a bastard all his life, and he's still one now!"

"Vasya, how can you say that about your own father?" The old woman drew herself up in reproach.

"I can."

"About your own father!"

"A fine father he is to me!"

It was ridiculous and absurd. Ahead of him lay death, while here something petty, futile, and useless had arisen, and the words cracked like empty nutshells underfoot. Almost weeping with anguish at the perpetual lack of understanding that had stood like a wall between him and his family all his life and that now, in the last few hours before death, had appeared again in all its terrible absurdity, Vasily shouted: "But don't you see, I'm going to be hanged! Hanged! Do you understand or don't you? Hanged!"

"But you shouldn't have harmed anybody; then they wouldn't have . . ." shouted the old woman.

"My God! What is this? Even wild animals don't do this! Am I your son or aren't I?"

He began to weep and sat down in the corner. The old woman began to weep in her corner, too. Incapable, even for a moment, of coming together in a feeling of mutual love and setting it against the horror of imminent death, both wept the chill tears of loneliness that fail to warm the heart.

The mother said, "You say I'm not a mother to you; you reproach me. But I've gone really gray these past few days; I've turned into an old woman! And you say things like that and reproach me!"

"All right, all right, Mother. I'm sorry. Now it's time for you to go. Give my brothers my love."

"Aren't I your mother? Don't I feel sorry for you?"

Finally she went away. Weeping bitterly and wiping her eyes with the ends of her shawl, she could not see which way she was going. The farther she went from the prison, the more bitterly she wept. She retraced her steps, then, absurdly, lost her way in the city where she was born, had grown up and grown old. She wandered into a deserted little park with a few old, broken trees in it and sat down on a wet bench where the snow had thawed. And all of a sudden she realized that tomorrow he would be hanged.

The old woman sprang to her feet and tried to run, but her head suddenly began to swim, and she fell down. The icy path was wet and slippery, and she could not get up at all: turning round and round, she raised herself on her elbows and knees but then fell over on her side again. Her black shawl had slipped to reveal a bald patch amid the dirty gray hair on the back of her head, and for some reason she imagined that she was at a wedding feast: her son was getting married, she had drunk some wine, and now she was very tipsy.

"I can't. Really, I can't, I swear it!" she said, shaking her head and refusing more wine, and crawled over the icy, wet snow. But still they kept pouring her more wine, pouring and pouring.

Already her heart was beginning to ache with the drunken laughter, the food and drink, and the wild dancing—but still they kept on pouring her more wine. Pouring and pouring.

VI
The Hours Fly

In the prison where the condemned terrorists were held, there was a steeple with an old clock. Every hour, every half hour, every quarter hour rang out with a slow, mournful sound that gradually died away high above, like the distant, plaintive cry of birds of passage. During the day this strange, sad music was lost amid the noise of the city and drowned by the hubbub of the big, crowded street that ran past the prison. Trams went rumbling by, horses' hooves clopped on the roadway, and swaying automobiles blared far ahead. Many peasant cabbies had come into the city from the surrounding districts specially for Shrovetide, and the little bells on the necks of their small horses filled the air with tinkling. There was the sound of voices, too—the gay, slightly tipsy voices heard at Shrovetide—and in perfect harmony with all these very different sounds were the young spring thaw, the muddy puddles on the pavements, and the trees in the public gardens that had suddenly turned dark. A warm wind blew off the sea, its gusts sweeping and humid, and it was as if one could see with the naked eye the minute, cool particles of air whirling away together in friendly flight, into the boundlessly free expanse of distance, laughing as they went.

At night the street grew quiet, flooded with the cheerless brilliance of its big electric lamps. And then the immense prison, without a single light in its sheer walls, was sunk in silence and darkness, separated from the perpetually busy city by a barrier of silence, immobility, and gloom. Then the striking of the clock became audible—the slow, mournful birth and death of a strange melody alien to this earth. Again it was born, and deceiving the ear, it rang out softly and plaintively, suddenly stopped, then rang once more. Like great, limpid drops of glass, the hours and minutes seemed to fall from an unknown height into a bowl that was ringing softly. Or it sounded like the cry of birds of passage.

Day and night this sound alone was heard in the cells where each of the condemned sat in solitude. Through the roof, through the thick stone walls it came, making the silence quiver, then retreated imperceptibly, only to return just as imperceptibly once more. Sometimes they forgot about it and did not hear it; sometimes they waited for it with despair, living from one stroke to the next, no longer trusting the silence. This prison was reserved for important criminals, and it had its own special rules—strict, harsh, and rigid like a corner of the prison wall itself. If there is nobility in harshness, then the profound, dead, solemnly mute silence in which every rustle and breath could be heard—that was noble.

In this solemn silence, broken only by the sad sound of the minutes ebbing away, five people—three men and two women cut off from every living thing—waited for nightfall, dawn, and execution, and each prepared for it in his own way.

VII
There Is No Death

Just as throughout her life Tanya Kovalchuk had thought only of others and never of herself; so, even now, she worried only about the rest and felt profound anguish for them. She imagined death insofar as it was something agonizing that was imminent for Sergei, Musya, and the others, but as for herself, it seemed not to concern her in the slightest.

As though recompensing herself for the control she had shown at the trial, she wept for hours on end as only old women who have known much sorrow or young, compassionate, good people can weep. The idea that Sergei might not have any tobacco or that Werner might perhaps be going without the strong tea he was used to—and all this added to the fact that they must die—tormented her no less perhaps than the thought of the execution itself. The execution was something inevitable and incidental that was not worth even thinking about, but if a man who was in prison—and what's more, awaiting execution—had no tobacco, then that was quite intolerable. She recalled and went over the fond details of their life together and felt weak with terror at the thought of Sergei's meeting with his parents.

She felt particularly sorry for Musya. For a long time now she had thought that Musya loved Werner, and though this was completely untrue, she still hoped fervently for something fine and joyous for them both. Before her arrest Musya had worn a little silver ring engraved with a skull and crossbones surrounded by a crown of thorns. Tanya would often look at that ring with a feeling of pain, seeing it as a symbol of doom, and half seriously, half jokingly would beg Musya to take it off.

"Give it to me," she implored her.

"No, Tanechka, I won't. Anyway, you'll soon have a different ring on your finger."

For some reason they all thought she was sure to get married before very long, and this offended her, for she had no wish for a husband whatsoever. Recalling her half-serious conversations with Musya and knowing that now she really was doomed, she choked with tears of motherly pity. Each time the clock struck, she lifted her tearstained face and listened, wondering how this long, insistent call of death was being received in the other cells.

But Musya was happy.

With her arms behind her back in the prison smock that was too big for her and made her look strangely like a man or a teenage boy dressed in someone else's clothes, she paced the cell with even, untiring strides. The sleeves of the smock were too long for her; so she had turned them back, and her thin, slender, almost childlike arms emerged from the wide sleeves like the stems of flowers protruding from the mouth of a crudely made, grimy jug. The coarse cloth irritated and chafed her slim, white neck, and from time to time, with a movement of both arms, she would free her throat and carefully feel with her finger the place where the chafed skin was red and smarting.

Back and forth she paced and, growing agitated and blushing, tried to justify herself to others. She justified herself by the thought that she, who was so young and insignificant, who had accomplished so little and who was not in the least like a heroine, would suffer the same honorable, beautiful death that real heroes and martyrs had suffered before her. With an unshakable faith in people's goodness, in their sympathy and love, she imagined how worried they felt about her now, how troubled and sorry they were—and she felt so ashamed that she blushed. It was as if by dying on the gallows she were committing some enormous blunder.

At their final meeting she had asked her defense lawyer to get her some poison but had suddenly thought: "What if he and the others think I'm doing it out of bravado or cowardice and, instead of dying humbly and inconspicuously, want to create more of a sensation?" And she had added hastily, "No, it's all right; you needn't."

Now she desired only one thing: to explain to people and prove clearly to them that she was not a heroine, that it was not in the least terrifying to die, and that they should not feel sorry for her or worry about her. She wanted to explain to them that she was not at all to blame for the fact that she, who was so young and insignificant, was suffering such a death and that so much fuss was being made over her.

Like someone who is actually being accused, Musya searched for excuses, trying to find something at least that would ennoble her sacrifice and lend it real value. She said to herself, "Of course, I'm very young and might have lived a long time yet, but . . ."

As a candle fades in the brilliance of the sunrise, so her youth and life seemed dim and pale beside the magnificent, resplendent halo that was to illumine her humble head. There was no excuse.

But perhaps that special feeling she had in her soul was infinite love, infinite readiness for heroism, infinite disregard for herself? After all, it was not really her fault that she had not been allowed to do all she could or wished—she had been slain on the threshold of the temple, at the foot of the sacrificial altar.

But if that were so, if a person were valuable not only for what he had done but also for what he had wanted to do, then—she was worthy of a martyr's crown.

"Am I really?" she thought with embarrassment. "Am I really worthy of that? Worthy enough that people should weep for me or worry about me when I am so small and insignificant?"

And she was filled with ineffable joy. There was no hesitation, no doubt, for she had been received into the bosom of her peers, she had stepped as if right into the ranks of those sacred souls who from time immemorial have passed through fire, torture, and execution to ascend to the heights of heaven. There they enjoy serene peace, rest, and boundless, quietly radiant happiness. It was as if she had already left this earth and were drawing near the mysterious sun of life and truth, soaring incorporeal in its light.

"And this is death! How can one call this death?" she thought blissfully.

If all the scholars, philosophers, and executioners in the world had gathered in her cell, laid their books, scalpels, axes, and nooses before her, and begun to prove that death exists, that men die and kill one another, that there is no immortality—they would only have astonished her. How could there be no immortality when she was now already immortal? And how could one speak of immortality, how could one speak of death, when she was already dead and immortal at this moment—alive in death, as she had been alive in life?

If they had carried a coffin into her cell with her own body decomposing in it and filling the room with its stench, and said, "Look! This is you!" she would have looked and answered:

"No, that's not me."

And if they had begun trying to convince her that it was she—she!—attempting to frighten her with the sinister sight of decay, she would have replied with a smile: "No. It's you who think that *this* is me, but *this* is not me. How can I, the woman you are talking to—how can I be *this?*"

"But you will die and become this."

"No, I shall not die."

"You will be executed. Here's the noose."

"I will be executed, but I shall not die. How can I die, when I am already immortal?"

And the scholars, philosophers, and executioners would have stepped back, saying with a shudder, "Do not set foot on this spot, for it is sacred."

What else did Musya think of? She thought of many things, since for her the thread of life was not broken by death but went on being calmly and evenly woven. She thought of her comrades, both those far away who felt pain and anguish at the imminent execution and those close at hand, who would mount the scaffold together. She was surprised at Vasily. Why was he so frightened? He had always been so brave and could even trifle with death. Last Tuesday morning, for example, when Vasily and she were strapping around their waists the explosive devices that in a few hours' time would blow them up, Tanya's hands had been shaking with agitation, and the others had been obliged to stop her helping them. But Vasily had joked and played the fool, spinning round and round and behaving so carelessly that Werner had said sternly, "You shouldn't take liberties with death."

So why was Vasily frightened now? But that incomprehensible fear of his was so alien to Musya's soul that she soon stopped thinking about it or seeking the reason for it. She suddenly felt a desperate urge to see Sergei and have a laugh with him about something. She thought for a little, then felt an even more desperate urge to see Werner and convince him of something. And imagining Werner was walking beside her with his precise, measured tread that drove his heels into the ground, Musya said to him:

"No, Werner, my dear, that's all nonsense, it doesn't matter a jot whether you killed X or not. You're clever, but it's just as if you're always playing that chess of yours: take one piece, then another, and the game's won. What matters here, Werner, is that we ourselves are prepared to die. Do you see? After all, what do these people think? They think there's nothing more terrible than death. They themselves have invented death; they're afraid of it themselves; so they try and frighten us with it. Now this is what I'd like to do: walk out by myself in front of a whole regiment of soldiers and start firing at them with a Browning. There'd be just one of me and thousands of them, and I mightn't kill a single one of them. But that's what matters—there are thousands of them. When thousands kill one, it means that the one is the victor. It's true, Werner, my dear."

But this, too, was so clear that she did not want to try and prove it any longer. Anyway, Werner probably understood now himself. Or perhaps her thoughts simply did not wish to dwell only on one thing—like a lightly soaring bird that can see boundless horizons and reach the whole expanse and profundity of the sky, all the joyously caressing, tender immensity of azure. The clock struck again and again, making the dead silence quiver. Into that harmonious, distantly beautiful sound flowed her own thoughts—they too beginning to ring—and the images slipping rhythmically through her mind themselves became music. Musya felt as if she were driving somewhere down a wide, smooth road on a still, dark night, with the soft springs of the carriage giving gently and the little harness bells jingling softly. All her anxiety and agitation had receded; her weary body had dissolved in the darkness, and in its joyous fatigue, her mind calmly brought forth vivid images, reveling in their bright colors and quiet peace. She recalled three friends of hers who had been hanged not long ago, and their faces were serene, joyful, and dear to her—dearer, even, than those of the living. So in the morning a man thinks with joy of his friend's house, which he will enter that evening to find a welcome on smiling faces.

Musya was very tired of walking up and down her cell. She lay down carefully for a while on her bunk and went on dreaming with her eyes barely closed. The clock struck again and again, making the mute silence quiver, and between the banks of its ringing sound, radiant, melodious images drifted gently by.

She thought to herself: "Is this really death? My God, how beautiful it is! Or is it life? I don't know, I don't know. I'll watch and listen."

For a long time now, ever since her first days in prison, her ears had been playing tricks on her. She was very musical, and her hearing had become more acute with the stillness. Against the backdrop of scant, fragmentary sounds coming from the reality around her—

the footsteps of guards in the corridor, the striking of the clock, the whisper of the wind on the iron roof, the creaking of a lantern— her ears created entire musical tableaux. At first she was afraid of them, driving them away as delusions of a sick mind, then she realized she was quite well and not ill at all and began to give herself to them quite calmly.

Now, suddenly and with total clarity, she caught the sound of martial music. She opened her eyes in astonishment and looked up— outside the window it was night and the clock was striking. "Again!" she thought calmly and closed her eyes. And as soon as she had closed them, the music began to play again. She could clearly hear soldiers—a whole regiment of them—coming around the corner of the building to the right and marching past her window. Their feet beat regular time on the frozen ground: left, right! left, right!, and she could even hear a leather boot squeaking occasionally and someone's foot suddenly slipping, then immediately righting itself again. The music came nearer: it was a completely unfamiliar but very loud, briskly festive march. There was evidently some special occasion in the prison tonight.

Now the band had drawn level with her window, and the whole cell was filled with cheerfully rhythmic yet discordant sound. One trumpet, a big brass one, was playing shrilly and badly out of tune, first lagging behind the others, then racing ahead in a ludicrous fashion. Musya could see the earnest expression of the little soldier playing it, and she laughed.

Everything moved away into the distance. The footsteps died away; left, right! left, right! From a distance the music was even more beautiful and gay. The trumpet shrieked once or twice more in its loud, brazen voice that was so happily out of tune, then everything faded away. Once again the clock rang out slowly and sadly from the steeple, making the silence quiver very slightly.

"They've gone!" thought Musya with sadness. She felt sorry for the departed sounds that were so funny and gay, sorry even for the departed soldiers, because those earnest men with their brass trumpets and squeaking boots were quite different from the ones she would have liked to fire at with her Browning.

"Well then, more!" she begged in a caressing voice. And now more images come. They bend over her, surround her in a transparent cloud, and lift her up to where the birds of passage are flying by and crying like heralds. To left and right, above and below, they cry like heralds. They call, announce and proclaim their flight far and wide. They spread their broad wings, and the darkness supports them as the light does, too; and on their chests, thrust out as they leave the air, the shining city gleams blue with light reflected from below. Musya's heart beats more and more steadily, and her breathing grows more and more calm and gentle. She is falling asleep. Her face looks tired and pale; there are dark shadows under her eyes, and her slender, girlish arms are so very thin, but there is a smile on her lips. Tomorrow, at sunrise, this human face will be distorted by an inhuman grimace, her brain will be flooded with thick blood, and her glazed eyes will start from their sockets—but today she sleeps quietly and smiles in her great immortality.

Musya has fallen asleep.

But in the prison, life goes on, a life of its own that is deaf yet quick to catch every sound, blind yet ever vigilant, like perpetual anxiety itself. There is the sound of footsteps somewhere. Whispering can be heard. A gun rattles. Someone gave a shout, it seems. But perhaps no one shouted at all—one only imagines it because of the stillness.

Now the grating in the door falls open without a sound, and a swarthy face with a big mustache appears in the dark opening. For a long time it stares at Musya in surprise, then disappears as soundlessly as it came.

The striking clock rings out its melody for an agonizingly long time. It is as if the weary hours are climbing a high mountain as the hands creep toward midnight, and the ascent grows more and more difficult and painful. They suddenly stop, slip, fall back with a groan, and crawl agonizingly on once more toward the dark summit.

There is the sound of footsteps somewhere. Whispering can be heard. And the horses are already being harnessed to the black carriages that bear no lights.

VIII
There Is Death and There Is Life

Sergei Golovin never thought about death, looking upon it as something incidental that did not concern him at all. He was a strong, healthy, cheerful young man, endowed with that calm, serene joie de vivre that makes any evil thought or feeling injurious to life rapidly disappear without trace in the organism. Just as any cuts, wounds, or stings he received healed quickly, so everything painful that injured his soul immediately rose to the surface and faded away. To every undertaking or even pastime—whether it was photography, cycling, or preparation for an act of terrorism—he would bring the same calm, cheerful earnestness: everything in life was gay, everything in life was important, and everything had to be done well.

He did everything well: he handled a sailing boat magnificently and was an excellent shot with a revolver; he was as steadfast in friendship as in love, and believed fanatically in one's "word of honor." His friends laughed at him, saying that if a detective, an agent, or a notorious spy gave him his word that he was not a spy, then Sergei would believe him and shake hands with him as a friend. He had just one failing: he was convinced that he had a good voice, whereas he had not the slightest ear for music, sang abominably, and was out of tune even in revolutionary songs; and he was offended when people laughed.

"Either you're all asses or I'm an ass," he would say in a serious, injured tone.

And after thinking for a moment, they all concluded in a tone that was just as serious as his, "It's you who's the ass; you can tell by your voice."

But as is sometimes the case with good people, they loved him perhaps even more for his failing than for all his good qualities.

So little did he fear death, so little did he think about it, that on the fateful morning of the planned assassination, before they left Tanya Kovalchuk's flat, only he ate a proper breakfast and enjoyed it: he drank two glasses of tea half diluted with milk and ate a whole five-kopeck loaf. Then he looked sadly at Werner's untouched bread and said: "Why aren't you eating? Go on, eat; you've got to keep your strength up."

"I don't feel like it."

"Well, I'll eat it then. All right?"

"You've certainly got a good appetite, Sergei."

Instead of replying, with his mouth full of bread, Sergei began to sing in a voice that was muffled and out of tune: " 'Cruel blizzards are blowing o'er our heads . . .' "

After his arrest Sergei began to feel sad; they had made a bad job of it and failed, but then he thought, "Now there's something else that must be done well—dying," and he cheered up. However strange it may seem, even from his second morning in prison, he had begun to do gymnastic exercises according to the unusually efficient system of a German called Müller that he was very keen on: he stripped naked, and to the amazement of the guard anxiously watching him, conscientiously performed all eighteen prescribed exercises. The fact that the guard was watching him and was evidently amazed by what he saw was gratifying for Sergei as a propagandist of the Müller system. Though he knew he would get no reply, he still said to the eye peering at him in astonishment through the peephole: "It does you good, old fellow; it gets your strength up. This is what they should start making you do in your regiment," he added in a loud but gently persuasive voice, so as not to frighten the guard, unaware that the soldier simply thought he was mad.

The fear of death began to manifest itself in him gradually, in fits and starts somehow: it was as if someone kept taking hold of him, and, with his fist, jolting his heart from below with all his might. It was pain he felt rather than fear. Then the sensation would fade, and a few hours later it would return, growing more and more prolonged and marked each time. It was already clearly beginning to assume the dim shape of immense, even intolerable, fear.

"Can I really be afraid?" he thought in astonishment. "What nonsense!"

It was not he who was afraid but his strong, young, vigorous body, which could not be deceived, either by Müller's gymnastics or by sponging down with cold water. And the stronger and fresher his body became after being rubbed down, the more unbearable was the momentary sensation of fear. Precisely at those moments when, before his arrest, he used to feel a particular upsurge of strength and joie de vivre—in the mornings, after a sound sleep followed by physical exercise—it was then that he felt this acute, seemingly alien fear. He noticed this and thought: "You're stupid, Sergei, old fellow! So it's easier for your body to die, you should make it weaker, not stronger. You're just stupid!"

And he gave up his gymnastics and cold sponge-downs. By way of explanation and justification he shouted to the guard: "Don't you worry about me giving it up! It's still a good method, my friend. Only it's no good for people who are going to be hanged. It's fine for everyone else, though!"

And in fact things seemed to get easier. He tried eating a little less, too, so as to grow even weaker, but despite the lack of fresh air and exercise, his appetite was still enormous and hard to satisfy, and he ate everything he was brought. Then he began to do this: before beginning his food he would tip half of it into the waste bucket. That seemed to help; a dull, sleepy lassitude took possession of him.

"I'll show you!" he said, threatening his body, but then ran his hand tenderly and sadly over his soft, flabby muscles.

But soon his body became accustomed to this regime, too, and the fear of death appeared once more—not as acute or as searing as before, it is true, but even more achingly wearisome, like nausea. "It's because they're taking a long time over it," he thought; "it would be better to spend all the time till the execution asleep," and he tried to sleep as much as possible. To begin with it worked well, but after a while, either because he slept too much or for some other reason, he began to suffer from insomnia. With it came painful, vigilantly wakeful thoughts, and with them a longing to live.

"Am I really afraid of it, damn it?" he asked himself, thinking of death. "It's losing my life I regret. It's a magnificent thing, whatever the pessimists say. What would a pessimist say if he were being hanged? Oh, I feel sorry about losing my life, very sorry. And why's my beard grown since I've been in prison? It wouldn't grow for ages, and now suddenly it has. But why?"

He shook his head sadly and heaved a few long, heavy sighs. A silence—then a long, deep sigh; another brief silence—then again, an even longer, heavier sigh.

So it went on till the trial and the terrible last meeting with his old folk. When he woke in his cell with the clear realization that life for him was over and that before him were only a few hours of empty waiting and death, he felt strange. It was as if he had been stripped completely naked, stripped in an unusual way—not only had they taken off his clothes but had also snatched sun and air from him, together with noise and light, actions, and the power of speech. There was no death yet, but there was no longer any life, either. There was something new and staggeringly incomprehensible, though, something half devoid of all meaning yet half possessing meaning, but it was so profound, mysterious, and superhuman that it was impossible to discover it.

"My God!" said Sergei in agonized amazement. "What is all this? And where am I? I . . . what I?"

He examined the whole of himself attentively and with interest, beginning with his big prisoner's shoes and ending with his belly, which protruded in his prisoner's smock. With his arms spread wide, he walked up and down the cell, continuing to examine himself, like a woman in a new dress that is too long for her. He turned his head around and around and found that it did in fact turn. And this thing that for some reason was rather frightening was himself, Sergei Golovin, and soon it would no longer exist.

And everything became strange.

He tried walking about the cell, and it seemed strange that he was walking. He tried sitting down, and it seemed strange that he was sitting. He tried drinking some water, and it seemed strange that he was drinking, swallowing, and holding the mug, strange that he had fingers and that those fingers were shaking. He choked, began to cough, and, as he coughed, thought, "How strange that I'm coughing."

"So am I going out of my mind, then?" he wondered, turning cold. "That would be the last straw, damn them!"

He wiped his brow with his hand, but that seemed strange, too. Then, without breathing, he sat motionless for what seemed like hours on end, suppressing every thought, stopping himself from breathing loudly, and avoiding all movement—for every thought was madness, every movement was madness. Time ceased to exist, as if it had been transformed into space, transparent and airless, into an immense expanse that contained all things, earth and life and people. All this could be seen at a glance, all of it to its furthest limits, to the brink of that mysterious abyss—death. The agony of it lay not in the fact that death was visible but that both life and death were visible at the same time. A sacrilegious hand had drawn back the curtain that from time immemorial had hidden the mysteries of life and death, and they had ceased to be mysterious. But they had become no more comprehensible than a truth written in an unknown language. There were no concepts in his human brain, no words in his human tongue capable of encompassing what he saw. And the words "I am afraid" sounded within him only because there were no other words and because there neither was nor could be any concept in keeping with this new, superhuman condition. So it would be if a man, remaining within the bounds of human understanding, experience, and feelings, suddenly saw God himself—saw him and did not understand, even though he knew that this was called God. And he would shudder in an unprecedented agony of unprecedented incomprehension.

"There's Müller for you!" he said loudly with extreme vehemence, and shook his head. With that sudden, complete change of feelings of which the human soul is so capable, he began to laugh sincerely and gaily: "Oh, Müller! Oh, my dear Müller! Oh, my splendid German! All the same, you're right, Müller, and I, my friend Müller, am an ass!"

He walked quickly up and down the cell several times and, to the renewed, supreme astonishment of the guard watching through the peephole, quickly stripped naked, then cheerfully and with extreme diligence performed all eighteen exercises. Bending and stretching his young body, which had grown rather thin, he squatted on the floor, breathing in and out, then stood on tiptoe and flung out his arms and legs. After each exercise he said with pleasure: "That's right! That's the way, Müller, my friend!"

His cheeks became flushed; beads of hot, agreeable sweat emerged from his pores; and his heart beat strongly and steadily.

"The point is, Müller," Sergei argued, sticking out his chest so his ribs were clearly visible under the thin, taut skin, "the point is, Müller, that there's a nineteenth exercise—hanging by the neck in a fixed position. And that's called execution. Do you understand, Müller? They take a live man, let's say Sergei Golovin, swaddle him like a doll, and hang him by the neck till he's dead. It's stupid, Müller, but it can't be helped—it has to be done."

He leaned over onto his right side and said again, "It has to be done, Müller my friend."

IX
Terrible Solitude

To the same striking of the clock and separated from Sergei and Musya only by a few empty cells—but just as desperately alone as if he were the only man in all the universe—the wretched Vasily Kashirin was living out his life in anguish and terror.

Covered with sweat, his wet shirt sticking to his body and his once-curly hair now straight and disheveled, he rushed convulsively and hopelessly about his cell like a man with an excruciating tooth-ache. Sitting down for a moment, he began to run about again, pressing his forehead to the wall, stopping and looking for something, as if seeking a remedy for the pain. He had changed so markedly that he seemed to have two different faces: the former, youthful one had disappeared, and in its place was a terrible, new one that had emerged from the darkness.

The fear of death had manifested itself in him straightaway and taken complete possession of him. On that fateful morning, heading for certain death, he had trifled with it, but by evening, when he was imprisoned in his solitary cell, he was whirled away and overwhelmed by a wave of mad terror. While he himself, of his own free will, was going to meet danger and death, and while his death, terrible though it seemed, lay in his own hands, he felt calm and even gay: in this sense of boundless freedom and the firm, bold assertion of his audacious, fearless will, the wrinkled, almost old-maidish shred of fear within him was lost without trace. With the infernal machine strapped around his waist, he seemed transformed into an infernal machine himself, containing within him the brutal reasoning of dynamite and conferring on himself its lethal, fiery power. Walking down the street amid bustling, everyday people preoccupied by their own affairs and hurrying quickly out of the way of cabs and trams, he felt like a stranger from another world, where fear and death were unknown.

Suddenly, all at once, there was an abrupt, preposterous, stupefying change. He no longer went where he wanted to go but was taken where others wanted him to go. He no longer chose where he wanted to be but was put by others in a stone box and locked up like a mere object. He was no longer able to choose freely between life and death, like everyone else could, but was doomed to inevitable, certain destruction. Having been for an instant the embodiment of will, life, and strength, he had become a pitiful example of unique impotence—a man transformed into a beast waiting for the slaughter, a deaf and dumb thing that could be displaced, burnt, or broken at will. Whatever he said, they would not listen, and if he began to shout, they would stuff a rag in his mouth; even if he tried to walk himself, they would still take him away and hang him; and if he began to resist, throwing himself about and lying on the ground, they would overpower him, lift him up, tie him up, and carry him like that to the gallows. The fact that it was people who would perform this mechanical task on his person, people just like himself, lent them an unusually novel and sinister appearance: half apparitions, specters of something illusory, and half mechanical dolls on a spring, which would take him, lay hold of him, lead him away, hang him, and pull him by the feet. Then they would cut the rope, lay him in a coffin, take him away, and bury him.

From his very first day in prison, people and life became for him an incomprehensibly frightful world of apparitions and mechanical dolls. Almost out of his mind with terror, he tried to imagine that these people had tongues and could speak, but he could not, for they seemed dumb. He tried to recall their speech, the meaning of the words they used in their dealings with one another, but he could not. Their mouths opened and sounds came from them, then they dispersed by moving their legs, and there was nothing more.

So a man would feel if, at night, when he was alone in the house, all the things around him came to life, began to move, and acquired over him, a human being, unlimited power. Suddenly a wardrobe, a chair, a desk, or a sofa would begin to pass judgment on him. He would shout and rush about the room, imploring them and crying out for help, but they would say something to each other in their own tongue, and then the wardrobe, the chair, the desk, and the sofa would take him and hang him. And the other things around him would look on.

To Vasily Kashirin, a man sentenced to death by hanging, everything began to seem toylike and small: his cell, the door with the peephole in it, the striking of the clock, the neatly designed prison, especially the mechanical doll with a rifle who stamped his feet in the corridor and the other dolls who frightened him by glancing at him through the peephole and handing him his food without a word. What he felt was not terror in the face of death, for he even wished for death: in all its age-long mysteriousness and incomprehensibility, it was more accessible to the intellect than this world that had been transformed in so preposterous and fantastic a way. Moreover, death seemed to have been completely destroyed in this mad world of apparitions and dolls, losing its great, mysterious meaning and itself becoming something mechanical and, only for that reason, something terrible. They would take him, lay hold of him, lead him away, hang him, and pull him by the feet. Then they would cut the rope, lay him in a coffin, take him away, and bury him.

A man would have disappeared from the face of the earth.

At the trial the nearness of his friends had brought Kashirin to his senses, and for a moment he again saw people as they really were: they were sitting there trying him and saying something in a human tongue, listening and apparently understanding. But already during his meeting with his mother, with the horror of a man who is beginning to go out of his mind and realizes it, he distinctly felt that this old woman in her black shawl was no more than a skillfully fashioned mechanical doll, like those that say, "da-da" and "mama," only a better-made one. He tried to talk to her but thought with a shudder: "My God! But she's just a doll, too! A mother doll. And that's a soldier doll over there, and at home there's a father doll, and this is the doll Vasily Kashirin."

A little longer, it seemed, and he would hear the clicking of the mechanism, the squeaking of unoiled cogs. When his mother burst into tears, for a single instant he again caught a fleeting glimpse of something human in her, but with the very first words she uttered it vanished, and it was curious and terrible to see water running from the doll's eyes.

Later, in his cell, when the terror had become unbearable, Vasily Kashirin tried to pray. Of all that in the guise of religion had surrounded him in the merchant home of his youth, there remained only a loathsome, bitter, irritating taste, and he had no faith. But once, far back in his early childhood perhaps, he had heard five words, and they had filled him with tremulous emotion, remaining full of gentle poetry for the rest of his life. Those words were "Comfort of all that mourn."

Sometimes, at painful moments, he would whisper to himself without praying or being really aware of what he was saying, "Comfort of all that mourn," and suddenly he would feel better and want to go to someone who was dear to him and complain softly, "Our life—but is this really life? Oh, my dear one, is this really life?"

Then suddenly he would feel ridiculous and want to ruffle up his hair, stick out his knee, and bare his chest for someone to hit it: "There you are: hit that!"

He told no one, not even his closest friends, about his "Comfort of all that mourn" and seemed not even to know of it himself, so deeply was it hidden in his soul. And he would recall it rarely, and then only with caution.

Now that terror at the clearly apparent, insoluble mystery had covered him from head to foot, as water covers a young willow on the riverbank during the spring floods, he felt a desire to pray. He wanted to kneel but felt embarrassed in front of the soldier and, folding his arms across his chest, whispered softly, "Comfort of all that mourn!" And filled with yearning, uttering the words with tender emotion, he said again, "Comfort of all that mourn, come to me, give strength to Vaska Kashirin."

Long ago, when he was in his first year at the university and still used to go on the spree, before he knew Werner and joined the revolutionary group, he used to call himself "Vaska Kashirin" in a vain and pitiful way. For some reason he felt like calling himself that again, now. But the words sounded unresponsive and dead: "Comfort of all that mourn!"

Something stirred within him. It was as if someone's gentle, sorrowful image had floated by in the distance and softly faded away without illuminating the darkness before death. The clock on the steeple was striking. The guard in the corridor rattled something, his sword or his rifle perhaps, and gave a long, gasping yawn.

"Comfort of all that mourn! But you are silent! Have you nothing to say to Vaska Kashirin?"

He smiled imploringly and waited. But all was emptiness, both in his soul and around him, and the gentle, sorrowful image did not return. Unnecessarily, agonizingly, he recalled the lighted wax candles, the priest in his cassock, the icon painted on a wall, and his father bending, then straightening again, praying as he did so and watching distrustfully to see whether Vaska was praying or getting up to mischief. And Vasily felt even more terrified than before he had begun to pray.

Everything vanished.

Madness was creeping painfully over him. His consciousness was dimming like the dying embers of a scattered campfire, turning cold like the corpse of a man who has just died and whose heart is still warm but whose hands and feet are already stiff with cold. Once more, flaring blood-red, his failing senses told him that he, Vaska Kashirin, might go out of his mind, might experience torments for which there was no name and reach a degree of pain and suffering never known by a single living creature before; that he could beat his head against the wall, put out his eyes with his finger, say and shout whatever he liked, assure them with tears that he could not bear any more—and nothing would happen. Nothing would happen.

And nothing did happen. His legs, which had their own consciousness, their own life, went on walking and supporting his trembling, wet body. His hands, which had their own consciousness too, tried in vain to close the smock that hung open on his chest and to warm his trembling, wet body. His body was shaking and cold. His eyes were open. And he felt almost at peace.

But there was another moment of wild terror. It was when some people came into his cell. He did not even think what this meant—that it was time to go for execution—but simply saw the people and took fright, almost like a child.

"I won't go! I won't go!" he whispered inaudibly with numbed lips and moved quietly away to the back of his cell like he used to as a child, when his father raised his hand.

"It's time to go."

They were talking, walking around him, giving him something.

He closed his eyes, swayed, and in anguish began to get ready. His consciousness must have begun to return, because he suddenly asked an official for a cigarette. And the man obligingly opened his silver cigarette case, which had a smutty picture on its lid.

X
The Walls Crumble

The anonymous prisoner nicknamed Werner was a man weary of life and the revolutionary struggle. There was a time when he had been passionately fond of life, enjoying the theater, literature, and contact with others. Gifted with a splendid memory and strong will, he had studied several European languages to perfection and could easily pass as a German, Frenchman, or Englishman. He usually spoke German with a Bavarian accent but could, if he wished, speak like a native Berliner. He liked to dress well, had beautiful manners, and alone of all his comrades could appear at fashionable balls without running the risk of being recognized.

But for a long time now, without his comrades noticing it, a somber contempt for mankind had been ripening in his soul. In it there was both despair and painful, almost mortal fatigue. A mathematician rather than a poet by temperament, he had so far never known inspiration or ecstasy and at times felt like a madman trying to square the circle in pools of human blood. The enemy against which he struggled daily inspired no respect in him, for it was a close network of stupidity, treachery, falsehood, filthy defilement, and vile deceit. The final thing that had destroyed forever, it seemed, his desire to live was the murder of an agent provocateur that he had carried out on the instructions of the organization. He had killed the man quite calmly, but when he saw the deceitful, dead face that was now so peaceful and so pitifully human, he suddenly ceased to have any respect for either himself or his cause. It was not that he felt repentance but that he simply lost his self-esteem, becoming uninteresting, insignificant, and tiresomely trivial in his own eyes. But being a man of single, undivided will, he did not leave the organization and remained outwardly unchanged, except that something chill and terrifying now lay deep in his eyes. And he said nothing to anyone.

He possessed another rare quality, too: just as there are people who have never had a headache, so he had never known fear. When others were afraid, he looked upon it without censure but also without any particular sympathy, as if fear were a rather widespread disease that he himself had never suffered from. He pitied his friends, especially Vasya Kashirin, but it was a cold, almost formal pity that even some of the judges were probably not devoid of.

Werner realized that execution meant not just death but something else, too. Nevertheless, he decided to face it calmly, as if it were something incidental, and to live to the end as if nothing had happened or would happen. Only in this way could he express his supreme contempt for the execution and preserve his essential, inalienable freedom of spirit. At the trial—and even his friends who were well acquainted with his cool fearlessness and superciliousness would perhaps not have believed it—he thought neither of life nor of death. Instead, calmly, intently, and deep in thought, he tried to work out a difficult game of chess. An excellent chess player, he had begun the imaginary game on his first day in prison and went on playing it all the time. The verdict that sentenced him to execution by hanging did not move a single chessman from its place on the invisible board.

Even the fact that he would probably not be able to finish the game did not stop him, and he began the morning of his last day on earth by correcting a move of the day before that had not been entirely successful. Pressing his hands between his knees, he sat for a long time without moving, then got up and, deep in thought, began to walk about the cell. He had a peculiar gait: bending the upper part of his body forward a little, he struck the ground firmly and precisely with his heels, so that even on dry ground his feet left a deep, visible imprint. Softly, under his breath, he whistled a simple little Italian aria, and this helped him to think.

But for some reason things were going badly this time. With the unpleasant feeling that he had made some serious, even gross, error, he went back over his game several times and checked it almost from the beginning. There was no error, but the feeling that he had still made one not only failed to disappear but grew more and more strong and annoying. Suddenly the unexpected, offensive thought occurred to him: did his mistake not lie in the fact that by playing chess he wanted to divert his attention from the execution and shield himself from the fear of death that was apparently inevitable in the condemned man?

"No, why?" he replied coolly, and calmly folded the invisible chessboard in his mind. With the same profound concentration with which he played, as if he were answering questions in a difficult examination, he tried to take stock of the horror and hopelessness of his position: looking around the cell and trying not to miss anything, he counted the hours left until the execution and conjured up an approximate but fairly accurate picture of the hanging itself, then shrugged his shoulders.

"Well?" he replied to someone in a half-questioning tone. "That's all. So where's the fear, then?"

There really was no fear. Not only was there no fear, but something that seemed to be the opposite of it was growing within him— a feeling of ill-defined yet immense, courageous joy. And the mistake, still undiscovered, no longer provoked either annoyance or irritation but spoke loudly of something fine and unexpected, as if he had thought a dear, close friend was dead; then the friend turned out to be alive and well and was even laughing.

Werner shrugged his shoulders again and felt his pulse: his heart was beating fast but strongly and evenly, with particularly audible force. Again, as attentively as a man who is in prison for the first time, he examined the walls, the bolts, and the chair screwed to the floor, and thought:

"Why do I feel so good, so happy, so free? Yes, free! I think about the execution tomorrow, and it seems not to exist. I look at the walls, and they seem not to exist, either. And I feel so free that it's just as if I weren't behind bars at all but had just come out of some prison where I'd spent my whole life. What is it?"

His hands were beginning to shake—something he had never known before. His thoughts raced in more and more frenzied confusion. It was as if tongues of fire were flaring up in his head, as if the fire were trying to break out and illumine with a great light the expanse around that was still shrouded in the darkness of night. And then it did break out, and the illumined expanse of distance shone far and wide.

The dull lassitude that had wearied him for the last two years had vanished, and the heavy, cold, dead snake with its closed eyes and ghastly closed mouth had fallen from his heart. In the face of death his beautiful youth was returning in all its gaiety. But there was more than just his beautiful youth. With the amazing lucidity of mind that comes to man at rare moments and raises him to the heights of contemplation, Werner suddenly saw both life and death and was astounded by the magnificence of this unprecedented spectacle. It was as if he were walking along a very high mountain ridge, narrow as the edge of a knife blade; on one side he could see life, and on the other death, like two deep, beautiful, glittering seas that merged on the horizon into a single, infinitely wide expanse.

"What is this? What a wondrous sight!" he said slowly, automatically rising and drawing himself up as if in the presence of a superior being. And destroying walls, space, and time with his swift, all-penetrating look, he cast a sweeping glance somewhere far into the depths of the life he was leaving behind him.

That life appeared in a new light now. He no longer tried, as before, to translate what he had seen into words, and anyway, there were no such words in the still-meager, scant language of men. The paltry, filthy, evil thing that had aroused contempt in him for his fellow men and at times had even caused him revulsion at the sight of a human face—that had vanished completely. So it is for the man who ascends in a balloon: the litter and dirt in the crowded streets of the small town he has left behind him disappear from sight, and ugliness turns into beauty.

With an involuntary movement, Werner walked to the table and leaned on it with his right hand. Though proud and commanding by nature, never before had he adopted such a proud, free, masterful pose; never had he turned his head like that; never had he looked in that way—for never had he been so free and commanding as here in prison, only a few hours away from execution and death.

His fellow men appeared in a new light, too, seeming unexpectedly charming and good to his lucid eye. Soaring above time, he saw clearly how young mankind really was—mankind that only yesterday had howled like a wild beast in the forests. What had once seemed unforgivable, terrible, and vile in people now suddenly became touchingly endearing—as endearing as a child's inability to walk like an adult, as his incoherent prattle shining with flashes of peculiar genius, as his funny slips, blunders, and painful bruises.

"You are my dear ones!" said Werner suddenly with an unexpected smile, and he immediately lost all the impressive quality of his pose, becoming once more the prisoner who feels cramped and uncomfortable under lock and key and is rather tired of the annoying, inquisitive eye peering at him from the flat surface of the door. It was strange: he forgot almost immediately what he had just seen so vividly and distinctly. What was stranger still, he did not even try to recall it. He simply settled himself a little more comfortably, avoiding his usually stiff position, and with a faint, gentle smile that was quite unlike his normal one, examined the walls and the bars on the window. Then something else happened that had never happened to him before: he suddenly began to weep.

"My dear friends!" he whispered, weeping bitterly. "My dear friends!"

By what mysterious paths had he come from a feeling of proud, boundless freedom to this tender, impassioned pity? He did not know and did not even think about it. And did he really pity them, his dear friends, or did his tears hide something else that was more lofty and passionate still? His heart, which had suddenly risen from the dead and broken into emerald leaf, could not tell him this, either. He wept and whispered, "My dear friends! You are my dear friends!"

In this man who wept so bitterly and yet smiled through his tears, no one would have recognized the cool, haughty, audacious, world-weary Werner—not the judges, his friends, or he himself.

XI
They Are Taken

Before being seated in the carriages, all five condemned were assembled in a large, cold room with an arched ceiling that resembled an empty waiting room or an office that was no longer used. They were permitted to talk to one another.

But only Tanya Kovalchuk took advantage of this permission straightaway. Without a word, the others shook hands firmly—hands that were as cold as ice and hot as fire—and trying to avoid one another's eyes, huddled awkwardly and distractedly together. Now that they were all together, they seemed to be ashamed of what each had felt while alone; and they were afraid to look at one another, so as not to see or show the peculiar, new, rather shameful thing that each felt or suspected lay behind him in his recent past.

But they glanced at one another once or twice, smiled, then immediately felt relaxed and at ease, as before; no change had taken place, and if something had happened, then it had affected them all so equally that for each of them individually it was imperceptible. They all talked and moved in a strange way, jerkily and in fits and starts, either too quickly or too slowly. Sometimes they choked on their words and repeated them many times; sometimes they did not finish a sentence they had begun—or thought they had already finished it but did not notice. They all screwed up their eyes, inquisitively examining familiar things without recognizing them, like people who normally wear glasses and suddenly take them off. They all kept turning around sharply again and again, as if someone behind them was calling to them all the time and showing them something. But they did not notice this either. Musya's and Tanya's ears and cheeks were burning hot; Sergei was rather pale at first, but he soon picked up and became his old self.

Only Vasily attracted their attention. Even here, among the others, he looked extraordinary and terrible. Werner roused himself and said quietly to Musya with tender concern, "What's wrong with him, Musya? Is he really afraid, eh? What do you think? We'd better go to him."

From somewhere a long way off, Vasily looked at Werner as if not recognizing him and lowered his eyes.

"Vasya, what have you done to your hair, eh? But what's wrong? It's all right, old fellow, it's all right; it'll soon be over. You must keep a grip on yourself—you must, you must."

Vasily said nothing. When it had already begun to look as if he would not say anything at all, there came a belated, toneless, terribly distant reply, as the grave might respond to long appeals: "But I'm all right. I've got a grip on myself."

And he said again, "I've got a grip on myself."

Werner was glad.

"That's it, that's it. There's a good fellow. Right, right."

But he met Vasily's somber, leaden gaze, which was fixed on him from far away in the distance, and thought with momentary anguish: "Where is he looking at me from? Where is he speaking from?" And with profound tenderness, as people speak only to the dead, he said: "Can you hear me, Vasya? I love you very much."

"And I love you very much, too," replied Vasily, his tongue moving with difficulty.

Suddenly Musya took Werner by the hand and, expressing her amazement in an earnest way, like an actress on stage, said: "Werner, what's wrong with you? Did you say 'I love you'? You've never said 'I love you' to anyone before! And why are you so . . . happy and gentle? Why is it?"

"Why's what?"

And like an actor, expressing what he felt in an earnest way, too, Werner squeezed Musya's hand hard and said: "Yes, I love people very much now. But you mustn't tell the others. I feel ashamed of it, but I love people very much."

Their eyes met and shone with brilliant light, and everything around them grew dim. So all other lights grow dim in the momentary flash of lightning, and even the heavy, yellow flame of a candle casts a shadow on the ground.

"Yes," said Musya. "Yes, Werner."

"Yes," he replied. "Yes, Musya, yes!"

They had understood something and confirmed it forever. His eyes shining, Werner roused himself again and stepped quickly toward Sergei.

"Sergei!"

But it was Tanya Kovalchuk who answered. Delighted and almost weeping with maternal pride, she tugged furiously at Sergei's sleeve.

"Just listen, Werner! Here I am weeping for him and grieving over him, while he does gymnastics!"

"The Müller system?" asked Werner with a smile.

Embarrassed, Sergei frowned.

"You shouldn't laugh, Werner. I've finally convinced myself that . . ."

They all burst out laughing. Finding strength and fortitude in one another's company, they were gradually becoming their old selves, but they did not notice this either, thinking they were all still the same as before. Suddenly Werner stopped laughing and said with extreme seriousness: "You're right, Sergei. You're perfectly right."

"No, you see," said Sergei gladly. "Of course, we—"

But just then they asked them to get into the carriages. They were so obliging that they let them take their seats in pairs as they wished. And in general they were very obliging, even inordinately so, trying either to display their humane consideration for the condemned or to show that they were not in the least responsible for what was taking place and that it was all happening of its own accord. But they were pale.

"Musya, you go with him," said Werner, pointing to Vasily, who stood motionless.

"All right," Musya nodded. "but what about you?"

"Me? Tanya can go with Sergei and you can go with Vasya . . . I'll go by myself. It doesn't matter; I'll be all right, you know."

When they went out into the courtyard, the damp, warm darkness blew softly but strongly into their faces and eyes and took their breath away, gently pervading their trembling bodies and swiftly cleansing them. It was hard to believe that this amazing thing was simply the spring wind, a damp, warm wind. This astonishing, real spring night smelled of melting snow as the sound of dripping water rang out in the boundless expanse of air. Briskly and busily, hard on one another's heels, the little drops fell rapidly and in concert, tapping out a ringing song; but suddenly one would get out of tune, and all the rest would be caught in merry plashing and hurried confusion. Then a big drop would sound its firm, stern note, and the hasty spring song would ring out its melody once more. And over the city, above the roofs of the prison, hung a pale glow from the electric lights.

"Oh-ah!" Sergei Golovin heaved a deep sigh, then held his breath, as if reluctant to let such fresh, beautiful air out of his lungs.

"Has the weather been like this long?" Werner asked. "It's very springlike."

"Only since yesterday," came the obliging, courteous reply. "There's still a lot of frost about, though."

One after the other the dark carriages drove softly up, took two passengers each, and rolled away into the darkness to where a lantern swung beneath the gates. The gray shapes of the escort surrounded each carriage, and the shoes of their horses clinked on the stones and slipped on the wet snow.

As Werner was bending and about to get into the carriage, a guard said to him vaguely, "There's somebody else in here who's going with you."

Werner was astonished. "Going where? Where's he going? Oh, I see! Somebody else? But who is it?"

The guard said nothing. And indeed, in a corner of the carriage, in the darkness, crouched something small and motionless but alive— its open eye flashed in the slanting ray of light from the lantern. As he sat down Werner nudged the man's knee with his leg. "Sorry, friend."

The other did not reply. Only when the carriage began to move did he suddenly ask haltingly in broken Russian, "Who are you?"

"My name is Werner, sentenced to be hanged for an attempt on the life of X. And you?"

"I'm Yanson. You mustn't hang me."

In two hours this journey would bring them face to face with that great, unsolved mystery, the passage from life to death—and still they were becoming acquainted. Life and death were moving in two different planes at the same time, yet to the very end, down to the most absurd and ludicrous trivialities, life was still life.

"What did you do, Yanson?"

"I killed my boss with a knife. And stole his money."

From the sound of his voice, it seemed as if Yanson were falling asleep. Werner found his limp hand in the darkness and squeezed it. Just as limply Yanson took his hand away.

"Are you afraid?" asked Werner.

"I don't want to be hanged."

They fell silent. Werner found the Estonian's hand again and pressed it tightly between his own hot, dry palms. It lay there motionless, like a little piece of planking, but Yanson no longer tried to take it away.

It was cramped and stuffy in the carriage, and there was a smell of soldiers' greatcoats, mustiness, manure, and wet leather boots. The young policeman sitting opposite Werner breathed hotly on him, his breath smelling of onions and cheap tobacco. But the keen, fresh air outside forced its way through chinks here and there in the sides of the carriage, and because of this, spring made itself felt even more strongly inside the stifling moving box than outside. The carriage kept turning first to the right, then to the left, and then seemed to go backward; sometimes it felt as if they had been circling round and round for hours on the same spot. At first, bluish electric light penetrated the thick curtains drawn over the windows; then suddenly, after one turning, it grew dark, and from this alone they guessed that they had turned into remote streets on the outskirts of the city and were nearing the S——sky station. Sometimes, when they turned sharply, Werner's bent knee bumped in a friendly way against the policeman's and it was hard to believe that execution was imminent.

"Where are we going?" asked Yanson suddenly.

He was rather dizzy from the prolonged swinging motion of the dark, boxlike carriage and felt slightly sick.

Werner told him and gripped the Estonian's hand more tightly still. He felt like saying something particularly friendly and affectionate to this sleepy little man whom he already loved more than anyone else in the world.

"Dear friend! You seem uncomfortable sitting like that. Move up here close to me."

Yanson was silent for a moment then answered, "No thanks. I'm all right. Will they hang you, too?"

"Yes!" replied Werner with sudden gaiety, almost laughing, and he waved his hand in a particularly free-and-easy, simple gesture. It was as if they were talking about an absurd, foolish trick that some dear but awfully silly people were wanting to play on them.

"Have you a wife?" asked Yanson.

"No, nothing of the kind! I'm single."

"So am I," said Yanson. "So am we," he said, correcting himself after thinking for a moment.

Werner was beginning to feel dizzy, too. At times he felt as if they were on their way to some festive occasion. It was strange, but nearly all the others felt the same, and together with their anguish and terror they were filled with a vague sense of gladness at the extraordinary thing that was about to happen. Reality was intoxicated by madness, and coupling with life, death gave birth to apparitions. It was quite possible that flags were flying on the buildings.

"Here we are at last!" said Werner gaily when the carriage stopped, and he jumped down, light. But with Yanson things took rather longer: silently and very limply, somehow he resisted, not wanting to get out. He seized the door handle, and a policeman loosened his feeble fingers and pulled his hand away. Then he grabbed hold of a corner of the carriage, of the door or the high wheel but with a slight effort on the policeman's part immediately let go. Without a word, he clung sleepily to things rather than clutched at them, and allowed himself to be pulled away easily and without effort. In the end he stood up.

There were no flags flying. As usual during the night, the station was dark, deserted, and lifeless. Passenger trains were no longer running, and the train that was silently waiting on the track for these passengers needed neither bright lights nor noisy bustle. Suddenly Werner felt bored. Not afraid or depressed but bored—an immense, slow, deadly boredom that makes one want to go away somewhere, lie down, and shut one's eyes tightly. He stretched and gave a long yawn. Yanson stretched, too, and yawned quickly several times in succession.

"If only they'd hurry up!" said Werner wearily.

Yanson said nothing and shivered.

As the condemned walked down the deserted platform cordoned off by soldiers and went toward the dimly lit carriages, Werner found himself next to Sergei Golovin. Pointing to something, Sergei began to speak, but only the word *lantern* was clearly audible, while the rest of the sentence was lost in a long, tired yawn.

"What did you say?" asked Werner, he too answering with a yawn.

"That lantern. Its lamp's smoking," said Sergei.

Werner looked around: it was true; the lamp was smoking badly, and the glass at the top was already black with soot.

"Yes, it's smoking."

And suddenly he thought, "But what does it matter to me if that lamp's smoking, when . . ." The same thought evidently occurred to Sergei, too: he shot Werner a swift glance and turned away. But they both stopped yawning.

They all walked to the carriages of their own accord, except Yanson, who had to be taken by the arm. At first he dug his heels in, and it seemed as if the soles of his shoes were stuck to the planks of the platform. Then he bent his knees and hung on the policemen's arms, his feet dragging along the ground like those of a drunk and his toes scraping the platform. It took them a long time to push him through the carriage door, but they did it without saying a word.

Vasily Kashirin walked unaided, vaguely imitating the movements of his friends and doing everything as they did. But as he climbed the steps to the carriage platform, he fell back, and a policeman took him by the elbow to steady him. Vasily began to shake and, jerking his arm away, uttered a piercing cry: "A-ah!"

"Vasya, what's the matter?" shouted Werner, rushing toward him.

Shaking violently, Vasily made no reply. Embarrassed and even upset, the policeman explained, "I tried to hold him up, but he . . ."

"Come on, Vasya; I'll help you," said Werner, and he tried to take him by the arm.

But Vasily jerked his arm away again and shouted more loudly still, "A-ah!"

"Vasya, it's me, Werner!"

"I know. Don't touch me. I'll go by myself." And still shaking, he climbed into the carriage unaided and sat down in a corner.

Bending forward and indicating Vasily with his eyes, Werner asked Musya softly, "Well, how is he, do you think?"

"Bad," replied Musya, just as softly. "He's dead already. Tell me, Werner, does death really exist?"

"I don't know, Musya, but I think not," replied Werner gravely and thoughtfully.

"That's what I thought. But what about him? I was so worried about him in the carriage; it was just like riding with a corpse."

"I don't know, Musya. Perhaps death does exist for some people. For the time being, that is—but later it won't exist at all. It used to exist for me, for instance, but now it doesn't."

Musya's rather pale cheeks flushed scarlet.

"Used to, Werner? Used to?"

"Yes. But now it doesn't. Just as it doesn't exist for you either."

There was a noise in the doorway of the carriage. Stamping his feet, breathing loudly, and spitting, Mishka the Gypsy came in. He flung a glance around him and stopped short, acting in a deliberately obstinate way.

"There's no room here, Mister Policeman!" he shouted at the weary officer who was looking at him angrily. "You make it so there's space in here for me, or I'll not go, and you can hang me right here from that lamp. They gave me a carriage, too, the sons of bitches, but d'you call that a carriage? The devil's guts, yes, but not a carriage!"

But then he suddenly bent his head, stretched out his neck, and walked forward toward the others. Framed by his disheveled hair and beard, his black eyes were wild and piercing, with a slightly mad look in them.

"Ah! Ladies and gentlemen!" he drawled. "So here we are! How do you do, sir?"

He thrust out his hand at Werner and sat down facing him. Leaning forward close to him, he winked and quickly ran his hand across his neck.

"You as well, eh?"

"Yes!" smiled Werner.

"But not all of you, surely?"

"Yes."

"Oho!" said the Gypsy, baring his teeth in a grin, and his eyes probed them all, his glance pausing for a moment on Musya and Yanson. And again he winked at Werner and said, "Because of that minister?"

"Yes. And what about you?"

"I'm here, sir, for something different. What do we want with a minister, eh? I'm a thief, sir; that's what I am. A killer. It's all right, sir; you can make room for me. It's not my fault they've shoved me in here with you folks. There's plenty of room for everybody in the next world."

Looking out wildly from under his tousled hair, he swept them all with a single swift, mistrustful glance. Without saying a word they all looked at him seriously and even with apparent concern. The Gypsy grinned and quickly slapped Werner several times on the knee.

"So that's how it is, sir! Just like the song goes: 'Rustle not, mother forest, with your green oak leaves.' "

"Why do you call me 'sir,' when we're all . . ."

"True," agreed the Gypsy with satisfaction. "What kind of sir can you be if you'll be hanging next to me? Now him—there's a sir," he said, pointing to the silent policeman. "But that one of yours over yonder, he's no better than us," he added, indicating Vasily with his eyes. "Sir, hey sir! Are you afraid, eh?"

"I'm all right," replied Vasily, his tongue moving only with difficulty.

"What do you mean, 'all right'? You're nothing of the kind! Don't be ashamed; there's nothing to be ashamed of! It's only a dog that wags its tail and grins when it's being taken off to be hanged, but you're a man, aren't you? And who's that there, the lop-eared one? He's not one of your lot, is he?"

His eyes skipped quickly over them all, and with a hissing sound he kept spitting out the sweet saliva that filled his mouth. Crouching motionless in the corner like a small bundle, Yanson moved the flaps of his shabby fur cap slightly but made no reply. Werner answered for him: "He killed his boss."

"Good Lord!" said the Gypsy in surprise. "How can they let folks like him go around killing people?"

For a long time now, out of the corner of his eye, the Gypsy had been scrutinizing Musya. Turning quickly, he suddenly stared straight at her.

"Miss, hey, miss! What are you doing here, eh? She's got little pink cheeks and she's laughing! Look, can't you see her laughing!" he said, grasping Werner by the knee with strong fingers that seemed made of iron. "Look, look!"

Blushing and smiling with slight embarrassment, Musya returned the Gypsy's direct gaze, looking into his piercing, rather mad eyes, which were so full of wild, grave inquiry.

No one said a word.

The wheels clattered with their staccato, businesslike rhythm as the little carriages jolted along the narrow track and ran diligently onward. On a curve or near a level crossing, the little engine gave a thin, painstaking whistle, as if the driver were afraid of knocking someone down. It was ridiculous to think that so much ordinary human conscientiousness, so much effort and care were being applied in taking people to be hanged and that the most senseless act on earth was being carried out in such a simple, reasonable way. The carriages ran onward, and in them people sat as they usually sit, traveling as people usually travel. Later there would be a stop as usual—"the train stops for five minutes here."

Then would come death, eternity, the great mystery.

XII
They Are Brought

The little carriages ran diligently onward.

For several years Sergei Golovin had lived with his parents in the country near this same railway line. He had often traveled this way, both in the daytime and at night, and knew the line well. If he closed his eyes, he could imagine he was going home this time, too—he had stayed late with friends in town and was coming back by the last train.

"It won't be long now," he said, opening his eyes and glancing out of the dark, barred window that revealed nothing.

No one moved, no one replied, and only the Gypsy quickly spat out his sweet saliva over and over again. His eyes began to wander over the carriage, probing the windows, the doors, and the guards themselves.

"It's cold," said Vasily Kashirin with stiff lips that seemed and really were almost frozen, and the word *cold* sounded like "co-a-d."

Tanya Kovalchuk began to fuss about. "Here, take this shawl and tie it around your neck. It's very warm."

"Round my neck?" asked Sergei suddenly, and he took fright at his own question. But as all the others were thinking the same, no one heard what he said. It was as if no one had said a thing or as if they had all said the same thing together.

"Never mind, Vasya; put it on, put it on, and you'll feel warmer," Werner advised him, then turned to Yanson and asked affectionately, "Dear friend, aren't you cold?"

"Werner, perhaps he'd like a smoke. Would you like a smoke, my friend?" asked Musya. "We've got some cigarettes."

"Yes!"

"Give him a cigarette, Sergei," said Werner, overjoyed.

But Sergei was already taking out a cigarette, and they all watched lovingly as Yanson's fingers took it. They went on watching as the match burned and a puff of blue smoke rose from Yanson's mouth.

"Thanks," said Yanson. "That's good."

"How strange!" said Sergei.

"What's strange?" asked Werner, turning around. "What's strange?"

"Well this—a cigarette."

He held the cigarette, an ordinary cigarette, in his ordinary, living fingers and with a pale face looked at it in amazement and even, it seemed, in horror. They all stared at the slender little tube with the smoke rising from its tip in a curling blue ribbon that was swept aside by their breath, while the ash grew dark as it lengthened. The cigarette went out.

"It's gone out," said Tanya.

"Yes, it's gone out."

"Oh, what a nuisance!" said Werner, frowning and looking anxiously at Yanson, whose hand with the cigarette in it hung down like a dead man's. Suddenly the Gypsy turned quickly and, bending his face close to Werner's and showing the whites of his eyes like a horse, whispered:

"Sir, what if we—the escort . . . eh? Shall we have a go?"

"You mustn't," replied Werner, his voice a whisper, too. "Drain your cup to the dregs."

"What for? It's a lot more fun dying in a scrap, isn't it? I give him one, then he gives me one, and you don't even notice they've finished you off. Just like you've not croaked at all!"

"No, you mustn't," said Werner and, turning to Yanson, asked, "Dear friend, why aren't you smoking?"

All of a sudden Yanson's flabby face crumpled pitifully: it was as if someone had suddenly jerked a string that set the wrinkles on his face in motion, and they had all become distorted. As if in his sleep he began to whisper in a dry, tearless, almost affected voice: "I don't want to smoke. Ah-ha! Ah-ha! Ah-ha! You mustn't hang me. Ah-ha, ah-ha, ah-ha, ah-ha!"

They began to fuss around him. Weeping copiously, Tanya Kovalchuk stroked his sleeve and straightened the dangling flaps on his shabby cap: "My little one! Don't cry, my dear one! My poor little one!"

Musya looked away. The Gypsy caught her eye and grinned.

"His Honor's a queer fish! He drinks hot tea but his belly stays cold," he said with a short laugh. But his own face had turned bluish-black, the color of cast iron, and his big, yellow teeth were chattering.

Suddenly the carriages gave a jolt and slackened speed noticeably. Everyone except Yanson and Kashirin stood up, then just as quickly sat down again.

"It's the station!" said Sergei.

It became so hard to breathe that it seemed as if all the air had been suddenly pumped out of the carriage. Their swollen hearts burst from their breasts, rising into their throats and pounding madly, crying out in terror as they choked with blood. Their eyes looked down at the quivering floor, while their ears listened as the wheels turned more and more slowly, slipped, turned again, then suddenly stopped.

The train had come to a halt.

What followed was a dream. It was not that it was very frightening: it was illusory, delirious, and alien somehow, for the dreamer himself remained elsewhere, and only his ghost moved immaterially, spoke soundlessly, and suffered without pain. In the dream they got out of the carriage, divided into pairs, and smelled the unusually fresh spring air of the forest. In the dream Yanson put up a feeble, pointless resistance and was dragged from the carriage without a word.

They came down the steps.

"Do we really have to go on foot?" asked someone almost gaily.

"It's not far," replied someone else just as gaily.

Then, in a big, dark, silent crowd, they walked through the forest along a rough spring track that was soft and wet. From the forest and snow came waves of cool, pungent air; their feet slipped, sometimes sinking into the snow, and their hands clutched involuntarily at their friends; breathing loudly the escort walked beside them, struggling over the fresh snow. Someone's voice said angrily: "They might have cleared the path! You could go head over heels in the snow here!"

Someone else explained apologetically: "They have cleared it, Your Honor. It's just the thaw that's the trouble; it can't be helped."

Consciousness was returning, but only incompletely, in snatches and strange fragments. First, in a businesslike way, the mind suddenly acknowledged the fact: "No, it's true: they couldn't really clear the path."

Then everything went dim once more, and only the sense of smell was left, bringing them the unbearably strong odor of air, forest, and melting snow; and then everything became extraordinarily clear— the forest, the night, the track, and the fact that very soon, in just a moment, they would be hanged. Snatches of restrained, whispered conversation could be heard:

"It's nearly four."

"I told you we set off too early."

"It gets light at five."

"Yes, that's right. We should have . . ."

They stopped in the darkness in a small clearing. Some distance away, through the thin trees with their bare winter branches, two small lanterns were silently moving. That was where the gallows were.

"I've lost one of my galoshes," said Sergei Golovin.

"What?" asked Werner, not understanding what Sergei had said.

"I've lost one of my galoshes. I'm cold."

"Where's Vasily?"

"I don't know. Oh, there he is, standing over there."

Vasily stood somber and motionless.

"Where's Musya?"

"I'm here. Is that you, Werner?"

They began to look around, trying not to look toward where the small lanterns went on silently moving with terrible meaning. To the left the bare trees seemed to thin out, and something big, white, and flat showed through them. From the same direction there came a damp wind.

"It's the sea," said Sergei Golovin, sniffing and filling his mouth with air. "That's the sea."

Musya replied in a sonorous voice, " 'My love, wide as the sea!' "

"What did you say, Musya?"

" 'The shores of life cannot contain my love, wide as the sea.' "

" 'My love, wide as the sea,' " repeated Sergei pensively, surrendering to the sound of her voice and the words of the song.

" 'My love, wide as the sea,' " echoed Werner, and he suddenly said in gay surprise: "Little Musya! How young you still are!"

All of a sudden, close by his ear, Werner heard the Gypsy's hot, breathless whisper: "Sir, hey, sir! Is this a forest, then? My God, what is all this? And what's that over yonder where those lanterns are? Is it a gallows, then? What is all this, eh? What is it then, eh?"

Werner looked at him: the Gypsy was filled with mortal agony.

"We must say good-bye . . ." said Tanya Kovalchuk.

"Wait a moment; they've still got to read out the sentence," replied Werner. "But where's Yanson?"

Yanson was lying in the snow, and people were busy with something beside him. Suddenly there came the acrid smell of liquid ammonia.

"What's going on there, doctor? Will you be long? asked someone impatiently.

"It's all right, he's only fainted. Rub his ears with snow. He's already coming around; so you can read the sentence."

The light of a shaded lantern fell on a sheet of paper and white, ungloved hands. Both paper and hands were trembling slightly, and so was the voice:

"Ladies and gentlemen, do I need to read out the sentence? You all know what it is, don't you? What do you think?"

"There's no need to read it," said Werner, answering for them all, and the lantern quickly went out.

They all declined the services of the priest, too. The broad, dark silhouette moved swiftly and silently away into the depths of the forest and disappeared. Dawn was evidently approaching: the snow had turned white, the shapes of people had grown dark, and the forest had become thinner, sadder, and more ordinary.

"Ladies and gentlemen, you must go forward in twos. You may choose your own partners, but do please hurry."

Werner pointed to Yanson, who was already on his feet, supported by two policemen.

"I'll go with him. Sergei, you take Vasily and go first."

"All right."

"Shall we go together, Musya?" asked Tanya Kovalchuk. "Well, let's kiss, then."

They all quickly kissed one another. The Gypsy kissed so hard that they could feel his teeth; Yanson kissed softly and limply with his mouth half open, but he seemed not even to understand what he was doing. When Golovin and Kashirin had already moved a few steps away, Kashirin suddenly stopped and said loudly and clearly, but in a voice that was completely unfamiliar and quite unlike his normal one: "Good-bye, friends!"

"Good-bye, friend!" they shouted to him.

They went away. It grew quiet. The lanterns beyond the trees became still. Those waiting expected to hear a shriek, the sound of a voice, a noise of some kind—but it was as quiet beyond the trees as it was in the clearing, and the lanterns shone yellow and motion-less.

"Oh, my God!" cried someone in a strange, hoarse voice. They looked around: it was the Gypsy suffering in his mortal agony. "They're hanging 'em!"

They turned away, and it grew quiet once more. The Gypsy clutched at the air and cried: "What's all this, ladies and gentle-men, eh? Have I got to go by myself, then? It's more fun with a bit of company! Ladies and gentlemen! What's all this?"

He seized Werner by the arm with fingers that tightened, then relaxed their grip almost playfully, and asked: "Sir, dear friend, won't you go with me, eh? Do us a favor, don't say no!"

Filled with pain, Werner replied, "I can't, my friend; I'm going with him."

"Oh, my God! So I've got to go by myself, then! How can that be? My God!"

Musya stepped forward and said softly, "Come with me!"

The Gypsy started back, and rolling the whites of his eyes wildly at her, said, "With you?"

"Yes."

"Just look at you! You're so little! Aren't you afraid? No, it'd be better if I went by myself. What a thought!"

"No, I'm not afraid."

The Gypsy bared his teeth in a grin.

"Just look at you! But I'm a thief, you know! Don't you mind? No, it'd be better if you didn't. I won't be angry with you."

Musya was silent, and in the faint light of dawn, her face looked pale and mysterious. Then she suddenly went quickly up to the Gypsy and, flinging her arms around his neck, kissed him firmly on the lips. He took her by the shoulders, held her away from him, shook her, and then with a loud, smacking sound kissed her on the lips, nose, and eyes.

"Let's go!"

All of a sudden the soldier nearest them swayed and unclasped his hands, letting go of his gun. But he did not bend down to pick it up. Instead he stood motionless for a moment, then turned sharply and like a blind man walked away into the forest over the untrodden snow.

"Where are you off to?" whispered his companion in alarm. "Stop!"

But the other went on struggling through the deep snow just as silently as before. He must have stumbled against something, because he threw up his arms and fell flat on his face. And he remained lying on the ground.

"Pick up your gun, you miserable devil! Or I'll pick it up for you!" said the Gypsy threateningly. "You don't know your job!"

The lanterns began to move about busily again. It was Werner's and Yanson's turn.

"Good-bye, sir!" said the Gypsy loudly. "We'll meet again in the next world, so if you see me, don't turn away. And bring me a drop of vodka sometime—it'll be a bit hot for me there!"

"Good-bye."

"I don't want to be hanged," said Yanson limply.

But Werner took him by the arm, and the Estonian walked a few steps by himself. Then they saw him stop and fall into the snow. People bent over him, lifted him up, and carried him along, while he struggled feebly in their arms. Why did he not cry out? He had probably forgotten he had a voice.

Again the yellow lanterns became still.

"I'll go by myself, then, Musya," said Tanya Kovalchuk sadly. "We've lived together, and now . . ."

"Little Tanya, my dear one—"

But the Gypsy intervened passionately. Holding Musya by the hand as if afraid she might still be taken away, he said in a rapid, businesslike way:

"Oh, miss! You can go by yourself; you're a pure soul, you can go wherever you like by yourself! Don't you see? But I can't. A thief like me—do you understand? I can't go by myself. 'Where are you off to,' they'd say, 'you murderer?' I used to steal horses too, you know, I swear it! But with her it'll be like . . . like being with a little child, you see. D'you understand?"

"Yes. All right then, off you go. Let me kiss you once more, Musya."

"Kiss, kiss," said the Gypsy encouragingly. "With this business you've got to say good-bye properly."

Musya and the Gypsy went forward. The woman trod carefully, slipping occasionally and holding up her skirts out of habit. Supporting her firmly by the arm, telling her to take care, and feeling for the path with his feet, the man led her to her death.

The lanterns became still. Around Tanya Kovalchuk all was quiet and empty. Gray in the pale, soft light of the new day, the soldiers were silent.

"There's only me left," said Tanya suddenly and sighed. "Sergei's dead, Werner and Vasya, too. There's only me left. Soldiers, dear soldiers, there's only me left. Only me . . ."

The sun was rising over the sea.

They laid the corpses in boxes. Then they took them away. With necks stretched out, eyes staring wildly, and swollen blue tongues protruding like terrible, strange flowers from lips flecked with bloody foam, the bodies were carried back down the same track along which they had come when alive. The spring snow was just as soft and fragrant, and the spring air just as fresh and keen as before. And the wet, worn galosh that Sergei had lost showed up black against the snow.

So it was that men greeted the rising sun.

1908
—Translated by Nicholas Luker

EDITOR'S NOTE

I want to thank those whose efforts and generosity of spirit have made this book possible, my husband Henry Carlisle, my agent Gloria Loomis, and my editor, Marie Arana-Ward. The patience and scholarship of Richard Davies of Leeds University are deeply appreciated—singlehandedly he has saved for posterity Leonid Andreyev's photographic legacy. My gratitude goes also to my aunt Nathalie Reznikoff, to my brother Alexander Andreyev, to Beth Vesel, to Professor Lazar Fleishman, and to Milan Kundera. I bear full responsibility for any errors this book may contain—a gap of more than seventy years separates us from Andreyev's "fabulous years."

Olga Carlisle